MURDER
BY JURY

MURDER
ON THE
APHRODITE

Ruth Burr Sanborn
(Courtesy Robert Carter)

MURDER
BY JURY

MURDER
ON THE
APHRODITE

(AND, "THE TRAIL OF THE CHITIGAU")

Ruth Burr Sanborn

COACHWHIP PUBLICATIONS
Greenville, Ohio

Murder by Jury / Murder on the APHRODITE
© 2020 Coachwhip Publications
Introduction © Curtis Evans

"The Trail of the Chitigau" first published 1923
Murder by Jury first published 1932
Murder on the APHRODITE first published 1935

Ruth Burr Sanborn (1894-1942)
No claims made on public domain material.
Cover design: 1931 houseboat, *Onika;* gavel © Grishina
    Tatiana

CoachwhipBooks.com

ISBN 1-61646-495-X
ISBN-13 978-1-61646-495-0

RUTH BURR SANBORN
Curtis Evans

In April 1935 popular American short story writer Ruth Burr Sanborn (1894-1942) published, in the glossy illustrated pages of *The American Magazine*, a short story entitled "Peach Crop." The story detailed, in a practiced tender fashion guaranteed to move the hearts of the magazine's feminine readers, the pure love that blooms between a handsome, earnest young man laboring in a peach orchard to earn tuition for his final year at medical school and an impoverished but beautiful and plucky sharecropper's daughter. Accompanying the story, one of Ruth Sanborn's trademark tales of ardent young love's strenuously won triumph, was an evocative color illustration by Norman Rockwell. Decades later, filmmaker George Lucas purchased Rockwell's original painting for "Peach Crop," which has been praised as "a statement of love and virtue . . . done . . . with tremendous skill. . ." Lucas has identified "Peach Crop" as his favorite piece among Rockwell's work.

Today the name of Ruth Burr Sanborn is all but forgotten, much in contrast of course with those of Norman Rockwell and George Lucas. Yet when in 1942 the writer died at the untimely age of forty-seven, her obituary was carried nationally in newspapers, including the *New York Times*. In the two decades between 1923 and 1942 Ruth Sanborn is said to have published over one hundred short stories, in such lucrative popular periodicals as

The Saturday Evening Post, Collier's, McCall's, Maclean's, Cosmopolitan, The American Magazine, Liberty, Woman's Home Companion and *Ladies' Home Journal.* A story by her from *LHJ,* "Professional Pride," achieved the distinction of being chosen, along with polished tales by Dorothy Parker, Sherwood Anderson, Stephen Vincent Benét, Louis Bromfield, Kathleen Norris and Wilbur Daniel Steele, as an O. Henry Prize Story of 1929. (It lost to Dorothy Parker's "Big Blonde," which I recall first reading in a college freshman English class.) Remarkably, Ruth Sanborn managed to find time as well in her life to publish three novels, including two lauded mysteries, *Murder by Jury* (1932) and *Murder on the Aphrodite* (1935), which now in 2020 have been reprinted, for the first time since their original publication, by Coachwhip Publications. (Her lightly humorous 1923 short story about boarding house life, "The Trail of the Chitigau," originally published in *Everybody's Magazine,* is included here as well, as an example of her magazine writing. In it is a wonderful character, Miss Laura Pennell, who resembles Ruth's mystery series spinster, Angeline Tredennick. Miss Laura, we learn, "was not above reading an occasional detective story, if the victim were killed in some quite nice way. . . .")[1]

Ruth Burr Sanborn was born in Woodville, New Hampshire, on July 13, 1894, but by the turn of the century she was residing with her parents in Framingham, Massachusetts. The only child of Wilbur James and Julia Eliza (Hobart) Sanborn, both of whom were nearly forty years old when she came into the world, Ruth for most of her early life resided in Massachusetts, although she later wryly recalled having lived in no fewer than two dozen houses in a dozen cities in five states. She came of old New England Puritan stock, on her mother's side descending from Reverend Peter Hobart of Magdalen College, Cambridge, who settled in Hingham, Massachusetts in 1635, so recording in his diary: *I with my wife and four children came safely to*

*New England June ye 8: forever praysed be the god of Heaven
my god and king.*

The thankful Reverend Hobart ultimately would sire
eighteen children by two successive wives and serve as
minister of Old Ship Church in Hingham for forty-four
years. Another of Ruth's Hobart ancestors, David Hobart,
served in the French and Indian War and as a Captain
at the Battle of Bennington in the American Revolution
commanded the 12th regiment of the New Hampshire
militia. Captain Hobart co-commanded the assault on the
Tory breastworks which saw the most desperate fighting
of the battle, as one source tells it: "The Tories expected
no quarter and gave none—fighting to the last like tigers.
They were completely surrounded within their fortifica-
tions, and the work of death was finished with bayonets
and clubbed muskets."

In milder days a century later, both of Ruth's grandfa-
thers were unremarkable rural Yankee farmers. However,
Ruth's father, Wilbur, his three brothers, Melvin, Mar-
ston, and Herbert, and his single sister, Amy, were all employed in trade. (The stylishly handsome Amy, who died
in 1904 at the age of forty-five, was a millinerist.) Wilbur,
a dry goods merchant, did well enough to send his only
child to Radcliffe College at Cambridge, Massachusetts,
thus making Ruth a Cambridge woman just as her distant
ancestor Reverend Peter Hobart had, in England, been a
Cambridge man. From Radcliffe Ruth received both her
AB, magna cum laude, and her MA, in 1918 and 1922 respectively. She took further graduate courses there in the
'Twenties, although she never obtained a PhD.

Among the faculty then at Radcliffe the greatest influence upon Ruth was exercised by a young English literature
instructor and native of Maine, Kenneth Payson Kempton,
who was but three years Ruth's elder. Kempton later taught
a short story class at Harvard University that another of
Kempton's students, the late journalist and critic Charles

Ruth Burr Sanborn
(Courtesy Robert Carter)

Champlin, lauded as "almost legendary." Champlin recalled Professor Kempton, "a slight, thin man, whose skin
seemed to be stretched taut over prominent cheekbones,"
as a Harvard "anomaly":

> He was a successful commercial writer of short
> stories, having sold dozens of them, many to
> the toughest market of all, *The Saturday Eve-
> ning Post.* I found his stories to be skillfully
> written, but far too touched with humanity
> to be dismissed as slick. I wondered how he
> got on with the academics on the faculty, who
> had no audience outside of academia. When
> I later saw Kempton bundled up against the
> cold, walking across the Yard toward the class-
> room from wherever he lived in the suburbs,
> he struck as being very much a loner.

Yet another post World War Two Kenneth Kempton
student, short story writer and novelist Alice Adams, received a C in Kempton's course (Champlin got an A) and
was far less favorably impressed with Kempton. She later
related of his dismissively telling her, "Miss Adams, you're
an awfully nice girl. Why don't you stop this writing and
get married?"

However, to Ruth Burr Sanborn, a spare woman with a
prominent jaw who decidedly favored the men in the Sanborn family and never married, Kenneth Payson Kempton
became an adored literary mentor. Ten years after receiving her MA at Radcliffe, Ruth acknowledged her hefty
debt to her gaunt former professor in the front matter to
her first novel, the mystery *Murder by Jury*, declaring that
Kempton "taught me to write in the beginning, and has
somehow, ever since, kept me at it." Ruth dedicated her
next novel, *Murder on the APHRODITE,* to Kenneth Payson
Kempton, "with thanks for help in boats and books." (Her

Ruth Burr Sanborn
(Courtesy Ron Bouvier)

first novel had been dedicated to her parents, who, she modestly avowed, "deserve a better book.")

Although Ruth seems to have published her first documented commercial short story, "The Poor Old Nincompoop," in the *Saturday Evening Post* in 1923, not long after she obtained her MA at Radcliffe, later that year she described her rocky climb to the height of a remunerative career in professional creative writing:

> I can claim . . . to have had five different professions in five years.
>
> First, I taught fifty pupils to a class, six classes to a day, with no time for lunch. I did newspaper reporting in a place where French was the principal language spoken. I do not speak French, but I can count in any tongue the six mahogany clocks that go with a wedding. I did advertising—in a factory town where there was a cubic foot of gossip to every square inch of sidewalk, and two means of entertainment, the "show" and the other "show." And I edited—I still do, in fact, for half of every day. In the other half of the day I write.

Write Ruth did. By 1932, when she joined the serried ranks of myriad other between-the-wars authors by publishing a detective novel, she had become one of the staples of what hard-boiled crime writer Raymond Chandler dismissively termed American "slick" fiction, which ran, it must be admitted, to a formula of the love of nice people conquering all, without ever offending the sensibilities of respectable white middle class readers. For this reason Chandler damned "all slick fiction" as "artificial, untrue and emotionally dishonest." Yet within this admittedly restricted ambit Ruth proved an able and entertaining

writer. A *New York Times* reviewer (male) of Ruth's third
and final novel, *These Are My People* (not a detective story
this time), praised Ruth, rather backhandedly to be sure,
as "a practiced writer of magazine fiction" who had "spared
none of her highly polished arts—from a photographic eye
for domestic interiors to a deft mastery of light dialogue—
to make her first novel [sic] a pleasant and ornamental job."

One generation's "pleasant and ornamental" fiction
tends quickly to be forgotten by the next, however popular it may have been, but fortunately in Ruth's pair of
detective novels the spice of murder lends piquancy to the
proceedings, despite the bland presence of comely young
lovers inevitably headed to a happy life together of holy
wedded matrimony. Ruth herself revealed a more puckish
sense of life when she explained why she had turned to
writing mystery fiction in 1932:

> It really is rare fun, I find, to write mystery
> stories. There is so much excitement in the
> planning—for of course you plan the murder,
> and then you stand the murder on its head
> and plan the mystery, with a slow leakage of
> clues. It gives one such a grand feeling of om-
> nipotence. So few of us ever really have an
> opportunity to commit a murder in person.
> And it never is really well looked on. But
> think of the vicarious satisfaction of killing
> off on paper the man who poisoned your cat
> or the dentist who pulled your tooth!

The impish sense of humor evinced by Ruth in this
passage happily finds its way into *Murder by Jury*, leav-
ening the novel's sentimentality. The novel also benefits
from what was then a highly original situation (something
that already was becoming in short supply in detective
fiction): murder in the jury deliberating room. There had
been novels about juries deliberating verdicts in murder

trials before, like Eden Phillpotts' *The Jury* (1927) and Tiffany's Thayer's sensationalistic bestseller *Thirteen Men* (1930) (later titles include Gerald Bullett's *The Jury*, 1935 and Raymond Postgate's *Verdict of Twelve*, 1940, recently reprinted), but an actual murder committed in the jury deliberating room while the jury is deliberating its verdict in a murder trial was something new. Contemporary reviewers naturally picked up on this point, and praised the novel accordingly. "[I]t may seem almost unbelievable when you are informed that this new story is a novelty in detective tales," observed a jaded *Boston Globe* reviewer of *Murder by Jury*, but it was really true of this mystery, which the reviewer pronounced "clever and worthwhile." "This is Miss Sanborn's first novel," observed an impressed Isaac Anderson in the *New York Times Book Review*. "In it she displays ingenuity, skill and a delightful sense of humor, qualities that should carry her far."

Murder by Jury concerns the twelve men and women, good and true (or not), who have assembled in the jury room of the courthouse in the town of Sheffield to determine the verdict in the trial of Karen Garetti, who is charged with the murder of her lover, blackguardly bootlegger Sebastian Como. With one exception, the dozen jurors are dominated by the tellingly named Mrs. DeQuincey Vanguard, a massive wealthy matron whose imperious presence has permeated all of Sheffield society, Mrs. Vanguard being "President of the Civics Club, the Woman's Auxiliary, the Town Betterment Society, the Association for the Enforcement of Prohibition, the Association for the Suppression of Vice, and the Crematorians." The other men and women on the jury are:

- furniture store proprietor Simon Gilley, the nominal foreman
- fluttery Angeline Tredennick, a spinster with an insatiable appetite for both sweets and gossip

- retired teacher Gideon Hawes, a health-
  obsessed pedant
- jaded flapper Damaris Lee, who chain
  smokes and scoffs
- meek nanny Mary Madras
- stolid dairy farmer William Apple
- flashy furniture salesman Charles Kashaw
- self-effacing Emanuel Biggs, a gentleman's
  valet
- nondescript Oliver Elding, a business clerk
- Leo Rinschy, a radical working man
- lovely young Cornelia Van Horn, the one
  juror who steadfastly resists Mrs. Vanguard's injunctions for a guilty verdict.

Just as it may appear to readers that they are perus-
ing an early, bi-sexual version of the famed 'Fifties film
Twelve Angry Men, one of the jurors collapses to the floor,
evidently the victim of some sort of fit. A doctor in the
courtroom, handsome David March, is called into the
jury room and ministers to the fallen one, who promptly
expires. It seems that the juror has been poisoned! Thus
begins a mystery within a mystery, investigated by the
unfeeling and uncouth District Attorney Pitt and his more
sensitive and astute assistant, young Garey Brennan. Soon
D.A. Pitt, no respecter of persons, has spotlighted Dr.
March and Cornelia Van Horn as his prime suspects. Being
what he is, he determines to third degree them into sub-
mission, most unpleasantly.

Ruth may have derived inspiration for her portrayal
of Italian bootleggers and the law enforcement personnel
who pursue them by means of a slightly older cousin, Ethel
Mae Sanborn, the only child of Ruth's uncle Melvin. Ethel
Mae wed Leslie Baxter Wotten, a burly motorcycle officer
in the Hyde Park division of the Boston police who had
earlier been employed as a chauffeur. Leslie's exploits as
a policeman included taking a chicken thief into custody,

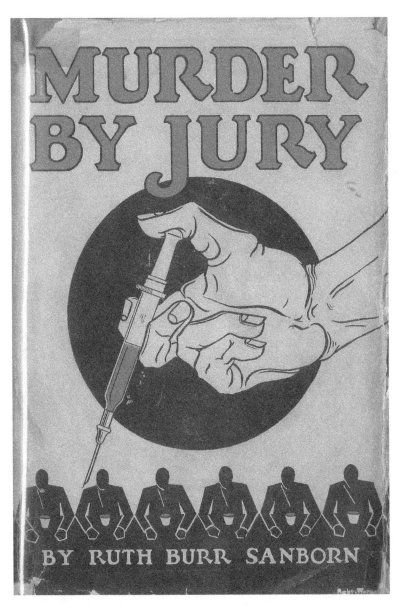

Front Cover, *Murder by Jury* (1932)
(Curt Evans collection)

Back Cover, *Murder by Jury* (1932)
(Curt Evans collection)

collecting a streets-wandering old man (probably suffering from dementia) and returning a runaway boy to his orphanage, during which latter operation he let the lad ride in his side car. However, Leslie on one reported occasion also participated in the arrest of two Italians, Patsy DelGrosso and fruit merchant Pietro Zampella, for bootlegging, recalling the Italian characters in *Murder by Jury* (who on the whole are sympathetically, if somewhat patronizingly, portrayed).[2]

In *Murder by Jury* it proves fortunate for the novel's leading pair of lovers, David and Cornelia, that both D.A. Pitt's assistant and the irrepressible Miss Tredennick have other, more original ideas than the blustering D.A. about who actually committed the crime. Before the novel is over, not only the juror's murder but that of Sebastian Como will be solved, in a cunningly (if at times improbably) designed mystery that amply deserved its plaudits from reviewers. *Murder by Jury* has merit beyond its novelty value, both in its clever plot and its compellingly drawn characters, who show the hand of a talented mainstream writer. Especially winning is Angeline Tredennick, who ultimately solves the mystery of the juror's murder and promptly enters the ranks of classic "inquisitive spinster" sleuths (led, of course, by Agatha Christie's Miss Marple). Happily, Miss Tredennick returned three years later in Ruth Burr Sanborn's second detective novel, *Murder on the* APHRODITE.

Like *Murder by Jury*, Ruth's second and final detective novel takes place in an enclosed setting, this time a disabled luxury houseboat beached on an unpopulated island off the coast of Maine. Like its predecessor, APHRODITE was lauded by reviewers. In the *New York Times Book Review*, for example, Isaac Anderson pronounced the book an "uncommonly good mystery tale," singling out for praise "the facility with which the author [like Mary Roberts Rinehart—CE] feeds into the action unexpected developments that bear obliquely, but definitely, toward the

denouement." Similarly, in the *Saturday Review* William
C. Weber (aka Judge Lynch) declared that *APHRODITE* "has
atmosphere, zip, good characterizations" and in the *LA
Times* the reviewer deemed the novel "clever, snappy and
surprising at the end."

In *APHRODITE* the murder victim is another obnoxious,
wealthy female, this time twice-widowed, jewel-mad Mrs.
Christine Van Wycke. For some reason Mrs. Van Wycke
has assembled an odd and ill-assorted trio of guests, all
male, on her fabulous houseboat, the *Aphrodite*:

- Professor Dante Burge, an eminent and
  odd psychiatrist
- Ewell Choate, a handsome and hot-blooded
  Virginian
- Max Varro, a mysterious foreigner of dubi-
  ous background

Then there is Mrs. Van Wycke's retinue of ill-treated
minions:

- lovely Jane Bridge, her circumspect secretary,
  who seems to have some secret agenda of
  her own
- Toombs, her butler
- Annie Budd, her cook
- Catriona Cooley, her maid
- companion Beulah Mullins, a constantly
  agitated cousin
- our old friend Angeline Tredennick, who,
  we learn, quixotically decided, after her
  involvement in the infamous Jury Murder
  Case, to give up keeping a boarding house
  with her bossy friend Marilla in order to
  become Mrs. Van Wycke's housekeeper.
  (Angeline's new employer fatally failed to
  appreciate that Angeline is one of those

people whom Murder relentlessly follows
in her wake.)

Into this mix comes stalwart and hunky insurance investigator Bill Galleon, fearlessly on the hunt for a purloined ruby which he believes is illegally in Mrs. Van Wycke's possession. The novel opens with Bill deliberately sinking his own boat so he will have an excuse to board *Aphrodite* and recover that ruby. Before long, however, Mrs. Van Wycke has been shot to death on the boat in the dark, during a bizarre demonstration by Professor Burge of the unreliability of people's perceptions, and her bag of jewels stolen. (This part of the novel reminded me of a 1939 John Dickson Carr mystery, *The Black Spectacles*.) Bill, aided by the still cheerfully prying Angeline Tredennick, who never tires of reminding him that she has already been involved in a murder case, sets out to discover whodunit. His investigation is complicated, however, by, among other things, the disturbing presence of Jane Bridge, with whom, it seems, he *shares a past*. Will Bill not only catch a killer, but get the girl? Not if Ewell Choate has anything to say about it, seemingly!

The most interesting character (Angeline aside) only pops up around the final third of the novel. He is Constable Amasa Loose, of Trusett, a nearby town on the mainland. To sophisticated outsiders Constable Loose may appear something of a Yankee yokel, but we learn that "behind those small bright eyes, shining through their scrub brows, there lurked a native shrewdness, a keen judgment of human nature, that under better auspices would have carried him very far." In any event Constable Loose is thrilled to have a glamorous detective story sort of murder on his hands, Trusett not being what you would call a hotbed of thrilling criminal mayhem:

There wasn't much crime in Trusett—game
violations sometimes, or a quarrel over a

boundary fence, and sometimes the boys
would lug off a hitching post and burn it
come Hallowe'en. Mostly [Loose] played pinochle down back of Berry's store, keeping
the peace and the like of that; adding to the
sunburn from his summer lobster pots the
airtight stove-burn of winter.[3]

Despite the praise for *Murder on the* APHRODITE, some
reviewers complained that the mystery suffered from
excessive love interest. Canadian reviewer F. H. Howard,
who commended the author for combining "mystery, psychology and romance in an individual and effective style,"
nevertheless requested that Ruth forgo romance in her next
opus, explaining: "A lot of us [mystery] addicts are funny
that way." For his part Choctaw mystery writer and reviewer and "confirmed bachelor" Todd Downing, a marked
sourpuss when it came to melding mystery with amour (at
least of the heterosexual variety), definitely was not taken
with the book. When he reviewed APHRODITE in the *Daily
Oklahoman*, he commented amusingly if acidly: "We are
reminded of a sign seen over a five-foot pile of mysteries
in a department store: 'The Ideal Gift for Your Week-end
Hostess.'"

In my view, the novel is inferior to the splendid *Murder
by Jury*, in part because the situation is far less original
and the characterization rather more superficial, but it
still makes for an enjoyable read, in great part because
of the winning presence of Angeline Tredennick—though
the author should have given the snoopy spinster a bigger role, commensurate with her marvelous scene-stealing
performance in *Murder by Jury*. A third Angeline Tredennick mystery would have been most welcome, but sadly
such was not to be.

Ten years before the publication of *Murder on the*
APHRODITE, in 1925, Ruth Burr Sanborn, then thirty
years old, left New England with her parents, upon the

retirement of her father, who was nearly seventy, from
the grocery business. The trio took up primary residence
in Southern Pines, North Carolina, although they main-
tained a summer vacation home in Maine. Southern Pines
was a lovely little resort town that underwent a commercial boom in the 1920s, as more and more northerners
like the Sanborns wintered there, many settling there
permanently. Between 1920 and 1930, the population of
Southern Pines increased by 240%, from 743 to 2524.
Ruth's Uncle Melvin, a building contractor, constructed
many of the new homes in Southern Pines. Here Ruth
struck up a new relationship with another literary mentor, psychiatrist and writer of pulp mystery fiction Ernest
M. Poate, her elder by ten years. In *Murder by Jury*, she

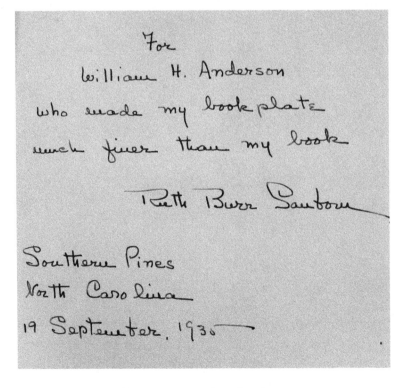

Inscription by Author

Ruth Burr Sanborn (channeling her inner Wednesday
Addams?) with her parents in Southern Pines
(Courtesy Robert Carter)

expressly thanked Poate, who helped influence her to take up mystery fiction, for allowing her to "use his wisdom and experience as if they were my own."

When a handsome colonial style public library opened in Southern Pines in 1939, Ruth was named its director, a fitting tribute not only to Ruth's prominent literary standing but to her elderly mother, Julia, who back in 1870s had served as a director of the Young Ladies' Circulating Library of Plymouth, New Hampshire. The same year Ruth bought a fine house on Dogwood Road and installed herself there with her parents and a cook. Two years later, in September 1941, she published another novel, this time a romantic melodrama set in North Carolina called *These Are My People*, with yet another heroic young doctor protagonist becoming rather smitten with a lovely, virtuous girl of humbler station. However, in early 1942 Ruth tragically was diagnosed with cancer of the liver, from which she rapidly expired on June 29, just two weeks shy of her forty-eighth birthday.

Ruth was survived by her aging parents, Julia and Wilbur, who passed away at Southern Pines in 1943 and 1950 respectively. All three New Englanders are interred by each other in modest graves at Mount Hope Cemetery in Southern Pines, North Carolina, that peach of a town where Ruth did the great bulk of the fiction writing that for a time gave her fame.

NOTES:

[1] THE FICTION MAGS INDEX credits Ruth Burr Sanborn with the publication of eighty-eight short stories, a score of which appeared in the *Saturday Evening Post*.

[2] Leslie's brother Perley met an altogether more dramatic end than Leslie, who died peacefully at nearly eighty years of age in 1971. A fireman in Freetown,

Massachusetts, Perley was killed in the line of duty
in 1941 after parting from his wife and six children
on the family's way to church to respond to a fire
alarm. En route to its destination the fire engine
on which Perley was riding struck a deep pothole.
Perley, who was holding his soft church hat with one
hand, lost his grip on the rail and was thrown off
the engine into the road, where he fatally fractured
his skull. Today Freetown devotes a webpage to Perley's memory.

[3] Possibly of interest here is that the Perley Wotton,
Sr., the father of Leslie Wotton, husband of Ruth's
cousin Ethel Mae, was an old Maine lobsterman. In
1927 he was discovered dead in in his bunk on his
lobster smack *Trimemoral* in the Hyde Park district
of Boston, having been poisoned by carbon monox-
ide gas from the smack's galley stove.

Ruth Burr Sanborn
(Courtesy Robert Carter)

MURDER BY JURY

(1932)

For
My Father and Mother
who deserve a better book

I wish to acknowledge my indebtedness to two good friends: to Kenneth Payson Kempton, who taught me to write in the beginning, and has somehow, ever since, kept me at it; to Ernest M. Poate, who for this book has let me use his wisdom and experience as if they were my own.

Ruth Burr Sanborn
San Diego
January, 1932

I

Tuesday, September 23, 1930

"Guilty," said Mrs. Vanguard decidedly.

Angeline Tredennick nibbled little half circles from a bar of chocolate, and watched uneasily. Somehow the sight of Mrs. Vanguard standing up there opposite, high-headed and high-handed, glaring round as if she defied them, every one, to disagree with her, made Karen Garetti seem guiltier than ever.

They were all gathered about the long table in the jury room of the Sheffield court house, and the thirty-seventh ballot in the trial of Karen Garetti for the murder of Sebastian Como was in progress. Simon Gilley, jury foreman, made a check beside Mrs. Vanguard's name and went on calling the roll.

"Mr. Kashaw."

"Guilty."

"Miss Lee."

"Guilty."

"Mr. Elding."

"Guilty."

"Mr. Hawes."

There was a delay while Mr. Gideon Hawes pottered back from the wash room with a paper cup of cold water and resumed his seat. "Pardon me; one moment," he said. "I must take my capsule. My kidneys. . . . One must not neglect the kidneys, must one?" He drew a square apothecary's box from his pocket, removed the elastic band, took

off the cover, selected a capsule, replaced the cover, replaced the band, replaced the box in his pocket. He put
the capsule gravely in his mouth and swallowed it. They
were large capsules, and went down hard. He drank the
cup of water.

"Now then," he said. "Every one so far has voted guilty?
Yes."

"And for the love of virtue, hurry up and vote guilty,
too," said Damaris Lee impatiently. "I'll never get to that
tea dance if we're hung up here much longer."

There were others who agreed with her sentiments,
though they disapproved of her manner. It was nearly
noon. The jury had been out all night, and every one was
edgy.

"I hope you will not think me obstinate," said Mr.
Hawes primly. "I am quite ready to be persuaded. I am, in
fact, eager to be with the majority. But I have not yet been
able to convince myself that Karen Garetti is the logical
person to have murdered Sebastian Como. I trust I may be
able to do so before the next ballot. In the meantime I will
repeat tentatively my former vote. Not guilty."

Mr. Gilley made a noise in his throat expressive of
annoyance, and went on up the other side of the table.

"Guilty, yes sir," said Biggs.

"Guilty," said Rinschy sullenly.

"Well . . . yes, I guess she must be guilty," said Mary
Madras with some hesitation.

"Sure, that's right; I guess so too," said William Apple.
"Guilty."

"Miss Tredennick?"

Angeline Tredennick straightened the fall of lace down
the front of her dress, and settled her real cameo brooch
more symmetrically on her little round bosom. It had
seemed like running an awful risk to wear Grandmother
Hawthorne's brooch. But she was glad now that she had
it; it gave anybody confidence in a trying situation. It had
not been so bad, of course, when you could write down

your vote on a slip of paper and hide it with your hand—
even though afterwards it came out in discussion what
your vote must have been. But to have Mrs. Vanguard demand, the way she had, that you stand up and say right
out how you were voting made it a lot worse. Angeline did
not like to look toward Cornelia Van Horn.

"It's kind of hard to know what to say, isn't it?" she
murmured. "With everything the way it is. But the more
I think it over, the more it seems to me as if so many
people couldn't be wrong. If it was just one or two now . . .
but there, it's pretty nearly everybody. I guess I'd better
change over and vote guilty, too."

"That's fine, that's fine," said Mr. Gilley approvingly,
rubbing his hands together in the peculiarly soapy way he
had. "My vote will also be guilty, of course." He made a
little bow in the direction of Mrs. Vanguard, as if Karen
Garetti's guilt were a special favor to her. "That makes
us ten to one, so far, for conviction. And now, Miss Van
Horn?"

Cornelia Van Horn lifted her eyes from the quiet hands
clasped in her lap. Enormous, troubled brown eyes, they
were, in a small bright face.

Angeline was already imagining Cornelia in the role
of her favorite heroine in her favorite love story; she had
thought of it the minute she saw her wave across the court
room to Dr. David March.

"Not guilty," said Cornelia clearly.

Everybody whirled upon her. It was characteristic of
the whole situation that it was she, not Gideon Hawes,
whom they held responsible for the deadlock. Gideon
Hawes was negligible: already half convinced; willing, by
his own statement, to be convinced altogether. He could
be disposed of any time. But Cornelia Van Horn was different. Under a gentle manner, Cornelia had displayed
from the beginning an unexpected firmness. *Not guilty* she
had voted on the first ballot—Angeline knew, because she
had watched Cornelia's pencil trace the words; *not guilty,*

unwavering, untouched by argument or persuasion or bullying, she had voted ever since.

"But I just don't think she did it," she said now unhappily. "It would be terrible if we made her be—be executed, and then it turned out that she didn't do it after all."

Mr. Gilley rubbed his hands together. "Now Miss Van Horn," he said suavely. "You're letting your feelings run away with you. Of course we all deeply regret the necessity for making any one suffer for her—ah—sins. But in the interests of law and order . . ."

Damaris Lee lighted a fresh cigarette from her last one, and ground out the stub under the spiked heel of her red slipper. "Come on, be a sport," she said, "and let's get out of here."

"You're just being stubborn," said Mrs. Vanguard sharply. "And it won't do you any good, either."

Angeline Tredennick found it hard to keep her mind on arguments that she had heard a hundred times already. She was a little bouncing person, with a round, sweet-tempered face, two chins, an inquiring nose, a fondness for ruffles, and gray curls wound up neatly on top of her head. Gossip was meat and drink and breath and sunshine to her. It had been a great stroke of luck for Angeline when she was drawn on the jury.

Of course there had been bad things about it that she had not foreseen. That pretty girl, Karen Garetti, murdering her lover and getting electrocuted for it, maybe. Still, she wasn't a really nice girl; they had said so right out at the trial. She was sorry for Cornelia Van Horn, too—she took it so awfully hard. And they had had to stay awake and quarrel practically all night, and it was hot and the windows stuck and wouldn't open. She looked at the long tight row of them in the wall opposite, the yellow distempered walls, stained with the smoke and angers of a thousand juries before theirs; a locked door into the court room, a guarded door into the corridor, a door into the wash room; one long table, twelve hard chairs, and a ventilator. Not a pretty room.

Still, you can't have everything. And it did seem good to be away from Marilla for once; have a chance to find out a few things, and eat all the butter you wanted, without a lot of talk about curiosity and a body's getting fat. Angeline drew a chocolate nut marshmallow caramel bar from her bag and popped half of it in defiantly. *That* for Marilla!

"It seems strange to me," Mrs. Vanguard was saying unpleasantly, "that a girl in your position should pretend to know more about this than anybody else."

"I don't pretend to," said Cornelia.

Angeline did not like Mrs. Vanguard. She suspected that, in private, nobody liked her; though it was the thing to say in public how much Good she had done. Angeline thought it more than likely that she should have changed her vote long ago if it had not been for deserting Cornelia Van Horn and going over to Mrs. Vanguard. Still, it really did look as if Karen Garetti had killed him. . . .

2

The Como case had not seemed, first off, like one that would keep a jury out for more than twenty hours. It was one of those deceptively simple cases that often prove so confusing.

The Como family was large and complicated. There were the two brothers: Luigi, an honest, hard-working bootlegger; and Sebastian, a handsome, hard-drinking scamp about whom, even after his death, no one could say a good word. There was Sascha, Luigi's wife; Matha, Sebastian's wife; a number of oddly assorted children; and Karen Garetti—politely called a niece. They lived just outside of Sheffield, on the edge of the foreign quarter, conveniently located for the bootlegging industry; and Sebastian carried on a number of profitable side-lines: junking stolen

cars, a little discreet blackmail, an occasional bad bill. In
spite of his wildness—perhaps because of it—he had a way
with women.

On the night of August eighteenth, Sebastian had complicated things still further by bringing home a new mistress named Rose, a little merry, round-faced girl, as pretty as nobody's business. Rose had promptly found herself
in a lot more trouble than she had bargained for. Sascha
had hysterics and went to bed. Karen had a tantrum and
threatened to kill Sebastian. All the children cried. Matha
poured out an acid stream of abuse and refused to cook
supper for anybody. Luigi, who had perhaps suffered more
than any one else from the vagaries of his brother, was
the only one who kept his head. He tried to reason with
Sebastian, without avail; he tried to reason with Rose. And
in the end Rose burst into a torrent of repentant tears and
went forlornly home. It was well for Rose that she went.

After Rose's departure, Sascha's hysterical seizure took
a turn for the worse; it culminated in a heart attack, and
she died before morning. At breakfast time Sebastian's
body was found in the bushes near the road, with a knife
wound between his ribs. All the Comos were angry enough
at Sebastian to have killed him, and plainly some one had.
Events, however, pointed to Karen.

Karen had been much angrier at Sebastian than anybody else. The others were accustomed to his ways; even
Matha, his wife, whose position, such as it was, was secure enough in spite of the new arrival. But Karen saw
herself supplanted—turned out, perhaps, without a name.
She had openly threatened Sebastian's life; nobody denied
that. But threats, they gave you to understand, were only
Karen's way. It had rained during the night, and Sebastian's own knife had been found beside him, washed clean
and bright. But Karen had a knife just like it, recently
scoured. There was blood on Karen's dress, which she said
came from Sascha's nosebleed. She had been away from

the house a long time and had no alibi; she told an inco-
herent story of being picked up by a car and going for a
ride. Nobody really believed it; Karen herself said she had
been upset and didn't remember very good—maybe she
might have got it mixed up.

In the court room the Comos were excitable and loqua-
cious, bent on getting Karen off. The evidence was chiefly
circumstantial. But Karen herself was her own best argument. She was a tall, handsome young woman, deep-breast-
ed and deep-eyed, with the free carriage of those who have
borne burdens on the head, and strong, fine hands that
hung quiet at her sides. She looked clearly at her questioners, unafraid, as if she did not believe that they could find
her guilty of this thing.

On the first ballot, the jury had stood nine to three in
favor of acquittal. And an acquittal it would have been,
forthwith . . . if it had not been for Mrs. Vanguard.

After that it might have been a conviction . . . if it had
not been for Cornelia Van Horn.

It was a strange thing, when you stopped to think of
it, that these two should have been the leaders of the opposing factions. Sitting there side by side at Mr. Gilley's
right, no two could have been more different.

Mrs. DeQuincy Vanguard was a big woman, in fact and
in reputation. She was tall, with a public-platform manner, a swelling figure sternly repressed by the right kind
of corsets; they gave to her person an appearance of unnatural hardness that matched the polished granite of her
face and her slate-gray eyes. There was a massiveness about
her, impressive but unlovable, like a glacier or a precipice.
It was her own force, rather than the force of the fortune
that Mr. Vanguard had gathered under her direction, that
made her influence.

There was no corner of Sheffield where that influence
had not been felt. Mrs. Vanguard was President of the
Civics Club, the Woman's Auxiliary, the Town Betterment

Society, the Association for the Enforcement of Prohibition, the Association for the Suppression of Vice, and the Crematorians. She was a member of the purchasing committee at the town library, and the board of trustees at the Home for the Aged. She headed committees on Safer Highways, Greener Parks, Less Loafing, and More Eggs. She believed in large Improvements. If individuals went under in pursuit of the Greater Good, that was the fault of the individuals. If her husband was nervous and dyspeptic, that was the fault of her husband. Mrs. Vanguard was always right and she could prove it.

Beside Mrs. Vanguard, Cornelia Van Horn looked very little and very lovely. She was a slim, bright slip of a thing, with a way of looking at you straight and tilting up her chin. That dauntless chin pointed a small, heart-shaped face under a cloud of copper hair caught up at the crown with one pin, like a child playing grown-up; one curl out in the back of her neck, one gay curl in front of an ear. In the tight, high-belted brown suit, with the close cream-colored blouse banded with russet and gold, she was like nothing so much as a nice young sprite right out of the autumn woods. A hat with an orange feather lay on the table before her. She looked terribly young, terribly alive: all spirit and brown eyes.

Cornelia Van Horn was brave. She was brave enough to stand up even against Mrs. Vanguard. But there was deep trouble in those brown eyes.

Mrs. Vanguard had voted for conviction on the first ballot and said so. She wasn't, she said, one to be ashamed of her own opinion. Only two others had voted with her. Mary Madras and William Apple were not subtle enough to conceal very long afterwards that they had been the two. But perhaps this fact was not so significant as it should have been. For Mary Madras was a pretty, blowzy little nursemaid, who could not keep her mind made up either way for two minutes together. And William Apple was a great big blundering, heavy-handed fellow, good-natured and slow-witted, who knew more about cows than crime, and felt that Mary must be right whichever way she voted. They had changed sides a dozen times during the proceedings.

Mrs. Vanguard looked round scornfully at the others: Biggs, Rinschy, Mr. Hawes, Mr. Elding, Mr. Gilley, Mr. Kashaw. . . . "Everybody knows," she said tartly, "that it's always hard to get a lot of soft-hearted men to convict a pretty girl."

How much this taunt had to do with subsequent events will always be a question.

On the second ballot there were four votes for conviction—and Mr. Gilley whispered to Mrs. Vanguard in a pleased way that he was responsible for the increase. Mr. Gilley was proprietor of the Sheffield Furniture Company—Everything to Make Home Homelike—and Angeline could not help wondering whether he thought it would be good for business to identify himself with the Vanguard interests. Perhaps she would not have thought of it, if it had not been for that peculiarly soft-soapy smile, that ingratiating rubbing of the hands—as if he advanced across a salesroom floor to meet a choice customer.

Damaris Lee was the next to change. "After all," she said flippantly, tossing her unfolded ballot down the table, "what's the fun in being on a jury if you can't convict somebody?"

Mr. Kashaw was the next. He was an automobile salesman and very sure of himself, but perhaps he did not have much chance sitting there between Mrs. Vanguard and Damaris. Angeline, however, would have had more faith in his conversion if he had not mentioned to Mrs. Vanguard in the same breath with Karen Garetti's guilt the fact that the Bustard Twelve was a pretty darn fine car, and Mrs. Vanguard could not go wrong if she bought one.

There was nothing very subtle about Mr. Kashaw—not even in his attentions to Damaris Lee. He was the kind of man who has to devote himself to somebody or drop dead.

Cornelia Van Horn had gently but definitely repulsed his advances that first day in the court room. Mary Madras might have been more to his taste, really, but he was not one to waste his talents on a woman who could not get him anywhere. And Damaris Lee was not above flirting with any man, just to pass the time away. They exchanged cigarettes and *sotto voce* wisecracks, convinced that they had done their duty by the commonwealth.

After that the others came harder, but one after unwilling one they came. Mrs. Vanguard brought them round by a combination of legitimate argument and skillful bullying, terribly difficult to stand against. Her words dropped, cold and hard, deadly in the hot silence of the jury room. There was something almost threatening about them. More than one showed apprehension before the votes for guilt mounted.

Cornelia Van Horn was very quiet at first, watching the faces round the table. But when the balance had swung from acquittal to conviction until it hung even, six to six; when it tipped down the other way, seven against five, then Cornelia spoke out. "I don't believe she did it," she said flatly.

Cornelia was not an orator. Against the power of Mrs. Vanguard she had only her charm and her young earnestness. But she spoke as if from some inner compulsion not to let the thing happen that she saw happening. And all Mrs. Vanguard's sarcasms could not stop her.

"Now Mr. Apple," she would say, leaning toward him across the table, her red lips tender with compassion and her clear eyes shining; putting out her hands, as if she held the matter up quite frankly, just between the two of them and his conscience. "Now Mr. Apple, think how you'd feel if Karen Garetti were your sister, or your sweetheart, or something. Do you think we ought to take her *life* away, when we don't *know* she did it?"

"Can't rightly say I do," admitted William Apple, crimson, squirming inside his clothes with pleasure at her notice.

He formed a laborious *not* in front of his word *guilty*.

"Sex appeal," murmured Charles Kashaw delicately.

"Mr. Apple," said Mrs. Vanguard harshly. "She isn't your sweetheart. She's a wanton woman. The facts are all against her. Do you want to be counted on the side of law and order and respectability? Or do you want to be known as one who favors illicit relations, loose morals, contempt of law, contempt of home, contempt of decency, violence and bloodshed? If that is the kind of man you are, who do you think will buy your milk?"

"I d'know," muttered William Apple heavily, not understanding a word of it except the last sentence. He crossed out the *not*.

Hard reasoning. Cold fact. An unkindly eloquence.

And so they came to the thirty-seventh ballot—and ten to two in favor of conviction. Eleven to one, you might as well say, with Gideon Hawes wavering. They bore down hard on Cornelia, going over the evidence.

3

"The facts are all against her," repeated Mrs. Vanguard. "She made threats."

"But she didn't mean them," said Cornelia eagerly. "She's excitable, and she said wild things without thinking. A lot of those Mediterranean people are like that. It wouldn't be the same at all as my threatening you, for instance, or your threatening me . . ."

"What do you mean by that?" demanded Mrs. Vanguard.

"Why I didn't mean anything," Cornelia said helplessly. "I just meant . . ."

"A nice way to talk then!" said Mrs. Vanguard. "I suppose next you'll be saying it didn't mean anything to have her clothes all covered with blood."

"But she got that from Sascha's nosebleed," Cornelia protested. "Sascha did have a nosebleed. They—they said so at the trial."

"And what about that knife?"

"But they all had knives." Cornelia was gently defiant. "Sebastian's own knife was right there beside him. He might have been killed with that. He might have killed himself. Why—why almost *anybody* might have done it."

"Anybody that was there," said Rinschy sullenly.

"Don't talk foolish," said William Apple, holding his swimming head. "She was there all right. I don't hold much with this story about her going off to ride. . . ."

"It might be true though," said Cornelia valiantly. She wasn't going to give up; the set of her chin said that. "You don't think she did it, do you, Mr. Hawes?"

Mr. Hawes took time before replying to drink off another cup of water; he had to drink a lot of water for his kidneys. "It does not seem logical," he said then deliberately. "Still, if she did not do it, I am at a loss to know who did. It does not seem logical for any one. If you will permit me to read a few paragraphs from my book. . . ."

Gideon Hawes was writing a book called "The Logic of Behavior," and on the slightest provocation he read excerpts. The manuscript was spread before him—he had chosen the free end of the table opposite Mr. Gilley to give himself space—and from time to time he added a note or two. He turned the pages now, cleared his throat with a small dry rasping: "In determining the logic of any single human action, it is necessary first . . ."

He never got any further; his prim voice was drowned in babble.

"Now then, Miss Van Horn, your one friend's gone back on you . . ."

"Even the professor says he doesn't know who could have killed him if Karen Garetti didn't . . ."

"I know just how you feel, Cornelia," said Angeline soothingly. Miss Van Horn had been Cornelia ever since the first day in the court room when Angeline had asked her a few questions about her poor dead Papa. "I know it's terrible hard to think that Karen did it. But there, somebody must have. People don't get dead all of a sudden, with knives stuck in them and all, without somebody's having a hand in it. . . ." She ran on rather nervously, because she thought Cornelia looked reproachful. In the clear, virginal depths of her own mind, Angeline could not really believe that any one had ever murdered anybody.

For relief, Angeline peeped into her bag at the chocolate bars—there were only four left. She took out Grandaunt Ermentrude's silver watch and eagerly snapped open the cover.

"Why it's almost twelve o'clock," she said brightly. "Mr. Gilley, don't you think we'd better have lunch pretty soon? I believe if we had a little something to stay our stomachs, things might all look clearer."

"That's the ticket," said Charles Kashaw heartily. "No food, no fight. How about it, 'Maris?"

Damaris Lee gave an indifferent shrug, fitting a fresh cigarette into her long red holder. "Mud and water and hardtack, like what we had for breakfast!"

"I could do with a bite myself," admitted William Apple, flushed with his own daring.

"At a time like this," said Mrs. Vanguard austerely, "I am the last to think of my own comfort."

Mr. Gilley agreed deferentially, though he was conscious of a gnawing under his own stout watch-chain. "Quite so, quite so. None of us, I am sure, would consider his own feelings. But as Miss Tredennick suggests, perhaps after lunch our dissenting members may be able to see matters in a more reasonable light."

Put in this way, Mr. Gilley's duty was clear; and he meant to do his duty. He rose with the dignity becoming a jury foreman, and flung open the door into the corridor.

In the performance of his duty, Mr. Gilley had been perhaps a shade too abrupt. Deputy Sheriff Trollope, squatting on his heels in the hall with his ear against the keyhole, was precipitated into the room with more than seemly violence; he saved himself from falling by ungainly movements suggestive of an amateur swimmer. He was a round, red man, with a shiny surface like a blown balloon.

"What d'you want?" he demanded, recovering himself.

"What were you doing?" countered Mr. Gilley.

"I ain't got no chair," stated Sheriff Trollope, trying to reduce the shine of his face with a large gray handkerchief. "A man can't stand up straight as an arrer day after day, without leaning onto something."

He glared at Mr. Gilley as if it would be his pleasant duty to arrest him for his very next crime. Mr. Gilley glared back.

"Lunch," said Mr. Gilley.

"It ain't hardly twelve yet," objected the sheriff. "I mostly bring in lunch at one."

"We will have lunch now," said Mrs. Vanguard, "and no nonsense."

"Yes, ma'am," said Sheriff Trollope.

He went out, moving as slowly as is humanly possible to move, in the hope of picking up a tid-bit of news. But there was dead silence. He slammed the door behind him finally, and went downstairs to the restaurant, passing through the court room on his way, and mentioning that it looked to him like they was weakening and he guessed it was going for conviction.

As soon as the door closed, the discussion was resumed. Mrs. Vanguard was frankly bullying.

"I wouldn't hold out if I were you," she said.

"But she didn't do it," cried Cornelia, a trifle wildly. "I just know she didn't."

"How do *you* know?"

"She doesn't look like a—a murderess," said Cornelia, and even that argument did not sound absurd with Cornelia's belief and brave brown eyes to back it. "Why I don't know how you could see her and say that; the way she stood up there in court and looked right straight at everybody. . . ."

"I guess if you had the nerve to kill a person," said Mrs. Vanguard coldly, "you could as much as look at anybody afterwards."

"Could—could you?" said Cornelia.

She was tired, you could see that. There were faint shadows under her eyes, a faint sharpening and tensing of the warm curves of her mouth. She unlocked the hands folded in her lap, slowly, as if they were stiff, and pushed back her hair with a gesture of utter weariness. But her back was just as straight as ever, and her chin was just as high.

"I wouldn't hold out . . . *if I were you,*" repeated Mrs. Vanguard.

4

The arrival of the lunch put an end to things for the moment. Sheriff Trollope rolled forward in sulky silence, and slapped it down in front of Mr. Gilley: a tray of ragged sandwiches and a huge pot of coffee, drooling untidily through the snout.

"Here comes the dole," said Charles Kashaw.

"Doleful, all right," agreed Damaris Lee. "What did I tell you?"

Mr. Gilley passed the drizzling pot over to Cornelia at his right; he was afraid of getting coffee stains on his light trousers, and spoiling his dignity. "I guess I'll let you pour," he said, with the air of conferring quite a favor under the circumstances.

"There aren't any cups," said Cornelia.

"You'll have to use paper ones," said Sheriff Trollope and slammed the door behind him.

Biggs, the perfect servant always, rose up on silent rubber soles and brought cups from the wash room. He had spoken only once since morning. Valet to Mr. Douglas Britten, he knew his place, he hoped, in a company of ladies and gentlemen; but here was a proper service to perform. He ranged the cups neatly in front of Cornelia.

Angeline was examining the sandwiches.

"I'd rather a-had some good hot frankforts and rolls," said William Apple.

"Well, I don't know," said Angeline. "These look real tasty. See, Mr. Apple, do you think that's American cheese in the one this way?"

"No coffee, thank you," said Gideon Hawes, stopping to speak to Cornelia on his way to the wash room. "My kidneys, you know. . . I must drink water instead. I must take my drops. My heart . . ." He trotted away and brought a brimming cup; he took a small vial from one pocket, a medicine dropper from another, and counted out his dose meticulously: "One, two, three, four, five, six . . . ten. There." He drank it off gravely. "Now I must have more water. I will bring some for the rest of you, too. There is nothing like water to prevent kidney trouble. Mr. Elding, will you help me, please?" He and Elding brought water for everybody, and with Biggs' help, handed it around.

Angeline, meantime, had bustled up from her place and begun to pass the sandwich plate. She stopped for a word with Charles Kashaw about automobiles; a word with Damaris Lee about the tea dance, and how many would attend.

"Will you have a sandwich, Mr. Hawes?"

"Plain lettuce, if you have one," he conceded. "No meat, thank you. Meat is very trying for the kidneys."

They held a whispered conference about kidney trouble, not quite delicate, Angeline was afraid, but kind of fascinating. She helped Mr. Elding with his selection. He was a frail, jerky man, with a habit of contradicting himself; he hesitated between egg and olive, and decided on marmalade. She asked Biggs if the Douglas Brittens entertained a great deal; and Rinschy if he thought socialism was gaining any headway in America; and Mary Madras if the Buckley children were subject to croup, and had she ever tried hot oil packs. But even as she talked, Angeline did not forget to rotate the sandwich tray, so that the fat-test, ham-iest, cream-cheesiest, and butteriest slices still remained.

"I hope there's mustard on the ham," she murmured. She selected one sliced chicken and one egg and mayon-naise—just to begin on. She took a swallow of the coffee, and her neat round face puckered in spite of her. "It's got a kind of an odd taste," she said. "Maybe the pot needs boiling out with soda. But there," optimistically, "it's real hot."

Biggs and Mary Madras drank their potions without comment, and William Apple tossed his off in one great gulp and passed his cup for more. Others, however, were less charitable.

"Do you know how they make this?" said Charles Kashaw. "They take a basis of good rich dish-water, and they put in . . ."

"Don't," said Mr. Elding feebly, pushing his cup away.

Mrs. Vanguard drank a few swallows, and set her cup aside also. "It's positively bitter," she said harshly. "I shall take this up with the authorities."

"Something ought to be done about it," agreed Mr. Gilley.

"All you can do about coffee as bad as this," said Dam-aris Lee, "is to put gin in it. Then you don't notice the coffee so much." She whipped out a small flask of red enamel, with a pattern of black lightning flashes, and un-screwed the cap. "Here, Charles. Some for you? Pass down Mrs. Vanguard's cup; I'll fix it for her."

In spite of her strong corsets, Mrs. DeQuincy Van-guard, president of the Association for the Enforcement of Prohibition, had the appearance of swelling; you could see the seams of her blue tailored dress visibly stretch and strain. "Insulting!" she cried, outraged. "You let my cup alone."

Damaris Lee, in the act of tipping up the red flask over the cup that Kashaw had mischievously passed, tipped it down again. "There's no point in wasting it," she said with a careless shrug.

"Here, try mine," said Kashaw to Damaris, pulling out his own flask—a flat silver one, commodious, worn about the corners as if it had seen much service. He pushed hers away, laughing. "Keep it. I don't like your brand of poison. It tastes of arsenic."

Mrs. Vanguard took up the cudgels promptly in her favorite cause. "It is people like you," she said magnificently, "flouting the laws of their country, putting to rout the forces of righteousness and order, who make possible crimes such as the one which calls us here together. Drink, as the Bible says, is the root of all evil. It gives rise to misery and unhappiness, violence and death, poverty . . ."

"And wealth," said Damaris Lee flippantly.

Mr. Gilley rubbed his hands together pacifically. He prided himself on his tact. "What you say is true, Mrs. Vanguard," he said, his mouth watering at sight of the flasks. "But your reference to the Como-Garetti case recalls us to the painful duty that lies before us. Why wouldn't it be a good idea, Mrs. Vanguard, while the others are finishing, for you to make a speech, summing up the evidence. I feel sure that under your masterly exposition . . ."

"I will," said Mrs. Vanguard.

No one had ever asked Mrs. DeQuincy Vanguard to make a speech and been met with denial. She rose. She took a small, professional drink of coffee, careless of its bitterness in the interests of oratory. She arranged her ringed hands tellingly before her. Mrs. Vanguard was tremendous on her feet, lofty and impregnable.

"It is a marvel to me," began Mrs. Vanguard, "that any one can be so callous to the Greater Good as to wish to impede the course of justice. Nevertheless, since such there be"—her glance at Cornelia was as if a mountain had looked askance down its nose—"I shall endeavor to put before you, clearly and incontrovertibly . . ."

She hesitated. Mrs. Vanguard was not given to hesitation.

"I shall endeavor to put before you . . . in . . . con . . ."

She stopped, supporting herself heavily against the table. "I am not well," she said in a different, more hurried tone. "I—I think I must be faint."

"Kidneys . . ." murmured Mr. Hawes.

Mr. Gilley sprang to her assistance; he was absurd, like a pebble in an avalanche, when Mrs. Vanguard's bulk collapsed against him. Angeline darted round from her side of the table to help him lower her into the chair. Cornelia tried to draw Mrs. Vanguard's head against her shoulder, but Mrs. Vanguard pushed her away and leaned on the table instead. Mr. Gilley was frightened; his suave voice cracked on a high note.

"Sheriff," he cried. "Sheriff, quick. Get a doctor."

"I saw Dr. March in the court room," said Cornelia.

5

It seemed a long time, but it was actually less than five minutes, before Deputy Sheriff Trollope bounded back again, looking rounder and redder and more important than ever, with Dr. David March behind him. Dr. March had been in the court room still, as Cornelia had said. He carried his black professional bag in his hand.

"What's the matter? Somebody fainted?" he asked quietly.

Angeline did not know Dr. March very well but she knew of him. Sheffield was one of these in-growing towns where everybody knows everybody else, at least by sight or reputation. And of course Dr. March was better known than most.

He came forward quickly, with a firm, light tread; he had that indescribable ease of motion that makes a man seem taller than he is. Dr. March was tall, too—tall, and keen, and thin, with too sensitive a mouth; you knew at once that he would be capable of suffering with his

patients. He had the brave, permanently tired eyes that all
good doctors have, humorous and wise.

Angeline saw that his glance flew to Cornelia before it
came to rest even on Mrs. Vanguard. Cornelia's hand went
up in a little unconsidered gesture, half welcome, half distress; and he smiled back swiftly.

Nobody else noticed. But Angeline had not read ten
thousand novels for nothing. Romance, in her own person,
had passed Angeline Tredennick by; but it had made her
inordinately sensitive to the romance of others. In that
brief look that flashed between them, she saw more than
Cornelia or Dr. David March ever guessed.

In Dr. March's eyes she saw a frank eagerness to be with
Cornelia. More than admiration; more than glamour; a
longing to cherish and protect, a question that had never
been asked.

In Cornelia's eyes she saw a heart-shaking surge of relief because Dr. March had come; a slackening of the tension round her lips. She saw an unreasoning faith that
anything he did was right, because he did it. A hint of
reserve, too, as if from fear of taking for granted more
than had been offered her, or asking for more than she was
meant to have.

The look was gone in a moment; the trouble was back
in Cornelia's face, an inscrutable quiet in his.

Dr. March was lifting up Mrs. Vanguard's head with
thin, kind hands. She scowled at him a little, making a
feeble gesture as if she would have pushed him away, too;
but she was too ill really to resist. Angeline helped to clear
the litter from their lunch, and Charles Kashaw gave Dr.
March a hand while he lifted Mrs. Vanguard to the table.
Angeline, always at her best and brightest in an emergency,
rolled up her gray coat and put it under Mrs. Vanguard's
head. She was obviously bursting with information.

"She was making a speech," she began, "when this faint-
ness came on. You see everybody was for conviction except
just two. . . ."

Mr. Gilley silenced her. "Dr. March is not a member of the jury. It is not proper to discuss the proceedings with him."

"Isn't it?" said Angeline in surprise. "I didn't mean any harm, I'm sure. I just thought he'd like to know."

Dr. March looked up quickly at Cornelia, while his fingers found Mrs. Vanguard's pulse. *"How many?"*

"Two," said Cornelia, low. She came close up to him so that her shoulder brushed his arm and whispered something that Angeline did not quite catch. "I think she knows . . ." That was what it sounded like.

"Don't worry," said Dr. March.

Angeline pushed her way a little nearer. "Worry about what?" she asked curiously.

Dr. March lifted his eyes with a cool gravity from Mrs. Vanguard's wrist. "Don't worry," he repeated. "She'll be all right. We'll fix her up." He bent down again, with a reassuring smile for his patient. "Just lie quiet for a minute, Mrs. Vanguard, and I'll bring you something to take."

He lifted his bag to the table edge and snapped it open; his accustomed fingers found the bottle that he wanted without searching, and he hurried to the wash room.

Angeline stayed behind long enough to take the coat out from under Mrs. Vanguard's head and put it back again; to arrange her skirts in a more seemly way about her ankles, and set her feet neatly upright on their heels. Then she flounced out after Dr. March; her little round person, in its tight gray silk, bouncing over the floor like a ball.

"Can I do anything, Doctor?" she asked helpfully.

"Thank you," said Dr. March. "I believe there isn't anything now. I'm getting on very nicely." He smiled, his grave, kindly smile, pulling a cup from the cup machine, drawing water into it, tilting up the bottle.

Back at Mrs. Vanguard's side, he slipped his hand expertly under the coat and lifted up her head in the crook of his arm. "Now if you'll just drink this. . . ."

Mrs. Vanguard tried weakly to pull away after the first taste, but he held the cup firmly to her lips; after that she drained the contents without protest, making a wry face; and he laid her head back again, pushing the empty cup aside. His fingers returned to her pulse.

Everybody crowded round the table to watch, in that uneasy silence that a sudden illness brings. Rinschy took a surreptitious swig from a black bottle. William Apple twisted a jackknife in his great red hands.

"Stand back away from her," Dr. March ordered. "And get those windows open. It's hot enough in here to make anybody faint."

Everybody knew, of course, that the windows were stuck tight; but in the relief of having something definite to do there was a rush for them nevertheless. They pulled and pried and pounded, standing on chairs and growing red in the face; Charles Kashaw profanely broke a fingernail against a catch.

"If I can't start 'em, nobody can't," said William Apple, proud of the muscles swelling before Mary Madras' round blue eyes.

Angeline fluttered over to the windows and fluttered back again. Cornelia had stayed behind with Dr. March; she dropped down on the edge of a chair, watching anxiously. Angeline stood by, ready to help; she prided herself on her efficiency in illness.

Mrs. Vanguard looked very ill indeed. She had not roused after the medicine that the doctor had given her; indeed she seemed to be sinking more deeply into stupor. Dr. March did not look at Cornelia now. His eyes were on Mrs. Vanguard: watchful, intent. Perhaps he was worried. Only of course you never could tell with a doctor.

"See if you can loosen her corsets," he said to Angeline.

Angeline fumbled among the intricacies of Mrs. Vanguard's costume, keeping her exploring hand discreetly covered with a fold of skirt. She did her best, but without making much headway. Dr. March did not wait.

"Here, let me," he said. He turned Mrs. Vanguard a little, easily, flipping back the skirt; Angeline was impressed and faintly shocked at the dexterousness of his quick fingers among the corset strings. "There."

He drew out his stethoscope and bent down over the heaving chest. His face was very grave, his lips pulled straight. He moved the little disk, here, there, but his eyes did not leave the patient's face. Mrs. Vanguard's pupils were dilated until only a tiny rim of iris showed; she breathed heavily, puffing out her cheeks. Dr. March straightened abruptly, and beckoned to Mr. Gilley.

"I don't like the look of this," he said in a low voice. "It's something more than just a fainting fit. I want to get her to a hospital right away."

Things happened quickly after that. Mr. Gilley, hurrying to the door as fast as his dignity would let him. Deputy Sheriff Trollope bounding in and bounding out again, all agog with excitement, his feet thumping down the hall on the way to a telephone. The jurors huddled together at the end of the table, all facing one way, like sheep in a brewing storm, restless and uncertain. Dr. March watching his patient, his fingers at her wrist. Cornelia watching Dr. March, as if she, more than the others, could read in his face what was really happening. And on the table, dominant even in collapse, Mrs. Vanguard. Mrs. Vanguard with her big, hard body shaken by gusty breaths. Mrs. Vanguard with her hard gray eyes black with the dilatation of the pupils. Mrs. Vanguard, relaxed and helpless, dropping into unconsciousness. Her harsh, irregular breathing was loud in the still room.

Then there was the clang of the ambulance in the street. There was the shift and hurry of feet when the men brought the stretcher. Dr. Hummell, the ambulance surgeon, stepped in smartly, looking brisk and antiseptic in his clean white coat. He and Dr. March spoke together briefly in low voices. Mrs. Vanguard, quite unconscious, was lifted onto the stretcher. The stretcher was carried out.

Dr. March picked up his bag. He touched Cornelia's shoulder lightly as he passed, without stopping to speak to her. Then he followed Dr. Hummell. The door closed behind them. It was all over.

6

"Well," said Angeline, letting out the breath that she might have been holding for all the ten minutes since the ambulance was summoned, and absently taking the last ham sandwich on the plate. "Well, what do we do now?"

"We wait for Mrs. Vanguard to come back," said Mr. Gilley.

"But what if she doesn't come back for a long time?" inquired Angeline. "What if she doesn't come back for—oh, for all day?" She did not like to put it more definitely than that.

"What if she's just sickening for something?" chimed in Mary Madras. "It's as much as my place is worth to be away much longer."

Damaris Lee suffered from no inhibitions. "What if she goes to heaven," she said cheerfully, "where the murderers cease from troubling and the jurors are at rest?"

Mr. Gilley frowned at her levity.

Charles Kashaw held his lighter to her cigarette. "Then they'd call it a mistrial and let us all go home."

"What's a mistrial?" asked Angeline, quietly helping herself to the sandwich that Mrs. Vanguard had left.

"A flash in the pan," said Charles Kashaw.

"A trial for any reason declared illegal," said Mr. Gilley. "An abortive attempt to secure a verdict," said Mr. Hawes, "requiring a re-presentation of evidence."

Cornelia took pity on Angeline's wide-eyed confusion. "If we couldn't, all twelve, say whether Karen Garetti was guilty or not guilty," she explained, "then they'd discharge us, and draw a new jury, and try the case all over again. And that would be a mistrial."

Angeline beamed at her. "You put things so nice and plain," she said comfortably, gathering in an odd half sandwich that did not seem to belong to anybody. "What I want to know is how we're going to pass the time till Mrs. Vanguard gets back. I wish I'd brought a good love story. Maybe you could read to us, Mr. Hawes. Isn't there any of your book that would be kind of interesting?"

"I have a chapter on 'The Logic of Love,'" said Mr. Hawes, hesitating.

"I guess that ought to be good."

But Mr. Hawes never read "The Logic of Love." They were all too restless to listen; and for once even Mr. Hawes did not insist.

There was never such a curious sight in any jury room. They milled about uneasily, with a strange reluctance to settle down again about the table. They peered out of the windows into the hot September street. They fetched dozens of drinks of water for their clamorous ham sandwiches. William Apple said over and over that he wanted to go home. It dried cows up something terrible, he told Mary Madras, to have a stranger milk them. Mary Madras said shyly that she had always thought it would be awful nice to live on a farm. Biggs carried a chair to one corner and sat by himself; he reflected that Miss Van Horn was the only one who acted like a real lady—so quiet and reserved-like. Mr. Hawes took an extra capsule. He said so much excitement was very bad for the kidneys, and put his hand anxiously to his side. Mr. Elding said he couldn't help thinking about Mr. Vanguard, now his wife was sick. He admired him more than any man living.

"More than any man I know, that is," he qualified his statement. "Of course I admire Lindbergh and President Hoover. DeQuincy Vanguard is a great man, too. Not great, exactly—but, yes, he might have been. . . ."

Damaris Lee offered to shoot craps with Kashaw and Rinschy and was reproved by Mr. Gilley. Rinschy muttered something in reply about boot-lickers and belly-benders that Mr. Gilley thought it better not to notice. He went to the door instead and told Sheriff Trollope to telephone the hospital every half hour.

Angeline was the only one who made any pretense of enjoying herself. She moved briskly about the room, from one group to another, a bar of chocolate peanut in her hand, her round pink face a-quiver with the questions she wanted to ask. How long had Cornelia known Dr. March; and didn't he have an awfully big practice for such a young man—he couldn't be more than thirty, could he, if he was that? Did Mr. Gilley think that business conditions were better; and what would he advise about material for re-upholstering a parlor chair? Didn't Mr. Apple have some trouble with his cows a year ago; what was that? Had Mary Madras always lived in Sheffield? When she was a child, too? Oh. What was the truth about that riot. . . . "Oh my no, Mr. Rinschy, I wouldn't mention it to a soul. . . ." How many servants did the Douglas Brittens keep? How had Mr. Hawes happened to write a book? Was Miss Lee the same who was engaged to Mr. Montgomery Walen? How much commission did Mr. Kashaw get when he sold an automobile?

And nevertheless Angeline always managed to be nearest the door when Trollope opened it with a report from the hospital. The reports did not vary much.

Mrs. Vanguard was still unconscious.

Mrs. Vanguard's condition remained the same.

Mrs. Vanguard was still unconscious. . . .

It was after three when they heard Sheriff Trollope come running. He flung the door wide. He tried to look impressive, and succeeded only in looking as if he were about to burst with excitement.

"Mrs. Vanguard is dead," he cried.

In the terrific silence that followed his words, they could hear the water dripping in the water cooler, and Mr. Elding muttering under his breath, "Thank God, now De-Quincy will have a chance."

"What—what happened?" asked Cornelia, in a small level voice.

"She was poisoned," said Trollope.

II
Tuesday (Continued)

"Owing to the death of a juror," intoned the Judge, "I must declare a mistrial in the case of the State against Karen Garetti." His voice was low; to the farthest corner of the packed court room people craned forward, tense with held breath, to hear him. "Mister clerk, make the record, and put this cause at the head of the docket for a new trial. The jury is excused from further attendance at this term, but all jurors will hold themselves at the disposal of District Attorney Pitt, for his investigation into the circumstances of the death of Mrs. Vanguard, and will not leave the court until excused by him. . ."

Pitt, assisted by young Garey Brennon of the detective force attached to the district attorney's office, herded the jurors back through the connecting door into the jury room.

"Where's that man March?" demanded Pitt. "I want him along too."

"I'm right here," said David March quietly.

And there he was, right there beside Cornelia Van Horn. He looked tired and rather sorry; Angeline remembered sympathetically that he had just lost a patient under peculiarly trying circumstances. It must be hard, sometimes, to be a doctor. But he smiled at Cornelia.

"Don't feel too badly," he said. "It couldn't have been helped."

"I'm sure it couldn't," said Angeline, with a comforting pat for both of them. "It's kind of upsetting, isn't it? But of course we all know you did everything you could."

"Thank you," said Dr. March gravely.

The jury room was just the way they had left it—and still it was different. It seemed stuffier; dingier; somehow vaguely menacing. Perhaps the difference was epitomized by the sharp way Pitt turned the key in the court-room door and stuck it into his pocket. That door had been locked all the time, of course. But now it seemed more completely locked than ever. The windows seemed more completely stuck. Deputy Trollope, at the door into the corridor, seemed more like a guard and less like an obliging errand boy who brought fresh supplies of chocolate. There was a threat in the long table, with its litter of paper cups and the cleared space where Mrs. Vanguard had lain.

"Take the places round the table where you sat for the jury proceedings," ordered Pitt with authority.

In unaccustomed silence they obeyed: Mr. Gilley at the head, Mr. Hawes at the foot; Cornelia Van Horn at Mr. Gilley's right, then Mrs. Vanguard's vacant place, then Charles Kashaw, and Damaris Lee, and Mr. Elding; opposite Mr. Elding, Biggs, then Rinschy, Mary Madras, William Apple, Angeline, and so back to Mr. Gilley.

Angeline could not pretend to be very sorry that Mrs. Vanguard was dead; nobody could. But it gave one a queer feeling, all the same, to see her empty chair beside Cornelia. Angeline was glad when Dr. March took it. "May I sit here?" he said to Pitt.

"Suit yourself," said Pitt shortly. "No accounting for tastes."

He had Dr. March's bag in his hand. "Picked it up at the hospital," he explained to Garey Brennon. "Thought we'd better nab it first, before he had a chance for any monkey-business." It was plain that to Pitt every one was guilty until he was proved innocent.

Pitt was a big, ripe man, with a hoarse voice and a red necktie. He had a drooping left eyelid, which gave him an air of seeing everything in a slightly underhanded way; the whole left side of his face drooped with the weight of his unlighted cigar. A single lower tooth, like one picket in a picket fence, served the sole purpose of holding this cigar in place; when things were going well, Pitt bit a piece off the end. He had a large, untidy nose, and loose lips, with too much cruelty in their shape for weakness. He was blustering and badgering—without mercy. It was his boast that in the course of six cigars he could get a confession every time. And he didn't care how he got it.

Garey Brennon was as different from Pitt as possible. A tall, red-headed youngster, with surprised blue eyes and a grin that he tried to discipline with a scowl of professional sternness. He was having his first chance on a big case, and he simply could not wait to begin. Garey Brennon lacked dignity. He lacked calm. He lacked patience and moderation. But he made up for everything by an unquenchable zest, a burning eagerness for this business of detecting.

"Not more'n six," Pitt repeated his boast to Garey Brennon, "and I get a confession. Never knew it to fail."

He lounged over to the table, with his hands in his pockets, and gave to each of them in turn a hard, unfriendly look. There is nothing quite so difficult to bear as silence: it is almost impossible not to answer back to accusations that have not been made. More than one was shifting nervously in his chair when Pitt's cigar gave the jerk that presaged speech.

"Mrs. DeQuincy Vanguard was murdered," said Pitt heavily. Angeline jumped at the sudden loudness of his voice. "She was murdered right here in this room. Somebody right here in this room murdered her. The best thing for whoever did it is to come clean, and no shilly-shallying. It'll save a lot of trouble. I'll get you in the end, whoever did it, and *don't you forget that.*"

This speech closed the preliminaries, and Pitt was ready for business.

"My, isn't he cross!" murmured Angeline.

Garey Brennon spoke to Pitt before he could go on. "Now who do you suppose wanted the Como-Garetti case declared a mistrial?" he asked eagerly. "Had you thought of it from that angle?"

"No," said Pitt shortly.

"Well, I had," said Brennon. "I wanted to know. . . . I say, sir, do you mind if I ask a few questions?"

Pitt eyed his young assistant with a nice mixture of amusement and contempt. "If you want," he said. For himself, he was content to do a little more looking. A guilty lot, too, the way they struck him; maybe they were all in on it.

"Now what I'd like to find out," said Garey Brennon, turning to the group about the table, and trying not to let his voice sound too friendly, "is how everybody stood in the jury balloting." His glance fell upon Angeline, sitting with her fingers pressed tight against her lips, as if to check the fountain of information bubbling behind them. "You tell me. You're Miss Tredennick, aren't you?"

"Yes," said Angeline. "But I don't know as I ought to tell you about how we voted and all, as long as you're an outsider." She glanced uncertainly at Mr. Gilley, remembering his rebuke.

Pitt was down on them in a minute. "Tell you to keep still, did he?"

"Why yes," said Angeline. "You see . . ."

"That was different," protested Mr. Gilley. "Dr. March . . ."

"I *see*," said Pitt, without waiting for him to finish.

"Of course," said Garey Brennon honestly, "I can't make you talk if you don't want to. But . . ."

"If you can't, I can." Pitt was never a stickler for the niceties of the law. A confession was a confession, no matter. "Go on," he ordered. "Tell him what he asked you."

"Well all right, I will," said Angeline, a trifle nettled. "It's nothing to be ashamed of, I'm sure. I never in the

world would have changed over to Mrs. Vanguard's side, if
I hadn't thought Karen Garetti killed him. . . ."

"What do you mean by Mrs. Vanguard's side?"

"Why, *guilty*, of course," said Angeline. "She was real
set on it. She voted that way the very first time round—she
said so herself. Of course we weren't supposed to tell, but
it was pretty hard to keep anything secret, the questions
Mrs. Vanguard would ask you. That first time Mr. Apple
and Miss Madras"—she indicated them beside her—"were
the only ones that voted with Mrs. Vanguard; she found
that out right away. But then Mr. Gilley changed, and
Miss Lee and Mr. Kashaw. She had talked over most all the
others, too, by the time she made us take that open vote. I
was the last one"—Angeline was not without pride—"and
I felt real bad, then, I can tell you. It seemed kind of like
going back on Miss Van Horn."

"What do you mean by that?"

"Why, she was for *not guilty*, of course," said Angeline.
"She said so as soon as it began to look bad for Karen
Garetti."

Cornelia Van Horn lifted clear brown eyes to Garey
Brennon's face. "I voted for acquittal every time," she said
simply. "I didn't think Karen Garetti did it."

"Why?"

"She didn't look like a murderess."

The weak little argument was not without its effect on
Garey Brennon. Evidently he thought there were others
who did not look like murderesses, either. It was easier to
question Angeline. . . .

Angeline rattled on cheerfully. "So there were the two
of them: one on one side, and one on the other. Sometimes Miss Van Horn would get somebody away from Mrs.
Vanguard: Miss Madras and Mr. Apple changed quite a
lot, and Mr. Elding did once, but he changed right back
again. By lunch time, this noon, there wasn't anybody left
with Miss Van Horn for acquittal except Mr. Hawes, and
he didn't count so much, because he was half persuaded

anyway, and he said himself if Karen Garetti didn't do it
he didn't know who did. . . ."

"Then you would say that Mrs. Vanguard and Miss Van
Horn were the leaders of the opposing factions?"

"Oh yes."

"And was there any animosity between them?"

"Oh heaps of it," said Angeline cheerily. "Mrs. Vanguard kept saying real mean things to Cornelia. She said it
was a wonder to her how a young girl like Cornelia could
pretend to know more about the case than anybody else,
and Cornelia said she didn't pretend to; and Mrs. Vanguard said, 'I wouldn't hold out . . . if I were you.' She
said that twice. And Cornelia said, 'But she didn't do it—I
just know she didn't.' And Mrs. Vanguard said how did she
know; and Cornelia said . . ."

"Oh thunder!" cried Pitt. "Shut it off. You're not getting anywhere, Brennon, letting her go on like that."

"I think I found out quite a lot," said Brennon, in rather a troubled way.

"Well, I found out that Miss Van Horn and the de-
ceased were at swords' points," conceded Pitt, taking to
himself, after a way he had, the one point that he considered of value.

"Oh I didn't say that," cried Angeline. "At least . . ."

"You said Miss Van Horn was putting up a fight against
Mrs. Vanguard, and Mrs. Vanguard was trying to break her
down. You said that, didn't you?"

"Why in a way I suppose I did. But . . ."

"Mrs. Vanguard was threatening her, and Miss Van
Horn . . ."

"Oh I didn't say anything about threats, I'm sure. The
only time threats were mentioned was when Cornelia said
Karen Garetti's threats didn't mean anything, because she
was from the Mediterranean and was excitable; she said,
'It isn't a bit the same as if I should threaten you, or you
should threaten me'; and Mrs. Vanguard asked her what

she meant by that; and Cornelia said she didn't mean any-thing."

"H'm," said Pitt portentously. "H'm." He left it at that for the moment. "This was round about lunch time, you say. And those are the cups from your lunch? I see some-body's taken good care to get them all mixed up."

"We pushed them one side," volunteered Mr. Gilley, "when we lifted Mrs. Vanguard to the table. Maybe we could straighten them out, if it makes any difference. I know that one's mine, because of the broken place in the rim."

Angeline was simply invaluable about this. It was she who remembered that this cup must have been William Apple's because it was all dry inside; he had drunk the cof-fee off quick and turned it upside down to show her it was empty. This was hers, because there was the little piece of ham gristle that she had dropped into it. This was Mrs. Vanguard's; there was just that much gone after the drink she took before her speech—pretty near half. The water cups were harder, but they got those straight, too, finally. Only the cups at the upper end of the table, where Mrs. Vanguard had been laid, were disturbed; the others stood unmistakably at their owners' places.

Pitt turned them all over to Garey Brennon. "Mark them for identification," he said, "and get them down to Pulsifer. Tell him to rush the analysis. We got to know if there was poison in the drinks. Now then. Didn't you have anything but coffee and water for lunch, huh? What was that about ham?"

"Sandwiches," said Angeline tenderly. "Ham sandwiches and cheese sandwiches and egg sandwiches and chicken sandwiches and lettuce sandwiches and olive sandwiches and marmalade sandwiches. And they weren't poisoned, either."

"How do *you* know?" barked Pitt.

"Because I ate them up," said Angeline, "and they didn't poison me."

2

Angeline came tripping back from the matron's room, where she had just been searched. There had been no end of trouble over the matter. Rinschy said sullenly that it wasn't legal. Mr. Hawes said if they took away his capsules or his drops, he could not answer for the consequences. His kidneys and his heart . . .

"You can search *me,*" said Damaris Lee idly. "It won't take long. I couldn't hide anything bigger than a pin." She put out her arms as she spoke, and the sight of her thin body in the dress so fashionably skin-tight that it lay like black varnish to every line of her, told them that what she said was true.

Mr. Gilley cut her off short; he didn't think it was decent. "I feel a search to be a personal indignity," he said. "But I am willing to do all in my power to cooperate with the law."

"I won't unhook my corsets, not for anybody," muttered Angeline. "How do I know I could hook them up again?"

Nevertheless, now that it was over, she came back looking pleased, like a kitten that has stolen cream and not been noticed. "Did I miss anything?" she asked brightly.

Pitt scowled at her. He did not like Angeline, and showed it.

But Garey Brennon had realized already that Angeline might prove useful. The qualities that made her rather a nuisance—her insatiable curiosity, her endless questions, her talent for always being everywhere and seeing everything—were the very qualities that might also make her valuable. Angeline was not really clever at putting two and two together, but there was nothing she could not find out about one and one and one and one. It was these isolated facts that Garey Brennon wanted to know about. He grinned at Angeline kindly. "You didn't miss much," he said.

They were just taking Dr. David March to the wash room for questioning. Trollope had carried in extra chairs and placed them opposite the door: one facing outward to the light, two facing that for Pitt and Garey Brennon. "It's as good as any place," Pitt said. "They can't hear us outside if we keep the door shut. Now then, March."

David March rose promptly when he was called. He smiled at Cornelia, and Angeline saw his fingers close for an instant over hers—there and gone again. "It's just a form," he reassured her. He crossed the room with his long, light stride, and passed through the wash-room door.

"He looks real nice," Angeline said. And Cornelia nodded, turning in her chair to watch him go, with a little prideful lifting of the chin.

David March did look nice, too. The high, clear forehead, with the dark hair growing back in points above the temples; the dark eyes under their straight brows, brooding even in laughter, cognizant of suffering; the lean, clean line of the jaw with its slight forward thrust, gave him a look of valor. It was a strong face; strong and purposeful. You saw that he had the power, which all good doctors must have, to make hard decisions quickly. You saw that he had the will to carry through to its just conclusion whatever it was that he had undertaken. But it was the mouth that held you: straight-lipped, with fine lines at the corners. A mouth exquisitely sensitive, humorous and tender; and yet so severely disciplined not to show emotion that you might have thought it stern at first—until he smiled. That smile of his was like a flash of light in a dark room, indomitable and gay.

Dr. March looked tired. He was always tired, with lack of sleep and the anxieties of a practice already beyond his strength. It was a very mixed practice—the houses on the Hill, and the foreign quarter; a large practice, that nevertheless would never make him rich. Nobody knew how many free patients he carried; how many people poured out their troubles and borrowed money of him. Perhaps he did not know himself. He had enemies, of course. He had unshakable friends in places where you would least expect

to find them. Cornelia Van Horn was not the only one in
Sheffield who thought that whatever Dr. David March did
was right because Dr. March did it.

He leaned back in the chair that had been set for him,
his long legs crossed, his long, clever surgeon's fingers
quiet on his knee. There was something a little quizzical
in the direct look he gave back to Pitt's glare. He answered
the questions that were put to him forthrightly.

Angeline had been much afflicted of late by the light
from the windows shining in her eyes, and now she tiptoed
across the room to inspect the curtain arrangements. This
brought her directly outside the wash-room door. "Sh!"
she whispered back over her shoulder.

Pitt began at once, without preamble. "Did you know
Mrs. Vanguard was poisoned when you took her to the
hospital?"

"I did not know," said David March quietly. "I thought
it possible. I spoke of it at once to Dr. Hummell, the ambulance surgeon, and he agreed with me. Afterwards, at
the hospital, the diagnosis was confirmed."

"What kind of poison did you tell Dr. Hummell had
been used?"

"I *suggested*"—the slight emphasis on the word corrected Pitt's phrasing—"I suggested hyoscine. The symptoms—extreme dilatation of the pupils, harsh, irregular
breathing, dryness of the throat, rapid pulse, and stupor—
were characteristic of hyoscine poisoning."

"Yeah. You gave her some medicine, didn't you?"

"Yes."

"What was that?"

"Aromatic spirits of ammonia."

Pitt's voice was a sneer. "Is that what you always give
for hyoscine poisoning?"

The lines at the corners of Dr. March's mouth deepened
just ever so slightly, but he permitted himself no other
recognition of Pitt's insolence. "I did not at first—I believe naturally—consider poison. I took Mrs. Vanguard's

attack to be an ordinary fainting fit, such as would not have been remarkable under strong excitement and in such a close room. Aromatic, as you probably know, is usually effective in such cases. When I saw that Mrs. Vanguard did not react to the stimulant, and when, on examination, I found no cardiac condition that would explain her symptoms, I began to be suspicious. I was then anxious to get her immediately to a hospital, where there would be facilities for dealing with the case, and where I might have another opinion."

"When'd you say you first thought of poison?"

"Soon after I administered the aromatic."

"Yeah. Quick, weren't you?" Even more than his words, Pitt's manner implied that Dr. March had been a little *too* quick, a little too ingenious, in his diagnosis. "How'd you happen to come in here anyway?" he added after an instant.

"The deputy sheriff called me. I was in the court room."

"Hang out there much, do you?"

"No." David March did not elaborate his statement. The word lay cold and bald between them.

After a moment's hesitation, Pitt decided to leave it at that. "Then you weren't sent for because you were Mrs. Vanguard's regular doctor?"

"No."

"Never attended her?"

"Yes. I was formerly the Vanguards' physician."

"Oh you were, were you?" Pitt's cigar gave a triumphant jerk in his red face, as if he had surprised Dr. March in a damaging admission. "What'd they fire you for?"

"I suppose they preferred another doctor," said. David March dryly. His professional pride was touched now, and for the first time he showed that he was irked by Pitt's questions.

But Pitt only bore down on him the harder. "Oh come now," he blustered. "You can't get away with any hocus-pocus like that. Out with it. What was the row about?"

Again the lines about Dr. March's lips deepened just perceptibly. "There was no row," he said evenly. "Mrs. Vanguard was displeased with a statement that I made in regard to her husband's health, and asked me to resign the case."

"Give him the wrong medicine, did you?" suggested Pitt slyly.

"It was not a question of medicine," said Dr. March, evenly still. "Rather the contrary. Mr. Vanguard was suffering from chronic nervous indigestion, and I said that what he needed was a . . . rest."

Angeline was finding the acoustics inadequate. Now she thrust open the wash-room door. "I just wanted to wash my hands . . ." she began. Then, at Dr. March's last words, she broke into a small, irrepressible giggle.

"I beg your pardon, I'm sure," she said, when Pitt and Brennon whirled upon her. "But really it *was* funny. I remember all about it at the time; the Vanguards' second girl told our cook. Mrs. Vanguard was fit to be tied. You see what Dr. March said was that Mr. Vanguard needed a rest from his wife. I thought it was too brave of him for anything, myself," she added generously.

"It was too honest," said Dr. March, soberly.

"Then you had reason to be sorry for it?" Pitt took him up in a flash, forgetting even to put Angeline out in his eagerness not to let the moment slip.

"I was very sorry," said Dr. March. "It was inexcusable."

"I suppose she did you quite a lot of harm in your business—an influential woman like her, turning you off herself, and likely making talk?"

"I couldn't say as to that. I was thinking of Mr. Vanguard. It made things harder for him."

"Yeah!" said Pitt skeptically.

But Garey Brennon turned eagerly to Angeline. "How did Mrs. Vanguard and Dr. March seem, when he was called in this noon? Did you notice anything?"

"Well, there, that was it, wasn't it?" said Angeline brightening. "I didn't think at the time. Mrs. Vanguard acted real put out. She tried to push him away at first. But afterwards I guess she didn't notice. I didn't pay much attention, because she was sick and kind of crotchety; she tried to push Cornelia away too. Dr. March didn't act any way special that I know of. Like a doctor, that's all. I guess he was willing to do for her. . . ."

"*Glad* to 'do for her,' huh?" said Pitt.

"She was ill and needed me," said Dr. March simply.

Garey Brennon conducted Angeline back to the door and pushed her gently outside; he explained that one did not interrupt the examination of suspected persons or other witnesses even to wash one's hands; he closed the door upon her. But Pitt sat still, his big body humped over and his big hands hanging; you could see from the way he bit a piece off his cigar that things were taking on a pattern in his mind.

"Then it comes down to this," he said finally. "You told Mrs. Vanguard where she got off, and she flared up and gave you the boot. There's been no love lost between you ever since. When she flopped, you barged in and gave her some medicine, and three hours afterwards she croaked. That it, huh?"

"Your summary is terse but misleading," said Dr. March coldly.

3

"Mr. Gilley," called Pitt, through the wash-room door.

Mr. Simon Gilley advanced with a smooth tread, a soapy rubbing of his hands, as if he were walking across his own salesroom floor, and took his place facing Pitt and Brennon. For all his self-importance, he was only a smallish, pompous man in buttons; buttons of orders on his coat, button of a nose, a mouth buttoned over prominent teeth, a heavy watch-chain buttoning in a prominent stomach, shoe-button eyes. Once he had been president of the Sheffield Board of Trade, and he had never forgotten it. It was in his manner now.

"Simon Gilley, proprietor of the Sheffield Furniture Company," he stated grandly, as if he were a butler announcing himself at a drawing-room door.

"Known Mrs. Vanguard long?"

"For years. I furnished her house for her when she was married." It was characteristic of the Vanguard domestic situation that Mr. Gilley did not regard it as in any degree the house of Mr. Vanguard.

"Wasn't any trouble over it, I presume?"

"On the contrary," said Mr. Gilley. "Mrs. Vanguard was very pleased. From time to time, when there have been changes to make, Mrs. Vanguard has always come to me."

"Know her any outside of business, did you?"

"At the time when I was president of the Board of Trade," said Mr. Gilley, with a pause to let the item sink in, "Mrs. Vanguard was president of the Civics Club, and we were associated in many enterprises of public betterment. We always worked together, I may say, in the greatest harmony. Mrs. Vanguard was a noble woman. She did a great deal of Good in Sheffield." After a moment he added: "Mrs. Vanguard was about to do her house over again. I suppose now . . ." He stopped, his face puckered comically; it was plain that Mr. Gilley was in the throes of honest emotion.

"Uh-huh," said Pitt. The cigar was very still. Even he could find nothing much against Mr. Gilley—he was not the type to kill off a good customer.

"May I ask a question?" put in Garey Brennon, popping up and down with impatience, like a hot corn on a griddle. "How did you vote on the Como-Garetti case?"

"On the second ballot, and on all succeeding ballots, I voted for conviction."

"And for acquittal on the first. Why did you change?"

"I became convinced that Karen Garetti killed Sebastian Como," said Mr. Gilley, in the patient voice of one who humors a young child.

"Who convinced you?"

"I was convinced of my own judgment. Mrs. Vanguard had been going through the evidence. . . ."

"Was it before or after you changed your vote that Mrs. Vanguard spoke of having her house done over?"

"I . . . don't remember," said Mr. Gilley. But his sudden flush betrayed him.

"What's that got to do with it?" asked Pitt impatiently.

"I don't exactly know," said Garey Brennon. "I just thought it might have something."

4

"Miss Tredennick," called Pitt, not without hesitation.

Angeline flounced into the wash room, settled herself in the chair, spread her gray skirts decorously round her ankles, and made sure that Grandmother Hawthorne's real cameo brooch was safely fastened. It was a talent of Angeline's that she could sit in the hardest, straightest, most rock-bound chair in the world, and make it look like a piazza rocker; it was something in the way she moved her body in rhythm with her speech.

"Yes, I'm Angeline Tredennick," she began, before any one could get in a word. "I live with Miss Marilla Holinshed, 32 Grove Street, and we take paying guests. Marilla is a real good woman, and I wouldn't say a word against her, but she is inclined to be a little bit bossy. I am fond of Marilla, but sometimes I can't help wondering, if I had it all to do over, if I could ever get so fond of her again. It is kind of aggravating to have her always harping on gravy, and saying that white rolls are fattening and I ought to eat dark bread, and taking my library books back to the library before I've had a chance to find out whether He married Her or not . . ."

"How old are you?" interrupted Garey Brennon meanly.

"I'm thirty-nine, young man, and not a day over, if it's anything to you," said Angeline with a toss of her head. "My hair is prematurely gray. I wouldn't have it dyed for anything, because I like gray hair, especially if it is naturally curly. I never had a wave in my life; I just put it up in combs at night, and in the morning . . ."

"Did you know Mrs. Vanguard?" interrupted Pitt.

"Know her! I should say I did, and her living in our back yard all these years—though she always did act as if it was her back yard we lived in. The two houses back up together, you see, and so one isn't any more in the back yard of the other than the other is. Of course I know Washington Avenue is more fashionable than Grove Street, but as I said to Marilla, what of it? And I guess paying guests are just as respectable as stocks and bonds, if they don't pay as well. Sometimes I wonder what Mr. Vanguard would have done if she hadn't got him started in the brokerage business. Something with fishes, I suppose, and I guess he would have been happier . . ."

"Ever have any trouble with Mrs. Vanguard?" interrupted Pitt.

"Trouble? I should say so, and who could help it with her carrying on the way she did? She acted as if paying guests were some disease and she was afraid she'd catch it. Hardly a day, there was, that she didn't have a complaint. Our dead leaves were coming over into her yard, and why didn't we have them raked up? Or Mrs. Noonan's parrot— Mrs. Noonan has our second floor, rear, the big room with the two bays—was swearing out the window, and she didn't think the children ought to hear him. Or the smoke from our incinerator was blowing right onto her terrace and she was going to have a tea. And then if I so much as asked her who was going to be at the tea, off she'd go with her nose in the air without hardly answering. I said to Marilla . . ."

"Oh Lord!" groaned Pitt. "Shut it off."

5

"William Apple."

William Apple lumbered forward apprehensively, his great hands twitching at his sides as if he more than half expected to find the chair awaiting him wired for electricity. He was a tow-headed giant, with a broad, flat face, burned darker than his hair, and dazed eyes under sunscorched brows. Not inordinately brilliant at the best, he was simply putty in the hands of Pitt; his natural taciturnity reduced to nods and shakes and unwilling monosyllables.

"What's your business?" began Pitt.

"Farmer."

"What kind of farmer?"

"Cows."

"Run a milk route?"

"Not now."

"But you did? How long since?"

"Year."

"What made you stop?"

"Couldn't sell the milk." William Apple's smoldering resentment betrayed him to an unwonted loquacity. "Have to sell it to the creamery. Creamery don't pay nothing. Folks is afraid. No sense to it."

"What you talking about?" demanded Pitt. "What they afraid of?"

"Tubercles."

"Oh I know what he means," cried Garey Brennon with enthusiasm. "You know that Cleaner Cows Commission that they had a year ago, when all the cattle were tuberculin-tested. Wasn't that it, Mr. Apple?"

William Apple nodded.

"And you lost part of your cows?"

"Most all."

"And I say!" cried Brennon again. "Didn't Mrs. Vanguard have something to do with that Commission? Wasn't she . . . ?"

"Head-pusher," said William Apple. "She come out there to my place. . ." He choked into silence. The old uncomprehending anger of that day a year ago blazed up again, like a fire nursed in secret under ashes. It burned in his pale eyes and knotted his mouth. His great hands twisted together suddenly in a gesture like strangling. William Apple did not look any more like the patient plodder of his wont, slow-witted and mild-mannered. He looked powerful and fierce. He looked . . . murderous.

"Did you hold Mrs. Vanguard personally responsible for your loss?"

"Huh?"

"Did you think Mrs. Vanguard killed your cows?"

"Sure she killed them," said William Apple fiercely.

Angeline opened the door again at this point. If a body needs a handkerchief, she needs a handkerchief, that's all—and Angeline thought she might have dropped hers while she was being questioned. "That doesn't prove anything," she broke in brightly. "Mrs. Vanguard killed my cat, too, but I didn't kill her."

The door was open behind her, so that the room heard. Charles Kashaw burst into a big delighted roar of laughter. The tension, that had been winding them all tighter and tighter into silence, broke suddenly. It seemed as if everybody were talking at once.

"Why didn't you say so?" snapped Pitt.

"I presume I would have," said Angeline rather crossly, "if you hadn't cut me off so short. I presume there are a lot of things I might have told you, if I'd had half a chance. He was a real nice little cat, too. Edmund Spenser, I called him, because he had blue eyes and white whiskers, and looked kind of poetic, like the Faerie Queen. Only I couldn't name him Faerie Queen, because . . . well . . . you see he was a gentleman kitty. That's what Mrs. Vanguard didn't like. He made noises on the back fence at night. I didn't mind it myself. I thought it sounded kind of cheer-

ful, as if he was having a good time. But Mrs. Vanguard
was real hateful about it always. And finally she gave him
rat poison, and . . ."

"Have any trouble over it?"

"Trouble? I should say we did have trouble! The minute
I found out, I put on my things, and I marched myself over
to Mrs. Vanguard's, and I said to her, 'Mrs. Vanguard,' I
said, 'a woman that's mean enough to poison a little innocent cat, ought to be poisoned herself. . . .'"

"He never had a fair chance, Mr. Apple didn't," Mary
Madras was saying. "The state didn't allow him half what
was right for his cows, and then after he got new ones,
people wouldn't buy the milk. I know, because of Mrs.
Buckley, where I work. She has three children and she
uses a sight o' milk. But after that Report came out, with
William Apple's name in it and all, would she buy another
drop off him? She would not. Mrs. Vanguard wrote the
Report. Her name was right onto the end of it. *I* wouldn't
be the one to blame Mr. Apple. . ." She stopped, her hand
clapped over her mouth.

Damaris Lee and Charles Kashaw were making a limer-
ick. They chanted it in joyful unison:

> There was a young Tom-cat named Spense'
> Who made love on the back garden fence.
>   Mrs. Vanguard with rat-bane
>   Administered cat-bane;
> And so Edmund Spenser went hence. . . .

Again Garey Brennon pushed Angeline gently outside;
again he explained to her that one did not interrupt. . . .

"How did you vote on the Como-Garetti case?" he asked
William Apple as he closed the door after her.

"Different ways," said William Apple.

"But you voted guilty last?"

"Yeah."

"Why was that?"

"Mrs. Vanguard said nobody wouldn't buy my milk if I didn't." William Apple rubbed the back of his hand across his mouth in a puzzled way. "I don't rightly know why. But that's what she said. . . ."

"You thought same as Miss Tredennick, didn't you?" broke in Pitt.

"Huh?"

"You thought a woman that would poison a cat ought to be poisoned too?"

"Oh. Yeah. I guess so."

"Or a cow?"

"Yeah."

"So you did it." Pitt thrust his purple face almost into William Apple's; the cigar wobbled under the fellow's dazed eyes. "You killed her. Come on, now; don't try to get out of it. You as good as said so. You killed her, didn't you?"

William Apple drew his hand again across his mouth. "Huh?" he said. "Who? Me?"

6

The search was over. The matron who had searched the women, and the officer who had searched the men brought in such articles as they thought might have a bearing on the case and turned them over to Pitt and Brennon. It was an odd assortment. There was Damaris Lee's enameled flask with the red and black lightning flashes; Charles Kashaw's flat silver one; a stout black bottle belonging to Leo Rinschy; an assortment of pocket knives—William Apple's big one with a tool for removing stones from horses' hoofs, Mr. Gilley's gold one off his watch chain, Rinschy's, Biggs', Mr. Elding's, Mr. Hawes', Charles Kashaw's, and a tiny pearl one of Cornelia's. Pitt tossed them all contemptuously back to their owners.

"You don't stick in poison with a knife," he said.

There was a small packet wound up in a paper towel that the matron passed to Pitt with a whispered word of explanation; he stuck it in his pocket without comment. There was an automatic. "Rinschy's," said the officer.

"Oo!" squealed Angeline. "See the pistol!"

"What you doing with this, huh?" demanded Pitt. "You got a permit?"

"Ye'," said Rinschy sullenly—then thought better of it. "No."

"You could do six months hard, fella, just for this," Pitt assured him. "Like enough the judge'll hold you for carrying concealed weapons, if you ever get out of this mess."

He tossed the matter to one side, paying no attention to Rinschy's furious, half-intelligible protestations: "I am not do wit' heem any harrm; she is for protect only. . . ." After all, you don't shoot in poison with a gun, either.

There was also a bottle of cheap perfume marked *La Tulipe Noire* from Mary Madras' bag; a bottle of Kow Kolic Kure of William Apple's; Angeline's sweet chocolate; and Mr. Hawes' capsules and his bottle of "drops." Pitt examined these last carefully.

"I beg you not to take those away from me," cried Gideon Hawes tremulously. "With my kidneys and my heart in this condition, it is a matter of the very gravest import for me to have them. I could not miss a single dose without serious results. I am dependent on them. I need them. I must have them. I . . ." His thin voice cracked and quavered.

"H'm," said Pitt, sniffing at them in a gingerly way. "How do I know they're not all full of poison?"

"But I take them. The prescription is on them. You can read for yourself. . . ."

"How do I know you didn't doctor them up with poison after you got them from the drug store?"

"But I take them," Hawes repeated. An idea came to him and he advanced it anxiously. "If you like, you could keep them for me, and give me out my doses when they are due. I . . ."

Garey Brennon was sorry for the little man's evident distress. "I tell you what," he suggested. "Here are the prescription numbers right on them. Why can't we copy them off and get Trollope to have them refilled? Then we could keep these. . . ."

Pitt shook his heavy shoulders in a gesture of impatience; Brennon was too soft-hearted by half, his manner said. But he did not openly object. "All right. Mark the rest of this stuff and get it off to Pulsifer. And tell him to get a move on with those drinking cups. Wait a minute, though, before you do it. There might be something else."

He turned back to the wash room, picked up the black professional bag that he had kept constantly under his eye, and plumped it down in one of the empty chairs. He beckoned to Dr. March.

"That yours?"

"Yes."

"Let's see the bottle you gave Mrs. Vanguard that dose out of."

David March bent over the bag. Just as he had done earlier in the day, he snapped it open; just as unhesitatingly he drew out a bottle. They had forgotten, all of them now, about the open door. But Angeline, though she gave her ears to what was going on inside, was looking at Cornelia. Cornelia sat leaning forward against the table edge, still, very still, even her quiet eyes unchanging, as if she were caught in the pause between two breaths.

"This one," said David March promptly, holding it out to Pitt. It was a two-ounce bottle, a little less than half full, with a label: Aromatic Spirits of Ammonia.

Pitt drew out the cork and held the bottle to his nose. The result was more than satisfactory. He choked, passing the bottle on to Brennon. "Ammonia, all right," he reluctantly admitted. "Where'd you get it ready for her? Out there?"

"No. Here in the wash room."

"Alone, were you?"

"I was alone at first. Afterward Miss Tredennick came in to see if she could help me."

"That right?" Pitt turned to Angeline.

"Why of course it's right," said Angeline. "Why shouldn't I come in, I'd like to know? There wasn't anything I could do, though. Just as I got here, Dr. March stepped over to the cup machine, and pulled out a cup, and measured out some of that medicine. . . ."

"This was the bottle?"

"Oh I'm sure it was."

"But see here!" cried Garey Brennon, flinging himself headlong into the conversation. "According to what Miss Tredennick says, you didn't prepare the medicine until after she came. What were you doing before that?"

"The cork in the aromatic bottle stuck," said David March calmly, "and I was getting it out. You'll see where it's a little broken at the side."

"You can't rattle him," muttered Garey Brennon to himself. "That's what you get, working with doctors."

"And so then you took it out and gave it to her," Pitt resumed. "Say now, where's the cup?"

For the first time, Dr. March seemed at a loss. "Why I don't know," he said slowly. "As I remember it, I set it right down beside me."

"Be there now, then, wouldn't it?"

"Maybe it went out with the ones we sent to Pulsifer," suggested Brennon.

"Not unless they fooled us," said Pitt sharply. "They accounted for those. Just a pattern, all round, and no extras."

It was Angeline, of course, who solved the difficulty. "Why I remember now," she cried. "Dr. March did set the cup down beside him, the way he said. But it was pretty near the edge of the table, and afterwards, when he leaned over to listen to Mrs. Vanguard's heart, his coat swung out against it and knocked it off. I remember thinking at the

time it didn't matter, because it was empty anyway, and so
I didn't pick it up. It must be under the table now." And
with the words, Angeline scuttled down the length of the
room, and vanished under the table herself, head-first, as
quick as a conjuring trick; they could see her little round
gray back, and her sensible low-heeled shoes showing their
soles a-tiptoe. She emerged very red in the face, with a
gray curl over one eye . . . and a cup in her hand. "There!"
she said, and stood triumphant, tidying her hair.

Pitt took the cup, smelled it, and passed it to Brennon.

"That's the one," cried Brennon excitedly. "It smells of
ammonia." He stood turning it in his hand; an ordinary
paper cup, slightly flaring, with fluted sides and a stiffening round the top to held the shape. "I say!" he exclaimed.
"Here's a queer thing."

It was a queer thing, too. He and Pitt bent over it together, plainly puzzled. Under one of the paper flutings,
close to the top of the cup and slanting a little downward,
there was a tiny round hole like the prick of a pin. The
hole was smooth on the outside, but inside they could feel
a slight roughness. Pitt closed the door abruptly; held the
cup out toward David March.

"What did you do that for?" he demanded.

"I didn't do it."

"How did it get there then?"

"I couldn't say."

"Miss Tredennick saw you take it out of the cup machine herself. You didn't let it out of your hands, did you,
till after you gave Mrs. Vanguard the dose of . . . medicine?"

"No."

"Well then!" cried Pitt. "Talk straight, now, and no
hedging. What did you make the hole with, and what did
you make it for?"

"I have no information to add," said David March. It
was at times like this, when he did not smile, that you saw
the sternness of his mouth.

To Brennon's surprise, Pitt appeared to let the matter drop. "Then perhaps you'll show your usual hearty cooperation by letting us see your bottle of hyoscine."

"Certainly," said David March calmly. He took out a small metal box, containing perhaps half a dozen bottles clamped in holders; made an unerring choice. "This one," he said, just as promptly as before.

It was a tiny yellowish vial that he held out, not so big around as a child's finger, with three minute white tablets at the bottom, and a bit of cotton thrust in at the top. There was a label running lengthwise:

Soluble Hypodermic tablets
No. 129
HYOSCINE HYDROBROMATE
1/100 grain

And, round the vial at right angles to the rest of the printing, the red word *Poison*.

Pitt looked from that vial to the two-ounce bottle of aromatic. "Not easy to confuse the two," he said meaningly. He peered at David March from under his drooping eyelid. "Is it customary for a doctor to carry hyoscine in his bag?"

"Why no," said David March frankly. "No, I shouldn't say it was customary. It can't be very uncommon, though. As a matter of fact, I had that for a case of Parkinson's Disease—paralysis agitans—about a month ago; I gave two hypodermics in one day, after which the case was removed to a hospital and I was no longer in attendance. But I left the hyoscine in my bag, and it has been there ever since."

"H'm," said Pitt. He rattled the vial in his hand, as if to shake its secret out of it. "How many tablets to a full bottle?"

"Twenty-five."

"How many for a dose?"

"One—one one-hundredth of a grain—would be a good large dose; I more frequently give half a one."

"And how many would be fatal?"

"Oh . . . ten, certainly. Probably less."

"You say you have given two doses of half a tablet each. But there are twenty-two tablets gone from your bottle. How's that?"

David March's quiet face did not change by so much as a flicker of the lids. "Oh yes," he said easily. "I've had that bottle a long time. I did not mean that the case I spoke of was the only occasion when I had used it—simply that that was when I put it in my bag."

"Yeah!" said Pitt again—and again he seemed to leave the subject. "You spoke about hypodermics. Usually give hyoscine hypodermically, do you?"

"Yes. The tablets are highly soluble."

"And you were alone with Mrs. Vanguard, weren't you, while she was there on the table?"

"Alone with eleven exceptions," said David March dryly.

"I thought you sent the others away."

"I believe not. Or yes—wait; I did ask them not to crowd round the table and shut off the air. And I asked them to open the windows. Most of them went then. Afterwards they were back and forth. I don't remember—"

"You're quick," said Pitt—and the words were not a compliment. "You're clever with your fingers. While those folks were *back and forth,* you could have given Mrs. Vanguard a hypodermic without their seeing you, couldn't you, huh?"

"I really don't know," said David March. And now at last he let his annoyance flash out in eye and twist of lip. "I have no way of knowing, because I didn't try."

"But you have a hypodermic syringe?" persisted Pitt.

"Oh yes."

"Where is it?"

"In my bag."

"Let's see it."

Again Dr. March reached inside the bag before him. "Why that's queer," he said after a moment. "I don't . . ."

seem to find it. It doesn't . . . seem to be here. This is the case it belongs in. . . ." He held it out, with the cover raised, showing the empty space where the syringe fitted. "I don't see . . ."

"Is this it?" Pitt spoke with unwonted softness. He took from his pocket the package that the matron had given him; it was folded round with a paper towel, and his heavy hands lingered tenderly over the wrappings as he undid them. He laid it out flat at last in front of Dr. March, with a hypodermic syringe in the middle. "Is that yours, huh?"

"Yes," said Dr. March slowly.

He did not move to touch it, and Garey Brennan leaned down excitedly over his shoulder and picked the syringe up. It was just as it had been used, with the needle still screwed in. He examined it with a layman's curiosity. Mrs. Vanguard's medicine cup he still held in his other hand. And then suddenly . . .

"*Look!*" he cried.

Garey Brennon was holding the hypodermic syringe in his right hand, with the needle pointing down. He was holding the paper cup in his left. He was inserting the needle under the fluting of the cup, directing it inward and downward, through the hole that was like a pin-prick. The needle passed through the hole sweetly, without friction. It was an exact fit.

"What did I tell you?" demanded Pitt, taking the credit neatly to himself. "*Now* we know something." And he bit a whole inch off his cigar.

"Now they know something," reported Angeline outside. And on that the door came open.

Nobody spoke while Garey Brennon collected the bottle of hyoscine, the bottle of aromatic, the cup, the syringe, and added them to the other things that were to go to Pulsifer for analysis. Even Damaris Lee, for once, had no flip comment to offer; even Kashaw had no wisecrack. Rinschy, glowering under black brows, forgot the automatic. William Apple forgot his cows. Mr. Hawes

forgot his capsule. They were watching David March coming back again: watching him . . . watching . . .

Only Cornelia did not look. She sat with her head high
and her chin firm—but her hands were tight together in
her lap. They showed white across the small brown knuckles. There was a tension in her very stillness, a straining
after quiet, as if she could not have moved without breaking.

Angeline couldn't stand it. She simply couldn't. Not
even if they knew she had been listening. "Where did you
find the hypodermic?" she burst out.

And Pitt, in very jubilation, answered her. "In Miss
Van Horn's bag," he said.

It was then, before the eyes of all of them, that a shocking thing happened. Dr. David March was looking straight
at Pitt, and the controlled expression of his face did not
change by so much as the least tremor of a muscle. But at
Pitt's words he turned suddenly, completely, very terrify-
ingly . . . white.

III
Wednesday

"I'm just as strong for justice as the next person," declared Angeline, flouncing into her chair, "but I draw the line at cockroaches."

It was Wednesday morning. They were gathered again in the jury room after a night in jail, where they had been held as material witnesses in the murder of Mrs. DeQuincy Vanguard. They had been offered bail, of course, but Simon Gilley was the only one who had availed himself of the offer. Damaris Lee might have done so, but she said she was too late for the tea dance anyway and she thought that being in jail would be more fun than a circus. All Damaris' crowd prided themselves on the number of times they had been arrested for speeding, but they always got off with fines and costs; you could see that her actual incarceration was going to make a grand story the way she would tell it at parties.

But it had not turned out to be any fun at all. Jails, it seems, are very jail-like. Cells are very cell-like. There was no society. There was no pep. The beds would not bear mention. And the food . . .

"Canned milk!" snorted Angeline. "Anybody might as well *be* a murderer, and done with it."

Their treatment, of course, had been the same. But there was one thing that was significant. The bail demanded of the others had ranged from five to ten thousand dollars, but this sum had soared abruptly to forty thousand in

the case of Cornelia Van Horn and Dr. David March. The
fact set them aside from the others, ringed them round
with a blacker wall of suspicion, a more intricate tangle
of doubt. It didn't seem right to Angeline, somehow. They
were so young. They were so alive. There was so much
capacity in them for laughter and living. They walked so
lightly, to have their feet tripped by the law. They spoke
so freely, to be whispered of with murder on the lips. And
yet . . .

But then they looked at you so straightly, with so much
candor, so much faith. Surely those concerned with killing
did not look at you like that? A dreadful thought came to
Angeline: a memory of something Mrs. Vanguard herself
had said. "I guess if you had the nerve to kill a person,
you could stand looking at anybody afterwards." Angeline
shivered a little, though the morning had come up hot and
clear out of a breathless night.

David March seemed no different than he had the day
before. A little pale, perhaps, grave, composed, his quiet
eyes resigned to sleeplessness, as if a night in the town jail
were only one more wakeful night in a doctor's wakeful
life. If he was worried about whether Dr. Larensen, who
was taking care of his practice, would bring the Hum-
bolt baby out of its next convulsion, or spend quite the
time and patient sympathy that the state of poor Miss
Meggs' taut nerves demanded, he showed it no more than
he showed the more immediate anxieties of his own situation. The pressure of his fingers over Cornelia's, when he
found them for an instant, was hard and comforting.

Cornelia's healthy young body, however, was not tuned
to loss of sleep. The print of that long night, when she sat
erect on her prison cot with her back against the wall—as
if she must face the horror that lurked in the dark and have
time to seize it before it lay hold on her—was in the faint
shadows underneath her eyes, the ever so slightly pinched
look round her nostrils. But she trod proudly still, her
chin tilted to a fine defiance. Despite the miserable jail

facilities, she had contrived to step forth looking as if she had just come from her maid and her hairdresser, her laundress and her presser and the man who shines boots. The brown hat was pulled down tight; and if the severity of its line, shutting away her hair, made her small bright face seem a shade less bright, a shade more keenly pointed, still the tiny orange feather at the crown waved like a banner. She returned the quick pressure of David March's fingers.

"Don't worry about me," she said. "I'm all right." Angeline walked over with them, just to show she didn't take too much stock in the way things looked.

"Now, David," she said, drawing him aside—it seemed a little more friendly to call him by his first name—"of course I don't think for a minute that you and Cornelia *did* it. But I *can't* help wondering how your hypodermic got into her bag."

"It put on its cap," said David March whimsically, "and walked out of my bag into hers."

Nevertheless it was no laughing matter.

And now, back in the jury room, David was not being whimsical any more. He was being very serious. And he was doing no whit better at explaining how the hypodermic syringe came to be in Cornelia's bag than he had done the night before.

Last night they had made him tell the story. Now they made him tell it again. Over and over. Over and over. As if they could wear him down by repetition, like dropping water in the old Inquisition. Angeline had performed a miracle with a hairpin and a bit of caramel so that today the wash-room door would not latch. While the questioning went on within, she strolled up and down outside—for exercise, she said; so much sitting gave her prickles.

"One night," David March was saying, "I was driving Miss Van Horn home. On the way I stopped to make a call. It was necessary to use my hypodermic. I was in a hurry, and I stuck it in my pocket. I was afraid I might break the needle, which I had left screwed in. I handed it to Miss Van Horn and asked her to put it in my bag. But my bag I had dropped over into the back seat of my car, and she could not reach it. 'Just put it somewhere safe till we stop,' I said to her, 'and then I'll fix it.' She tucked it into her purse. I forgot all about it . . ."

Yes, that was some time ago. Perhaps a month.

No, he had not asked for it. Didn't he say he had forgotten?

No, he had not had occasion to use it since.

No, he did not pretend to say that he had not given a hypodermic for a month. He had another syringe in his office.

"I guess you didn't know"—Pitt ground out the words slowly—"I guess you didn't know that Miss Van Horn confessed you gave the syringe to her yesterday noon, and told her to get rid of it."

"She couldn't have," said David March, "because I didn't say it."

Over and over. Over and over again. They let him go finally and took Cornelia.

"I had had it in my bag quite a long time," Cornelia said. "Dr. March gave it to me to put away one night when I was riding with him. I couldn't reach his bag, because it was over in the back seat; but my own bag was in my lap"—it was in her lap now: a tan-colored tweed one, with a cream and orange hand and a brown wooden top—"and I put it into that. Afterwards I forgot."

Yes, that was quite a while ago. Several weeks, maybe.

No, she had not thought it queer that he didn't ask for it. She just didn't think about it at all. If she had, she would have given it back.

No, she did not pretend that she had carried it round with her every day. She did not use that bag often.

Yes, perhaps she had used it once or twice. But it was a deep bag they could see—and it had a lot of little odd things in the bottom. She had not taken them out.

"What you got to say to March's admitting that he gave it to you here in the jury room yesterday noon?"

"Oh but he couldn't have said that," said Cornelia staunchly. "That wasn't true."

"He told you to get rid of it. Didn't he?"

"No."

"He told you to sneak it back in his bag if you got a chance."

"No."

"No, you didn't get a chance?"

"No, he didn't tell me that."

"He told you to hide it somewhere else."

"He didn't tell me anything. We had both forgotten that I had it. . . ."

Over and over. Over and over. Pounding. Jeering. Hammering. Trying to break down defenses. Trying to catch them in a misstep.

"Stick to it, if you want," snarled Pitt. "I'll get you in the end. You got your story cooked up good between you, but it won't hold forever."

"Oh they didn't cook it up between them," cried Angeline anxiously. "Honestly, Mr. Pitt. Why I asked Dr. March myself how the hypodermic got in Miss Van Horn's bag, and when I told her afterwards what he said, she kind of laughed and acted real surprised."

2

"Mary Madras," bawled Pitt.

Mary Madras was the type who is terrified by the law, and shows it. She crept into the wash room timidly, twisting a button on her coat; the color in her face had gone off a little, so that the freckles across her short nose showed in a peppering of round gold spots; her blue eyes were round too with a child's frank fear of the unknown. Mary Madras was pretty in a somewhat too full-blown way. Her black hair was a little untidy, as if she never had the time to dress it properly, but it waved rather nicely off her forehead. There was too much lace on her blue silk dress, and too much imitation fur on her coat, and the pearls round her throat were too large even to imitate pearls, and her reptile shoes had never seen a reptile. But there was something appealing in her frank fumbling after beauty, something wholesome and satisfying in her healthy natural color. Later she would be stout, perhaps. But now she looked only pleasantly rounded, and touchable, and hearty. In her manner there was that curious mixture of shyness and bravado that marks women who have had to fend for themselves always and have not always had good fortune in their fending. She had the anxious eyes and apologetic speech of one long accustomed to reprimand.

"Yes, sir, I'm Mary Madras," she began timidly. "Nursemaid. I work for Mrs. Buckley, on Cardigan Avenue?"

"Know Mrs. Vanguard?"

"I knew who she was, sir." Mary Madras' voice was careful. "But I never had a word with her in my life until I saw her here."

"You had words here, then, you say?"

"Only good-morning, or the like of that. And of course about how I voted."

"How did you vote?" put in Garey Brennon.

"Well, I guess maybe you'll think I changed my mind a pretty good many times," Mary said with becoming embarrassment. "Seemed as if one minute it'd look as if Karen Garetti killed him, and the next . . ."

"But you voted guilty in the end?"

"Yes, sir."

"Why was that? Who persuaded you?"

"Why I guess in a way you might say Mrs. Vanguard did. I was kind of afraid to do any different."

"What do you mean, you were afraid?"

"Well, I don't know as I can rightly tell you," said Mary Madras with pitiful frankness. "But Mrs. Vanguard, she was an awful woman. Seemed as if she could do people harm without hardly knowing she did it, kind of off-hand, as if they weren't real people. I was afraid she'd lose me my job with Mrs. Buckley, or the like of that, if I went against her. And then I didn't want she should do any more harm to Mr. Apple, the way she said she'd see there didn't nobody buy his milk if he didn't vote like she said. . . ."

"You were soft on Mr. Apple, weren't you?" interrupted Pitt with his usual delicacy.

Mary Madras' round cheeks flushed crimson; there was the shine of unshed tears behind the china-blue eyes. "He was real nice to me," she said, with unconscious pathos.

"And you thought Mrs. Vanguard hadn't treated him right?"

"Oh she treated him awful bad. Mr. Apple didn't hardly ever have no luck after that Report and all; he told me so himself. I thought if we could just not have any trouble with her, and kind of keep out of her way like, why then that would be best."

"You didn't think if *she* was put out of *your* way, that would be best?"

"I wasn't hardly sorry when she died," said Mary Madras, not realizing her terrible indictment. "I guess there wasn't anybody. But I wouldn't have killed her, if that's what you're meaning. Oh indeed I wouldn't, sir. Why I wouldn't hardly have known how to go about it if I'd wanted to."

"Maybe Apple might have known."

"I don't think Mr. Apple is hardly the kind of a man to think of killing anybody unless he was to be put up to it," said Mary Madras, with surprising insight into William Apple's character. "He didn't do it, sir, you can be sure of that."

"I guess you wouldn't tell me if he had."

"I guess I wouldn't tell nothing if I knew," admitted Mary shrewdly, "but I don't know nothing to tell. Oh he didn't do it, sir, indeed, indeed he didn't." There was the shine of tears again behind her lashes. She twisted the brass chain on her tapestry bag.

It was at this point that Angeline knocked at the door and walked promptly in. "I'm real sorry to interrupt you," she said, meeting Pitt's black look with a beaming smile. "And of course I know I'm not supposed to, because Mr. Brennon explained it all out to me. But Mr. Hawes wanted some water. You know with his kidneys so bad, it isn't right for him not to have it. He felt awful delicate about coming in himself, but I told him I knew you wouldn't mind when you understood about it, and I'd just as soon as not. . . ." She took a cup from the machine and pressed the lever on the water cooler with a firm, plump thumb. Over her shoulder she examined the situation. "Now you must be nice to Mary," she said, "and not make it hard for her. She's had trouble enough already, being brought up in an orphan asylum and all. . . ."

Pitt turned back from Angeline to Mary Madras. "You didn't say anything to *me* about an orphan asylum."

"You didn't ask me," said Mary Madras. "It's nothing to be ashamed of, I should hope."

"Well there, of course it isn't." Angeline stopped on her way to the door, with the cup of water in her hand, and waited to see how things were coming out. "An orphan asylum is just as respectable as anything. And I guess the Refuge was a real nice place. . . ."

"Nice!" Mary Madras flared out at that in a burst of uncontrollable bitterness. "Oh it was awful *nice,* I can tell you. They gave us *nice* boiled *rice* every day."

Angeline made a little clicking noise of sympathy with her tongue; bad food was a form of hardship that she could understand. "You don't say!" she cried. "I hate boiled rice myself, as if it was the plague. But I always thought from what Mrs. Vanguard said . . ."

"What?" exploded Pitt. "Who? What's that? Who'd you say?"

"Why, Mrs. Vanguard. She was on the board of directors. And she always gave me to understand . . ."

"You told me you never knew Mrs. Vanguard," Pitt boomed at Mary Madras. "You told *me* . . ."

"And no more I didn't, either," said Mary, frightened, but sticking boldly to her guns. "The orphans didn't chum round much with the directors, and don't you think it. The only times I ever saw Mrs. Vanguard was when she'd give out the presents of a Christmas—a new gray gingham dress and a little wizzley orange to each one—and even then she'd hand them to the matron to hand to us, as if she was afraid she'd get dirty off'n us or something. Why I didn't even see her that time she kept me from getting adopted. . . ." She stopped, her hand clapped across her lips, as if she had said something she had not meant to say.

"What? What's that? She kept you from being adopted?"

The memory of past injustices over-rode Mary's caution. "It wasn't anyways fair," she cried. "And all for an old pitcher. And all the time they liked me better than Katherine, because I had curly hair. And Katherine got everything: all silk ribbons in her underclothes and pink roses to her wallpaper, and I don't know what. And I . . ." She choked, and the tears that she had held back for present misfortunes streamed down for the sorrow of childhood; they made little bright streaks on her face like rain on some flamboyant flower—a dahlia or a peony.

"What was that about a pitcher?" put in Garey Brennon. There was honest interest in his voice, honest sympathy; if the genuineness of his concern betrayed Mary Madras to her own undoing it was hardly his fault.

"Oh, I didn't scarcely break it anyways," she sobbed. "It only kind of slipped. . . ."

"You mean to tell me Mrs. Vanguard actually interfered in your adoption"—Garey Brennon was frankly shocked—"because you broke a *pitcher?*"

"She said it was because I lied about it," Mary Madras confessed. "But oh honestly, Mr. Brennon, sir . . ."

"Oh-ho!" Pitt's cigar showed agitation. "So *that* was it. If you'd lie then, you'd lie now. Come, my girl, tell me how much of what you've been saying is all lies anyhow."

"Oh it's all God's truth, every word of it," cried Mary Madras. And she added ingenuously: "There wouldn't be anything to lie about now. I don't want to be adopted any more."

"Maybe you want to keep out of the electric chair, though."

At Pitt's words, full realization of all that she had said swept upon Mary Madras like a storm. Her features drew together in a pucker; she looked blue and pinched as if with cold. "Oh I never done it," she cried. "As God's my witness, Mr. Pitt, sir, I never did. Never. I hated Mrs. Vanguard, and may Mary, Merciful Mother of God, forgive me. But I never would have killed her. I would have been afraid for my soul. . . ." She flung herself down on the floor before Pitt in an ecstasy of pure terror, clutching, sobbing, clinging to his knees. "Oh Mr. Pitt, sir, I beg you before God to believe me, when I say I didn't do it. I didn't, I tell you. I didn't. I *didn't!*" Her voice rose in a breathy scream. "And William didn't either."

3

Mary Madras was sobbing herself into quiet on Angeline's shoulder when they sent for Gideon Hawes. Mr. Hawes finished taking a capsule before he replied to the summons; he replaced the cover on the apothecary's box, replaced the elastic band, replaced the box in his pocket, drained his cup of water. Things had to be done in order when Gideon Hawes did them. He rolled up his manuscript, made sure that his pen and pencil were clipped to the edge of his pocket, and pattered over to the wash room with his short precise steps.

Gideon Hawes was the most careful, puttering little man in the world: the kind who wears suspenders and a belt and carries a safety-pin in his pocket besides; the kind who has two pairs of spectacles, in case one breaks, and an extra set of false teeth packed in cotton. His tidy gray suit that matched his hair fitted as exactly as if he had been melted and poured into it; the neat blue tie that matched his eyes was tied as precisely in the middle as if its position had been charted by rule and compass. His white linen was immaculately white; his black shoes immaculately black. But his gray-hued face wore the anxious look of one who thinks too much about his health, and he held a hand nervously to his side. His small features were all crowded together in the middle as if from lack of space—puckered mouth, spare nose, tight mustache, skimpy gray brows . . . and above them, startling atop that economical face, soared his forehead, big, and high, and broad, and bulging; towering, enormous. An ugly little man. An absurd little man. And yet a little man whom you could never quite pass by, because he was so persistently, so fussily and irritatingly and minutely present.

He settled himself fastidiously in the chair facing Pitt and Brennon, testing it before he trusted himself to it as if he doubted its ability to bear him up, and unfolded his manuscript across his knees. "I consider myself more than ordinarily fortunate," he began, "to have been drawn on this jury. The opportunity which it has given me to be actually present at a murder, to observe at first hand, if I may so phrase it, the locutions of the criminal and anti-criminal mind, has meant more to me than you can realize. It has enabled me greatly, I believe definitively, to extend my chapter on 'The Logic of Crime,' thus rounding out my work. With my kidneys and my heart in the condition in which they are, I cannot expect to live long. But I have done a public service. And I shall leave behind me a permanent record, a contribution to human knowledge. My book . . ."

"Say, look here," Pitt succeeded in interrupting him at last. "We came in here to talk about murder, not literature."

"But my book is about murder," insisted Mr. Hawes, with the professional patience of the schoolman. "The chapter on 'The Logic of Crime' deals primarily with murder, since murder is the primary crime of all crimes, and the logic of the emotions underlying it is the logic,

intensified in degree but similar in essence, to that underlying all lesser crimes and misdemeanors. If you will read
this chapter with an open mind, I think it will help you to
solve this mystery—and not only this mystery, but all mysteries henceforward. Being, as you may say, on the ground
from the beginning, I have had an opportunity to observe
the case in all its ramifications. These observations I have
set down in as much detail as time permitted. I shall be
glad to put them at your disposal. And I believe that you
will find them of the greatest value. I should even, if you
like, be glad to go over them with you . . ."

"You needn't trouble yourself," said Pitt shortly. "What
I want to find out . . ."

"Oh it's no trouble," said Gideon Hawes. "A pleasure,
rather, to discuss the case with you; for I am curious to see
in how far your views coincide with mine. This crime, in
my opinion, is the most logical of recent years. Its solution, if it is to be solved, must therefore be by following
the same logical pathway originally followed by the murderer. While the case is in some ways extraordinarily complicated, in other ways it is simple. That is, while there are
twelve people who could have committed the crime, there
is logically only one who would. Perhaps you will see more
clearly what I mean if I read to you from my book . . ."

That Gideon Hawes ever read as far as he did, was
due to the entrance of Angeline. "I beg your pardon, I'm
sure," she said. "But I wanted to dampen this handkerchief
to cool Mary Madras' face off with. Poor child, she's all
fevered up over this. I don't think you were very nice to
her. . . ." She rinsed her handkerchief at the bowl, making
rather a business of getting it just right; not wet enough
to be soppy, not too dry to be cool and comforting; and
all the time her head was cocked over one shoulder like a
bird to catch what was going on behind her. Pitt, with a
look of grim amusement at Garey Brennon, let Mr. Hawes
go right on reading.

". . . It has been customary," read Gideon Hawes, "in the attempt to solve any given crime, to consider three things: the means, the motive, and the opportunity. To these three a fourth must logically be added: the inhibition. The inhibition is the antithesis of the motive. The motive represents what is to be gained; the inhibition, what is to be lost. It is only when the motive overbalances the inhibition that a crime results. For there are normally certain checks—certain considerations for the future—which function against murder. It is when these checks cease to function that murder takes place. . . ."

Angeline gave her handkerchief a final squeeze and flounced out. "There's nothing going on at all," she reported. "Just Mr. Hawes reading."

But already the reading was over. "Cut the lecturing," commanded Pitt shortly the minute the door closed, "and get down to facts. What's your business?"

"From now on—when my book is finished, that is, and already it is practically complete—I shall have no occupation. Until my retirement two years ago, I was a teacher of logic in the Sheffield High School."

"What'd you retire for? Don't you have to support your family?"

"I have no family. I am quite alone. I have not even formed close friendships, for the reason that . . ."

"I said what'd you retire for?"

"Pardon me. My health, even two years ago, was not what it should have been. My heart . . . my kidneys . . . When the school board felt that my ideas were becoming too . . . ah . . . logical for the minds of the young, it seemed best for me to withdraw."

"You mean they fired you?"

"By request, I withdrew."

Angeline scurried in again, as the sound of their voices indicated that things were livening up. "I didn't get my handkerchief quite wet enough," she explained, running water briskly. "Yes, I remember all about that affair at the school. Mrs. Vanguard said . . ."

"What's that?" cried Pitt. "What had Mrs. Vanguard to do with it?"

"Why she was on the school board," explained Angeline. "I don't think she treated Mr. Hawes quite right, either, talking about his corrupting the minds of the young. It seems he lectured about following impulses to their logical conclusions. But as I said to Marilla, if anybody just has the right *impulses* . . ."

"Oh-ho!" said Pitt. "Then you and Mrs. Vanguard had trouble as far back as two years?"

"Our theories were in conflict, yes," said Mr. Hawes. "But there was no open breach. Logically . . ."

"Oh cut the logic, and get down to brass tacks. She got you fired, didn't she?"

Gideon Hawes seemed uncertain how to answer; he turned to Angeline. "Do you think she did?" he asked anxiously.

"Oh I guess she did, all right, though I supposed you knew it or I wouldn't have said a word. You see I heard all about it, because the Vanguards' chauffeur, John his name was, was keeping company with our cook—not the cook we have now; Delia Scoggins, and a fine cook too, but Marilla couldn't get along with her, and now we have a new one named Sue Wessel, and not half so light-handed with the pastry. I used to find out things from John. John heard Mrs. Vanguard say she'd get rid of you if it was the last thing she ever did. . . ."

There was no doubt about the honesty of Gideon Hawes' amazement; his gray brows lifted, his blue eyes opened wider, even his close mouth fell a little apart, so that for a moment his whole face seemed more spacious: a very picture of surprise. "That is very interesting," he said slowly. "Though of course I did not know she felt so strongly. Mrs. Vanguard—I do not wish to speak evil of the dead—but Mrs. Vanguard was not very logical. She allowed herself to be blinded by the proximity of events, without looking forward to their logical fulfillment. My removal no doubt seemed more important to her than the propagation of logic through the schools. . . ."

"Did you like to teach?" demanded Garey Brennon suddenly, with that unfocused eagerness of his that did not always discriminate between relevant and irrelevant detail.

"Yes," said Gideon Hawes inflexibly. He added: "It was the only life I had known. Naturally I was sorry to have it end under, if I may use the expression, a cloud. Still, no doubt it was for the best. Under existing circumstances I have been able to do more for the service of humanity than I could have done by teaching. Had I continued, with my ill health and the heavy demands upon my time, I could never have written my book. This book, and all that it stands for, will, I feel sure, do much for the dissemination of the principles of logic. My thesis is more conclusively developed than is possible in the class room. . . ."

"Oh come," admonished Pitt. "You're not teaching now. What I want to find out is how much you know about Mrs. Vanguard's murder."

"To the best of my belief," said Gideon Hawes modestly, "I know all about it. Working the case out according to my theory of logic . . ."

"Can the logic and talk sense. Way it looks to me, you had a down on Mrs. Vanguard. Now then, did you give her poison or didn't you?"

"No." Mr. Hawes brought the word out stiffly, as if he were annoyed at the affront to his logic rather than to his character. "I certainly did *not*. If you will permit me . . ."

"Do you know who did then?"

"I have a suspicion," said Mr. Hawes, "which in my own mind amounts to a certainty. Naturally I do not wish to incriminate anybody. But it seems incredible that the whole thing is not as obvious to others as to me. I have

said that of us all, there is only one who *would* have done
it. Perhaps I can show you most clearly what I mean by
reading from my book."

It was a tribute to Gideon Hawes' implicit power that
he succeeded in reading almost a whole paragraph. He
mouthed the words with the relish of an author and a philosopher:

> "Your logical murderer must be a man of
> strong will, of strong purpose. He must have
> patience to wait for his time. He must have
> decision to act unhesitatingly when the time
> comes. He must be able to look ahead to the
> conclusion of events and make ready to direct
> that conclusion. He must have a care for de-
> tail, lest he be ruined by a break in the pat-
> tern of his logic. He must be fitted by nature
> or training to a command over his own per-
> son, lest he betray himself by word or expres-
> sion. Above all he must be able to weigh mo-
> tives against inhibition—what he has to lose,
> if anything, against what, if anything, he has
> to gain—deciding logically. . . ."

"Logical bunk!" said Pitt.

4

"Well, he did say," Angeline was reporting to the others,
"that there was only one person here that would have done
it. He didn't name right out who it was. It sounded to me
kind of like . . . But there, I guess it's better not to say it."
She looked down at the floor in a troubled way, not meeting the eyes of any one. "They want you again, Cornelia.
I'll go in with you, if you'd like to have me, and kind of
get you settled."

Angeline never forgot to the last day she lived how
Cornelia Van Horn looked that morning, sitting in the

wash room facing her inquisitors. She saw her afterwards in harder times and more distressing places. But somehow that once always stood out as if it was an emblem of all that followed.

Cornelia looked very little, sitting there, with Pitt's unwieldy bulk, Garey Brennon's bony height, looming over her. But it was not that which moved Angeline so profoundly. It was not even her beauty, though she was very beautiful, and Angeline was wistfully susceptible to the lure of youth and slenderness. Cornelia had pulled off the brown hat again, and the riot of her bright hair, pinned up away from her small close-set ears, waving in elf-curls of her forehead, was a charm in the dun room. It caught every snatch of sunlight through the smudged window and quickened it to glory. It gave a strange poignancy to the intent face. But it was the eyes that mattered: clear eyes, enormous eyes, too big almost, stretched too wide under turned-back lashes. They looked straight at her questioners, unyielding. But there was something in their expression that Angeline did not quite like. It did not match the rest of her: that young, untouched look, like a new leaf; that gay, undaunted mouth. It wasn't a denial, exactly. It certainly wasn't an admission. It was something terribly like fear.

There was fear in Cornelia's body, too. Angeline sensed it without knowing why. Cornelia sat quietly, her hands folded in her lap like a good child's, her small brown brogues crossed carefully before her. But underneath that conscious quietness, Angeline saw that she held herself rigid as if to withstand a blow.

"That'll be all for you, Miss Tredennick," Pitt said pointedly.

Angeline flounced out, muttering. The door did not quite latch because of the caramel. Angeline brought a chair, set it down outside the door, and planted herself in it.

"I guess we're not so modern," she said, "that a young girl doesn't need *some* chaperon, shut up all alone in there with two big men."

Garey Brennon was kind to Cornelia, impressed, in spite of his resolve to be a bold bad hard-boiled detective who wouldn't be impressed by anything, by a hint of defenselessness in her manner. Pitt was without mercy; if Cornelia was defenseless, why then so much the better. But between them in no time they had the rags and tags of Cornelia's life all spread forth.

Cornelia began her story soberly in answer to their questions; her voice was a little husky, so resolutely firm over this hard first part that it would have seemed almost without expression if it had not been for that small betraying quiver in the drop at the end of a sentence.

"Yes," she said. "Cornelius Van Horn was my father."

Angeline knew what that meant; there was a whole history in the brief statement. The Van Horns were one of the oldest families of Sheffield; Laren Van Horn and his wife Julia had come there on horses when Sheffield was a fort, before the Wilson Massacre; when there were real beavers in Beaver Brook and Wildcat Hill was something besides a name. They had settled with the permanence that was in the Van Horn blood, a fine, stern family, prospering justly, without bowing to any man. Afterwards their wealth was only an incident in their power, their power an incident in their own exact uprightness. Seven generations they had lived there; and then the family, by a series of misfortunes, had gone to pieces. Cornelia was the only surviving Van Horn.

"My mother died when I was little," she was saying steadily. "William and Janus—they were my two older brothers—were killed in the war. William was an aviator. He was very brave. Janus was a gunner. Sometimes it is hard to remember that Janus is dead. He was only eighteen when he went away, and he was always laughing."

She hesitated, the choke in her throat actually visible in the tightening of muscles. "After that, my father and I lived alone together. He said he ran his business for me and I ran the house for him, so it was even. We were very fond of each other." She smiled a little, as if sorrowfully acknowledging her own under-statement, and went quickly on. "When the stock-market crash came a year ago, my father lost everything he had. The—the shock killed him. I don't think it was losing the money so much," she added, as if she could not bear to have any one think her father a weak man even in the manner of his death. "It was losing his faith in his own judgment, more, and—and all he had planned for me."

Garey Brennon took out a very large white handkerchief, and blew his nose loudly. But Pitt did not so much as blink.

"Yeah?" he prompted her.

"Dr. March took care of my father while he was sick," said Cornelia, "and he was very kind. He helped me straighten things out afterwards. There wasn't anything left, of course, and I had to go to work right away. Dr. March found me a place." She brought David March's name into the story quite simply, as if it could hardly have been told without him. Her tone was as completely impersonal as if she added a foot-note to an historical document; but there was a faint brightening in her face nevertheless when she spoke his name, less of color than of light, a faint deepening and softening of her voice, as if the very name itself was sweet upon her lips.

"Yeah?" said Pitt. "Who'd you work for?"

"Mrs. Vanguard."

"The devil you say!" cried Pitt, and Angeline snorted audibly outside the door. "Why didn't you tell me so before?"

"I hadn't come to it," said Cornelia. "I thought you wanted me to tell things in their order."

The very reasonableness of her reply irritated Pitt, so that his manner became more intimidating; he thrust his face close to hers, and the smell of his damp cigar was in her nostrils. "You say Dr. March got you the place? But he and Mrs. Vanguard had had trouble. How . . ."

"This was a year ago, you know. Before that happened. I was Mrs. Vanguard's secretary."

"You still with her at the time of her death?"

"No. I left three months ago."

"She fire you too?" It was characteristic of Pitt to take for granted that every one who changed his occupation had been discharged.

"Yes," said Cornelia calmly.

"What for? Incompetence?"

"No. It was . . . a personal matter." There was more restraint in her manner since Mrs. Vanguard's name had been brought forward. Sometimes she hesitated rather a long time, as if she turned her answer over to see the other side before she let them have it.

"Something to do with Mr. Vanguard?" It was inconceivable to Pitt that a personal matter should be other than an illicit love affair.

"Oh I say . . ." began Brennon. And Angeline started up from her chair and made for the door. Then she sat down again.

"Yes," Cornelia was saying.

"You saw a lee-tle too much of him, I reckon."

"Of course I saw quite a good deal of him while I was working there." The color came up in Cornelia's face—not the steady brightness that David March's name had brought her, but a harder, more searching flush. "He didn't have any regular business to take him away from home, so he was always about the house. We used to talk together sometimes. He used to tell me about deep-sea fauna—that was what he was really interested in, you know—and it was very fascinating the way he could tell it. And then he would ask me how things were going. I think he was sorry for me, because of my father. I was sorry for him, too," she added impulsively.

Pitt caught up her last phrase. "What were you sorry for?"

"Well . . . I didn't think Mrs. Vanguard was very nice to him." Cornelia obviously repented her rash speech, but she was forced now to go through with it. "She wasn't much interested in deep-sea fauna, and she used to say cutting things right before people."

"Say things about you and him too, did she?"

"I don't believe she liked to have us together very well," said Cornelia honestly.

"Did he ever make love to you?"

"What?"

"Did he ever kiss you?"

Poor Cornelia was crimson. She caught her breath a little, lifted her hands as if to push back the painful thing that crowded down upon her. "Once," she said, low.

"Ah-h-h! And when was that?" Pitt's voice was soft, oily.

"The—the day I was discharged," said Cornelia.

Outside the door, Angeline's hands pinched so hard together that Aunt Sabethany's signet ring cut into her third finger. She saw it all so plainly: Cornelia Van Horn, gentle, kindly, talking to Mr. Vanguard because there was no one else for him to talk to, taking an interest in fishes because Mrs. Vanguard did not care for things like that . . . little Cornelia, round-eyed and innocent, letting Mr. Vanguard kiss her simply because she was sorry for him.

But it did not look like that to Pitt; to him it was a black affair indeed. Kisses stood for illicit relations. Triangles. Love nests. Entanglements. Murder. . . .

Garey Brennon did not see it either way, exactly. He saw only the lovely curve of Cornelia's lips, the long sweet line of her throat down the open neck of her jersey. . . . He took out his handkerchief again and wiped his palms, which were suddenly rather moist. "And what did you do after you left Mrs. Vanguard?" he asked, to give her a minute's relief from Pitt's relentless pounding.

Cornelia threw him a quick look of gratitude. "I worked in the bank."

Pitt took things promptly back again into his own hands. "Who got you *that* job? I guess Mrs. Vanguard didn't recommend you."

"Dr. March found that place for me, too."

"Did you keep on seeing Mr. Vanguard after you went to the bank?"

"Why yes, I saw him sometimes," said Cornelia. "He was a director, you know, and he used to stop by at my desk on his way to directors' meetings."

"Where were the meetings held?"

"Upstairs."

"And where are the stairs? Right inside the door, aren't they?"

Pitt leered at her from under his drooping lid. "Did most of the directors go past your desk on their way up those stairs?"

"No."

"But you tell me Mr. Vanguard did?"

"He used the other stairs," explained Cornelia.

On and on. On and on. Pitt sneering, insinuating. Cornelia making her damaging admissions with a fine unreserve, as if she did not half realize how damaging they were.

"Mrs. Vanguard ever catch you and Mr. Vanguard together?"

"She came in one day to cash a check while Mr. Vanguard was there."

"And what did she do?"

"She called to Mr. Vanguard, and he went right out and got into the car. After that she went upstairs."

"There was a directors' meeting?"

"No, the meeting was over."

"Who was upstairs, then?"

"Mr. Halburton, the president, was up there in his office."

"Better get Vanguard down and see what he says about this," Pitt put in an aside to Garey Brennon. "Have Trollope telephone for him. Young woman"—he leaned over and tapped Cornelia's knee with a blunt forefinger. "Young woman, didn't it occur to you that Mrs. Vanguard might

make trouble for you there at the bank? That you might
lose your job?"

"I thought of that," said Cornelia frankly.

"And you were worried about it?"

"No."

"Why not?"

"Dr. March said not to worry, so I didn't. He could
have found me another place."

"Ah-h-h!" Pitt's breath came out in a long note of satisfaction. "So this is where March comes into it again. I
was wondering. You were seeing a good deal of him, too,
weren't you?"

That *too* was an insinuation. It was an out-and-out insult. He was onto her now, Pitt's manner said. Having an
affair with a married man. Having an affair with a doctor.
Oh he knew her kind, all right, all right. The kind you
could expect anything of. And Mrs. Vanguard was the one
who threatened her security.

Garey Brennon gritted his teeth in a wholly unprofes-
sional manner. But it was as if Cornelia herself were unconscious of the implication that lay behind Pitt's words;
as if she did not see, until it was too late, the pitfall opening under her feet.

"I saw him now and then," she said.

"He was very . . . *kind*, you say?" That *kind* was a mockery. But again it was as if Cornelia were unaware of mocking.

"Oh yes, very kind," she said readily. The difficult
flush that had come up in her cheeks with the mention
of Mr. Vanguard's name fell away again and left her ten-
der-lipped and eager. She betrayed herself in that look, as
if she would have been glad to put a better name to it than
kindness. "He was kind to all his patients. He would do
anything for them. . . ."

Angeline Tredennick found herself standing up without
knowing she had risen; sensing catastrophe without understanding its form. With a desperate urgency she beckoned
to David March to join her there at the wash-room door.

David came quickly. As if he could have stopped it then; as if any one could have stopped it.

"You were a patient of his?" It was always a dangerous sign when Pitt spoke softly.

"He was our family doctor."

"You sick a good deal?"

"Oh no." Cornelia's voice was faintly amused. "I am never sick."

"But you saw a lot of him all the same?"

"He was always very busy"—pride in this—"but sometimes he would take me riding while he was making calls."

"He would do anything for you too, then? He was paying you marked attention, wasn't he?"

Cornelia's face was drained suddenly of color. The question that she had never quite dared to ask herself loomed over her, demanding to be answered, here, aloud, before unfriendly people. And now, at last, she saw where Pitt was tending. But she never had to answer after all. It was David March, flinging wide the door, striding across the threshold, towering over all of them, brave and tall, who answered for her. "I was paying her marked attention," he said gravely.

If Pitt was surprised at the interruption, he did not show it; the thing happened too patly to his purpose. "Then you would *do anything* for her?"

Across the narrow room David's look met Cornelia's: closer than the touch of hands, that look, warmer than caress; a strange, tortured, happy look, quick with knowledge. Angeline held her breath; for with that look it was as if the little drabbled room fell away into nothing, and there were left only Cornelia Van Horn and David March, they two, alone, shoulder to shoulder for all the space between them, dauntless, undeterred.

"I would do anything I could for her," said David March.

And Pitt's words were not a question any more. Just a statement.

"Even murder."

IV
Wednesday (Continued)

Parr chewed another inch off his second cigar. "We got 'em," he said to Garey Brennon. "They're right in together on this, March and the Van Horn girl. Either she did it, and he's trying to cover it up; or he did it for her; or they both did it together."

"I don't feel so sure," said Brennon, in rather a worried way. "Miss Van Horn doesn't look to me like the type."

She did not look like the type. She looked like a tired child, a little bewildered, a little shocked; she looked as if nothing would comfort her so much as sobbing out her trouble on David March's shoulder: and perfectly incapable of doing it. Her smile was resolutely gay. She talked in a clear bright voice, trying to give an air of naturalness to an unnatural situation: small, inconsequential things that any one might have heard. It was warm, wasn't it? Too bad the windows wouldn't open. She'd like something with ice, that would rattle, and a large green tree. . . .

David March looked as if nothing would help him so much as gathering Cornelia right up in his arms and comforting her, and just as incapable of such a gesture as she. He looked older, Angeline thought, without being able to say why; perhaps from a conscious effort to look exactly the same. His voice was as cheerfully off-hand as Cornelia's. Yes, it was warm. Maybe Trollope would make them lemonade. Maybe Mr. Gilley would send down to his furniture store for a hat tree. . . .

And yet for all the other people present, it struck Angeline again that they looked strangely alone. It wasn't in any open word—not yet. Not in any expressed suspicion. But there were whispers. Sly looks. Mary Madras saying something to William Apple behind her hand, and his prompt betraying glance across the table. Rinschy eyeing them covertly, as if he could have said a lot if he had wanted to. Gideon Hawes watching them with too much concentration, too much speculation as he penciled a note in his manuscript. Damaris Lee cracking her hard little jokes: "Let's write a mystery story, Charles, and call it *Medicinal Murder.*" Oliver Elding, starting uneasily when Cornelia asked the time, as if just to tell her might somehow implicate him. Mr. Gilley, at the head, blandly disapproving.

From the far end of the room, Pitt and Brennon as they talked watched them too—closer than any one.

"Type!" Pitt scoffed, taking up Brennon's word. "There isn't any such thing as a killer type. Everybody's a killer when he comes to want somebody killed. You see a baby-doll face and you don't look for the wheels that make it open its pretty eyes so wide. But I tell you, boy"—Pitt was in good humor because things were going so well against his chief suspects—"I tell you it's the baby-doll faces gets the men to do their dirty work."

"But I don't see where the Como case comes in," began Garey Brennon anxiously.

"It doesn't come in, that's where. It doesn't have to. We don't care who killed Mr. Sebastian Bootlegger Como out there in the bushes. What we want to know is who killed Mrs. DeQuincy Vanguard right here in this room with a shot of hyoscine. Did you get hold of Vanguard?"

"Mr. Vanguard's sick. Prostrated. Shock. The doctor says he can't come before tomorrow."

"Tell him if he doesn't show up tomorrow, we'll send a man after him," said Pitt with his usual sympathy. "Maybe he can tell us something. . . ." He broke off abruptly. "Hey, what you doing?"

It was Angeline Tredennick whom he thus addressed. And Angeline was certainly doing something strange. She had a tiny bottle in her hand, and from its contents she was moistening a scrap of cotton. She did not even trouble to look up from her absorbing task. "I'm fixing toothache medicine," she said.

Pitt was down the length of the room in half a dozen heavy strides. He snatched the bottle from her hand. "Where'd you get that?"

"Get it?" said Angeline rather crossly. "I got it at Robbot's drug store, if you want to know, and it cost thirty-five cents. Don't spill it. I do think myself that things are a little more expensive at Robbot's, but as I said to Marilla, the place to economize isn't on your drugs. If you need any drugs at all, you need them good and druggy. . . ."

"Say! That isn't what I'm asking you, and you know it. I'm asking you how this bottle got in here."

"Got in here?" repeated Angeline, speaking indistinctly because she was tucking the cotton round a rear molar with a toothpick. "Why I brought it, of course. I was never much for dentists myself, for all Marilla says. Not that I'm not just as brave about being hurt as the next person, but I don't like the noise that buzzer makes. This most always stops toothache. It's got oil of clove in it. . . ."

Pitt was sniffing skeptically at the bottle. "Answer me what I ask you, and that's all I want to know. Weren't you searched?"

"Why of course I was," Angeline still spoke thickly round the cotton. "And such goings-on I never did see in my life. The matron . . ."

"Why didn't you give her this then? Afraid it might incriminate you?"

"Well there," said Angeline cheerfully. "I didn't think a search was so you could give things to whoever was searching; I thought it was so she could find them. I didn't want to lose the toothache medicine for fear I might have toothache, and so I just put it away."

"You put it *where?*" Pitt was only too keenly conscious of the suppressed snickers proceeding from Damaris Lee and Charles Kashaw, the leer on Rinschy's lowering face, the secret, unfriendly interest of the others.

"Away," repeated Angeline. "In my hair."

"Didn't you have to take your hair down?"

"Well there, I did," Angeline admitted. "I never saw anybody in my life so suspicious as that matron. But . . . well, I suppose I might as well come right out and say it, though I think it's a pity if a woman can't have a *few* secrets. It isn't that I haven't got hair enough, either. But it's so fine it doesn't hold its shape very well, and so I always wear a little . . . support under it." She placed her hand on the firm bun of "prematurely gray" curls to indicate where the support was needed. "I put the toothache medicine in there. I kind of wondered whether if anybody *did* have something to hide, he could hide it so it wouldn't get found. I guess"—blithely—"anybody could."

Pitt chose to ignore something in the atmosphere that was too near applause for comfort. "We found what we wanted," he said. "We found that hypodermic."

"Well yes," said Angeline brightly. "But of course the things you didn't find, you don't know about."

2

This passage with Angeline put Pitt into a terrific humor; if others questioned that afternoon found him harder to deal with than his wont, it was not to be marveled at.

"We'll run the rest through fast," he said to Garey Brennon, with an assumption of nothing untoward having occurred. "And by that time we ought to have something from Pulsifer. If there was poison in that medicine cup."

"But I don't see . . ." began Brennon.

"You don't have to," snapped Pitt. "Miss Lee, come in here."

Damaris Lee was an ill choice for Pitt to begin on. She scratched a match with great nonchalance on the sole of her red shoe, and with a sly glance at Pitt's unlighted cigar offered him one also.

Pitt ignored the match, but no one could ignore Damaris Lee. Thin to emaciation, husky-voiced from too many cigarettes, black-haired, black-eyed, tense, high-pitched, she imposed herself upon the attention by the very brilliance of her person. There was something dramatic about her, calculated in every least detail: her hair parted in the middle, brow to nape, slicked down tight, with only a mathematically exact wisp pasted to her cheeks before each ear; the little upward fleer at the outer corners of her eyes emphasized by a pencil. She wore no rouge, but her mouth was bright with exotic lipstick—more orange than scarlet—as startling in her white face as the red of her purse and shoes with the deliberately plain black dress. Not really beautiful, not really charming, Damaris Lee had nevertheless a certain fascination, a dashing, devil-may-care way, and an utter recklessness in her eyes. It was part of her code never to take anything seriously.

"Who are you anyway?" Pitt demanded, uncomfortable in spite of himself before her mocking gaze.

"Damaris Lee." There was something pert in the simple statement.

"I know that," said Pitt sharply. "What I mean is, what do you do? Where do you hang out?"

"Oh I do my darnedest," said Damaris gaily. "And they don't hang in this state, do they? They electrocute."

Pitt was furious. "You'll hang yourself if you don't watch your step. What I want to know . . ."

"Well now I think the best thing," said Damaris Lee, blowing two thin streams of smoke composedly from her nostrils, "is for me to confess. As you say, it will save a lot of time and trouble if I tell you right out that I killed Mrs. Vanguard."

"You—you *what?* You—you *killed* her?"

"Sure," said Damaris cheerfully. "Didn't you know it? I never liked Mrs. Vanguard, because she was always right. And so I killed her with kindness. When the lunch came in, I choked her with butter."

Pitt's ripe face was abruptly purple. "Don't you be so confounded funny. What do you think this is anyway?"

"A bedroom farce," murmured Damaris Lee. "That's what it was last night. Take my word for it, my mattress was stuffed with cornstalks, with the ears left on."

"What do you mean, you killed her?"

"Why, *killed,*" explained Damaris Lee. "That's plain, isn't it? I strangled her with a bootlace."

"You haven't got any bootlaces." Pitt was betrayed into irrelevant argument—betrayed, in spite of himself, into a still more irrelevant glance down Damaris Lee's slim ankles to the slim red shoes.

"That's right," she said. "So I haven't. I borrowed one of Rinschy's. He's got them."

"He's got 'em in his boots," said Pitt heavily. Fear he understood, and protective lying, and evasion and the simple forms of deceit. But mockery, this light-hearted fooling, he was ill-equipped to cope with. The look he cast at Garey Brennon was the nearest thing to an appeal that he had ever made.

"When did you change your vote from not guilty to guilty?" asked Brennon promptly.

"Oh I was one of the early converts," said Damaris Lee easily. "I knew Mrs. Vanguard would get her own way in the end, because she always did; so I thought I'd speed things up."

"Mrs. Vanguard did not try to persuade you to change?"

"Why, sure she did. I thought you knew that. She put the works to everybody. That's why I *did* change."

Garey Brennon sighed hopelessly. These glib admissions were infinitely more misleading than any denial could have been. They left you dangling, not sure where you stood.

"She wasn't strangled," said Pitt half to himself, heavily matter-of-fact.

Damaris Lee laughed out. "Why so she wasn't. I forgot. I was going to strangle her, and then I changed my mind, so I put poisoned gin in her coffee instead."

Pitt was beside himself with rage. "You didn't either," he shouted. "You didn't do anything of the kind. You didn't kill her, and don't you say you did. You . . ." It was a surprising accusation for a district attorney to make.

"Well after all," said a voice behind him, "she *did* put gin in her coffee."

It was Angeline, of course, come again to fetch water for the unquenchable Gideon Hawes. And if anything were needed to complete Pitt's discomfiture, it was Angeline: plump and pink and kindly, with one cheek a trifle larger than the other from cotton and toothache medicine, and her eternal wonderment.

"The devil you say!"

"I didn't say anything of the kind," flared Angeline. "I said she put gin in Mrs. Vanguard's coffee, and she did. Or anyway she tried to. Mrs. Vanguard gave her quite a talking to about it; she was awful strong for prohibition. Miss Lee was going to put some in Mr. Kashaw's too; but he said hers had arsenic in it, so he put his in instead. . . ."

"Is that right?" Pitt was too bewildered even to shout.

"Sure. Looks bad, doesn't it?" said Damaris mockingly. "I forgot to say that Charles was my accomplice. I'm always forgetting some little thing like that. Arsenic was just his pet name for hyoscine."

"I must say I couldn't help wondering about it afterwards, the way things turned out," Angeline said. "But I hope I haven't got you into any trouble. Of course I wouldn't hold with your poisoning Mrs. Vanguard. But I can't say I blame you for being mad at her."

"Why?" asked Garey Brennon.

"The way she broke up Miss Lee's engagement to Mr. Walen," Angeline explained. "And married him off to her own niece, Irene Carstairs that was. As I said to Marilla at the time . . ."

The effect of her words was electric. From a careless figure of unconcern, as hard and shining and remote as a lady of lacquer, and as impervious to touch, Damaris Lee was transformed in an instant into a white flame of a woman, uncontrolled, blazing with some strange malice from within. "You keep still," she cried. And her unguarded voice jangled like the snapping of a taut string.

They were all startled. After her offhand nonchalance, her perverse mocking, this self-betrayal was the more complete. In the studied whiteness of her face two bright spots came up, high on her cheekbones, like the touch of fever; the hand that held her cigarette trembled so sharply that a spark fell, burning a tiny hole, like the prick of a pin, in the front of her black dress.

Damaris Lee had played around with every man in town—and prided herself on it. She had teased them and mocked them and eluded them, taking their kisses and letting them go with a kiss: careless, intemperate in the outward show of love. But underneath all her hardness and brightness, somewhere down deep where no one saw it but Damaris Lee, there was a capacity for falling in love . . . once. The man was Monty Walen, handsome, dashing, weak, irresistible Monty. They had been engaged when Mrs. Vanguard took him in hand and married him firmly to her niece, Irene Carstairs, whose pudgy inconsequence was becoming a burden to her family for all the Carstairs money. Damaris had let Monty go in scorn and bitterness. Not saying a word to hold him, when a word would have been enough. Hating herself for loving him . . . and loving him just the same.

Damaris Lee—all Damaris Lee's crowd—prided themselves on being good sports; it was their religion in a shaken world. Damaris was very sporting. She had smoked more cigarettes, that was all, and perhaps been a little more appreciative of quantity than of quality in her liquor and her men; she had laughed a great deal, and made others laugh, and danced at Monty's wedding, and cracked hard, truthful little jokes about her shattered life. The affair had not broken her courage. It had not broken her pride. But it had broken a more brittle, shining thing that we used to call faith.

Those days in the jury room with Mrs. Vanguard had been more of a strain to Damaris Lee than any one could know. Her words came out in a high thread of sound, infinitely shocking.

"I said I killed her," she cried wildly. "What more do you want? Why can't you let me alone? Do I have to wash my dirty lingerie in public just the same? Hate her? Of course I hated her. Everybody in Sheffield with any sense hated her. Lord, that woman had done more harm than an army. She ought to have been executed as a public menace. Poison? Poison was too good for her. She ought to have been flayed. God. . . ."

She stopped, dead. Her head was bent a little as if she were listening—as if for the first time she heard the dreadful words she had let loose in that silent room.

"There, there, Damaris," said Angeline helpfully. "You're all worked up. Here, take a good drink of this nice cold water."

"*Water!*" said Damaris Lee bitterly.

She drew out a fresh cigarette and lighted it. Her hands still shook a little, but otherwise, as abruptly as she had gone to pieces, so abruptly she was master of herself again. It was as if she had shut her real self, her living and vulnerable self, back into the hard bright case that she showed to a gaping world.

"If I killed her," she said composedly, "it was with the evil eye."

And to Pitt and Brennon and Angeline in turn Damaris Lee gave a deliberate, mocking look out of long black eyes that nobody could fathom.

3

Charles Kashaw was an automobile salesman, and a highly successful one, too, if you let him tell it. He was quite ready to confide how many cars he had sold the year before; how he had won the company competition for the largest total output; what Mr. Arthur Wainright, Division Sales Manager for Bustard Motors, Inc., had said when he presented the gold fountain pen with which Kashaw was to jot down fresh sales and greater triumphs. He did not suffer from an inferiority complex. If he slightly overestimated his success in salesmanship, along with his success with women, and the invincibility of his engaging manner, still he was so honest in his own good estimation that no one could take offence: you found yourself accepting him at his valuation.

Charles Kashaw had reddish hair and greenish eyes and freckles on the backs of his hands: a quick-speaking, persuasive man with a cheap kind of charm. He talked with his whole body—a shake of the shoulders to ward off adverse opinion; a tap of the foot to emphasize a point; two fingers clapped across an agile palm to clinch an argument. If his narrow eyes were a little too quick-moving to be quite dependable, if his speech was a little too glib, a little too spacious, to be aware of every inch and grain of truth, still you had to admit that he had a way with him. This way had carried him far. Too far, some said.

"Know Mrs. Vanguard?" Pitt began.

"Sure, I know everybody," said Kashaw, not without pride. "Mrs. Vanguard was on my prospect list. I tried to sell her a Bustard Twelve a while back, and didn't make a go of it. But I would have got her in the end."

"What do you mean, *got her?*"

"Sold her," explained Kashaw, emphasizing the word by striking down a slightly too yellow shoe smartly on the floor. "When I start out to sell anybody, I sell 'em. And Mrs. V. was just the ticket for one of those big Twelves; she had the style for it, you know, as if she owned the earth. That big Twelve is sure a bird: glassed-in shoffer's seat, speaking tube, flood light, siren, half an acre of nickle on the hood, and speed—boy! Make a nice police car, too," he added.

Pitt ignored the suggestion. "Have any trouble with her because she didn't buy?"

"She wasn't what you call cordial," said Kashaw with a grin. "But Lord, man, I didn't bump her off for that, if that's what you mean. If everybody that was saucy to a salesman got bumped off, who'd be left to drive the automobiles? No, I got to hand myself this: I don't ever get mad at a prospect. When I found Mrs. V. here on the jury, I was tickled. I got a seat next beside her, and began right where I left off."

"Any luck?"

"Well, I didn't get her on the dotted line," admitted Kashaw regretfully. "If I had, I guess I could hold the estate for it. But she talked turkey all right."

"Was that before or after you changed your vote to guilty?" Brennon asked.

"Might have been before, might have been after," said Kashaw, very off-hand. "Maybe both. We talked all up and down the line. But I would have changed anyway, if that's what you mean. I could see Mrs. V. was likely right; set a woman to catch a woman every time. That Garetti jane was sure a hot one. Vim, vigor and vitality; yes, sir. I guess Como was lucky while he lasted. But I let that kind alone myself, and aim higher up." He spoke with his usual subtlety; there was more than a hint in his words, in the avid gesture of his hands, that any woman would have come running for Charles Kashaw's whistle.

Garey Brennon felt a distaste for the man. "Then there wasn't any suggestion that Mrs. Vanguard would buy a car if you changed your vote?"

"I got something better to sell than votes," replied Charles Kashaw with his easy shrug. "But think so, if you want. It lets me out the other way. Nobody with sense is going to think I bumped off my top prospect." He grinned, rather engagingly, at Garey Brennan, and Brennan, for all he could do, found himself grinning back. There was that about the fellow: you didn't like him, and yet you smiled; you didn't want a car, and yet you bought one. It was all part of his invincible salesmanship. And now he was selling his innocence to Brennan and Pitt just as earnestly as he had ever sold a Bustard Twelve.

"You say so," said Pitt. "We got nobody's word for it but yours."

"Miss Lee'll tell you," suggested Kashaw good-humoredly. A successful salesman does not lose his temper just because some one doubts his word.

"Miss Lee's told us an earful already," Pitt shot at him. "What you got to say to her telling us you were her accomplice when she put the poisoned gin in Mrs. Vanguard's coffee?"

"I say she's a liar," said Kashaw promptly. If he had left it at that, he would have stood a first-rate chance of being believed. But he was suddenly alarmed, and his alarm—the fright of a ready talker—found vent in an uncontrollable flow of words. "Why the little devil!" he cried. "She said that, did she? She's a crooked stick, if I ever saw one. You have to look out for these high-flyers. They fly high, but they light low, and there's nowhere too low for them to light. Why the little liar! Accomplice, my eye! I don't know what she had in her gin bottle. I don't know whether she put any in Mrs. Vanguard's cup or not. I don't know . . ."

"You don't know much all of a sudden, do you?" said Brennon dryly.

"You handed Mrs. Vanguard's cup to her, didn't you?"

"Yes, but I tell you I don't know whether she put anything in or not. I tell you . . ."

"You're telling a lot more than you mean to. She offered you some too, didn't she?"

"Yes, but . . ."

"But you didn't take it. Miss Lee states it was because you said there was arsenic in it."

"But . . . but there wasn't any question of arsenic, was there? I thought it was hyoscine."

"You thought there was hyoscine in it?"

"No, I didn't. Wood alcohol, more likely."

"What made you think there was anything in it except gin?"

"Women have bum taste in liquor," muttered Kashaw.

"They have bum taste in men," muttered Garey Brennon.

"Miss Lee tells us," said Pitt, "that arsenic was just your pet name for hyoscine."

"My pet name for her is hell-cat," bawled Kashaw, and everybody in the jury room heard him.

4

"Emanuel Biggs, yes, sir."

Biggs was the most unremarkable man in the world; so completely inconspicuous as to be practically invisible. He had no eyebrows, no chin worthy of mention, no personality; there was not one in the jury room who could have mentioned the shade of his pale straw-colored hair or his pale, mud-colored eyes. He came and went on silent rubber soles, as quiet as a shadow and as unregarded. He was of the type born to serve; finding his satisfactions, if he ever found any, so deep below the surface that no hint of gratification ever reached his face. He never spoke except when spoken to, answering then with an uninspired docility.

"Valet to Mr. Douglas Britten, the philanthropist. Yes, sir."

"Know Mrs. Vanguard?"

"No, sir."

"Never see her before the trial?"

"Yes, sir. She and Mr. Vanguard came to the Brittens' sometimes. That was mostly when she wanted money for a charity." Biggs spoke without humor. "But Mr. Vanguard came more often, sir, by himself."

"What did he come for?"

"A glass, sir."

"A glass of what?"

"Chianti, Chablis, Pol Roger, Romanée Conti. Scotch mostly, sir. Mr. Britten has a very fine cellar. Sometimes Mr. Vanguard stayed all night."

"What for?"

"To sleep it off, sir," said Biggs practically. "He could not go home because Mrs. Vanguard was a prohibitionist. But he was always a gentleman, even when I had to put him into bed. Yes, sir."

To Biggs all the world was divided into ladies-and-gentlemen, and *others;* he felt the unquestioning admiration for the first, the unreasoned intolerance for the latter, which only those know who have never seen themselves even in imagination as anything but *others.*

"You changed your vote from not guilty to guilty, didn't you?"

"Yes, sir."

"Did Mrs. Vanguard tell you to?"

"Yes, sir."

"What made you do as she said?"

"I couldn't argue with her, sir."

"Why not?"

"She was a lady, sir."

And there you had it, pat, without argument, incapable of modification. Mrs. Vanguard was, technically, a lady, and one did not argue with ladies. As often as they went round the narrow circle, so often they came back to the same blank barrier. Mr. and Mrs. Vanguard were ladies-and-gentlemen. What had murder to do with it?

"Did Mrs. Vanguard offer you any money?"

"She and Mr. Vanguard were very liberal about tips. They were ladies-and-gentlemen, sir."

5

Leo Rinschy was born to be a murderer, and if he wasn't a murderer this time it was the greatest pity in the world. Garey Brennon, watching him slouch in, felt that if it came to a matter of types, then Rinschy was the type *par excellence:* a dark, bristly man—the kind who sprouts additional beard while you are looking at him and cannot keep his cuffs clean; arms too long for the heavy body set up on its absurdly short legs; a bull-dog's jaw, a ferret's eye, sharp rather than bright, an emotional mouth; an air half furtive, half brazen. It was as if the essentials of his face were skilfully concealed by a kind of camouflage: the untidy shock of black hair drawing attention from the low, slightly receding forehead; the heavy brows, oddly notched and pointed, like some special kind of brushes, tipped over the eyes; the bold nose hooking down, the bold beard curling up to hide the facile mouth. A born agitator, you saw him on a soap box, haranguing crowds of unemployed, himself immune to labor; you saw him in the back room of restaurants with dirty tablecloths, froth dripping untidily down his glass, froth dripping down his beard, blowing up the government with a well-contrived bomb.

Garey Brennon guessed that he was the sort who might tell everything or nothing; there was a capacity in the man for excess in any direction. "Mind if I begin?" he asked, fearing Pitt's methods.

"Suit yourself," said Pitt shortly. He felt no deep interest in Leo Rinschy, who looked too much like a killer, he thought, ever to be one. The absurdity of the episode with Angeline, the extravagances of Kashaw and Damaris

Lee, the wall-like aloofness of Biggs, had drained even his
vitality. He sank into a chair, mouthing his cigar aimlessly.

"Didn't I hear you make a speech once?" said Garey
Brennon to Rinschy on a venture.

"I cannot be arrezt for zat, no?" said Rinschy sullenly.
"I have ze right, yes?"

"Sure you have," said Brennon heartily. "I'd make
speeches too if I could do it the way you can." He stood
easily, teetering on his toes, hands in pockets, red head
flung back so that he looked at the ceiling instead of at
Rinschy with an air of fine unconcern. "That piece about
capitalism was darn good."

This was a straight shot in the dark. Only it seemed inconceivable, if Rinschy had ever made a speech at all, that
capitalism should not come into it somewhere. But Garey
Brennon was amazed at his success. It was as if that word
capitalism was the key that unlocked Rinschy; once the
word was said, the door was open: the real Rinschy stood
forth in front of his beard. He spoke with a running fluency, a hissing of z's and s's, that made him hard to follow.

"Oh zat capitalizm," he cried. "She is bad. She make
ze fool of good men. She wind round ze earth, like ze big
snake, zo and zo; she wind round ze man zat he lose his
job, and ze voman zat she lose her new radio w'at ze inz-
tallment man should take it avay, and round ze leedle baby
w'at he do not have ze hot milk wit' beer and get sick on
'em maybe zo and make ze doctaire bill. Ze rich pipple zey
do not care how harrd ze snake she squeeze, so she squeeze
out ze more money to make ze more capitalizm to make
ze more snake to squeeze some more. Ah ze rich ones, zey
t'ink zey are zo smart. Zey go in ze college and t'ink zey
are zo wize. Zey sit in ze soft chair and t'ink zey are so
nize zat ze park bench should make ze bone ache. Zey talk
themself over ze family and ze inherit' and ze leizure and
ze educate'. But I zay to you down wit' ze family and up
wit' ze effort. Down wit' ze inherit' and up wit' ze vages.

Down wit' ze leisure and up wit' ze work. Down wit' ze educate' and up wit' ze common sense. I zay take avay ze money w'at ze capitalizt he do not earn and give it to ze laborer, w'at he earn it, all equal, zo every one start even. I zay . . ."

"Quite a lot of capitalists right here in town, aren't there?" asked Brennan carelessly. He did not dare to look at Rinschy for fear of stopping him.

"I name you vone hund'ed," cried Rinschy. "Two hund'ed, maybe. I name you Meester Halburton to ze bank, w'at he lend you ze money for buy ze house zo he take ze house avay again. I name you Meester Britten, w'at zey call philantropiz', w'at he give you money zat you should earn for him. I name you . . ."

"Mrs. Vanguard," suggested Brennon softly.

"W'at she iz vone bad lot and downtrod ze poor," Rinschy swept on unmindful. "I name you . . ."

"So that's why you killed her?" Pitt was unable to resist taking such a juicy morsel to himself. "Because she was a capitalist?"

But upon that, in an instant, it was all over. Rinschy had been caught up by the ring of his own eloquence, so that he was no longer in the grimy wash room of the court house, but on the Sheffield Common, the pale growling faces of the unemployed turned up in applause about his soap box. Now, at Pitt's abrupt question, he was aware of himself again. He realized what he had been saying—to whom he had been saying it. And on the moment the real Rinschy stepped back again behind his beard and his hair and his eyebrows and his big nose, and left only a stolid, stupid fellow, who could not even understand any too well what was asked of him, and answered in monosyllables. It was exactly what Garey Brennon had feared. And now it had happened.

"So you killed her," Pitt repeated.

"No kill," said Rinschy.

Brennon swung into a casual line of questioning, designed to take Rinschy's mind from serious matters and make him talk again. But it was no use.

"Where do you live?"

"Wit' mine zon."

"What does he do?"

"He dig ze ditch."

"And what do you do?"

"I am retire'. Mine zon do vork. I live wit' mine zon."

Pitt was impatient at what he considered a gross waste of time. "You've got a tall lot of explaining to do," he broke in, playing on Rinschy's fears. "Here you are right where a murder's been committed, and you've got a bottle of illegal liquor, and you've got a gat and no permit. It doesn't look good."

It had seemed to Garey Brennon that Rinschy's face was inexpressive before; he had yet to learn what complete absence of expression means. At Pitt's words it was as if a curtain had been drawn down between Rinschy and a light, so that you saw only a silhouette; shape without detail. His eyes were as blank as two glass marbles.

"What you got to say, huh?"

Rinschy, it appeared, had just exactly nothing to say. He sat inert, like one of those lumpish idols carved in stone with their heads grown down between their shoulders.

"You come clean now on what you know about the murder, and maybe you'll get off easy on the other," Pitt promised craftily.

Rinschy's eyes were wary. He had the perverse conception of the American law common to the foreign born—it was as if he distinguished no difference in importance between murder and bootleg whiskey. "I am not know notting bout zat murder," he said. "Notting bout zat bottle. I am not do any harrm by carry zat zo leedle, leedle gun. She is by ze pocket only. Eet is not fair, eet is not right, zat I should be arrezt for zat I have not ze leedle zo foolish paper for say I am carry heem. For v'y I have ze paper anyvays? Vill ze paper shoot? V'en I am need ze gun, am I zen take out ze paper for vave heem in ze air? I am not do wit' ze zo small gun any harrm. I am carry heem for protect only. . . ."

"Don't you know you don't have to protect yourself in America? The law does that."

"Oh zat law!" Rinschy gave an eloquent shrug, spreading out his hands. "Zat law is for arrezt, not for protect. Alvays arrezt. Arrezt for nottings."

"How long since you were arrested last time?" asked Brennon negligently.

"Six . . ." He stopped. "Nevaire arrezt."

"Six months?" Brennon's mind went leaping back over events in Sheffield, and caught the essential fact. "I remember. You were one of those they pulled for stirring up the mill riot."

"No, no, no, no," cried Rinschy, suddenly voluble again. "No, no. I am not zere. I am innocent-bystanding only. I nevaire go near ze mill."

"The Vanguards were heavy stock-holders in the mill, weren't they?"

"No, no, no, no," reiterated Rinschy. "I nevaire know zo. I nevaire hear zo. V'en zey tell me, I shut mine ear like zat."

"Did Mrs. Vanguard threaten to tell something about the riot if you didn't vote the way she said?"

Again Garey Brennon was aware of that complete, that absorbing blankness in Rinschy's look; his face washed as clean of expression by Brennon's words as a wave washes a beach. "She do' know nottings to tell," he said, "about zat riot."

Garey Brennon was at a loss; there seemed no way to get past that wooden look. And yet he had a feeling that there was something here that was important, if he could

only reach it. He was still hesitating when he heard a noise
behind him. Around the edge of the door appeared one
blue eye and one gray curl that could mean nothing but
Angeline; one white forefinger crooked and beckoned. He
pushed back his chair quietly and went out.

Angeline stretched on tiptoe. "I was just wondering . . ."

When Garey Brennon came back again, he looked very
grave. He began without preamble. "The way I understand
it," he said, "when Washington Avenue was being repaved,
your son was on the road gang. He threw a lighted cigarette into a pile of leaves in front of the Vanguard house,
and Mrs. Vanguard got him fired."

"No, no, no, no, no, no," cried Rinschy. "Zey vas vet
leafs anyvays."

6

Oliver Elding was the kind of man who cannot say it is a
pleasant day without qualifying his statement; he had no
sort of chance from the beginning with the remorseless
Pitt. A pale, frail creature, with an oddly egg-like quality:
the long oval of his face, coming to a slight point at the
dome, had a brittle look about its paleness and smoothness, as if a careless touch might chip the surface; his large
pale eyes rolled in a too fluid way, as if their substance
lacked the stiffness needful to hold them still.

There are a thousand Oliver Eldings in every Sheffield.
Clerks who wear themselves shiny in the back in the interests of business not their own. Indecisive men, who eat in
cafeterias, and find themselves with great greasy braised
joints on their trays instead of the oysters they meant to
order. Timid men, who live in hall bedrooms and move
their beds in front of the closet door when it rains because
they do not dare to complain to the fierce landlady about
the leak in the roof. Little men, wistfully adventurous,
spending their evenings over volumes about explorers and
warriors and statesmen. Alone in his room Oliver Elding
had slain dragons and defeated armies, but he shivered on

his high stool in the Herrod Mercantile Company whenever a door slammed. He shivered now as he faced Pitt.

"When you heard that Mrs. Vanguard was dead," Pitt
began, "you said, 'Thank God, now DeQuincy will have a
chance.' What did you mean by that?"

"Why I didn't mean anything." It was probably the first
unconsidered remark that Oliver Elding had ever made,
and he had been repenting it ever since. "That is, not
anything definite. I just meant if God had seen fit to take
Mrs. Vanguard . . ."

"He didn't see fit to take her," said Pitt, with the air
of one who could tell you all about the private thoughts
of the Almighty. "She was poisoned, and you know it. You
meant you were glad she was dead, didn't you?"

"Oh no," cried Elding, shocked. "I didn't mean that. I
just meant if DeQuincy wasn't interfered with . . ."

"What do you mean, interfered with?"

"Well, perhaps not exactly interfered with," Elding
stammered, trying to remedy matters and making them
worse with every word he said. "Criticised, more. And—
and kind of made fun of. Mr. Vanguard was a scientist.
That is, he was before his marriage. He might have been a
Great Scientist. He could tell you all about the foramin-
ifera and coelenterata; the echinodermata—the crinoids,
star fishes and sea urchins; and the worms, vermes, both
round and flat, platyhelminthes and nemathelminthes; and
the cephalopods and the lamellibranchia. . . ." He rolled
the lordly words upon his tongue. "But Mrs. Vanguard
didn't like things like that around the house. She thought
they were—well, smelly, and not very dignified. . . ."

"Why didn't he go where they were then?" Garey Brennon could understand anything except immobility.

"Mrs. Vanguard didn't want him to," Elding explained.
"I think she was afraid he'd get to drinking. He wouldn't
have, though, not if he was doing what he liked. Not that
DeQuincy ever drank anyway; not what you call drink.
Only he used to take a glass for his stomach. He had

nervous indigestion. And sometimes he over-estimated. He used to come to my room then and . . . that is, rest up, and get over his . . . that is, his indigestion. . . ."

He hesitated, blundering and stammering, but his indecisive mouth was shaped to pride. DeQuincy Vanguard, who knew all about the vermes, both round and flat, and who had so much money that the very contemplation of it made him nervous, yet came to him, Oliver Elding, clerk, for aid and comfort.

The truth was that Oliver Elding had an insatiable capacity for hero worship. Himself an inconsiderable fellow, product of office chairs and lights under green shades and the fear of his superiors, it was as if he were tuned to a perception of greatness in others such as more successful men could not have had. He saw in his heroes attributes that he would have liked to possess himself and did not— attributes, even, that they hardly possessed themselves. Reality became smaller, farther away, like something observed through the wrong end of an opera glass, and the fancied likeness to reality became larger, more solid, until it bulked more true than truth.

So with DeQuincy Vanguard. Oliver Elding saw him a Great Man, triumphing over insuperable odds. He saw him sailing the seven seas in ships, his thin legs planted wide to the swing of the billows, his eyes burning with a triumph that poor DeQuincy's wavering gaze had never known. He saw him going down in diving suits, intrepid in shark-infested waters; dragging up the wonders of the deep; laying them bare under microscopes; writing books that shook the world; revolutionizing science. And all the time he saw himself nearby, in some capacity not quite defined—the great DeQuincy Vanguard's friend.

Some of this now in his blundering way he tried to put into words. He twisted his meager hands together as if imploring you to accept his version of the hero as scientist. "Mrs. Vanguard never appreciated him. She never understood him, that is. She didn't care for science. She told him how to make money, and he made money the way she said. But he would have been great by himself. Really great, I mean. He had a brilliant start—no, brilliant is not too strong. He had done notable work with cephalopods. When he talked about cephalopods . . ."

"You would have done anything, wouldn't you, to help Mr. Vanguard with his work?"

"Oh yes. I tried to persuade him to take it up again. I fixed a place in my room with his microscope. It was as if he didn't have the spirit for it, though, with his indigestion and all. . . . But he could have done wonders if things had all been right. . . ."

The pity of it was that through the over-eager words you saw DeQuincy Vanguard, not the way Elding would have made him, but baldly the way he was: a promising young man, marrying too ambitiously, without the strength to keep to the hard way. Giving up the work he loved to make money, until his very riches ruined him. An unhappy man, without will, ridden by a domineering wife. A neurotic. A dyspeptic. A secret drunkard. An idler with no way to spend his time. A millionaire with no way to spend his fortune. Taking his little underhanded pleasures secretly, in the way of small men: a kiss from his wife's secretary, a drink and a bed at the Brittens', a microscope in a hall bedroom, and the adulation of an unsuccessful clerk.

"Did Mrs. Vanguard like to have him go to your house?" Brennon asked.

"No, I guess not. No, I don't suppose she did."

"Was that why you changed your vote—so that Mrs. Vanguard would not interfere?"

"Oh no." He was lying pitifully, obviously; his great pale eyes rolling in his pale face, his hands fidgeting in his lap; repeating the feeble denial until it lost all force. "Oh no. Oh no."

"Mr. Vanguard felt like it was Mrs. Vanguard kept him from doing what he wanted, didn't he?" asked Pitt.

"She kept him from making his mark in science. That is . . ."

"He'll be glad she's dead, too, won't he?"

For once Oliver Elding answered without evasion, without qualifying statement. "He didn't kill her," he said, and his thin voice held a high note of triumph. "He wasn't even here."

"You were here," said Pitt.

And at his words, abruptly, betrayingly, Oliver Elding's egg-like face was drenched with sweat; it gathered on his forehead and on his chin, it shone across his cheek bones like a fine cold rain. It was an oddly distressing thing, to come so suddenly like that, so uncontrollably; it was grotesque, it was obscene, because it gave to his long pale face a false effect of heat. "I didn't kill her either," he said weakly.

"No?" Pitt spoke with bitter relish. "No? You said yourself you'd do anything to help Vanguard along with science. And now, Brennon, we got to get hold of Vanguard."

7

"That makes the lot of them," said Pitt. "While we're waiting for Pulsifer, we'll see what we've got. He said he'd have something here by four."

They sat down over it together with pencil and paper, listing possibilities: beginning with the foreman and going round the table. It was like this finally:

Simon Gilley. Not much against Mr. Gilley. Seemed to want to stand in with Mrs. Vanguard. They ruled him out.

Angeline Tredennick. Had had a lot of trouble with Mrs. Vanguard. Mrs. Vanguard poisoned her cat, and she said she ought to be poisoned too. Hid the "toothache medicine" when she was searched.

William Apple. Held Mrs. Vanguard responsible for the loss of his cows and the ruining of his milk trade. The type to harbor a grudge. Easily led. Probably not bright enough to conceive a murder, but vindictive enough to execute one conceived by some one else.

Mary Madras. Hated and feared Mrs. Vanguard: partly for the injury to William Apple, partly for interfering with her own adoption in childhood. An untrustworthy witness; a liar by her own admission. Had a great deal of influence with William Apple.

Leo Rinschy. Bad reputation; agitator, jail-bird. Carried concealed weapons. Had a grudge against Mrs. Vanguard because she caused his son, who supported him, to lose his job. Mixed up in mill riot, perhaps an attempt to get even with the Vanguards, who were stock-holders. Obviously concealing something.

Biggs. A nonentity. Might have been open to a bribe, but hardly capable of acting for himself. They practically ruled him out.

Gideon Hawes. Disliked Mrs. Vanguard. They disagreed in theory, and she caused his discharge at the high school. Claimed he knew the murderer through application of logic.

Oliver Elding. Thanked God when he heard of Mrs. Vanguard's death. Devoted to Mr. Vanguard. Thought Mrs. Vanguard stood in the way of his success. Admitted he would do anything for him. Just the type for a fanatic murder.

Damaris Lee. Tried to put something in Mrs. Vanguard's coffee. Threw sand in the eye by a lot of bogus confessions. But went to pieces badly when it came out that she hated Mrs. Vanguard for breaking up a love affair.

Charles Kashaw. Undependable character. Named by Miss Lee as accomplice. Betrayed excitement when accused.

Dr. March. Discharged Vanguard physician. Mrs. Vanguard showed dislike when he came in, tried to push him away. Alone in wash room while he prepared medicine. Immediately after dose, Mrs. Vanguard was taken worse.

Died three hours later. Had hyoscine in his bag; twenty-two tablets gone, but accounted for only two. His hypodermic found in Miss Van Horn's possession. Needle of hypodermic fitted hole in Mrs. Vanguard's medicine cup. Fond of Miss Van Horn; said he would do anything he could for her. Very self-controlled; hard man to judge.

Cornelia Van Horn. Discharged for affair with Mr. Vanguard. Afraid of losing position at bank through Mrs. Vanguard's intervention. Antagonism between two at jury proceedings. Veiled talk of threats. Mrs. Vanguard warned her to be careful, shrank from her touch. Hid hypodermic in her bag. . . .

Garey Brennon could not stand it any longer. "I don't care," he burst out unprofessionally. "Mrs. Vanguard got no more than she deserved. Talk about twelve good men and true! Why she just about corrupted this whole jury. She . . ."

"We're not deciding whether she ought to have been murdered or not," Pitt reminded him. "We're deciding who murdered her."

"Just the same it's got something to do with it," insisted Brennon stubbornly. "It ties it up to the Como case. About everybody that changed his vote did it because he was afraid of Mrs. Vanguard. And fear is a motive."

They were interrupted by the entrance of Deputy Sheriff Trollope, looking as usual as if he were about to burst. His words came explosively, as if they were barely in time to relieve a dangerous pressure. "Coroner's verdict, death from hyoscine poisoning," he gasped as triumphantly as if he were telling them something new. "This here's from Pulsifer." He held out a folded paper. "He said tell you it was only a partial report, but he'd have the whole thing in the morning."

Pitt ripped the paper open. The next minute he was stampeding out the door, all but upsetting Angeline, who leaned against the casing.

"Who poured the coffee?" he demanded.

"Trollope brought the pot to me," began Simon Gilley, "and I . . ."

"I poured it," said Cornelia clearly.

Pitt stood glowering down at her and David March together. His cigar had mysteriously disappeared, as if he had swallowed it whole. There was an evil triumph on his face.

"Hyoscine was found," he said, "in Mrs. Vanguard's coffee cup. Traces also in the cup used for aromatic. Now what you two got to say to that?"

V

Thursday

The next morning they had the final report from Pulsifer on the articles sent to him for analysis. They had also the result of the autopsy. Things became at once simpler and more complicated when these reports were in.

Pitt and Brennon went over them together in the wash room. The others dallied outside, with the restlessness of enforced waiting.

It was a dingy morning. The week's unseasonable heat had broken in a torrent of wild rain; it swept in horizontal waves along the streets, and the wind worried the old wooden court house, prying at the loose places in the roof and snarling down the gutters. It was very dark, so that they had had to turn on the overhead lights, like dirty bubbles in their fly-specked globes, and the feeble result, half day, half evening, was as uncertain as destiny. There was a dankness in the room that had been so hot the day before, like the dankness of an old cellar, and Angeline found herself wiping her fingers as if they were actually wet.

The spirits of the jurymen were dingy to match the day. Their first night in jail, unenjoyable as it had been, had had at least the excitement of novelty. But there is no novelty in repetition.

"It's like putting in the second sleeve of a dress," Angeline said, "when you know you've sewed the first one wrong and it's got to come out again."

The bad beds, the bad food, the cry of the wind, above all the cold weight of suspicion and uncertainty, the attitude of the jail authorities that no doubt they were all guilty, lay heavy upon them. Damaris Lee would have claimed bail now, if it had not been for her code of being a good sport; she had said she would stick it, and now stick it she would. She lighted one cigarette from another, dragging them out quickly, and the smoke hung foggily above her head like some unhealthy spreading growth, without the lightness to disperse in the dead air.

"I hate rain," said Angeline. She used the word heedlessly, without knowing what it meant; there was no capacity in Angeline's abounding spirit for hating anything. "Don't you?" She addressed Dr. March.

David March roused himself from a troubled reverie.

"They say it's good for crops," he replied pleasantly. "And I've noticed it will rain about once in so often. So I don't pay much attention. I just turn up my coat collar, and hope I won't have to change a tire."

"It isn't the rain I mind," said Cornelia. "It's the rubbers. The heels never will fit over the shoes you happen to be wearing."

They chatted on, as if they felt a compulsion to play up; but Angeline sensed an effort in it, a certain absentness, as if their minds were far away and only their lips framed words suitable to what was said.

For the life of her, Angeline could not help thinking that it was like that time she had the tooth out. The dentist had injected novocaine, and after that she had had to wait for fifteen minutes; he had sent her into a gray inner office—and there were no end of other people, all with novocaine at work round their aching teeth, all waiting fifteen minutes too. There had been the same strain in that dingy office as there was here in the jury room. There was the same pretense that everything was all right, an effort to put up a front before the others . . . and all the

time their ears were cocked to those sounds from the oper-
ating room: "Open pretty wide, please. Now don't move."
So here they were aware, under their own talk, of Pitt's
and Brennon's voices in the wash room. Something bad
was happening inside, and presently it was going to concern them.

Angeline still remembered the man who had read the
magazine so assiduously, his lips moving as if in deep concentration . . . and the magazine upside down. She remembered the one who had studied the calendar so hard,
his brow wrinkled as if he were sorting a multiplicity of
engagements . . . when all time stopped for him fifteen
minutes away.

It was like that now. People doing anything to fill the
space of waiting, trying to seem natural. Mary Madras
stood by the window watching the storm, her round face
and snub nose pressed so tight to the pane that the drops
coursing down outside were like great dirty tears on her
own cheeks.

"I'm glad I'm not at Mrs. Buckley's," she said. "It's awful when it rains. The children can't get out to play, an'
they just cut up something terrible. The last time little
James bit Dorothy and made red tooth marks."

William Apple lounged beside her with his hands in his
pockets. "I hope that fool don't let the cows to pasture,"
he said morosely.

Oliver Biding had found a bit of string and was making
a cat's cradle. Gideon Hawes wrote doggedly at the end of
his manuscript. His left hand he held rigidly to his side.

"Have you got a pain?" inquired Angeline sympathetically.

"Not exactly pain," said Gideon Hawes. "But of course
in a case like mine, one is never quite unaware . . ." He left
the sentence hanging, and finished with a smile of conscious patience. Angeline could not help feeling that there
was something not quite honest in it: a little affectation,

as if he did not mean to let any one forget that he was a constant sufferer. And yet she felt sorry for the little man, too, because he took his own infirmities so hard.

"Maybe you'll feel better when it clears," she suggested cheerfully.

"I fear I can hardly look for much change," said Mr. Hawes with resolute pessimism.

Angeline left him to his symptoms and his manuscript, and herself went to take a little exercise outside the wash-room door. Presently she came back. "May I borrow your pen?" she said. "I want to make a few notes myself."

Gideon Hawes' hand fluttered up again in its little nervous gesture. "I think you would find my pen rather unsatisfactory. I hold it in an odd position when I write, tipped, you see, to one side, and it makes it difficult for others to use.

"Oh I guess I can manage."

"I think perhaps some one else's . . . ." Gideon Hawes had obviously the very careful person's prejudice against lending his property.

"Oh all right," said Angeline, slightly offended. "Here's Mr. Kashaw's. He won't mind."

Charles Kashaw was already whipping out his gold pen, only too glad for another chance to show it. He had brought a deck of cards with him, but no one wanted to play, and he had been reduced to solitaire and cheated himself abominably. "This pen," he said, opening it with a flourish and indicating the spot where it was inscribed with his initials and the date, "was given me in person by Mr. Arthur Wainright, Division Sales Manager for Bustard Motors, Inc., in recognition of my having made more sales during the year 1929. . . ."

"Much obliged," said Angeline, taking it. She had heard all about Mr. Arthur Wainright, Division Sales Manager for Bustard Motors, Inc., about twelve times before; and she was in a hurry to get back to her station by the wash room. She perched on the edge of a chair, and made a series of holes and blots on the back of an old envelope balanced against her knee.

"The hyoscine was found in the contents of the stomach," she reported.

It was true. The hyoscine—all the hyoscine—had been found in the stomach contents. They had expected it, of course, in view of the drinking cups. But they had hoped also for some evidence of a hypodermic injection. And there was none. It made it hard to fit the hypodermic syringe to the crime.

Most of the articles that had been taken from the jury at large were reported harmless: the three flasks, Rinschy's, Kashaw's, and Damaris Lee's; Mary Madras' perfume; Gideon Hawes' drops and capsules; Angeline's toothache medicine and the cakes of sweet chocolate. Brennon set them aside to return to their owners.

"That lets them out," he muttered. "Makes no odds who *wanted* to kill her, as long as he didn't have anything to kill her with."

It didn't matter now that Damaris Lee had tried to put gin in Mrs. Vanguard's coffee. It didn't matter that Angeline had hidden the toothache medicine.

"But it doesn't let them all out," Pitt reminded him. He was examining a second group of articles—those that had to do with David and Cornelia—and his look was heavy with meaning. "Look here, Brennon."

Garey Brennon looked. He felt a chill as he bent over, a premonition that things were going to happen then and there. Five small objects: two cups, two bottles, and a hypodermic syringe, with their secret locked away inside of them—and the key to the secret in the paper that Pitt held in his chunky hand. "Well?" he said.

"Not so well," returned Pitt with satisfaction. *"Not—so well."* He handed over the objects one by one, checking them from the paper.

"This is the cup that had Mrs. Vanguard's coffee in it, and six tablets of hyoscine. . . .

"This is the aromatic cup, with hyoscine in it too. We knew that. The water cups and the other coffee cups didn't have anything. . . .

"Here's Dr. March's aromatic bottle. And it's nothing but aromatic. . . .

"This here's his hyoscine. And it's nothing, you bet, but hyoscine—with twenty tablets unaccounted for. Remember he told us ten was a killing dose? Looks as if they'd given her two doses, ten each, to make sure. . . .

"And"—he handled the thing with tender pride as if he fairly loved it—"and this hypodermic *was last used for hyoscine. . . .*"

Garey Brennon knew then that he should have to believe it. That gay and lovely child, that strong and steadfast man: somehow, between them, they had killed Mrs. Vanguard. But he would not admit it yet even to himself. He picked up Mrs. Vanguard's coffee cup, turning it in his fingers to hide his own hard thoughts. He had not foreseen that detecting was going to be like this.

The cups bore no finger prints that were of any value. The fluted surface, the moistening and softening of the paraffin with which they were coated, had effectively destroyed anything that might have been there. But under one of the flutings near the top, smooth outside, slightly roughened inside, pointing inward and downward, there was a tiny prick like the prick of a pin.

"This cup's got a hole in it just like the one in the aromatic cup," he said thoughtfully.

"Sure it has," said Pitt, who had not noticed it before. "Didn't you know that?"

"No," said Brennon. "I don't see . . ."

"He put it there, of course. March did."

"But he wasn't in the room when they had the coffee."

"That's so. *She* was, though—the Van Horn girl."

"But why would anybody get a dose of poison ready in a syringe, and then inject it into a cup, and give it that way? It doesn't make sense."

Pitt was at a loss too. But it wasn't like him to admit it. "Maybe he just schemed it out that way to mix us up, because it *doesn't* make sense. Maybe the Van Horn girl gave Mrs. Vanguard the first dose in the coffee. Then March came and gave her some more. First off he mixed it in the syringe; then something kept him from giving it like that, and he put it in the cup instead. Afterwards he might have poked a hole in the coffee cup too, just to throw us off."

"Why didn't he make holes in all the cups then?" demurred Brennon. "That would have thrown us off a lot more. It doesn't seem very sensible, when they must have known the syringe would be found."

"But they didn't expect it to be found. They meant to get rid of it. Remember how hard March tried to get those windows open? He meant to have the girl pitch the syringe out. It was glass, see, and it would have been smashed to smithereens there on the alley pavement, and likely all swept out before we got around to look."

"That isn't the whole thing, though," insisted Brennon. "Why put the poison in the side of the cup, when it could have been put in the top without leaving any mark? There's something queer about it that we haven't got onto yet."

There *was* something queer about it. But the queerest thing was that it could have happened. Cornelia Van Horn. . . .

Still, she and Dr. March had had hyoscine between them. They had had the syringe. There was hyoscine in the syringe. . . . There were holes in the cups. . . . There was hyoscine in the cups. . . The needle of the syringe fitted the holes. . . . Mrs. Vanguard had died from hyoscine poisoning.

"You've got to have a working theory," Pitt explained condescendingly. "When we know where the hypo comes in, then we'll know everything."

2

"Now you see!" said David March with a fleeting smile at Cornelia. "The hypodermic didn't have a thing to do with it." He had been quick to catch the significance of the stomach content.

"How do you know?" cried Pitt.

"How could it, if the hyoscine was in the stomach?"

"How do *you* know it was in the stomach?"

"It would have to be, wouldn't it," said David coolly, "if it was in the cups?"

He was not going to let Angeline down and tell where he got his information. She was grateful to him for that, and sent him a quick little smile of thanks. But the incident troubled her nevertheless. He covered it so neatly, with such a ready and reasonable explanation, with such a casual show of unconcern. If he could hide that, this time, so easily, what else might he not have hidden?

David's little triumph, however, if indeed it was triumph, and not the conventional red herring, was of short duration.

"The amount of hyoscine found," said Pitt, "was fourteen one-hundredths of a grain. Add that to six one-hundredths found in Mrs. Vanguard's coffee cup, and you've got the amount gone from your bottle and not accounted for." His eyes bored into David March's like a gimlet. "Come on, now, what you got to say to that?"

"No doubt I could account for it all if you gave me time enough," said David evenly. "I have had the bottle a long while, as I told you; I don't use the drug often. Twenty to forty doses would be a good deal to remember. But perhaps . . ."

"Perhaps *if you had time enough,* you could cook up something," sneered Pitt. "But you don't need to bother. The last two doses are all I want to know about. All I want to know about is why you used a hypodermic syringe to put poison in a cup."

"I did not use the hypodermic syringe here at all," said David March.

Those who had seen Dr. March under stress, those who had seen him when things were going wrong with a patient, when there was a hysterical family to be dealt with, when he bent for the first time over a bad accident, would have recognized that look in his face: the will to stand up to things without flinching. But Cornelia's brown eyes widened and deepened with a dreadful urgency. She put her hand on his arm.

"David," she whispered. "I think we'll have to . . ."

"Sh-h!" said David March. It was a command, and a terse one; but the touch of his fingers took away its sharpness. "Wait," he whispered back.

No one noticed—no one but Angeline. Pitt was already proceeding on his "working theory." "We'll go over that luncheon business again," he said to Brennon. "The catch is in there somewhere, and this time maybe we'll get onto it. He's smart; but that poker face won't get him by forever."

He turned back to David. "You admit you didn't let that aromatic cup out of your hands from the time you fixed the dose till you gave it to Mrs. Vanguard?"

"No, I didn't," said David March, gravely, steadily, and you saw that he was aware of everything that answer of his implied.

"And you admit you poured the coffee?" He turned to Cornelia.

"Yes, I did," said Cornelia: just as grave, just as steady, just as much aware.

They went over the whole scene from the beginning after that, reconstructing it. Angeline, as usual, proved perfectly invaluable.

"Sheriff Trollope brought in the coffee pot," Simon Gilley said, "and set it here in front of me. I handed it over to Miss Van Horn and asked her to pour. She said there weren't any cups, and Trollope said we'd have to use paper ones. Somebody went out and got some. . . ."

"Biggs," said Angeline promptly. "Biggs brought them. He brought a lot, stacked all together, and set them out in front of Cornelia; and then she poured it. . . ."

"Did you give the cup of coffee to Mrs. Vanguard yourself?"

"Why—I suppose I must have," said Cornelia slowly.

"Yes, you did," said Angeline helpfully. "Don't you remember? You gave the first one to Mrs. Vanguard to pass to Miss Lee; and the second to pass to Mr. Kashaw; and the third to keep. Mr. Elding and Mr. Hawes were out after water, and Biggs was bringing the cups, so that made a big gap at that end of the table and they couldn't pass them any farther. After that you handed the others to Mr. Gilley to pass down this way. Mr. Hawes didn't take any, because coffee is bad for his kidneys; and neither did Mr. Elding, because it makes him nervous if he drinks more than just the one cup in the morning. Biggs came up and got his own when he was ready to sit down; and I came and got mine after I passed the sandwiches."

"You passed the sandwiches?" asked Brennon.

"I certainly did," said Angeline, licking her lips reminiscently, and glancing at Grandaunt Ermentrude's silver watch to see if it was almost time for sandwiches again.

"But there wasn't any hyoscine in the sandwiches," said Pitt, disposing of that point.

"And you say Hawes and Elding brought the water?"

"Yes. And after he got the cups, Biggs helped them pass it round."

"There wasn't any hyoscine in the water, either," said Pitt, and disposed of that point also. "Then what?"

"Then we ate," said Angeline, with gusto. "Mrs. Vanguard didn't eat much, though. She hardly touched her sandwich, and it was a real good one too. But she was all worked up about the voting. And she said the coffee was bitter."

"*Was* it bitter?" Pitt pounced on that.

"Well, it wasn't very good coffee," Angeline admitted. "It tasted kind of dreggy, as if maybe the pot needed boiling out; but I wouldn't call it bitter."

"Did anybody else think it was bitter?"

"No. Weakish," said William Apple.

"Just plain vile," said Kashaw.

"That is, Mrs. Vanguard's was bitter, but nobody else's was. Would hyoscine have made it bitter, Dr. March?"

"Yes," said David March slowly.

"Then the hyoscine had been put in before that point anyway."

"Probably it was the poisoned gin in it she tasted," said Damaris Lee with a naughty grin. "The reason you didn't find any in the cup was because Mrs. Vanguard drank out the gin and left the coffee. Clever, don't you think?"

Pitt ignored her ill-timed fooling.

"You hush up," said Kashaw sulkily. There had been a noticeable falling off in his enthusiasm for Damaris Lee ever since she had claimed him as her accomplice.

"Well, anyway, that was why she didn't finish it," resumed Angeline, unwilling to relinquish her position as spokesman. "She just drank a few swallows. And then afterwards, when she was going to make the speech and all her water was gone, she drank maybe a couple of swallows extra. But it was more than half left."

"And then she was taken sick?" prompted Pitt.

"Yes," said Angeline. "And then Cornelia said prob'ly Dr. March was in the court room, and they called him in."

"Miss Van Horn *suggested* Dr. March? How did he act when he came—as if he'd been expecting it?"

"Oh he acted real pleased to see Cornelia," said Angeline without guile. "And Cornelia acted relieved, sort of. Dr. March told her not to worry."

"*Worry?*"

"I couldn't help kind of wondering about that myself," admitted Angeline. "So I asked him what he meant by it, and he said he meant not to worry about Mrs. Vanguard, because he'd fix her all right."

"Yeah! *Fix* her."

"So then he got Mrs. Vanguard up onto the table, and brought her the medicine."

"Did she say the medicine was bitter too?"

"Why no, she didn't say that," said Angeline, puckering her white forehead in an effort to remember. "But she did make an awful bad face. And once she tried to pull away, only Dr. March wouldn't let her; he held the cup right up to her mouth and made her finish what was in it. . . ."

"And then?"

"And then right off she was taken worse, and they carried her away," finished Angeline in triumph. In her satisfaction at being allowed to talk all she wanted to for once, it never seemed to occur to her that she was doing harm to that nice man David March with every word she spoke.

"What did you do after Mrs. Vanguard was taken to the hospital?" Garey Brennon asked abruptly.

"Oh nothing much. Just waited round for Mrs. Vanguard to come back—you know then we thought she would—and of course we talked."

"What did you talk about?"

"Oh different things. About everything, I guess. I remember first we talked about mistrials, and after that . . ."

"Mistrials!" cried Garey Brennon, starting into sudden animation at the word. "Who wanted a mistrial?"

"Why I don't know, I'm sure. *I* didn't even know what they were."

"Do you know now?"

"Oh yes. It's when a jury is dismissed, like us, and they have it all to do over again. A sight of trouble, too."

"Who explained to you what a mistrial was?" Garey Brennon could not keep that young, betraying eagerness from his voice.

"Oh different people. About everybody: Mr. Gilley, and Mr. Hawes, and Mr. Kashaw. . . . But they just mixed me up, talking about flashes in pans and abortive verdicts and I don't know what-all. But Cornelia made it real plain."

Garey Brennon turned unwillingly to Cornelia. "If you couldn't get an acquittal, you wanted a mistrial, didn't you?" he accused her soberly.

Cornelia Van Horn lifted her eyes slowly under the compulsion of his. "I didn't think . . . Karen Garetti did it," she said.

With the words they were back again to the point from which they had started: Tuesday, day before yesterday, a thousand years ago. Only now everything was different. Angeline felt it without knowing why it was. She saw the tell-tale throb of color in Cornelia's pale cheeks—a hot, betraying flush that beat upward to her temples; a tiny pulse flickering in her throat. She saw a hardening and tightening in Brennon's lively countenance. Garey Brennon was realizing now that detecting was not a lark; that crime was crime, no matter who the criminal, and a detective must find the truth no matter how little he liked it.

The fact was that at that moment Garey Brennon gave up the unmotivated belief to which he had clung: the belief in Cornelia's innocence. Whichever way you started out, he saw, whether by his theory or Pitt's, you came to the same point in the end. It didn't seem believable. It wasn't believable. Cornelia Van Horn, with her clear look, her lovely air of innocence and youth. But it was *so*.

Angeline saw only that from that time Garey Brennon seemed as anxious as Pitt to fix Cornelia's guilt. It was very upsetting.

Angeline herself did not believe for a minute that any one so pretty and gentle as Cornelia, any one so kind and courtly as David March, could have a thing to do with murder. But she just simply was not constructed so that she could keep silent. She never realized how things would sound until after she had said them.

"There's one thing I forgot," she said. "I don't suppose it makes any difference, but I couldn't help wondering about it at the time. . . ."

"What was that?"

"Well," said Angeline, "it was about when Dr. March first came in. You asked me if I noticed anything. Well, I did notice this, and it did seem kind of funny. You see I was telling Dr. March what had happened, because I thought anybody'd like to know, and Mr. Gilley made me stop because Dr. March was an outsider and it seems you don't tell about jury proceedings to outsiders. But right off Cornelia went up close to Dr. March, and he spoke to her, kind of quick and low, as if he didn't mean anybody else to hear. 'How many?' he said. And she said, 'Two.' 'Two?' he said. And then Cornelia whispered something back that I couldn't be quite sure about, because Mr. Gilley was talking."

"What did it sound like?"

"It sounded like: 'I think she knows.'"

Another segment vanished off the end of Pitt's third cigar. "Oh-*ho!*" he cried, whirling upon Cornelia. "You thought she, knew, did you? What did you mean? Know what? You meant: 'I think she knows I tried to poison her,' didn't you?"

"No," said Cornelia.

She spoke in such a small tight voice that not a soul believed her.

3

"The whole thing's as plain as your nose," Pitt was saying to Brennon in the wash room. "Listen here. The Van Horn girl was having an affair with Mrs. Vanguard's husband, and Mrs. Vanguard was onto it. She fired her herself, and when the affair kept on, it looked like she was going to get her fired at the bank. Mrs. Vanguard was fixed so she could do Miss Van Horn a lot of harm and keep her from hanging onto a job anywhere. That was what she meant, wasn't it, when she said, 'I wouldn't hold out . . . *if I were you*'? Miss Van Horn was worried. She talked it over with March, and they decided the only thing was to bump Mrs.

Vanguard off. March didn't get along with her either, and she had hurt his practice a lot since they had their trouble; so his interests and Miss Van Horn's fitted right in together.

"When Mrs. Vanguard and Miss Van Horn were both drawn on this jury, they saw it was their chance, and he slipped her the hyoscine and told her how to work it. When she poured the coffee, she dumped ten tablets in. But it turned out the coffee was bad, and the hyoscine made it taste worse than common, and so Mrs. Vanguard didn't drink it—not enough to kill her, anyway; just enough to make her sick.

"They talk a lot about how busy Dr. March was, and all, but he was hanging round the court room just the same, waiting to be called. Miss Van Horn knew he was out there, and she mentioned him so they wouldn't make any mistake and get somebody else. She was plumb scared for fear Mrs. Vanguard was onto her, and she whispered to Dr. March as soon as he came in that she thought Mrs. Vanguard knew she tried to poison her. March saw the only thing to do was to give her some more poison quick before she had a chance to talk. He told Miss Van Horn not to worry, and beat it into the wash room alone and fixed up a dose with ten more tablets in it. He made sure this time that Mrs. Vanguard got it all down—shoved it right into her when she tried to pull away. Mrs. Vanguard drank it and croaked. Simple, what?"

"It sounds simple," Garey Brennon admitted. "But there must be something more to it than that. We found out a lot, but we didn't find out about that hypodermic."

Pitt elaborated his working theory. "March meant to give the stuff hypodermically. He said he mostly did it that way. He had the syringe with him, and he had plenty of time to get it ready here in the wash room before Miss Tredennick came in—you know that line he pulled about breaking the cork in the aromatic bottle. But afterwards maybe there were too many round, or maybe he was afraid it would take too long to work and Mrs. Vanguard would get gay and do some talking. So he put it in the aromatic instead and made a quick job."

But Garey Brennon was an obstinate young man. "There's more to it than that," he insisted. "It looks as if she did it all right. That is, the two of them together. But . . ." After a moment he hazarded: "Still I've got a hunch it was mixed up somehow with the Como business. Miss Van Horn wanted a mistrial."

"How do you know she did?"

"Well, she wanted an acquittal, and she wanted it bad. She admits that herself. Mrs. Vanguard was the one that was keeping her from getting it. As long as there were enough more holding out so there was no danger of conviction, everything was all right. But when the whole crowd began to go against her, then the head one for conviction got killed. It looks queer to me. And now see this. If Miss Van Horn wanted a mistrial, then Dr. March knew why, and he wanted it too. Maybe it was on his account she wanted it; a doctor has a chance to get mixed up in a lot of funny business. Anyway he was right there in the court room, and there were rumors round that the jury was weakening and it was going for conviction. You don't have to guess at that—you can read it in the papers. Now what *I* say . . ."

"I can't see you've said much about the hypo, either," scoffed Pitt.

"N-no," agreed Garey Brennon.

"Tell you what," Pitt was saying presently. "You take your theory, and I'll take mine. You take the girl, and I'll take March. We'll tell 'em each we got a confession from the other. And we'll beat it out of 'em."

"You'd better take the girl," said Brennon unhappily.

"All right," agreed Pitt. "And believe me, I'll have that wash-room door fixed so it'll stay shut."

4

It was a terrible thing, that accusation. And then, after all, nothing came of it.

Garey Brennon wished himself out of it a thousand times. Cornelia Van Horn faced them with the gallant look they had grown to know so well; prideful setting of the lips, prideful lift of chin. He didn't like lying to her.

At first, though, it had seemed as if they would be successful. "The jig's up," Pitt began. "March has confessed."

Even Pitt, cruel old hand that he was, was startled at the transformation his words brought into Cornelia's face. It was not so much that color went out of it, though there was no color there. It was as if life itself had drained away and left her features cold and still: a beautiful ivory figurine, exquisitely carven, without breath. Only her eyes changed. Under the fire of her hair they widened slowly, terribly, until it seemed as if they must engulf her small white face—the wide, wide look of terror and despair.

"What do you . . . mean?" she said.

"I mean what I say," bawled Pitt. "I mean confessed. I tell you March blew the works, hypodermic and all, from the first time you talked about bumping Mrs. Vanguard off."

"But we didn't talk about it."

"You don't pretend it wasn't premeditated, do you, when you brought the hyoscine right in with you?"

"I didn't bring it with me."

"How did you get it in the coffee then?"

"I didn't get it in the coffee."

She was very self-possessed now. And though no color had come back to her face, she spoke quietly and firmly. Garey Brennon fancied that there was relief in her look. As if Pitt had not asked quite the thing that she had feared.

After that Pitt was pounding at her again, short, hard questions, like blows. Garey Brennon had the feeling that he was beating her with a bludgeon across that white, uplifted face.

"You better come clean. Make things easier in the end. It won't do March any good for you to hold out. He's confessed already."

"I haven't anything I can confess," said Cornelia.

"No? March gave you the hyoscine, and told you how to work it."

"No."

"You poured the coffee, and put ten tablets in it."

"No."

"March was waiting in the court room, expecting to be called. He brought in the hypodermic. . . ."

"Oh no. The hypodermic was in my bag."

Over and over. On and on. Bludgeon blows across that white, defenseless face. Unwavering denials.

No. No. No. No.

Very quiet. Very composed. Very, very unshakable.

In the end that was just exactly all they got out of her: one betraying look of terror and despair, when they told her that David March had broken down. What did it mean? Of course it meant something.

But finally they had to let her go without finding out. They had to let her go, feeling more sure than ever of her guilt—of her guilt and David March's together—and quite as unable to prove it. Quite as unable to fit that hypodermic to the chain of their other evidence.

The strange part of it was that that was exactly what they got from Dr. David March, too. One look.

"We had Miss Van Horn in here," Brennon began, "and she gave herself clean away. What do *you* know about what the Como case had to do with Mrs. Vanguard's death?"

David March's countenance was schooled to self-control; a whole life-time of training had gone into that rigid mastery. It was less, then, by any change of expression that he betrayed himself, than by the complete, the almost unnatural absence of change. It was as if every muscle of his face, every line and curve, set themselves in the precise shape that they held when Brennon's question was asked: consciously still, skillful not to show emotion. Only after an instant his dark eyes flicked up under their lashes and came to rest on Brennon's face. Keen eyes. Judging eyes. Garey Brennon had the odd feeling that they looked through his face into his mind and saw that he was bluffing. He had a feeling that they laughed at him.

"Nothing that I know of," David March said calmly. "Or Miss Van Horn either."

Garey Brennon knew then that it would be no use. And he was right. Question, accusation, insinuation; David March met them all with the same uncompromising denial.

"What did you make those holes in the cups for?"

"I didn't make them."

"How do you explain your hypodermic's fitting them?"

"I can't explain it."

"After you got the hyoscine fixed in the hypodermic, why didn't you give it that way?"

"I didn't fix any hypodermic. How could I? The syringe was in Miss Van Horn's bag all the time."

They had to let him go at last too.

"All they've got to find out is about the hypodermic," Angeline reported faithfully to the group outside.

She rose with great composure from her chair just under the ventilator. The wash-room door stuck fast today—perhaps because there was a chair tipped under the knob inside. But she had discovered that there was a ventilating system in the Sheffield Court House.

"Well, did you confess?" asked Damaris Lee merrily.

David March sank heavily into his chair. But he contrived a grin. "No," he said. "How could I?" And his eyes met Cornelia's.

"You'd better," Damaris advised him. "It's much the easiest way. I confessed half a dozen times, and nobody has said a word about murder to me since."

5

The worst of it was that public opinion was turning against David and Cornelia. First, everybody had suspected everybody else—anybody, to distract attention from himself. But now they began to take sides. They formed and reformed in shifting groups, discussing the thing among them.

"Well I don't know," said Angeline. She had her preconceived ideas of how murderers looked, and this idea
did not include pretty girls and handsome men like Cornelia and David March. "I kind of think Rinschy did it.
He had a pistol, didn't he?"

Gideon Hawes laughed at Angeline's logic. "But my
dear lady!" he protested. "Mrs. Vanguard was not shot."

"Well, no, I know she wasn't," admitted Angeline, all
in a twitter at being called Mr. Hawes' dear lady. "But just
the same, what I always say is, a man that will carry a pistol will do about anything. And then you know he's been
mixed up in riots and things. . . ." She stopped, clapping
her hand across her mouth. "Oh I forgot. I promised not
to say anything about that."

"But we didn't have a riot," Mr. Hawes reminded her.
"We had a murder. A murder by poison. And Mr. Rinschy
did not have any poison. He had nothing but a bottle of
whiskey, as pure and undefiled as bootlegging could make
it. You must consider the logic of the case, Miss Tredennick. According to logic there is only one possibility. If
you will permit me to read from my book . . ."

He was off again before any one could stop him:

> "In any premeditated murder—and this will at
> once rule out the impulsive crime, the crime
> of passion or of anger—one of two motives
> will normally be operable: either the admin-
> istration of vengeance or justice for some act
> of the past, or the hope of some gain for the
> future. By considering any given murder in
> turn, then, from these two points of view—
> the point of view of the past or the point of
> view of the future—it should be feasible so to
> balance possibilities against each other as to
> arrive at the probable motive.

(I have appended here a note on the Vanguard case:)

"Of those who had an opportunity to commit the murder, there were none who had anything to gain in a monetary way, nor in any personal way unless it be from Mrs. Vanguard's silence. But silence implies something to be silent about. That is, it implies an act of the past. The motive is, therefore, thrown automatically into the field of the past: the field of vengeance or of justice. But people normally look toward the future. And it is here that we must consider the inhibition. We must consider not only who had something to gain, but who had nothing to lose. We must consider fear. The person or persons who murdered Mrs. Vanguard had not only a reason for vengeance in the past, but either because he, she or they knew the crime to be incapable of solution, or for other reasons, no fear for the future."

"I believe I can show you . . ."

But already the talk had gone on and left him.

"Bughouse," said Damaris Lee.

William Apple scratched his head with a mighty effort at thought. He drew aside, forming a new group. "I guess prob'ly Miss Lee must a-done it," he muttered. "She said she did, didn't she? And look-it, Mrs. Vanguard got her boy friend away from her. I guess that would just about fix it the way Mr. Hawes says, wouldn't it? She's got cause for revenge, all right. And look-it, she couldn't lose nothing by it, neither, because she's a'ready lost him."

William Apple was pleased with this effort. It disappointed him when Mary Madras did not fall in with it.

The truth was that Mary Madras was not half listening. Nobody half listened to anybody else, because each was too busy with his own theory.

"I'm not any too sure myself," Mary said. "But it seems to me Mr. Elding acts awful jumpy. He's crazy about Mr. Vanguard, too. Mr. Vanguard gains money ways, and personal ways, and all ways. And I guess Mr. Elding likes Mr. Vanguard so well that if he had of done it for him it would of been just like he done it for himself."

Rinschy and Elding, being thus named—a fact of which they were cognizant by the expressive glances cast in their direction even when the words were not audible—were suddenly strong for March-Van-Horn guilt. Damaris Lee, too. After all it is one thing to "confess," but quite different to be accused by others.

"Don't be silly," she said. "We all know they did it. Pretty tough having to double for the parts of hero and heroine, *and* villain and villainess. Kind of crowding things. But there you are. Nobody else had poison."

"I don't like to accuse them," said Mr. Elding. "Of course I *don't* accuse them. It isn't for me to accuse anybody. But I can't help thinking that the weight of the evidence is against them."

"Ze doctaire, he is good feller," said Rinschy. "I razzer see anybody arrezt for murder nor heem, egcept me. You do not make me zay vone vord againz heem." He nodded several times profoundly, as if he could have said a good many words if he had been so minded.

"They're a pair of accomplices, if that's what you're looking for," muttered Charles Kashaw. Charles Kashaw was in a foul mood. Damaris Lee had done him dirt. Cornelia Van Horn was a stuck-up piece, crazy enough about her doctor for a murder, he hadn't a doubt. Mary Madras, who after all was a cute little skirt, had gone gah-gah over that big block of a Swede farmer. Angeline was fifty, if she was a minute. Charles didn't have a soul worth showing off

for. And for Charles Kashaw to show off was as necessary
to him as breathing "What do you say, Biggs?"

Biggs jumped. He was accustomed to the role of silent
listener, not to these sudden indusions in talk among his
betters. "I really hardly know, sir."

Simon Gilley cleared his throat ponderously. "Of
course," he said, "none of us likes to believe ill of anybody. Still, we have to look the facts in the face."

They were still looking the facts in the face when Angeline slipped over to Garey Brennon. Brennon was just returning from another round of telephone calls in pursuit
of Mr. Vanguard. Mr. Vanguard remained inaccessible. Tomorrow, his doctor said now, was the best he could promise. No, it wouldn't do any good to send a man up. Mr.
Vanguard was not able to talk with any one. Sorry, but he
really couldn't allow it.

"I was kind of wondering," said Angeline, "about those
holes."

"Yes?" said Garey Brennon. He was feeling about a
hundred years older than he had ever felt in his life, and
for once Angeline's youthful wonderings left him cold. He
did not even stop to ask how she knew. "So was I," he said
dryly.

"Well," said Angeline with gusto, unwrapping a fresh
cake of chocolate and offering a corner to Brennon, "you've
all been taking it for granted that the poison was put in
those cups right at the time they were used. But I was kind
of wondering why it couldn't have been put in before."

"You mean . . ." began Brennon. For an instant he
thought he had seen a great white flash of light. But it was
only Angeline, with the lamps winking on her little round
nose-glasses and her round blue eyes shining behind them
with questions and wonderment. "You mean . . ." he repeated breathlessly, and he made a dash for the wash room
with Angeline trotting happily behind him. "Couldn't be
done!" he argued with himself. "Not while they were in

the machine. Couldn't be. The holes would have been in the bottoms of the cups. Or . . . *wait!*"

Garey Brennon was examining that cup machine in a fever of impatience. It was one of a not uncommon type: a metal case, narrow and tall, with the forthcoming cup protruding a finger's grasp at the bottom; a glass plate was put on down the front with screws, so that through the glass you saw the stack of cups within fitted one inside another. One of the screws at the bottom Brennon pounced upon.

"It's scratched," he cried.

It was scratched: minute, almost invisible scratches, such as might have been made in an attempt to loosen it with a tool too fine for the job.

"It's loose," he cried again.

And it *was* loose. Once started, Garey Brennon turned it out easily with his fingers. It left a tiny hole. Through the hole they could see the upper edge of a paper cup beneath.

"Could you?" mused Brennon, almost too excited to think. Could you? A ticklish job. But . . . *couldn't it be done?* A hypodermic needle through that hole . . . under the fluting . . . at the top . . . in and down so as not to touch the next cup . . . more space as you go down because the cups get smaller . . . that's the way the holes went, in and down. . . .

"Here's my bosom pin," said Angeline helpfully.

Garey Brennon snatched it—Grandmother Hawthorne's real cameo brooch. But when he approached the hole, no human being could have been more careful. He slipped the pin gently through the hole, pressing softly, firmly, until he felt the slight give of tough paper under a sharp point. He drew it back quickly then, and began to take cups out of the bottom of the machine with a hand that shook. The first cup showed no mark. The second showed none. The third . . . and there under the fluting, inward and downward, just as it had been in Mrs. Vanguard's coffee cup, just as it had been in the fatal cup of aromatic, was a tiny hole, like the prick of a pin . . . or a hypodermic needle.

There was an awed look on Garey Brennon's face when he turned it to Angeline. He held the cup between his fingers as gingerly as if he held death itself there. And perhaps he did.

"Two cups and then the poisoned one," he said in a hushed voice. "What was it Dr. March said when he first came in? *How many?* And Miss Van Horn said: *Two.* Two cups and then the poisoned one. Oh my good God!" He raised a voice that was no steadier than the hand that held the shaking cup before him. "S-ay!" he called. "Say, Pitt! Look here. I've found out where the hypodermic comes in."

VI
Friday

Mr. Vanguard came the next morning. Pitt had sent a man for him as he had threatened, though it was less because he felt his evidence necessary to complete the case than because he had said he would have him, and now have him he would. Mr. Vanguard's physician raised objections, but he let him go finally on condition that he should not be kept.

They had been over and over that matter of the hypodermic and the cup machine.

"It complicates things after all," Garey Brennon insisted privately to Pitt. "We know now how the hypodermic was used and why. But if the poison was put into the cups before they were taken out of the machine, then anybody here might have done it. Dr. March wasn't in the room at first. The others were all in and out of the wash room a dozen times, and you couldn't possibly check up on it. You know Biggs was the one that brought the cups for the coffee. I've thought all along that fellow might be deeper than he looks."

"It doesn't complicate things at all," said Pitt. "The Van Horn girl was here, and she was the only one that had a hypodermic. She did have it all the time; they made a bad break when they admitted that. And don't you see the beauty of it is it didn't matter who took the cups out of the machine? All the girl had to do was make sure Mrs. Vanguard got the right one. When she saw it wasn't going to work, she had plenty of time to fix another. And the first thing March asks when he comes in is how many before the next poisoned one, and she tells him two."

"It does look kind of bad, doesn't it?" whispered Angeline to Mary Madras. She stole a look across at David and Cornelia.

Cornelia was excited. Her face was a white blaze of anger under the blaze of her gorgeous hair.

"Why can't they *believe* us?" she cried passionately. "We *told* them I had the hypodermic in my bag all the time, and just because it didn't fit with their old theory, they said I didn't, and that you brought it with you. And now all of a sudden they've got a new theory, and having you bring it doesn't fit with *that,* so they turn right round and say *I* brought it, and they act as if they'd made me admit something that I'd been covering up. As if . . ."

David tried to quiet her. He leaned forward and took her hands gently between his. But if his touch was professionally soothing, the look that burned in his eyes had nothing professional about it. The warmth of that look wrapped her round, shielding her from everything. "My dear," he said brokenly. Then he steadied himself. "You mustn't get all worked up," he said in the matter-of-fact voice of the physician. "You'll make yourself sick."

"*They* make me sick!" cried Cornelia stormily. Her hands between his were tight fists of rebellion. "Whatever we say, they twist it right around."

"That's what I've been telling you," said David March upon a note of lightness.

But . . . was there more in it than lightness? Did he *mean* something? If he did, there was no doubt that Cornelia understood. The defiance went out of her suddenly, and left her curiously relaxed and lifeless, with hunted eyes and unprotesting hands.

"Yes," she said in a small flat voice. "You—you know best, David."

David's smile was reassuring. Was it more than that? "That's the girl!" he said. "All we've got to do is keep the pecker up and tell them what they ask us. We'll pull out yet."

Angeline had not missed a word. "I can't help wondering . . ." she began breathlessly.

It was just then that Mr. Vanguard came.

Mr. DeQuincy Vanguard was a sad sight. His agitation may have been due more to excitement than to grief, as Pitt supposed, but Garey Brennon could not repress a pang of pity nevertheless, for there was no doubt that the man was ill. His eyes were sunken. His face was lined and drawn. His hands worked at his sides.

DeQuincy Vanguard was the wreck of a fine man—so much of what Oliver Elding said was true. But he was a very complete wreck nevertheless. A tall man, the stoop of his broad shoulders—lopped forward at the corners, like a figure made of paper without the weight to hold itself erect—took away from his height. His eyes were black, and must once have been piercing, but now they looked lost and hopeless in the great lonely caverns of his eye-sockets. His hair was white, startling above black brows. He had the high forehead, the long face, the mobile lips of the scholar; but the face was torn by nervous twitchings, the mouth hung slack like a false mouth held by an elastic which has spoiled. There was something fumbling and uncertain in every movement.

Mr. Vanguard had not loved his wife. But he had grown to depend upon her. Now he was like a lame man who has not loved his crutch, but who is at a loss when he finds that he must make shift to walk without it.

The deputy who had brought him closed the door, going out again, and Mr. Vanguard stood for a moment just inside, peering about blindly like one who has come from a dark place into dazzling light.

Outside it was still raining. The wild gale of yesterday had passed, leaving a business-like downpour in its wake; Mr. Vanguard, though he had walked only from the curb to the court-house door, was already wet through; his coat

lay soggy and black across his shoulders, and the hat that
he held in his twitching hands dripped down on his wet
black shoes. He looked at it with a dazed curiosity, as
if the dripping worried him and he was at a loss how to
account for it. Then he caught sight of Elding.

"Why Oliver," he stammered with a pathetic eagerness.
"Why Oliver! I'm glad . . ." He stumbled forward, holding
out his hands, hat and all.

"Good morning," said Oliver Elding. "That is . . . good
morning."

Oliver Elding admired Mr. Vanguard more than any
one in the world. But he had not in himself the capacity
for greatness sufficient to run the risk of being accused
of murder in the name of friendship. It was clear that he
wished to tone down, as much as possible, the evidence of
their intimacy.

Mr. Vanguard, however, who of course knew nothing
of what had happened in the course of the investigation,
was as anxious to display their friendship as Elding to
conceal it. He doddered round the table, still holding out
both hands as if, crutchless now, he needed even Elding's
physical support.

"I wanted you, Oliver," he said. "I wanted you, and
they wouldn't let you come. I wanted you to tell me . . ."

"Sh-h," said Elding hastily. "Not now, DeQuincy: Another time."

"My best friend," said Mr. Vanguard to the rest of them,
with a pitiful pride in having any friends at all. "My ve-ry
best friend. He would do anything for me, Oliver would.
Wouldn't you, Oliver?"

"Why, why almost anything," stammered Elding. "That
is, anything in reason. That is . . ."

"That's just his modesty," Vanguard explained. "He's
modest, Oliver is. He'd do anything. He's my best friend."

"You are very fortunate," said Gideon Hawes search-
ingly. "It isn't many of us who have friends who would do
anything." He made a footnote in his manuscript.

"There, there, DeQuincy," whispered Elding frantically. "Hush."

"Bes' frien'," repeated Mr. Vanguard.

Garey Brennon saw then what he had not realized before. Mr. Vanguard, in addition to his obvious illness and weakness was slightly befuddled by drink. He guessed what might have been the nature of the prostration following Mrs. Vanguard's death, that had made his physician so unwilling to grant an interview. And guessing, he slipped around the table and borrowed something of Rinschy. It was a mean thing that he meant to do, but he felt he had to do it.

"There might be something in it at that," he whispered to Pitt. "Elding was in the wash room—supposed to be getting water—around the time Biggs brought out the cups."

"Yeah?" said Pitt skeptically. "So was Hawes in there just as much. They went in together. I suppose Hawes just stood round and waited while Elding poisoned the cup, and then it just happened that March got the right one, and . . ."

"Still, Hawes couldn't have been in there all the time," Brennon argued. "He must have been in and out, passing the water round. Maybe . . ."

Pitt paid no more attention to him. "I'm the district attorney," he was saying to Vanguard. "This here's Brennon, my assistant in the investigation of the—ah—the unfortunate murder of your wife. We thought maybe you could help us. How many of these other people here do you know besides Elding?"

Mr. Vanguard looked about him in some surprise, as if he had noticed for the first time that there were others present. David March stood up at once. But if Pitt had hoped for anything spectacular from this meeting, he was disappointed. David March's manner was no more, no less, than that of any self-respecting doctor meeting a former patient, as devoid of embarrassment as it was of currying favor. He advanced with his hand outstretched, friendly, matter-of-fact.

"Hello, Mr. Vanguard," he said. "I'm glad to see you. Though I'm sorry it had to be like this."

"Hello, Doctor," said Mr. Vanguard. From the tragic flash of gladness in his face you saw that it was no will of his that had severed their connection. You saw, dimly, what Dr. March meant to his patients.

It was as if the warm strength of David March's handclasp steadied Mr. Vanguard. He tried to pull himself together. For a moment he stood taller, less slack. "It's been a long time since I saw you," he said, and flushed sensitively at his own ineptness.

"Yes," said David March, ignoring the awkwardness of it. "How's the indigestion?" His keen eye swept over the poor figure before him and knew all there was to be told, but he had the physician's instinctive impulse to protect a weaker man from his own folly. To do so in Mr. Vanguard's case, however, was more than humanly possible.

"It's worse," Mr. Vanguard lowered his voice, with a grotesque and dreadful smile. "You know, I didn't get that . . . rest."

It was unfortunate that the ill-timed joke—in such exquisitely bad taste that Mr. Vanguard, cold-sober, would have been of all men least capable of making it—should have been known to five of those present. But David March ignored that too, his quiet voice passing over it as if it had not been.

"Here's Miss Van Horn," he said.

Cornelia held out her hand too. "Good morning, Mr. Vanguard."

She was gently impersonal, but Mr. Vanguard flushed again, weakly, at the memory of former meetings. He tried to say something suitable, gave it up. "I—I have not been well," he muttered in apology.

"I'm sorry," said Cornelia simply. "I know this must have been hard for you."

Standing beside Cornelia, Mr. Vanguard looked slowly round at the others. In Mrs. Vanguard's wide civic activities

he had never taken an interest, and he was plainly in igno-
rance of William Apple and his cows, Mary Madras and the orphan asylum, Gideon Hawes and the Sheffield High School,
Charles Kashaw and Bustard Twelves, Damaris Lee and her
love affair. His eyes passed over them without knowledge.
He nodded briefly to Mr. Gilley, Mrs. Vanguard's interior
decorator as well as one of the town's leading business men;
and without much enthusiasm to Angeline, his rather too
nosey neighbor. "D'do, Biggs," he said.

Then his eye fell on Rinschy. "Why, hello, Ri . . ." he
began—and stopped dead, halted by the blank look without a hint of recognition which Rinschy turned to him.

"You know Rinschy?" Brennon asked.

"No," said Mr. Vanguard dully. "I thought he was somebody else."

"I wonder," murmured Angeline. But nobody heard her.
She subsided, thoughtfully sucking a butterscotch bar.

"Now Mr. Vanguard," Pitt was saying, "I'm sorry to
trouble you so soon after your—ah—bereavement. But of
course I understand there wouldn't anybody be more anxious to run down your wife's murderer than you would.
Naturally, you'll want to see justice done."

"Yes," said Mr. Vanguard confusedly. "Of course. Justice."

"I might as well say right out that I've got a working
theory," resumed Pitt with satisfaction. "But I want to see
if what you say supports it. And so I want to ask you a few
questions. If you'll just step this way. . . ."

"Yes," repeated Mr. Vanguard. "Of course. Questions."
He was making an obvious effort to control himself; to
conquer his weakness and meet the gravity of the situation
as it deserved.

"Now then," said Pitt. "There was quite a lot of hard
feeling between your wife and Dr. March, wasn't there?"

"Why—why, no," said Mr. Vanguard, taken unawares.
"I—I wouldn't say that." It was evident that whatever his
desire for justice, he had no wish to do harm to Dr. David
March.

But Pitt was inexorable. "He used to doctor you, didn't he?"

"Yes. He's a fine doctor. None better."

"And then he and your wife had trouble, and she turned him off."

"Oh not—not trouble," stammered Mr. Vanguard. "I wouldn't call it trouble."

"Not trouble; just a fight," said Pitt sarcastically. "Now Mr. Vanguard, it won't do any good to try to cover things up. I know all about it. March said what you needed wasn't medicine, it was a rest from your wife; and she was mad as fire, and told him to get out and stay out. Isn't that right?"

"Well, of course, in a way . . . yes. But . . ."

"And what was the situation after that?"

"Situation?"

"Your wife didn't get over being mad all in a minute, I guess. Did she ever talk about it?"

"Mrs. Vanguard was—was quite a talker," Mr. Vanguard admitted.

"Did she ever keep people from employing him?"

"N-no, not exactly."

"What do you mean, not exactly? She said things against him, didn't she?"

"Y-yes. just that he wasn't fit to practice, or nobody with any sense would have him, or things like that. But . . ."

"Think it hurt his practice much?"

"Oh I hope not," cried Mr. Vanguard, honestly distressed. "I'd hate to think . . . But I know he always had all he could do."

"Did you ever employ him again yourself?"

"N-no. I—I couldn't very well do that, though I had the greatest confidence . . . *She* . . ." He broke off.

"Did you ever see him?"

"Oh just on the street, or something like that. He was always nice to me." There was the anxious pride in his manner of one who has not had many people nice to him.

"Did you tell him what your wife said?"

"Why I—might have. I didn't want him to think . . ."

"And did he ever hint to you that if you didn't have any wife, then you would have the rest you needed and *so would he?*"

"Oh no!" cried Mr. Vanguard aghast. "He—he wouldn't have said a thing like that." He half started from his chair; settled back again impotently. He was in the unhappy situation of a man just sober enough to know that he is saying things he does not wish to say, and just drunk enough not to be able to help saying them.

"No, likely he wouldn't," agreed Pitt dryly. He had established the point he wished to make—that David March knew Mrs. Vanguard was doing all in her power to hurt his practice—and he was satisfied. "Now about Miss Van Horn. She was your wife's secretary, wasn't she?"

"Yes."

"How long?"

"Several months. Eight or nine."

"And then your wife fired her?"

"Why . . . y-yes."

"Why was that?"

"I—I don't know."

"Oh come now; think. It was because your wife caught you kissing her, wasn't it?"

"Oh I—I . . ." Mr. Vanguard's twitching face was washed with crimson. He started up again, wildly. "It—it wasn't her fault," he panted. "It—it didn't mean anything. We—we were just good friends, that was all. I—I . . ."

"You were such *good friends,*" pursued Pitt mercilessly, "that you kept right on seeing her after she went to the bank, didn't you?"

"I—I just stopped to speak to her once in a while. I—wanted her to know I was sorry for what happened."

"And your wife caught you at it?"

"She—she found me there."

"And did she say anything about it afterwards?"

From the wild look that swept Mr. Vanguard's ravaged face, it was evident that something, decidedly, had been said about it.

"Did she tell you that she had seen Mr. Halburton about discharging Miss Van Horn?"

"Y-yes, she did," cried Mr. Vanguard desperately. "She said she'd see she didn't keep a place anywhere in town. She said—oh, it was terrible. It was my fault. Miss Van Horn and Dr. March were two of the best friends I had, and I got them both into difficulties. I—I . . . ."

"How did you let Miss Van Horn know about this?" asked Pitt. "Telephone her?"

"Oh I—I wouldn't have dared to telephone," cried Mr. Vanguard, his defenses all swept away. "She might have heard me. I—I wrote her a letter."

Pitt nodded, well satisfied. Again he had established his point, more of a point than he had hoped for. Mrs. Vanguard had meant to get Cornelia discharged, and Cornelia had known it.

He spoke to her as they returned to the jury room. "Funny thing," he said, "about your forgetting to mention Mr. Vanguard's letter."

"I didn't forget," said Cornelia. "I thought it didn't matter."

2

"You know Rinschy, don't you, Mr. Vanguard?"

Brennon had been saving the question. Ever since that first betraying moment when Vanguard had come in, when he had begun a greeting cut off short before the stony unresponsiveness of Rinschy's look, Brennon had been sure that there was something here that would bear thinking of.

He had been thinking of it ever since. He had seen how studiously Mr. Vanguard avoided glancing toward Rinschy; no matter where his hunted gaze had wandered, it had not been there. He had seen, on the other hand, how

closely Rinschy watched Mr. Vanguard. During most of
the proceedings that had followed Mrs. Vanguard's death,
Rinschy had sat passive, sullen but unmoved, as if whatever he knew—if indeed he knew anything—were shut
away so tight that no force could shake it loose. But after
Mr. Vanguard came, he was restive: under the bristling
brows the small sharp eyes were in constant motion, scurrying now this way, now that, like rats in a trap—watching
Mr. Vanguard as if they had some cause to fear his words;
under the fury of his curling beard there was a small continued agitation, as if he gnawed his lips.

Garey Brennon was not a patient waiter, but he had
waited. Now when Pitt was through, satisfied, when he
would have let Mr. Vanguard go—when Mr. Vanguard himself was most completely demoralized—Brennon brought
out the question.

"You know Rinschy, don't you, Mr. Vanguard?"

"No," said Mr. Vanguard quickly—too quickly.

"No?" repeated Brennon. "Then what made you speak
to him when you came in?"

"I—I thought he was somebody else."

"Funny," mused Brennon. "Funny when you thought he
was somebody else that you called him by his right name."

"I—I didn't call him by his name. I—I don't know what
his name is."

"You began it all right, though."

"He fought I vas Rinaldi, down to ze Mill," said Rinschy instantly. "Eet is vone mistake mos' common. Rinaldi
an' me we are, ah, zo mooch alike, alike as brotherz. He
have ze black hair, zo, like me. He have ze beard. . . ."

"That—that's it," said Mr. Vanguard, snatching at the
explanation and repeating it parrotwise. "I thought he was
a man named Ri—Rinaldi, down at the Mill. They are
enough alike for brothers. Rinaldi has black hair, too, and
he has a beard. . . ."

Brennon walked negligently over to the door into the
corridor. "Trollope," he called. "Telephone the Sheffield

Woolen Mill and ask them to send up a man with black hair
and a beard named Rinaldi. I want to see if he's enough
like Rinschy here to be his brother."

"Rinaldi is not zere now a-tall any more," said Rinschy
quickly.

"N-no," Mr. Vanguard echoed. "He isn't there. He—he
went away."

"I hope he'll have a good trip," said Brennon pleasantly. "And now that little joke is over, Mr. Vanguard, tell me
how you happened to know Rinschy."

"I—I don't know him."

"But you've seen him before, haven't you?"

"Oh I might have seen him," Mr. Vanguard admitted.
"You—you see everybody in Sheffield sooner or later."

"Where did you see him?"

"How—how do I know? It might have been on the
street. It might have been . . ."

"Don't bother with the list," said Brennon coolly. "just
tell me where it *was*. Where did you see him last?"

"I—I don't know."

Mr. Vanguard began to pace the room, the absurdly careful pacing of a man not quite himself. He chose the side of
the table behind Rinschy, as if he wanted to hide himself
from those hurrying sharp eyes; but Rinschy swung in his
chair to watch him, unwilling to let him out of sight. Mr.
Vanguard's long damp hands were working at his sides, his
face was twitching and jerking. Rinschy's beard trembled
with the gnawing of his lips. Brennon could not quite
make it out. It was as if they were afraid of each other.

It was then that Garey Brennon did the thing he had
meant to do all along; the thing that, other methods failing, he felt he had to do. He took from his pocket the
black bottle that he had borrowed from Rinschy, and set
it on the end of the table. Rinschy half stretched a hand
for it, but Brennon stopped him. "Let it alone," he said
sharply.

Mr. Vanguard made his careful turn at the end of the room and started back again. He saw the bottle instantly. It is a curious fact that a man who has been drinking—a man who is dependent on drink—develops a kind of sixth sense that warns him of the presence of liquor. He will be drawn to it under no matter what strange circumstances.

So now with Mr. Vanguard. His black eyes, burning in their great lonely sockets, fixed themselves upon that bottle as if it were the only thing in the room. He came toward it as stiffly, as irresistibly, as if he were a puppet drawn by strings. He reached out and took it in a hand that was suddenly, wildly shaking with desire.

"Same bootlegger?" asked Brennon conversationally.

"Yes," said Mr. Vanguard. He was half hypnotized by the sight of the liquor, running up slantwise through the dark glass.

"The Comos?"

"Yes." Too late he saw from Rinschy's look what he had done. "No, no," he corrected himself. "I don't know the Comos."

"I do not has it by ze Como," said Rinschy swiftly. "I has it by zat man name of Toni Petronelli on ze ozzer side o' ze railroad trags."

Brennon ignored him. "So it was at the Comos' that you saw Rinschy last?"

"No," cried Mr. Vanguard frantically. "I never saw him. I never went there. I . . ."

"Now see here." Brennon spoke not unkindly but with deadly purpose. "I don't know why you're lying, or who you're lying for—yourself or Rinschy. But remember, you can't keep us from finding out the truth. We're bound to do it. It will be better for you and everybody else if you just tell us everything straight out. Come now, be a good fellow and tell the truth, and I'll let you have a drink."

It was devilishly clever. Mr. Vanguard was a neurotic and a weakling. Every raw nerve in him was crying out for the liquor that he held in his hands. He began to shake all over like a man with a chill. His trembling fingers fumbled at the cork.

"Y-yes," he said hoarsely. "It was there I saw him."

"When?" Brennon held back the bottle in restraining fingers.

"That—that night."

"What night?"

"The—the night Sebastian Como was murdered."

And DeQuincy Vanguard tipped the bottle in a long, long drink.

3

"I am not zere," cried Rinschy for the dozenth time. "I am not zere, I tell you."

He was standing up, gripping the table before him with dirty, claw-like fingers; his beard, his eyebrows, even his hair seemed all in movement, as if they were blown by the wind of his own agitation; and between them his face showed in patches of soiled white, like the crust of an ill-baked pie.

"No?" said Brennon. "And how did Mr. Vanguard see you, if you weren't there?"

"He is not zee me. He is make ze mistake. He t'ink he zee me only. He zee zombody else, and he t'ink . . ."

"No more Rinaldis," Brennon warned him. "What were you doing at the Comos' that night?"

"I am not zere," repeated Rinschy. "Meester Vanguard is lie. He is lie for get me in ze troubles. He is capitalizt, and he lie for get ze poor vork man . . ."

"What were you doing there?" insisted Brennon.

"He is drrunk," said Rinschy, changing his plea. "He is not know w'at he says. You zee yourself he is drrunk by ze bottle. You do not take vorrd of capitalizt, so drrunk, againzt vorrd of honest vork man, no? He . . ."

"What were *you* doing there?" It was the same question, but Garey Brennon asked it now of Mr. Vanguard. And this time he received a reply.

"I went to get a drink," said Mr. Vanguard. He lowered his voice craftily. *"Don't you tell."* It seemed to come to him then that Mrs. Vanguard was dead, and there was no one any more whom he had to keep from knowing. And as if the memory, or the warmth of the liquor he had taken, had loosened his tongue, he became suddenly confidential.

"I went to get a drink," he repeated. "I used to go, now and then. That was where I used to see Rinschy. Sometimes we had a drink together."

"Did you have a drink together that night?"

"No." Mr. Vanguard lowered his voice still farther. "That night I did not go in. There were people about and I was afraid I should see somebody I knew. One—one does not like these things talked about, you understand. So I drove up, and when I saw how it was, I drove away again. That was when I saw Rinschy. He was going out the Back Road, very fast. When he saw the car, he hid in the bushes. But I saw him by the headlights. . . ."

"What time was that

"I don't know exactly. It might have been eleven."

"Oh my goodness!" gasped Angeline. For shortly after eleven, Sebastian Como had left his brother's house, and he had never come back again. It was in those bushes, near the Back Road, that his body had been found.

Garey Brennon was excited. He had been right—the Como case had something to do with it after all. And he was on the point of finding out what.

They were all excited really, though they showed it so differently. Mary Madras giggled nervously. William Apple sat with his eyes bulging and his lips moist and greedy. Gideon Hawes took a capsule deploring the effect of so much tension on the kidneys and made hurried, voluminous notes at the end of his manuscript. Biggs twiddled his fingers restlessly, betraying for once the man inside the servant.

"*Now* who says Rinschy's bootlaces didn't come into it?" Damaris Lee jibed at Kashaw.

Cornelia laid careful plaits in the hem of her handkerchief and let them out and plaited them anew. Only David March listened impartially, with no visible emotion.

Angeline applied herself to the butterscotch bar with audible sucking noises and watched Garey Brennon. She fancied that his very hair flaunted redder than usual in triumph; certainly his eyes were bluer; his words came falling over each other in their eagerness to be said. But he tried to hold himself back to the pattern of a proper detective.

"What were you doing at the Comos' the night of Sebastian's murder?" he asked Rinschy again.

"I am not zere," began Rinschy. Then he realized that he was fairly caught. "I am not zere all ze vay," he amended. "I am go, but I am not like ze look, zo I am turn mineself back and go ze ozzer vay."

"That was where you saw Mr. Vanguard, then, in the bushes by the Back Road?"

"Yes. I zee heem. He is ride by wit' ze car."

"And that was where you saw Sebastian Como, too, wasn't it, *in the bushes by the Back Road?*"

"No, no, no, no." Rinschy's voice rose on a high, chattering note of fear. "I am not zee heem zat night. Not nevaire. I am go avay, I tell you."

"You waited for Sebastian there in the bushes?"

"No, no, no, no," repeated Rinschy. "I am not zee heem, I zay. I am not like ze look. Zere is too mooch excite', Meester Vanguard, he zee too mooch excite', an' he go avay. I zee too mooch excite', an' I go avay. Eet is all ze same by bot'."

"But if there wasn't any reason for it, what made you hide when you saw Mr. Vanguard?"

"I am not weesh to be seen. Meester Vanguard is capitalizt. He go avay by ze car, eet is all right, yes. But I am poor vork man, I go avay by ze foot. Maybe I get arrezt for innocent bystand only, like at ze Mill. . . ."

"What was going on that you didn't want to be mixed up in?"

"I do' know. Eet make ze loud talk."

"Who was talking?"

"I do' know."

"Was Sebastian Como in the house then?"

"Yes. He make ze loud talk. I do not zee heem. I hear heem only."

"So then you waited for him to come out?"

"No, no, no." Again Rinschy's voice soared in a frenzy of pure terror. "Eet is not vorse for me to be zere, no, than Meester Vanguard to be zere, yes? He is zere so mooch as me. . ."

"But you said yourself he went away."

"Yes, yes," said Rinschy, so lost now in the maze of Brennon's questions and his own fear that he no longer grasped the significance of what was asked him. "He go out ze road, out of sight, yes, by ze car."

"Then according to your own statement, Mr. Vanguard went away while Sebastian Como was in the house talking. But you . . . were still there."

"No, no. I am not zere. I go avay alzo. I am poor work man, I go avay by ze foot, zat no-vone zee me. But I go queek, yes. Queek I go. . . ."

"Where did you go to?"

A look of guile came into Rinschy's face, and he hesitated. "I go by Toni Petronelli," he said finally.

"What time did you get there?"

"Twelf, maybe zo. Twelf-t'irty. I do' know."

"You were at the Comos' at eleven, and it took you more than an hour to get to Petronelli's? What were you doing in between?"

"I am poor vork man," said Rinschy with dignity. "I do not haf ze vatch. Eet is elefen-fif', maybe zo. I do' know."

"What did you do at Petronelli's?"

"I am drrink ze preety-near ze beer. I am play ze game wit' ze poker. Bime-by I mak' ze spich."

"Who else was there?"

"I don' be so sure," said Rinschy carefully.

"You're not sure? First it takes you an hour or more to walk from the Comos' to Petronelli's, and then you're in such a state you don't know who you played poker with? You must have been a good deal upset."

"I am opset preety-near by ze beer. She is preety-near strong. Maybe zo Izzidor Weinnitz, he iz zere. Maybe zo Tori Farnoski. Maybe zo Meester Solares. I do' know. Bime-by I go home."

"And what time did you get home?"

"I am not haf ze vatch," repeated Rinschy. "Eet is late. I am poor vork man, and I am not haf ze car w'at I should ride home queek. I valk by ze foot. On ze vay I am meet wit' grreat mizfortune. I am valk by ze foot up ze currbing. Ze currbing she is zo high. She rize oop. She take me by ze foot zat I should fall down and mak' ze head ache. I am sit long time by ze currbing for rest ze head. Bime-by I go home."

"Did your son know when you came in?"

"Should I zen vake oop mine zon," inquired Rinschy regally, "w'at he is so tired for vork all day by dig ze ditch w'at mak' ze capitalizt, and haf heem look ven I come in and hold ze night-zhirt, maybe zo?"

Damaris Lee tittered. But Brennon was grave enough. "Give me those names again," he said. "Isidor . . . what'd you call him? We'd better have that alibi checked, hadn't we, Pitt?"

"Sure," agreed Pitt without enthusiasm. He never felt kindly toward any fact that got in the way of his theory, but he knew what his duty was. "I'll put Deering onto it."

Rinschy might have drawn comfort from Pitt's tepid manner, but he failed to do so. The idea of checking his alibi was evidently not one that appealed to him. "Eet is zo, alvays eet is zo like zat," he burst out. "Ze capitalizt, he come, he go, zere is no qvestion ask vere he go nex', but ze poor vork man zey is ac' like he is lie, v'at ze currbing zo high should reach oop and catch ze foot zat he should fall, poor vork man v'en he is valk home w'at he

am not haf ze car for ride heemself. Eet is not fair. Eet is
not legal, maybe zo. Eet is not vorse for me to be zere by
ze Como zan ozzers, no? Half ze town she is zere zat night,
maybe zo. . . ."

Garey Brennon was quick to catch the one significant
phrase in the torrent of unfocused speech.

"What do you mean? Who else was there that night besides Mr. Vanguard?"

But Rinschy was already repenting of his indiscretion.
"I do' know," he said flatly, and his beard closed with
finality over the words.

With the denial, Garey Brennon was aware again of
that utter blankness, that complete absence of expression,
that he had seen in Rinschy's countenance once before.
From an extravagant figure of fear and garrulity, mouthing
and gesticulating, he became in an instant as stony still as
a very sphinx. Brennon could not understand it. He had
not understood it that other time either, the key word had
been so lost in the crowding of other matters. But he knew
now. The blankness had come with the mention of the
bottle of bootleg whiskey found in Rinschy's pocket. That
bottle had involved the Comos—and he had not wanted
the connection to be discovered. But what could he have
still to hide? What was the key word here?

"What do you mean, half the town?" Brennan repeated.

"Notting. jus' pipple."

Rinschy did not look at Garey Brennon now. He sat
tightly still, staring straight before him—so intently that
Brennon turned involuntarily to see what he was staring at.
And the answer was—nothing. There was nothing before
Rinschy but a blank wall and the open door of the wash
room; no person except Dr. David March, half turned in
his chair, one arm thrown over its back, listening with as
little visible emotion now that things were going in his
favor and suspicion setting another way, as he had shown
when they were blackest. No, it must have been Rinschy's
own thoughts, Brennon guessed, that he watched in the

space before him. Some vision of a midnight road, perhaps, and dripping bushes in the dark and rain? Some vision of Sebastian Como, advancing unsuspecting to his
doom?

"What people?" he said sternly.

"Any pipple."

"What people?"

"I do' remember."

"What people?" Garey Brennon knew that for Rinschy's
emotional temperament there was nothing so difficult to
bear as this deadly reiteration. "What people?"

"I do' know. I am not zee any pipple."

"How do you know they were there then?"

"I zee cars."

"What cars?"

"I do' know. How am I tell? Any cars. I do' know w'at
cars."

"Now look here," said Brennon. "You're not fooling
me for a minute, Rinschy. You saw somebody at the Comos' that night that you knew. Somebody you haven't told
about. Now who was it?"

For an instant indecision hovered between Rinschy's
beard and his eyebrows. Then the look passed. His eyes
were as blank as glass. There was a pucker of determina-
tion in his beard.

"I am not tell," he said.

"Yes you will too tell." Pitt's advance down the room,
head lowered, arms swinging, was like the charge of a bull.
His voice was a bellow. With one gesture he swept Brennon aside, and all that Brennon had discovered. It was his
case. His evidence. He took it back into his own hands by
the sheer bulk and volume of his roaring. "I'll see that you
tell."

"No," said Rinschy. "V'en I tell, it do me not any good.
It do zombody harrm, maybe zo. No."

"I'll make you tell," roared Pitt. His mouth was very
terrifying, cruel. Mr. Vanguard hid his face in his hands,

shuddering. Even Garey Brennon looked away. "I got tricks to make folks talk you don't know anything about. Not yet. But I'll teach 'em to you. I'll teach 'em to you one at a time. I'll . . ."

"I am not tell," reiterated Rinschy stubbornly.

"If you don't," threatened Pitt, "you'll find yourself locked up for something a lot worse than carrying concealed weapons. You'll find yourself sitting in a hot, hot chair. You . . ."

Leo Rinschy's face was pasty-white, and his scurrying eyes were frantic. His fingers fumbled in his beard. But he never had to answer. Dr. David March answered for him.

David March had not moved. He still sat crosswise of his chair, one arm along its back, his slim surgeon's fingers quiet over its edge. His face was shadowed, unutterably weary, as if he had come to the end of something. But his voice was as composed as if the thing he had to say were to his own advantage.

"Don't get yourself into any more trouble on my account, Rinschy." Gravely, steadily, the words fell. "If you saw me at the Comos', say so. I was there that night."

For an instant there was silence. Tremendous. Shattering. Then it was broken.

"Oh-h-h!" said Cornelia. It was not a cry; hardly even a word. Just a little breath of sound, of endurance broken.

David March turned quickly. And Cornelia Van Horn, who had borne all the Vanguard frightfulness with unshaken courage, pitched forward into his arms in a dead faint.

VII
Friday (Continued)

The rest of that day was a nightmare. It was so bad that it actually took away Angeline's appetite. Such a thing had not happened before since Aunt Sabethany was killed in the railroad wreck.

David March had gathered Cornelia right up in his arms when she fainted. For an instant he stood quiet, holding her like that, looking down at the bright head tipped back against his shoulder. Angeline would have known then, if she had not known already, that David loved Cornelia. For in that instant his defenses were swept away; the rigid self-mastery in which he had schooled himself, the pride of profession, went down before a more natural, a more primitive thing that is in everybody. He was no longer a physician. He was just a man, any man, looking down at the one he loves, hurt because of him. There was such raw pain in his face that even Angeline turned away.

Charles Kashaw sprang to his feet, upsetting his chair with a clatter. "Here, let me help you," he cried.

But David March waved him back, holding Cornelia in one arm. "She is very light," he said sadly.

For a moment still he hesitated, as if he could not bring himself to lay Cornelia on that table where he had laid Mrs. Vanguard, under circumstances so similar, only a few days before. But there was nothing else for it. He stepped forward and put her down. Her limp body fell away from him, and he caught her hands to keep them from rapping against the boards.

Angeline bustled over to the peg which she had appropriated for the use of her gray coat, and brought the coat back with her, rolling it up as she came. She tucked it under Cornelia's head. She began to straighten her skirts, to arrange the feet in their small brown brogues more precisely on their heels. Then she stopped. It was too dreadful to do for Cornelia so exactly what she had done for Mrs. Vanguard.

"Not quite so high," said David March. "Let her right down flat. That's better. Thanks." His fingers flew to Cornelia's wrist.

Angeline was frightened. Cornelia lay between them so still, so white, her breath so imperceptible between the colorless lips, her whole young body so lax and helpless that it seemed as if she were already dead. You saw now, when there was no brave smile to cover it, what these last few days had done to Cornelia. You saw it in the faint hollows at the temples and under the cheek bones, in the tragic thinning and sharpening of the small pointed face. This white, exhausted little figure, stretched so inert before them, was the shadow of the bright nymph who had entered the jury box two weeks before, and waved across the room to David March.

David put down the wrist he held very gently. "She's fainted, that's all," he said. "May I have my aromatic?"

"Tell me how much, and I'll fix up the dose myself," said Pitt officiously. "We don't want any more accidents."

David March stepped back as if he had been struck. As if he had been struck the red came up across his face in a hard streak of crimson. His lips twisted. His eyes were burning points of light. For an instant Angeline thought he would have sprung at Pitt. Then he controlled himself. He brushed a thin hand across his lips, as if he would have turned them by force to the shape of quietness.

"Half a teaspoonful," he said, "in a little cold water."

He picked up a section of Gideon Hawes' manuscript, ignoring the shocked gesture of protest, and began to fan Cornelia. "If you would get some water. . . ." he said to Angeline. When she brought it, he passed the fan to her, and himself bathed Cornelia's head. Under his fingers the hair lay back from her forehead like a shining crown; where they grew damp, the elf-curls at the temples twined more closely in a parody of gayness—as if they alone, of all her body, retained life.

Pitt took out the aromatic bottle with a great show of efficiency, and strode into the wash room. He pulled a cup from the cup machine, peered into it suspiciously, shook it upside down, smelled it, and squinted round the top for signs of holes. Then he decided it was all right, poured the aromatic, drew the water, and brought the cup to the table.

Cornelia stirred a little as he came up, and a faint sigh touched her lips.

"Will you give it to her, please, Miss Tredennick?" David said. "I'll hold up her head."

It was plain enough to all of them that he could not bear the thought of Pitt, with his beefy hands and foul cigar, ministering to Cornelia. It was plain even to Pitt. It did not make things any better afterwards for Dr. David March. He lifted Cornelia's head in the crook of his arm with infinite tenderness. Her eyelids fluttered a little, but they did not open. "It's all right," he whispered softly. "This is David. Here's something for you to take. Drink it all down, will you, dear?"

Cornelia swallowed obediently. And presently a faint color returned to her lips, a more life-like hue to her cheeks. She moved a hand, gropingly, and David March's fingers closed over it in a hungry gesture of protection. At last her eyes opened. They opened very slowly, as if her lids were dragged up against a heavy weight, as if she came back reluctantly from far places to face the present. At first they were quite blank, enormous, still, like two

brown pools that carry no reflection. Then, as David bent
closer, they focused; recognition came into them. Another
instant and they saw the anxious faces clustered round,
and full knowledge swept them; knowledge and . . . fear.
She struggled to sit up.

"Lie still," said David March gently. Gently he held her
back.

"But I want to say . . ." whispered Cornelia.

"You mustn't talk."

"But I've got to tell them."

"Hush," ordered David firmly. "You mustn't say a word.
I'll do the talking."

And Angeline could not help wondering whether he
meant anything *special* by that.

2

Afterwards, when Cornelia was propped up again on two
chairs, with Angeline's coat behind her for a pillow, and
David's coat spread across her knees, then David had to
tell his story.

They let Mr. Vanguard go, after taking his deposition
that he had seen Dr. March that night at the Comos'; that
was why he had gone away, for fear of being recognized.
It seemed remarkable to Angeline that a man in his condition had been able to conceal so important a fact. But he
had done it. It was another of the queer loyalties that one
was always running onto where Dr. March was concerned.

Dr. March wanted to send Cornelia away too—home,
to a hospital, even to the jail: anywhere where there was a
bed, and quiet, and rest. But Pitt would have none of it.

"You say yourself she's all right," he insisted. "She only
fainted."

"She is exhausted," said David March.

"That isn't my fault," said Pitt without sympathy. "You
ought to have thought of that sooner." And something in
the tightening of David March's too sensitive lips showed
that the shot had struck home.

"I beg you for her own safety to let her go," he said tensely. "She could be recalled at any moment."

But Pitt was adamant. He was not above taking advantage of any circumstance favorable to his case, and perhaps he hoped that Cornelia, in her weakness, would betray facts which David March would have wilfully concealed.

Cornelia herself was opposed to going. "I want to stay. Please, David," she begged. "I want to stay with you."

So in the end she stayed, a wraithlike little figure in the two stiff chairs, with her fingers locked tightly in her lap.

And before Cornelia, David March told his story of what happened that night at the Comos'.

It was after office hours, he said—probably about ten thirty—and he was making a few late calls. His office hours were from seven to nine, though they often ran over the hour, and he almost always had calls to make afterwards. When he had finished, he stopped in at Robbot's drug store with a prescription that he had promised to leave for Mr. Tattersall to get the next morning. He found a message at Robbot's, asking him to telephone 0125M. People often left messages for him at Robbot's, when they could not reach him at his office or the hospital, because it was known that he was in and out there a good many times a day. He recognized the number as Luigi Como's.

"You were in the habit of going there then?" Pitt interrupted his steady speech.

"Oh yes," said David March. "I was their regular doctor—have been ever since I came to Sheffield. There are a number of children, you know, and I have attended all the younger ones at birth, and through the usual childhood diseases. The grown people, too. Saadi had just been having colic, so I had been telephoning every day. Besides, it happens that I have a good memory for numbers. . ."

"You've got a better memory for some things than others," Pitt commented tartly. "Well. Go on."

"I called Luigi Como from Robbot's pay station," David March continued, ignoring the thrust. "He seemed excited. I could not make out what was the matter. Saadi was no worse, he said, but it was very urgent. So I went right out."

It was a longish drive to the Comos', David March said. They lived at some distance from town, on the edge of the foreign quarter, and it must have been eleven before he reached there. The house sat a little back from the road. At the right there was a drive; it looked as if it ended at the house, but really it ran on past it—very narrow in a tangle of lilac bushes—and came out again through an untidy yard at the rear into what was known as the Back Road. The Back Road ran across country from the direction of Linesboro and was very rutty and grassgrown, but beyond the Comos' it was better, though still rough and deep with mud in wet weather; it joined the main road about half a mile nearer town. It was over this Back Road that most of the Comos' bootlegging activities were carried on.

"You knew they were bootleggers then?" put in Pitt.

"Oh yes," said David. "Sebastian ran the business. Everybody knew that." If there was just ever so slight an emphasis on that *everybody,* just ever so subtle a comment on the efficacy of the Sheffield police, perhaps David March was justified. He went on again quietly.

The bootlegging quarters were at the rear, where there was a bulkhead entrance. Sebastian did a thriving retail trade. He had a room fixed up in the basement, where you could buy anything you wanted by the glass. But most people bought it by the bottle or the case and carried it away. Sebastian didn't deliver. He didn't have to. As David March drew up, he saw the lights of a car, swinging to make a turn in the back yard. Then it went away. He thought nothing of it at the time, for there were always strange cars coming and going at the Comos' bulkhead, and it did not do to inquire too closely what pillar of society rode inside. He supposed now, from what he had heard, that it was Mr. Vanguard.

"Don't trouble with your supposings," said Pitt. "I want to know the facts."

"Very well," said David.

The Comos' front door, he said, was in the middle of the house, with a sitting room and kitchen on the left, and bedrooms at the right. The children all slept together in a loft—except the littlest baby, and Saadi, who had had a shake-down in the sitting room since she was sick. He saw a light in the rear bedroom, and concluded that his patient was there. He parked the car under the lighted window among the lilac bushes, and went in.

Inside there was a great uproar. He had heard the evidence in court, and his observations were substantially as the story had been told there.

"I don't want any hearsay," Pitt admonished him. "I don't want any 'substantially.' I want to know what you saw yourself and no fiddle-faddle."

"Very well," said David March. "I will try to tell you."

Sebastian Como, then, was obviously drunk. A hard and steady drinker, Sebastian nevertheless seldom lost control of himself. Long habit, a good head, and a shrewd judgment of his own capacity, kept him normally in the state, slightly exhilarated but quite sane, which he found best for business. That night, however, was different. He was in the quarrelsome stage; his eyes were blood-shot, his lips loose, his movements were jerky and ill-coordinated. A splash of spilled coffee on the floor and a broken cup and saucer gave evidence of at least one effort at conciliation and what had come of it. He kept waving his arms about and shouting loud and not very coherent remarks about his business being his business and nobody's interfering with it.

Karen was screaming. She was quite as excited as Sebastian was, though in a different way, and infinitely more alarming. Her hair had come down—she had very heavy black hair that reached to her knees—and with it all tangled round her face, and her black eyes big and flashing with anger, she looked like a wild woman. She was crying out threats at Sebastian.

Luigi Como was trying to quiet them. Luigi was a steady, downright fellow, very different from his lawless brother. Dr. March was sorry for him, because his domestic difficulties had so obviously got out of hand. His efforts to make peace seemed only to stir Sebastian to greater frenzy; Karen slipped from under his soothing fingers and screamed more wildly than ever.

Luigi was receiving no support from Matha. She stood apart, rolling forth a thick stream of vituperation, most of it polyglot and unintelligible; when she saw Dr. March, she cried out in English that she would never cook another meal for Sebastian and his rabble. Matha was Sebastian's wife, and she had long since given Sebastian up as a bad bargain; it did not even matter to her much any more who his latest mistress was, so long as she was sure of a home for herself and her children, and the protection of her kindly brother-in-law, Luigi. Sascha, Luigi's own wife, was not present; but Dr. March did not notice this at first, there were so many of them.

The children were an added complication. There were fourteen of the Como children, of whom the oldest was ten. Saadi and one of the babies belonged to Karen. Of the others he thought seven were Sascha's and five were Matha's; he wasn't any too sure himself. They were huddled in the corners, in their nightclothes, as they had come down from the loft to see what was going on; keeping out of the way of their raging elders by a kind of miracle, and crying, to the last child, with terror and bewilderment. Their wails increased the confusion. Besides, it was a shocking scene for children to witness.

"Scatter!" he said to them as soon as he came in. "Up those stairs with you, every one. Quick now, before I catch your toes."

He drove them before him up the steep stairs, pretending to snatch at their bare feet to make them hurry. He saw their bright eyes shining over the edge of the square hole in the loft floor where the stairs ended, but they were as quiet as mice. He believed they thought it rather a joke then.

He picked Saadi up out of her shake-down and carried her into the dark front bedroom. The littlest baby, incredibly enough, was sleeping, and he laid Saadi on the bed beside him.

"What's up?" he said to Luigi.

At first he could make nothing of it. They all talked at once, and the more they talked the less understandable it was. It was not till then that he noticed Rose.

Rose was the only one present whom he did not know. She was sitting by herself in a corner, sobbing as if her heart would break; she was bent right over, with her face hidden on her knees, and her whole figure shaken by the violence of her grief. They kept pointing at Rose and chattering, and he gathered that she was the cause of the disturbance. At last Luigi made him understand. Rose was Sebastian's new mistress. He had brought her home that night. And this was the result.

David March went over and put his hand on the girl's shoulder; she looked up at him at once. She was a pretty little thing, wholesome and rosy; but her round dark face was all streaked and blurred with tears. "I want to go home," she cried.

"Well, go home then, kid," he said. "That's the very thing for you. I'll drive you home myself."

No, no, Luigi Como said. The doctor must not do that. There was Sascha. They had sent for him for Sascha. She was in there. Sascha was sick. She had had a fit. She was bleeding. She was most dead maybe.

It was rather terrible, because in the excitement the whole Como family had evidently forgotten about Sascha.

"I'll go right in," Dr. March said. "You take Rose home yourself, Luigi."

He hurried toward the rear bedroom, which Luigi had pointed out as Sascha's. But Karen's condition, too, alarmed him. She was beside herself, and he felt half afraid to leave her, like that, and Sebastian, drunk, alone with only Matha. As he went by Karen, therefore, he took her by the arm and gave her a little shake. "Stop that noise," he said. "I want you to help me."

He went into Sascha's room and took Karen with him.

Presently he heard the tremendous reverberations which meant that Luigi was cranking his old car; a little more and it went pounding and racketing away. So he knew that Luigi was taking Rose home.

Sascha he found in a state of complete collapse. She was not strong. She did not like Sebastian anyhow; after all she had had a great deal to bear from him. Now at this fresh outrage she had let herself go altogether. She had had a violent attack of hysterics, and this had culminated in a very bad nosebleed. Her heart was not quite right either, had not been since the last baby was born. But he had not thought at first that it would prove so serious. After he had stopped the bleeding and made her comfortable he went out again to the sitting room.

When he returned, he found Luigi already back. Rose's boarding house was less than a mile away, and Luigi had seen her in the door himself. There was no doubt that this was correct. The matter had been checked afterwards, and half a dozen disinterested persons had sworn that they saw Rose come in; her room-mate knew that she had not gone out again until she went to work at the Mill the next morning. No, Rose was out of it.

"I didn't ask you who was out of it," said Pitt. "I'm trying to find out who was in." He chewed busily at his fourth cigar.

"Sorry," said David March briefly.

He was sensitively aware of all those faces, blurred into a wall—goggle-eyed, gape-mouthed, as the mesh of evidence tightened about him; morbidly curious to see his pain, like those who rush to watch an accident.

"As good as a show," Damaris Lee whispered to Kashaw.

Angeline saw the muscles at the corners of David March's jaw stand out in knots as he heard her. But he did not turn. When he looked away from his inquisitors, it was not at the crowding, curious faces. It was at Cornelia; biting her lips, twisting her fingers, bearing it with him. He flung her a heartening smile before he went on again.

When he left Sascha, he said, Sebastian was gone. Karen he had had with him all the time. He had kept her very busy: holding the basin, pouring fresh water from the pitcher on the wash-stand, tearing up cloths, putting a clean case on Sascha's pillow. As long as she was occupied, she behaved better. She had wound up her long hair on top of her head, and though she muttered from time to time under her breath, otherwise she seemed normal.

Now, however, when she found Sebastian gone, she broke out as wildly as ever. She ran across the room and jerked open the door, intent on following him. She was crying out and making threats.

Karen was a good girl. In spite of the informality of her manner of living, in many ways she was the best of the lot—except Luigi. But she had the hot blood of the South, the South's passion and temper and lack of control. David was afraid to let her go like that.

"I want you to come down to the drug store with me," he said upon an impulse, "and get some medicine for Sascha." It seemed the best solution for the moment.

He gave Luigi instructions about Sascha, told him to telephone if the bleeding started again, said good night to Matha, and went out to his car. He took Karen with him, holding her by the arm. She did not want to go at first, but they got off finally.

He drove slowly on the way back to town. It had begun to rain a little already—not heavily, but in a thin mist that gathered on the windshield. The Back Road was very dark.

"What were you sneaking out the Back Road for?" put in Pitt.

"One does not sneak in a car as old as mine," said David March whimsically. He grinned across at Cornelia, with the memory of past break-downs. "It's too rattly. I went out the Back Road for no reason except that it was more convenient. There was not much room to turn in the Comos' yard. I often went that way."

"You say so!" said Pitt. "Well. Get along with it."

Even after he reached town, David March said, he had not gone directly to the drug store. Karen was pretty unmanageable. She tried to throw herself out of the car. She tried to bang her head against the window frame. Her hysterics were as completely uncontrolled as ever Sascha's had been; but she was physically strong, very strong, so that her violence did her no permanent injury, as it had in Sascha's case. Still, he had an ado to prevent her from hurting herself. He drove round for some time, keeping to less frequented streets, before he dared to run the risk of leaving her in the car in front of Robbot's. It was five minutes of one when he reached there.

"Got it right down pat, haven't you?" sneered Pitt. "What were you, expecting you'd need to prove an alibi?"

"No," said David March composedly. "I am sure of the time, because I watched it carefully. I was afraid I should be too late. The drug store closes at one. I waited as long as possible before the closing hour."

"Yeah!" said Pitt.

At the drug store, he said, he bought Sascha a simple sleeping draught, and wrote directions on it for Luigi. After that he drove Karen straight home.

At the Comos' he turned the car in at the front drive, as he had done when he was there earlier in the evening. Everything was still. The house was entirely dark. Even the light in Sascha's room was out; so he judged she must be asleep and decided not to go in. He stopped the car at the corner of the house and let Karen out.

Karen was quiet by this time. After the violence of her outburst, she was sleepy and lethargic. He did not think

there was any danger now even if she met Sebastian. And
Sebastian, he imagined, would be sleeping off the effects
of his debauch. He waited long enough to make sure that
Karen got in all right, and saw her close the door behind
her. After that he kept straight ahead, through the narrow
drive by the side of the house, and out again into the Back
Road.

He paused, just perceptibly. Angeline was aware of
increased tension. It wasn't in David March's looks. They
had all given up, long ago, expecting betrayal there. He
was composed, as always, though perhaps there was the
least hint of tightness in the muscles of his jaw, the least
possible added pallor. But it was Cornelia whom Angeline
watched. Cornelia was still weak and unstrung; she was
under a terrific strain. It was not strange if her feelings
showed more plainly through the likeness of plucky unconcern she tried to put upon them.

Cornelia was frightened. She had been frightened before, Angeline knew. But this was a more poignant, a more
immediate terror. It pinched her small face to the shape
of dread, wilfully controlled; it widened her eyes to two
black holes burned in a white shield. Her fingers clutched
spasmodically at the collar of David March's coat lying
across her knees, as if it was only by holding hard to something of David's that she could steady herself. Her lips
moved over silent words, as if she rehearsed a set speech
that some time she must say.

Angeline guessed shrewdly that Cornelia knew what
David March meant to say next, and she was afraid to
have him say it.

Suddenly Angeline was afraid too. She was afraid because she saw Garey Brennon watching Cornelia.

Brennon worried Angeline. She had a wholesome awe of
his nimble wit. The very quickness of his ups and downs,
his young enthusiasms, his agile reconstruction of points
of view—and this with a certain stubbornness, as well, a
fine disregard for things that got in his way—made him

formidable. If you had anything to hide, Garey Brennon was a difficult man to hide it from.

Angeline hoped nothing she had said could have got Cornelia and David March into any trouble. She didn't see how it could have, really. Still, she meant to be more careful after this. Not that there was anything more to tell about them that she hadn't already told. She unwrapped a chocolate peppermint patty, and wrapped it up and put it away again.

David March did not look now at Cornelia. He looked straight at Pitt, and his eyes never faltered. After that breath's space of pause, it was as if he were in haste to get out what he had to say.

"Not far from the house," said David March steadily, "on the left hand side of the road, I saw a man. He was lying among the bushes, so that his body did not show; but his head stuck out a little into the road. At first I thought it was a stone, and turned out for it. Then the lights came on it and I saw what it was; it was raining hard by this time, and the face was wet so that it shone under the lamps. I stopped the car a short distance beyond, and went back. It was Sebastian Como, and he was quite dead."

3

To say that there was a sensation was to put the thing too mildly. Hours before the murder had been discovered, David March had stood over Sebastian's dead body there among the bushes by the Back Road—and he had not come forward to say so. It looked . . . pretty . . . queer.

"Gad, he's got nerve, I'll say that for him," Damaris Lee whispered to Kashaw. Nerve was the one thing she could respect.

"He's a cool hand," agreed Kashaw.

"You wouldn't hardly think it of'm, would you?" said Mary Madras, with a glance of admiration for David's towering height.

"I wouldn't put it past him," said William Apple jealously. "Doctors is used to dyin' and such. He likely wouldn't mind it."

Rinschy appeared actively unhappy. He had got Dr. March into this. Up to his neck, looked like. And the worst of it was if he tried to get him out, suspicion would turn right back onto him. Rinschy liked Dr. March, but he didn't want to be a hero. "I do' care who he is kill," he muttered to Biggs. "He is fetch mine zon's kid out o' ze fit and am not send ze bill v'en mine zon he haf no vork."

Even Gideon Hawes showed surprise; this was the more remarkable because a teacher and a philosopher and a logician does not usually betray emotion, surprise least of all. He chewed for some time at the end of his silver pencil before he made a note in his manuscript.

Angeline was silent. She was watching Garey Brennon—who was still watching Cornelia.

Pitt did not let David March go on any more telling his story at his own pace. He burst into a blast of questions that were themselves an indictment.

"You say he was dead?"

"Yes."

"When you got there, you mean, or when you left?"

"Both." David could not quite resist that. "He was dead when I got there," he specified.

"How do you know?"

"I examined him. I tried his heart, and when I could not get the beat, I turned on the flash light that I had brought from the car and held his hand against it. It was quite white. There was no pink line about the fingers as there is in the living. It was a dead hand."

"You say you turned on your flash light. Hadn't you had it on before?"

"No."

"Why not?"

"I hadn't needed it. The lights from the car were enough."

"Didn't need much light for your job, I presume," surmised Pitt. "How long do you claim he had been dead?"

"I couldn't say exactly. I did not make a thorough examination. I only made sure that there was nothing I could do to revive him."

"You mean to say you're a doctor, and you don't know whether a man had been dead two hours or two minutes?"

"Not two hours, certainly. Sebastian was in the Comos' sitting room about two hours before. Certainly more than two minutes."

"How do you know it was more than two minutes?"

"He was beginning to grow cold."

"You say so!"

"Yes, I say so."

"How long would that take?"

"Half an hour, perhaps. It varies a great deal. He might have been dead longer."

"H'm," said Pitt. "Took you quite a while to think that one up, didn't it? Hadn't got it figured out as well as you had the Vanguard case. Now then. Was Sebastian's body there the other time you went out the Back Road?"

For the first time, ever, since he had entered that jury room three days before, David March hesitated. "I believe not," he said. "I didn't see it."

"Then it couldn't have been there."

"No. I don't believe it could."

"Make it nice for you if you dared to say it was there all the time, wouldn't it? And you with your pretty little alibi all cooked up. I wouldn't advise you to swear to it, though. Somebody might have seen him alive after that."

"I don't want to swear to it," said David March. "I have said that I don't believe the body could have been there without my seeing it."

He had recovered his customary manner, cool and detached. But that short interlude, when he had seemed to be weighing what he said, considering chances, had made a bad impression. There was something not quite frank about it. Angeline saw Garey Brennon's look shift quickly from Cornelia to David March and back again. She couldn't help wondering.

But Garey Brennon had already caught the significant fact. "See here," he cried, jumping up in his impulsive way. "When Sebastian's body was found the next morning, it was in the bushes. It wasn't in the road at all. Luigi testified . . ."

"I moved the body back," said David March.

"You *what?*"

It seemed impossible that he had said it. But he had.

"I moved the body back," he repeated.

Pitt was beside himself with joy. He fairly gobbled at his cigar, his red dewlaps flapping, his tongue tripping on a dozen things he wanted to say at once. His heavy hands came up in a curious clutching gesture, as if he caught confessions in the air. "You got the nerve to stand there and tell me," he panted, "that you hid Sebastian Como's body in the bushes. . . ."

"I didn't hide it," corrected David March. "I moved it back out of the road."

"What did you do that for?" asked Brennon.

"It seemed better. It isn't pleasant to think of a dead man being run over by a passing car."

"*You* didn't run over him."

"I was going out, and naturally was on the right-hand side. The body lay at the left. Had I been coming in, I might have hit it. I came in the other way, you remember."

Garey Brennon said no more. There was a spark of unwilling admiration in his eyes for David March's readiness. But he did not look as if he believed the explanation for a moment.

No one did.

"You got the nerve," bawled Pitt again, "to stand up there and tell me you found Sebastian Como dead, and pulled him in the bushes, and went along home and said nothing to anybody . . . *and you didn't have a thing to do with killing him?*"

"Those are the facts," said David March, imperturbably.

4

"Well then, and so after you got the body fixed, what did you do then?"

"I got into my car and went home."

"Wouldn't it have been kind of natural to go back and tell Luigi Como his brother was dead?"

"Perhaps."

"But you didn't do it?"

"No."

"Why not?"

"There wasn't anything he could do. Sascha was sick. The children . . ."

"Kind of embarrassing interview. Yeah, I see." Pitt's voice was a study in sarcasm. "And so you went home and tumbled into your little bed where it was all warm and safe."

"I did not go to bed," said David March, unshaken. "I went up to my room. . . ."

"What time was that?"

"Twenty minutes after two."

"I thought you'd know," Pitt scoffed. "Trust you every time."

"There was a clock on the table beside my bed," said David March—and left it at that.

"But see here," broke in Garey Brennon again, irrepressibly. "The first time you went to the Comos', you say you were at Robbot's at ten-thirty, and after you had left a prescription, and got the message from Luigi Como, and telephoned, and driven out there, it was only about eleven. Less than half an hour for the trip. But this time you were at Robbot's at one, and it took you an hour and twenty minutes to drive out and right back. How do you account for the extra time?"

"I stopped to see Karen into the house. I stopped when I found Sebastian. I suppose I drove more slowly, because of the rain."

"And it took a little time to kill Sebastian," said Pitt.

"I did not kill Sebastian," said David March.

Angeline trotted out to the wash room and brought Cornelia a cup of water. She thought from the look of her that she might be going to faint again. But the water seemed to revive her. She sat up straighter, fingering the fall of lace down Angeline's dress. "He didn't kill him," she whispered brokenly.

"Of course he didn't," agreed Angeline, with more conviction than she felt.

"Why didn't you notify the police?" Pitt was booming.

"I know I should have," agreed David March. "I was wrong not to do it right away. I meant to. But I went into the bath room first to wash my hands. . . ."

"What did you do that for?" asked Brennon excitedly.

"To get the blood off them," said David March coolly. "I got them bloody when I felt for Sebastian's heart. I wiped them on my handkerchief, but I couldn't get it all off."

Again Brennon flashed him that look of hard-won admiration. God, the man had courage.

"What did you do with the handkerchief?" he asked.

"I put it in the laundry basket."

It was perfect. It was so exactly what an innocent man would have done. You couldn't get ahead of David March. He thought of everything.

"Who's your laundress?" bawled Pitt. "Get her name, Brennon. Tell Trollope. . . ."

Brennon grinned at David March, conceding a point. "She won't remember," he said. "Don't you suppose a doctor ever has blood on his handkerchiefs? And what could she tell us anyway that we don't know?" David March was as guilty as hell—but he couldn't help liking him. He was so gol-darned *adequate*.

And so presently Pitt went on again. "After you got scrubbed up, why didn't you call the police then?"

"I meant to," David March repeated. "But before I could do it, the telephone rang, and I was called out."

"You could have notified the police before you started, couldn't you?"

"It was an emergency. I left a note on the pad, and went straight on."

"An emergency? I don't know of any accident round then."

"It wasn't an accident. Mrs. Taftoloski, out at Bent End. It was her first baby. I thought I could notify the police from there."

"And why didn't you?"

"There was no telephone."

"You could have gone to the neighbors'."

"There were no neighbors."

"You could have sent somebody."

"There was no one to send."

"Say, look here! You tell me somebody telephoned to you, but there wasn't any telephone and nobody to use it."

"Mr. Taftoloski called me. I suppose he went somewhere to a pay station. But he didn't come back. I heard afterwards that he was down at Petronelli's, roaring drunk."

"Did you see him there?" Brennon asked Rinschy.

"I zee heem," agreed Rinschy with suspicious promptness. He added craftily: "Maybe zo he don' remember me ver' good. He is drink preety-near too mooch preety-near ze beer."

Brennon made a note of that for Deering. Deering was not getting on very well checking Rinschy's alibi. No one that Rinschy said he had played poker with seemed to remember it.

"Sounds to me like you'd found a good place to keep out of trouble, and you meant to stay there," Pitt was saying to David. "I guess likely you could have gone out to a pay station yourself if you'd been a-mind to."

"I might have," admitted David March. "But I didn't dare to run the risk. Mrs. Taftoloski begged me not to leave her. She was afraid."

"And you always stay with your patients when they're afraid, I suppose!"

"Yes," said David March.

Something in the simple monosyllable made a choke come in Angeline's throat. David March killing Sebastian Como . . . killing Mrs. Vanguard. . . . David March staying all night with Mrs. Taftoloski because she was afraid. It didn't seem right, somehow. But then there were a lot of things about this that didn't seem right. It wasn't right for Cornelia to have to look like that.

"The child was born the next afternoon," David March said. "After that I left Mrs. Taftoloski alone long enough to fetch a nurse. Then I went home."

"And I suppose you still *intended* to call the police."

"Yes. I meant to telephone Luigi Como, and the police right after that. But Luigi was waiting for me."

"In your office?"

"No. In the garage."

"Hadn't he been to the house? Wasn't there anybody there?"

"The housekeeper, Mrs. Aaron, was there, and Miss Maddocks, the office nurse. But he hadn't been to the house."

"How do you account for that?"

"I suppose he wanted to see me alone," said David March dryly. "And he thought I would drive directly into the garage when I came, as indeed I did."

"Didn't the housekeeper or the nurse see him come in?"

"I believe not. The entrance to the garage is not in sight from the house, and the drive is shaded by shrubbery. When I asked later for the people who had tried to reach me, neither of them mentioned Luigi Como."

"Oh. A *strictly private* interview!"

"Yes," said David March, more dryly still.

"And what went on at this private meeting?"

"Luigi told me what had happened. You know all that."

"You can tell me again," said Pitt. "I notice when you tell things they've got a way of sounding different."

It was a moment before David March continued—as if he were gathering himself. But when he spoke it was in short, matter-of-fact sentences.

"First," he said, "Luigi told me that Sascha was dead. She was alone when she died. Luigi had been in a number of times during the night to see if she wanted anything. She was quiet, and he thought she was sleeping. He did not light the lamp for fear of waking her. Just after daybreak he went in again. Sascha was lying half across the bed, as if she had started up—in pain perhaps—and fallen back again. Luigi telephoned me immediately, and when he failed to reach me, he called another doctor. Dr. Callam, who testified in court. Dr. Callam said that Sascha had died of a heart attack; she had been dead for several hours." He paused. "Luigi felt very badly. It was dreadful for him to think that Sascha had been already dead when he was tiptoeing in and out so softly, so as not to waken her. He . . . you see he loved Sascha." After a moment he added: "I felt very badly too. If . . . I had stayed there that night, perhaps it would not have happened."

He looked down, steadying himself, and Angeline saw the corners of his mouth twitching painfully. She marvelled again at what manner of man this was: who suffered over the accidental loss of a patient; who killed with un-impassioned coolness, overlooking nothing, brazening it out to the end. It didn't seem . . . She groped for a word and found Gideon Hawes'. It didn't seem *logical*.

Pitt, however, was burdened with no such metaphysical speculations. "And after all this love feast," he said coarsely, "did either of you happen to mention Sebastian?"

"Oh yes," said David March readily. "Luigi told me about that, too. They found the body rather early. When Sebastian didn't appear for breakfast, they sent the children to look for him. It was Germina who found him.

I was sorry about that," he added. "Germina is a high-strung youngster."

He could kill without compunction. But he was sorry about Germina. Angeline could not help wondering.

"And then of course," said Pitt, very heavily sarcastic, "you told him how *you'd* found the body in the middle of the night, and didn't mention it."

"Yes," said David March surprisingly. "I told him that. He said that Karen had been arrested. And I said at once, 'But Luigi, Karen couldn't have done it. She was with me. Sebastian was already dead when I brought her home.' And then of course I told him about it."

They were all incredulous.

"But look here! Do you know what you've done?" Brennon cried.

"Done?"

"You've made Karen a cast-iron alibi."

"Oh yes," said David March. "I know that."

"And you expect us to believe that you admitted as much to Luigi Como, and he didn't run with it to the police? What did you do to shut him up?"

"Nothing. I said to him, 'I must get in touch with the police right away. Then I'll come back with you, and we'll try to straighten things out.' But Luigi said no, I mustn't do that. I must stay away—not say anything. He had not mentioned my being there the night before, and Dr. Callam believed himself the only physician who had been called on the case. Luigi said it would look queer if we said anything then, and we'd better wait and see how things turned out."

"I'll tell the cock-eyed world it looks queer!" remarked Kashaw.

But Pitt swept David March a derisive bow, grotesque with his dumpy figure and worn cigar. "And may I ask," he inquired mockingly, "to what you attribute this remarkable piece of self-sacrifice on the part of Luigi Como?"

David March answered as carefully as if the question had been put in good faith. "Luigi and I were . . . friends," he said slowly. "I had attended his family a long time, and I had done what any doctor would have done. He was more grateful to me than I deserved. He didn't want to get me into trouble." He paused, considering this, as if to make sure that he had covered the point. Then he went on. "But that wasn't all of it. Karen had already been accused. If she were released, then some other member of the Como family might be arrested in her place."

"Do you mean to tell me," broke in Pitt, "that Luigi Como didn't think you killed Sebastian?"

"Oh no. He didn't think that," said David March. "I told him I didn't do it."

It was another of those perfect things. So exquisitely simple that an innocent man might have said it. Again Garey Brennon darted at him that grudging look of homage, a tribute to a better man than he.

But Pitt was practical always. "We'll get the Comos down and see what they've got to say about it," he promised. After that they labored on again.

David March had not realized, he said, until Luigi had pointed it out, how strange his own conduct was going to look. During the long hours at Mrs. Taftoloski's, every nerve had been stretched to the problem of bringing her out of danger, and he had not thought of anything else. He had been up the night before, too, so that he had not slept for nearly sixty hours, and perhaps outside the immediate circle of the present his mind was not working very well. Now he saw how hard it was going to be to explain his actions. The finding of Sebastian's body, alone there in the dark. His failure to let Luigi Como know. His failure to notify the police.

He and Luigi went over and over it. He didn't know what Luigi's suspicions were—whether he had any. It hadn't seemed fair to ask. To Luigi, with his patriarchal ideas of family, for one Como to be accused was no worse than for another. He didn't want the justice of the American law; he wanted to save his people.

They agreed that Karen could not have done it. If Karen didn't do it, Luigi argued, then she couldn't be convicted. If she wasn't convicted, then the case would be dropped. And that would be the best for every one. The thing to do was to wait and say nothing, and see how things came out.

David March had refused flatly at first. He was shocked and repelled by the suggestion. But in the end he had consented.

He interrupted when Pitt would have stopped him. "You must not blame Luigi Como for this," he said. "He is of foreign birth, and he does not understand the American law as I do. He did not realize the seriousness of covering up the truth. The responsibility is entirely mine."

"You're darn cahootin' it is," agreed Pitt with enthusiasm.

Then those hardest questions of all.

"You realized that you had information that would have freed Karen Garetti if you had brought it forward?"

"Yes." David was very white.

"But you chose wilfully to withhold this information?"

"Yes."

"You preferred to let her stand trial for a crime of which you knew her to be innocent?"

"Yes." He was whiter than white now. Ashy. Frightening. Did—did *men* faint, Angeline wondered?

"If Karen Garetti had been convicted . . ."

David March made a little protesting gesture. The white face broke in shame and pain. "If she had been convicted, then I should have told what I knew."

"Pretty likely!" said Pitt.

But Garey Brennon was watching Cornelia. "You knew this story?" he said now softly.

Cornelia wet her lips. "Yes."

"And so you didn't mean to let Karen Garetti be convicted?"

"Not—not if I could help it," said Cornelia.

"You would rather have had a mistrial, even, than a conviction." Garey Brennan spoke thoughtfully. It was a statement, not a question; and Cornelia did not answer it.

But even then, when he was sure of her, Garey Brennon tried to be merciful. He did not press her too much. Instead he turned shrewdly to Rinschy.

"How much did Mrs. Vanguard know about who was there that night?"

Rinschy too had suffered from the strain. He broke out emotionally, without his usual caution. "She is vone devil, zat voman," he cried. "She know everyt'ing. Meester Vanguard, he no good. She fin' out from heem, maybe zo. She mak' me vote like she zay, or she tell I am zere too. . . ."

Mrs. Vanguard was betrayed in an unlovely light. A woman who would have convicted Karen Garetti, guilty or not, at any price in threat and bribery—convicted her to keep the name of Vanguard from being so much as mentioned, no matter how innocently, in a sordid bootlegging tragedy. But that did not matter now.

Garey Brennon turned back to Cornelia. "That was what you meant," he said slowly, "when Dr. March came in after Mrs. Vanguard's collapse, and you said to him: 'I think she knows.'"

Cornelia's hunted look flew to David March. "Yes," she whispered.

VIII
Saturday

It was Saturday before they could collect the Comos. It is no simple matter to round up a family of seventeen. And with the Comos it was all or nobody.

No one had slept that night. Excitement, fear, remorse; guilty conscience or speculation on another's guilt—something had driven sleep from all their prison cots. Nobody admitted it except Kashaw, who yawned openly, but it showed in their faces. Damaris Lee looked haggard and emaciated. Elding looked as timorous as a rabbit. Gideon Hawes drank even more water than usual—always a sign of nervousness. Biggs looked positively human. Only Simon Gilley, who alone continued to enjoy bail, came in looking as if he had cantaloupe and hot muffins and scrambled eggs and bacon and coffee with real cream. He folded his hands over his stomach and looked virtuous.

Pitt was munching on his fifth cigar. He said that he should have a confession before night. But Garey Brennon, springing about like a man on wires, too completely everywhere to be anywhere in particular, worried Angeline much more.

Cornelia worried Angeline too, though she said she was all right. She was quite brisk really, and laughed apologetically about her collapse. Wasn't she silly to faint? She never had before. It must have been the weather! Nice to have it clear again, wasn't it? But Angeline thought she looked all eyes and resolution, as if nothing kept her going except the refusal to stop.

David March looked tired. He always looked tired, of course, but this was a more pervading weariness, as if somehow it had got inside him. It was not in his face so much—that is, not in line of mouth or droop of lid—as in his whole body; as if every movement were an effort to which he had to nerve himself anew. It is a sign of exhaustion in men of very strong will.

Otherwise he was just the same—too much the same, perhaps, to be quite natural. Almost as if he had thought out in advance how he must seem, and now was resolved to seem that way. He said good morning to everybody without a hint either of conciliation or defiance. He held chairs for the ladies. He made sure that Cornelia was comfortable, hung his coat over the chair slats to keep them from hurting her thin shoulders, grinned at her companionably, and said that everything would be all right yet if she kept a stiff upper lip.

"And you know what I mean by that," he whispered.

Angeline could not help wondering.

She examined his expression closely, and could make nothing of it. Under the points of his dark hair, brushed back smooth from the temples, his forehead was clear. His eyes, if watchful, had still the seeming of candor. His lips, if tense, were still not without the capacity for humor. A brave face. A strong face. A face admirably, if misleadingly, controlled.

It was as if to the pressure of weariness and discouragement from without there was opposed some hidden spring of energy within. "Like a camel," he said whimsically, when Angeline told him something of the sort.

She could not help wondering how he could joke, with two murders on his conscience.

Angeline tried to sort things out in her own mind, as all night, vainly, she had tried to sort them. David March had killed Sebastian. He had hidden his body in the bushes.

What else could his silence mean except that? He had
let Karen Garetti stand trial for his crime. That was bad
enough. But he had drawn Cornelia into it, and that
seemed even worse. He had left it to her to secure Karen's
acquittal. Failing that, he had given her the poison and
the hypodermic and taught her how to use them. When
Cornelia had not succeeded—when she told him that Mrs.
Vanguard knew—then he killed Mrs. Vanguard himself.

It was all so plain—and so incredible. She didn't believe it. And yet what else could she believe?

Pitt had Mr. Vanguard back again that morning, just in
case he should want him. It seemed best to get everybody
together now things were approaching a crisis. Pitt expected the weight of Como evidence to break David March
down at last.

Mr. Vanguard was better that morning—and he was
worse. He was more nearly sober, that is, and thus the
more desperately in need of a drink. Mr. Vanguard's weak-
nesses offset each other. The soberer he was, the more he
suffered from his own sobriety.

There was something not quite finished about Mr.
Vanguard. His tie hung loosely, as if he had not had the
strength for tightening the knot. One of the buttons of
his shirt was undone—yesterday's shirt. His socks were
not mates. He had skipped an eyelet in fastening his shoes.
His whole body jerked and quivered, like one of these
painted wooden toys which gyrates to the pull of a string.

"Good—good morning," he muttered, including everybody. Then, more warmly, to David and Cornelia: "Good
morning." And then, "Good *morning*, Oliver. What—
what's happened?" he quavered.

"You sit down there," Pitt instructed him, "and if I
want you I'll let you know."

Mr. Vanguard's eyes rolled pitifully toward Elding, and
Elding, evidently fearful of what he would say, slipped
over to his side and tried to quiet him.

"What . . ."

"It looks as if Dr. March killed them both," said Elding hastily.

"B-both?"

"The way it looks now he killed Mrs. Vanguard just to cover up about Sebastian."

"But—but why—why should he do that?" asked Mr. Vanguard foolishly.

Oliver Elding did not answer. There wasn't time.

2

Trollope opened the door as small a crack as possible, and stuck a perspiring face into the aperture. He looked deflated, as if the importance of his station had suffered an attack. He seemed to be struggling with the edge of the door.

"I d'know what to do," he said uncertainly. "There are some people here . . ."

The door burst away from him suddenly, under irresistible pressure from without, and the Comos entered.

The entrance of the Comos was in the nature of an invasion. A very large masculine Como in the van, marching like a general; holding a toddling Como by the hand. A very large feminine Como next behind him, clasping an infant to her blatantly maternal bosom. A rosy-faced young woman carrying baggage. A tide, a welter, of small and still smaller Comos surging in behind them.

"Oh goody!" shrilled one. "Here's my doctor."

And the next instant David March disappeared under such an avalanche of brown legs and short red skirts and small blue overalls and clutching grimy hands and curly heads, that you would never have known he was there at all save for his own long legs sticking out the bottom of the tangle.

"See my new shoes."

"Got your watch? Can I take your watch?"

"'Member that day we went to the drug store, and we got us ice cream? Mine was pink."

The child who had discovered him kissed him moistly on the cheek.

David March emerged from the mêlée with his hair on end and his tie askew. He looked a little fussed and a little pleased, a little shamefaced and a little proud; and then over the tops of the children's heads his eyes met Cornelia's, and they laughed. They laughed without tension, heartily, such unrestrained laughter as had not touched their lips since they entered that jury room. And with that, suddenly, irrepressibly, the room laughed with them: a burst of wholesome, natural mirth. Even Garey Brennon laughed. Even Biggs.

But Pitt was angry. You sent for some witnesses to convict a man of murder, and everybody got the giggles. He'd show them murder wasn't such a funny joke. "I'm the district attorney. . . ." he began in a big voice.

The leader of the Comos bowed. "You send for me?" he inquired politely. "Yes? I, Luigi Como. This"—he pointed an illustrative forefinger—"this, Matha Como, wife of brother Sebastian, who is dead. This, Rose Altrudo.

"These"—he continued to point—"François Como, Baptista Como, Valentine Como, Jesse Como, Eulie and Sylvie Como the twin, Germina Como, Fabian Como, David Como"—a flash of smile at David March—"Giusti Como, Zebina Como and Saadi Como, little Pietro Como and little Jehan Como." He ended with a flourish. "Do your manners."

The children, disentangled from David March, formed roughly into line. The boys bobbed their heads. The girls gathered their skirts bunchily and curtsied.

"Now look here," began Pitt. But it was a long time before he had command of the situation.

The Comos took possession of the room. It was a large room, but suddenly it was not nearly large enough—as over-crowded as a tenement house. The jurymen stood about in corners, amused or disgusted according to their natures.

Luigi shook hands with Dr. March, his dark face glow-
ing. "Glad to see, Doctor. Glad to see," he kept repeating.
Matha had to shake hands too. She was left-handed, and
awkward with the baby; David patted her shoulder, smiling a welcome. He had a word for Rose. A word for all the
children. His manner met theirs without constraint, as
if for them he pushed aside momentarily the horror that
hung over him

"I didn't ask you to bring half the town," Pitt said.

"We should bring young one when we come a-tall," explained Luigi. "This, Saturday. No school. We leave young
one home, he make mischief mebbe."

"Mischief!" exploded Pitt.

Eulie and Sylvie, the twins, had discovered the water
cooler and were running a pool on the wash-room floor.
François, the eldest, a skinny small boy with a wise, wiz-
ened face and the agile hands of a monkey, was trying to
climb high enough to look in the ventilator. Valentine
and Jesse discovered Angeline and her bag; she borrowed
Gideon Hawes' knife and divided the remaining chocolate bars. "Look out you don't cut yourselves," she warned
them. "The edge is kind of rough." When the chocolate
bars were gone, Angeline adopted Zebina. She was a fat
dumpling of a baby, with red cheeks and shining black
eyes and no neck; her round little head sat on her round
little body without visible connection. Cornelia picked up
young Jehan.

Germina was leaning against David March's knee. She
was a strangely quiet child in that noisy company, as thin
and brown as a twig, with a slow smile and adoring, liquid
eyes like a puppy's. Germina did not need to be entertained.
She was satisfied just to stand there and lean against her
doctor's knee. On David's other knee sat his namesake,
young David, a merry rogue with a beguiling chuckle.

Young David marked a new epoch in the roster of the
Como children. There was a largish gap between him and
Fabian, who was rising six. This interval represented the

epidemic of scarlet fever that had carried off all the infant Comos just before Dr. March came to Sheffield; if he had not come, Fabian would have died too, and François and Germina. His acquaintance with the Comos had begun with gratitude. Their homage showed now in Matha's dark gleaming eyes and white gleaming smile; in Luigi's hearty, unembarrassed friendliness; even in the shy admiring looks Rose cast up at him from under her curling lashes. Sascha, who was dead, had adored him. One saw what Dr. March meant to his patients when he was with the Comos.

Angeline had caught a glimpse of it before—and that with people as far apart as Mr. DeQuincy Vanguard and Leo Rinschy. She had seen it in the quivering eagerness of Mr. Vanguard's first greeting; his dread of making any statement that would be prejudicial to Dr. March; his concealment of the meeting at the Comos'. She had seen it again, even more strikingly, in Rinschy's stubborn refusal to implicate the doctor, when suspicion was gathering tightest round himself. And now, with the Comos, she saw it completely. David March's patients loved him.

It was not because of what he did for them, either. Though there was not a doubt in the Lord's world that those were David's boots the young Comos were walking in, or David's red berets on their black heads, it wasn't that. It wasn't his convenient forgetfulness about bills when times were hard. It wasn't even his skill; or his willingness to come, always, on the darkest, wettest nights, over the roughest roads, roads unbroken under snow, doing the things a nurse would have done when one couldn't afford a nurse—holding a body's hand when she was scared and wanted the comforting pressure of his kind, cool fingers. Not even that. It was because they felt him to be their friend. People all the way from the Hill to the foreign quarter were fiercely, unshakably loyal to Dr. David March. Angeline could not help wondering how he could be like that and still . . .

"Now look here," Pitt was bawling again. "I sent for
you to ask you some questions."

"Oo, look-it," screamed Fabian. "I can put my banana
up my nose."

David March removed the banana. "Now children," he
said, "Mr. Pitt is going to talk with your father. I want
you all to go over there by the wall and sit in a row and be
quiet. Will you do that for me? If not one of you speaks
till I tell you, it wouldn't surprise me if your father took
you to the drug store on the way home and bought ice
cream."

"Pink?" specified Germina.

"Pink," said David March gravely. "With a strawberry
on top."

Germina smiled her slow smile. "Aw right," she agreed.

Two minutes later the room was still. The children sat
in their row along the wall, uncannily quiet . . . as quiet as
only those children can be whose unquiet lives have taught
them necessity. Trollope brought in more chairs, and the
jurors found places. And with that it was as if they were
back again where they had been before the Comos came.
The tension was in the room again. The laughter had gone
out of it, and the fear and the pain were there. David
March swept his hands over the hair that the children had
left boyishly tumbled, and laid it severely flat. It was like
a symbol. He squared his shoulders, as if he took up again,
knowingly, a burden that for a moment in forgetfulness he
had laid aside. He lifted his head to the future.

"Now look here," Pitt was beginning.

"Luigi," David interrupted him. He spoke slowly,
stressing his words. "Luigi, Pitt knows that I was at your
house the night Sebastian was killed. You mustn't try to
cover up, now, anything about me. *Do you understand?*"

Luigi Como looked at him. A long, deliberate look,
inscrutable. Then he nodded. "Sure," he said.

3

Luigi Como fingered the black band sewed round the left sleeve of his best blue store clothes. He had done the occasion the unwonted honor of buttoning the top button of his shirt, and he looked hot and pressed. He was a stocky fellow, heavy-shouldered, of great strength; the broad, flattish face was too wide-spaced between the eyes, the heavy cheek-bones bulged too roundly under the seamed skin, the black hair was moist and untidy. But he looked good-humored; stolid and not unlikable. When he smiled his whole face split wide open like some enormous fruit, over a flashing show of white teeth.

"Now then," began Pitt. "Who do you think killed your brother?"

Luigi Como shrugged his shoulders. He spread out a pair of mighty calloused palms in a gesture of complete negation. He did not answer in words.

"Oh come now!" said Pitt. "You've got some idea. Do you think Karen did it?"

"No," said Luigi. "Never Karen. She cannot do." He considered, as if making up his mind whether it was all right to say it, and added: "She go with Doctor."

"All the time?"

"All time," agreed Luigi, nodding. "He take her Sascha room. He take her drug store. He bring home. She come in. I hear. She do not go out. No, she cannot do. I know." He closed the subject with a vast shrug.

"Well then," said Pitt, "admitting for the sake of argument that Karen didn't kill him. . . ."

"Wha'?"

"If Karen didn't kill him," repeated Pitt, raising his voice, "then who did? Somebody else in your family?"

"No," said Luigi Como somberly.

But Pitt went over them all just the same. "Not Matha?"

"No. She is not go out. I know."

"Not Rose?"

"No. I take home."

"Maybe you did yourself?"

"For why?" inquired Luigi with dignity. "He is brother."

"Sebastian rest by me all time Luigi go," Matha broke out excitably. "He stay in after. Crazy talk, he kill. Crazy talk. . . ." She was gesticulating volubly, more expressive with her hands than with her words. It was plain that though Sebastian had been her husband, she considered Luigi worth two of him.

"You keep still," said Pitt. "When I want to hear from you, I'll let you know. Maybe Sascha?"

Luigi Como's face was suddenly contorted—and Angeline remembered that he had loved his wife. "Sascha is sick to die," he said simply. A thought struck him and he added: "It is not to blame Doctor that she die. No. Doctor come. He make better. He go. She die after. Baby cry. She get up too quick, maybe. Sascha love Doctor. He make well many time. Sascha will not wish it to blame Doctor that she die. . . ."

"Oh I don't say he killed Sascha," agreed Pitt callously. "I only say . . ." He decided not to say it then. "If none of those people, then who?"

"Maybe tramp," said Luigi helpfully. "Maybe he have enemy."

"Your brother had enemies?"

"Oh sure." Luigi made a gesture indicating armies. "Make him in business. Sure." He was obviously pleased with his own suggestion.

"Who were his enemies?"

Luigi's enthusiasm waned instantly. His face dosed into dullness. "I d'know."

"Were there any of them round that night?"

"I d'know. I d'know who is they."

"Now look here," admonished Pitt again. "We know there were a lot of people there that night. If any of them had a grudge against your brother, now's the time to say so. We know Mr. Vanguard was there . . ."

Luigi Como's glance rested without favor on the quivering visage of DeQuincy Vanguard. He had the boundless scorn of the strong man for one who carries his liquor badly. But he was just. "No," he decided. "Mr. Vanguard come. He go. Early. Sebastian is in house. No."

"Rinschy was there too."

Luigi Como's look swung from Mr. Vanguard's broken figure to Rinschy's agitated beard and excitable hair. His face soured and darkened; it was evident that for reasons of his own Leo Rinschy was no favorite with him either. "You there then? Maybe you kill?" He sounded mildly hopeful.

"No, no, no, no," flared Rinschy. "I am zere zo early, yes; I come, I go, all ze same like Meester Vanguard. I am not zee Sebastian; I hear heem only make ze loud talk by ze house. I am honest vork man. I go avay. You know me, Luigi Como, honest vork man. . . ."

"I know you plenty," said Luigi Como dourly.

"He claims," explained Pitt, "that he was coming to the house, but he heard a lot of noise and saw some cars, and so he turned round and went back. Mr. Vanguard passed him on the way out, and recognized him. Then he says he went to Petronelli's, and the Lord knows where. We're checking his alibi. . . ."

"Wha'?"

But Pitt did not bother to repeat.

"I can't help wondering why they don't get it checked pretty soon," Angeline whispered. "I should think . . ."

"Mebbe he kill. Sure," said Luigi, pleased with this solution also.

"We're finding out where he was later on that night," explained Pitt. "But there's one man who doesn't even pretend he's got an alibi. And that man's Dr. March. He's the man that killed your brother."

"Wha'?" said Luigi.

"You know that, don't you? You know Dr. March killed Sebastian?"

Luigi Como registered profound astonishment. "Doctor?" he repeated. "Doctor is for cure, not for kill. Isn't it?"

"None of your back talk. After he brought Karen home, he sneaked out in the bushes and killed him "

"For why?" inquired Luigi, with a polite show of interest.

"You tell me why. Out with it. What did he have against Sebastian?"

"Mebbe t'ree dollar, for when he cut the thumb," suggested Luigi literally.

Pitt fairly frothed. "What did he want to kill him for?"

"He do not wish," said Luigi. "No. We are friend. All friend." His gesture might have been a token for universal brotherhood. "Doctor is good man. Ver' good man. Isn't it?"

He appealed suddenly to his family. And as if his gesture of invitation had released some hidden lever, they burst into such a chattering, such a piping and shrilling of eulogy for Dr. March, that it was like Babel.

Briefly, you couldn't beat the Comos. These Mediterranean families were units, to the third and fourth generation of their mistresses; subject to their private dissensions, but presenting a solid front to the American law. Even Rose was as much one of them now as if she had been a daughter. Every one had had a bad time with them in court, and you could not expect them to do better now that they were not under oath. They had their story pat to the last babe—right down to little Fabian—and nobody could shake it.

But when you came to the point, this was the sum of their argument: Dr. David March didn't kill Sebastian, because he was Dr. David March.

4

Nevertheless, as the day went on, and Pitt's questions went on also, thudding and tireless, things began to look darker and darker for David. It wasn't what the Comos said so much. It was what they didn't say.

Pitt was, of all things, persistent. He could ask the same question a thousand times for the sake of catching his victim tripping on the thousandth. There was no least coil in the whole tangled matter that he did not have out for a new turning.

"When did you find Sebastian's body? Who found him?"

"I found him," said Germina. Her face puckered suddenly in distress. She wiped her hands frantically on her skirt, as if she were wiping away a memory that clung to her small fingers.

François sprang to his feet. "I found him next after Germina," he cried shrilly. "I was right behind her all the time. I found him most as much as she did. He was all blood. Lots of blood. All over his shirt. . . ." He illustrated with gusto. "I got my hand in it," he added proudly.

"He was all blood," repeated Germina, in a small voice. She began to cry bitterly, clinging to David March.

"Don't think about it," he said gently, smoothing back the tumbled hair from her hot face. "See. I'm going to give you a bright quarter."

"Where did you find your uncle's body?" Garey Brennon was asking François.

"In the bushes. Beside the Back Road."

"It wasn't *in* the road?"

"No. It was right in the bushes."

"It was *hidden* in the bushes, you mean?" Pitt again.

"Yes. They was a grea' big sumac bush, and right in underneath . . ."

"Dr. March tells us," said Pitt, "that he moved the body out of the road, but he didn't hide it. But you say it was hidden. Now tell me."

François' sharp, bright-eyed face became suddenly as old as the hills, and very nearly as wise, and about twice as impenetrable.

"I do' know wha' you mean," he said.

Pitt turned back to Luigi. "As soon as you found Sebastian's body, you tried to get in touch with Dr. March, didn't you?"

"Sascha is die," said Luigi with dignity. "I call Doctor. Doctor is not home. I call som'other doctor. Dr. Call'm."

"And when did you call Dr. March again?"

"I do not call again. Sascha is already die. For what he come?"

"After Sebastian's body was found, and the police were there, you didn't telephone for fear somebody would hear you?"

"Who'?"

"You went to see Dr. March instead of telephoning, because you had things to say you didn't want to say over the telephone. You wanted to warn him that the crime was discovered, and he'd better keep away."

"I do' unnerstan' ver' good," said Luigi, wrinkling his wide brow.

Luigi Como upon occasion could curse in English with fine and vulgar fluency; he could trade automobiles, with a nice discussion of parts, and drive a hard bargain. The children were all American born; they went to an American school. At the Mill, Rose had a reputation as a chatterbox. Even Matha never had any trouble in dealing with Sebastian's American customers. But now they were beset, one and all, by a convenient incomprehension. Let you so much as drop a hint against Dr. David March, and they could not understand a word of it.

"When you went to see Dr. March, why didn't you go to the house?"

"Doctor is not in house."

"He wasn't in the garage, either."

"He come. I wait."

"Why didn't you wait at the house?"

"He come garage first. I wait garage."

"You didn't go to the house for fear the nurse or the housekeeper would see you?"

"I no want nurse. I no want housekeep'. I want Doctor."

"And what did you say to Dr. March in the garage?"

"I say Sascha is die. He feel ver' bad. He like Sascha."

"You told him Sebastian's body had been found, too, didn't you?"

"Ye'."

"And I guess he felt pretty bad about that!" Sarcastically.

"Ver' bad. He like Sebastian." The sarcasm all lost.

"And he liked Karen so well he wanted her to stand trial for what he did."

"Wha'?"

"You made him admit the murder, didn't you?"

"Wha'?"

"He told you he killed Sebastian in the night, didn't he?"

"He tell me he dead in night. He find. He dead."

"And you believed it, like thunder!"

"Like wha'?"

"You didn't believe it, did you?"

"He say. I believe. Sure."

"Yeah! And what did he say then?"

Luigi considered this and decided it wouldn't do any harm. "He say tell police. I say no. I say wait."

"Why?"

"For wha' good tell?" inquired Luigi practically.

"You knew the police would think he did it."

"P'lice is funny," said Luigi with commendable frankness. His gesture, taking in the room, indicated how excruciatingly funny the police could be.

"You knew he was present on the scene of the crime near the time the murder was committed. It is illegal to withhold evidence. You could be arrested as an accessory after the fact."

"I do' know them big word," said Luigi.

"Did Dr. March offer you a bribe?"

"Wha'?"

"What did he offer you if you would keep still?"

"Wha'?"

"You knew Karen had an alibi. If you could prove her innocent, what made you let them go ahead and try her?"

"She do not do," stated Luigi. "They cannot prove. They let go. All right."

Thus briefly Luigi summed up the Como view of the case. If Dr. March did not kill Sebastian—and he didn't, because he was Dr. March; and if Mr. Vanguard did not kill him—and he didn't, because he left before Dr. March came while Sebastian was still in the sitting room; and if Rinschy did not kill him—and he didn't, if it was true that he went away when he said he did . . . why then somebody else killed him. The Comos were the only others there. The police might blunder on the truth, and that would be bad. It would be much better for Karen to stand accused, because Karen didn't do it . . . and if she didn't do it, they could not prove she did . . . and if they could not prove she did, they would have to let her go. The case would be dropped, and that would be the best for everybody. This, untangled, was the Como reasoning.

"But what if they proved she *did* do it?"

"She do not do," repeated Luigi firmly. "The law, that make justice, isn't it?" The wide spread of his hands was a magnificent tribute to the infallibility of the American law.

"Something might have slipped though," said Pitt. "And something darn well would have slipped, too, if they hadn't murdered Mrs. Vanguard so it wouldn't."

"*Wha'?*" inquired Luigi. When Pitt did not explain, he felt that something more was needed. "If they say she do, then Doctor say she not do. Then he tell. Ye'."

"And if he decided not to tell, *then he'd take some other measures.*"

Cornelia Van Horn came half erect with a little strangled cry. Her face was all twisted; her eyes had the driven look of the wild thing, caught. She put out her hands in helpless, inarticulate appeal. "David . . ."

But David March was even quicker than she. He was beside her in an instant, his strong hands on her shoulders. "Hush, Cornelia," he said. "You mustn't."

"She mustn't what?" asked Garey Brennon watching.

"She mustn't excite herself," said David March defiantly.

Garey Brennon was not satisfied. "You were going to say something?" he prompted Cornelia.

"She's ill again," said David instantly. "She wants a drink."

5

But David March, as well as Cornelia, had borne too much already. It had been too hard. It had gone on too long. Every fiber of him was stretched too taut, so that his spent nerves winced and jangled to the impact of every word. The lines down his face, nostril to lip, were chiselled as sharply as if they had been cut in stone.

Angeline couldn't help wondering how long any human being could hold out.

Pitt, blissfully gnawing his cigar, knew that no one can hold out forever. The end was near now. He pounded on remorselessly.

He pounded at the credibility of the Comos as witnesses. They were all prejudiced. They were devoted to Dr. March. They would lie to keep him from getting into a mess. Pitt did it craftily, building it up by insinuation before he put it into words.

Dr. March had been kind to the Comos. They were indebted to him. They owed him money. They all liked him. Luigi, Matha, Karen, the children. Sascha had liked him most of all. Sascha wouldn't have wanted anything to happen to the doctor. Luigi wanted to do what Sascha would have liked.

Karen didn't run any risk—not really. No wonder she had shown no fear in the court room. They had it all worked out. Luigi promised not to tell. Karen promised to stand trial. Dr. March promised she should never be convicted. . . .

"And you'd lie your head off to save him," Pitt accused.

"I say true," said Luigi with dignity. "Or I say not'ing." He lapsed into silence.

But most particularly, because he saw that he could hurt that way the most, Pitt pounded at David's perfidy in allowing Karen to suffer for his guilt. David's haggard young face whitened and whitened under the sting of the lash that was laid across it.

He sat close to Cornelia now, his chair just a little behind hers. Over the chair back his hand rested on her shoulder. The knuckles were white, too, as white as his spent face—as if he held her quiet by actual strength.

Angeline could not bear to look at Cornelia. She felt the sting of tears behind her own lids.

"You know you could have freed her, just by a word, and you didn't say that word."

"No."

"You were there in court. You saw Karen Garetti stand before her accusers, unjustly charged; you saw her scorned of all men; reviled; her life made a mock of; her character defamed; you saw her very life endangered. . . ."

"Oh not that." The words were wrung out of him. "I would have . . ."

"You would have *killed Mrs. Vanguard first.*"

"*Not that.* I would have . . ."

"You saw these things, I say, and you did not come forward. You did not lift a finger to save Karen Garetti from shame and sorrow."

"I—"

"Hiding behind petticoats. Letting a woman stand the gaff so you could go free."

"I—"

"Coward," Pitt flung at him. "Coward. Sneak. . . ."

It broke Cornelia down at last, though it could not have broken David.

"David!" she cried. "I won't *let* you. . . ."

"Hush," said David softly. His lips were wry, but his hand was still steady over hers.

But Cornelia tore herself from his restraining grasp. She sprang up, away from him, away from everybody. She faced them alone. And now it was Garey Brennon who held back David March.

Standing there alone before them, suddenly the terror that had haunted Cornelia so long was swept away. The small white face bore the marks of suffering still—perhaps would always bear them; the brown eyes were shadowed by a bitterness of knowledge that nothing could ever take away. But the strain and the struggle were gone. She faced them with a toss of the bright head, as if she dared life to do any more to her. She looked at peace. She looked almost happy . . . because nothing could stop her now.

When she spoke it was with a ring like triumph in her voice.

"You shan't say such things of him," she defied Pitt. "It's a wicked lie. He's the bravest man in the world. He didn't tell because of me. *I was with him that night.*"

IX
Saturday (Continued)

David had to tell his story all over again after that, putting in Cornelia.

He told it in the wash room this time, alone with Pitt and Brennon. Pitt was now as anxious to keep Cornelia from hearing what was said as he had previously been to force her to listen. He regretted that. She knew too much to start with. Still, it didn't really matter. He had got what he wanted. He had broken her down and forced her to an admission. It would all be plain sailing after this. He put an offensive hand on David March's shoulder, as if he were already under arrest.

"I won't run away," said David sardonically.

"You're darn well right, you won't," said Pitt.

Angeline hurried in to draw a final cup of cold water for Gideon Hawes before they shut her out. Her mind flew back to the first time she had seen David March facing his accusers. It was so different now. . . .

She remembered how far above suspicion he had seemed to her then; how cool and untouchable. She remembered how he had resented little unimportant things that did not matter: a slur on his professional dignity, a hint of medical bad management. And all the time had it been just a part of a carefully thought-out role that he must play? It seemed incredible that he had believed he could cover up everything. He was not in a position to resent anything now.

She remembered even how she had admired his hands—
long, slim surgeon's hands, quiet and sure. But with those
hands . . .

David was fighting for his life now, his life and Cornelia's. He was forcing himself to a last effort. And no matter
what the man had done, you could not help respecting him
for the cold courage with which he faced it. He looked like
one who has been knocked down, and terribly hurt, and
who rises again, and shakes the blood out of his eyes, and
comes forward to meet his antagonist. He had the watchful look of the fighter. His hand was closed upon his knee
as if he held a weapon.

"Now see if you can tell the truth for once," said Pitt,
launching the attack.

"No word of what I have already said is untrue," said
David March proudly. "I have left out certain things. That
is all. Now I must put them in."

"You bet you got to," agreed Pitt.

In the jury room outside there was a curious quietness.
It was like that brooding hush that comes before a storm, a
dread and a premonition. People spoke in whispers, without knowing that they were going to; and were ashamed,
and said over again what they had to say, louder—and
then were shocked at the volume of their own voices. They
watched Cornelia furtively to see how she was taking it.

Cornelia was taking it well. It was as if in the vast relief of having *said* it at last, she did not quite realize yet
what she had done. Or perhaps it was not that. Perhaps
she would rather have been in danger with Dr. March than
to be safe by herself. Or perhaps . . .

She looked exhausted, but she looked calm. There was
still that gleam like triumph in her face.

"You're a good kid," said Charles Kashaw impulsively,
"no matter . . ."

Angeline liked him the better for that.

But Damaris Lee turned toward Oliver Elding. "It's
about as Mrs. Vanguard said," she remarked lightly. "Let a

girl come out with a good murder or two, and all the men are for her."

"Don't talk about Mrs. Vanguard," said Elding, with a look of horror. He felt at once that his remark might need explaining, "That is, not before Mr. Vanguard."

Angeline set the cup of water she had brought down beside Mr. Hawes. "I thought you might want it before the wash room was free again," she said. She added lingering: "Weren't you *surprised?*"

"Yes and no," said Gideon Hawes judicially. "I am very rarely surprised. I could have told you of course all the time who was responsible. In fact I did tell you. If you had listened carefully to the extracts which I read you from my book . . . wait, I will read that part again:

> Your logical murderer . . . must look ahead to the conclusion of events, and make ready to direct that conclusion. He must have a care for detail, lest he be betrayed by a break in the pattern of his logic. He must be fitted by nature or training to a command over his own person. . . .

"Look about you. Who of us the best conforms—has all the time best conformed—to this description? Who has been most heedful of detail? Who has commanded himself in such wise that certainty has been turned aside? Who has again and again trailed red herrings, if I may be permitted a colloquialism, so successfully across the path that even in the face of overwhelming evidence . . ."

"Clever, aren't you?" jibed Damaris.

"I have been called so," said Gideon Hawes complacently. "Afterwards."

Angeline was suddenly furious at the little man and his smug self-satisfaction. If he knew as much as he pretended, why didn't he come right out and say so? It was easy, as Damaris said, to be wise after the event.

"I don't care," she snapped at him. "You make me tired. Pretending to know it all. I don't believe David March killed Mrs. Vanguard nor Sebastian Como, either, so there!"

"But my dear lady," said Gideon Hawes in gentle protest. "Be logical. I have not said that Dr. March killed anybody. I have not, if you remember, mentioned any names whatever. I simply said . . ."

"And I simply said I didn't believe it," said Angeline unreasonably. After all, her nerves were worn thin, like everybody else's. She fluttered down the room and stood beside Cornelia, protectingly. It was a foolish gesture, and somehow oddly touching.

Cornelia's acceptance of it was more touching still. Such a dear look of relief and gratitude flamed in her face that more than one turned away with a thickening in his throat.

"Aw the poor kid!" muttered William Apple.

Cornelia was eager. "Oh he *didn't,*" she cried, setting her small palms together in a quick, unconscious gesture like supplication. "You *don't* think so, do you?"

"No I don't," said Angeline. She hoped that Whoever had charge of such things would forgive her the lie. If it was a lie.

"I am not mean zat I should bring on heem such troublez," Rinschy confided to Biggs. "I am not do eet, eezer, v'en he keep still. I am not tell, nevaire, nevaire. How am I know she is zere wit' heem?"

The young Comos were quiet, round-eyed against the wall. They did not understand a word of it. They knew only that something bad had happened to their doctor.

But Luigi went over to Cornelia's side, and laid on her shoulder a hard curved hand, of the size and shape of a shovel. Cornelia was half hidden under it. "He is good man," he said simply.

And at that Matha, who had been wiping her eyes on the corner of her shawl, paddled heavily over to Cornelia too, and threw herself down on the floor beside her, and flung her arms about Cornelia's waist, and wept into her lap. Rose snuffled in sympathy.

"There, don't cry," said Cornelia kindly, smoothing Matha's tremendous heaving shoulder.

"There is no cause for all this excitement," said Simon Gilley pompously, folding his hands over his stomach. "Those who have done no wrong, need have no fear. Justice will be accomplished."

"Justice!" said Mary Madras scornfully. "Who wants justice? There's been too much justice in this town already. Give 'em a break, why can't you?"

Biggs said nothing. But presently he slipped out of his place, and picked up Cornelia's scrap of a linen handkerchief that had fallen to the floor. He folded it twice neatly through the middle, and smoothed the creases, and handed it to her with a little bow. It was, from Biggs, the perfect tribute. He was not one of your glib men. He had no words of comfort or reassurance to offer Cornelia, but he knew how to wait on a lady.

The queer part of it was that while there had still been a reasonable doubt, they had all been quick with suspicion. But now, when doubt was closing down into certainty, they shut their minds and opened their hearts. Whatever she had done, whatever she had helped David March to do, they were sorry for Cornelia.

It was sentimental, if you like. But that is the way people are.

2

François Como stood on the back of a chair with his ear against the ventilator. Baptista and Valentine and Jesse and Fabian held the chair to keep it from tipping over. Angeline hovered close by so that the children should not get hurt.

"Why don't you come over here?" she said to Cornelia.

"Why should I?" said Cornelia defensively. "I know what he's saying."

"Well, all right, if you don't feel like standing up," conceded Angeline. "I'll let you know how it goes."

On the other side of the ventilator, David March was telling his story all over again. Pitt let him take his own gait. He could afford to now.

He was through his office hours early that night, David March said; about nine, he thought. Afterwards he had a few calls to make, but they were brief ones, and so he telephoned to Cornelia and asked her to ride. They often went together like that after office hours, if it were not too late and he had nothing important in hand; it was hard to find time when he could see Cornelia—she was working till five, and his own hours were irregular. It was nearly ten thirty when he finished with the calls. It had been oppressively hot all day, but a little breeze was springing up with a promise of rain in it, and after he had left the prescription for Mr. Tattersall at Robbot's, they planned to drive down to the Lake to catch a breath of air.

At Robbot's he found the message from Luigi Como. He was disappointed. The Comos' was not a place for a girl like Cornelia, and he knew that he ought to take her home.

"I wish to God I had done it," he said brokenly.

When he went back to the car and told Cornelia, she wanted to go with him. Her room was hot, she said, and she didn't feel like going in. She could just as well be riding to the Comos' as to the Lake. "It's a rough crowd that goes there," he told her. She would stay in the car, she said, and nobody would know that she was with him. It was a nice drive out Birch Road.

David had hesitated. It would be half an hour before he could take Cornelia home and leave her, and Luigi had sounded very urgent. If he did that and anything happened . . . Of course it was quite safe really, he told himself; he was being over-cautious. Against his better judgment, he let himself be persuaded.

When he reached the Comos', he parked the car directly
under the window where the light was, so that when he
was inside the room he would be only a few feet from
Cornelia. When he entered the house, however, he found
things in such a disturbed state—just as he had already
described it—that it was some minutes before he went into
Sascha's room at all. He took Karen with him, as he had
said, and left Sebastian and Matha together. Luigi went
out immediately to drive Rose home.

When he went into Sascha's room, he made an excuse about the air's being very bad, as indeed it was, and
opened the window wide. His car lights were shining outside, but the lilac bushes grew thick and close against the
house so that he could not see Cornelia. She could see
him, though—his shape against the window with the lamp
behind him—and she called "Hello" to him very softly, so
that he knew she was all right. Sascha's bed was in the far
corner of the room, against the inside wall, and when he
was with her he could not see the car at all. But he felt at
ease, Cornelia was so near.

He found Sascha in a bad way. The bleeding from the
nose was very severe, and he gave all his attention to stopping it. He kept Karen busy helping him. For a few minutes Sascha absorbed his thought completely. He was still
bending over her when Cornelia screamed.

Cornelia screamed once, the quick, high scream of panic, and called his name. David was terribly alarmed; all the
possibilities in the world flashed through his mind in an
instant—all but the right one. He thrust the basin into Kar-
en's hands, spilling the water on the floor, and dashed out.

"What he say about water?" asked Luigi sharply, straining his ears to listen.

"He spilled it on the floor." Angeline relayed the trifling information in a stage whisper.

Matha was in the sitting room when David went out,
and Luigi had just come in and was taking off his cap.

Sebastian was gone. David jerked open the door, and Luigi turned to follow him. But David pushed him back.

"Stay here. Look after Sascha and Karen," he gasped, and slammed the door behind him.

He didn't remember any steps or any path or anything, just running as fast as he could. He did not think he had ever moved so fast before. He was round the corner to his car in no time—much, quicker than he could tell it.

When David rounded the corner of the house, a man was just getting out of the car. He ran when he saw David, but he ran a little unsteadily; he ducked into the bushes as quickly as he could. But David had left the headlights on instead of just the parking lights and the man had to run straight in front of them to reach the shrubbery. David saw that it was Sebastian Como. He paid no attention to him at the moment, because he was thinking only of Cornelia. He wrenched open the door and flung himself inside. "What's the matter?" he cried. "Are you hurt?"

Cornelia was huddled in the far corner of the seat, with the robe that he always carried drawn up about her as if she had tried to hide behind it. At first she just clung to him and did not say anything, but after a little he made her tell him what had happened.

Cornelia had been sitting there waiting when Sebastian put his head in the car window. He said it was a hot evening. Yes, Cornelia had agreed, it was warm. Sebastian said then that he was the brother of the sick woman, and the doctor had sent him to stay with her until he came back. He opened the car door and got in. Cornelia had not tried at first to stop him.

But afterwards she was rather afraid of him. She saw that he had been drinking; his breath was heavy with liquor and his speech was thick. When he refused to get out, she moved along the seat away from him. Sebastian moved after her, until they were crowded into the corner. She hated to call David and make a disturbance; and she was not really much frightened as yet because she thought that if the man would not leave her, then she could leave him. But when she reached for the car door he put out a hand and stopped her. The gesture brought her almost into his arms. Immediately his advances became more objectionable. . . .

"What do you mean?" demanded Pitt.

"What do you think I mean?" asked David March curtly. "He . . . tried to kiss her. That was when she screamed."

David got into the car beside Cornelia, and soothed and comforted her. After a few moments she stopped trembling, and said she was all right. She even laughed a little, and said she had got scared and made a fuss about nothing; it was all over now and David could go back.

David was in a quandary. He did not dare to leave Cornelia alone again like that. And he did not dare to go away without another look at Sascha. He suggested that Cornelia come with him, but she dreaded the possibility of meeting Sebastian in the house and did not want to go. Finally he had an inspiration.

"I'll lock the car," he said, "and then no one can get in. If anybody comes near, blow the horn."

So it was arranged. David's car was a four-passenger sedan with two doors. He locked it on the outside and put the key in his pocket. Then he returned to the house. He had been gone perhaps ten minutes.

David was pretty mad, he said, when he went back to the house. He had done all he could for Sebastian in the past, and this was what he got for it. So when Luigi asked him what was the matter, he blurted out, "There's a friend of mine in the car and Sebastian assaulted her."

He was sorry the minute he had said it. It wasn't very nice or very tactful. But he came out with it quickly before he thought. Partly he supposed it was because he blamed himself so much for bringing Cornelia when he knew he shouldn't have done it. But of course that wasn't an excuse. He would have taken it back if he could. But you never can take anything back.

"What'd you want to take it back for? Wasn't it so?"

"It made more trouble for the Comos," said David frankly. "They were angry enough at Sebastian before—about Rose. But now they were more angry still, about Cornelia. And it was my fault."

"You were mad at him too. Mad enough to kill him." Pitt nodded at Brennon, as who should say: now we've got the motive.

"No," said David steadily. "Not mad enough for that."

"It's reason for plenty of killings."

"My business—as Luigi Como pointed out—is to cure and not to kill."

"None o' your back chat," warned Pitt.

"Very well," said David.

He went on again at once. He and the Comos, he said, with a shy deprecation, had always been good friends. He had tried to do what was right for them, and they had been grateful. Now when they found that Sebastian, in his drunken irresponsibility, had insulted the "doctor's girl," they were furious—furious with the hot, quick fury of the South. It wasn't so much that they thought Sebastian had done wrong. They felt their hospitality outraged, and that was a great point in their half-feudal view of the rights of strangers. More particularly it was because Cornelia had come with the doctor. Just the fact that she was with him made her forthwith the "doctor's girl," and subject to special protection. Sebastian had insulted one whom they would have delighted to honor.

Luigi Como felt it most, he thought, though he had said the least. He was the head of the family and took his responsibilities seriously. Matha was sorry of course; but her sorrow and anger were tinged by curiosity: her curses on Sebastian were so mixed with questions about Cornelia's looks, her prospects, her accomplishments, and David's intentions in regard to matrimony—he spoke a little more quickly, in embarrassment and a sorry perception of how little it mattered now what his wishes might have been—that it was hard to know just how to take her. He did not pay much attention really. But no one could help paying attention to Karen. Karen was beside herself. She was threatening to kill Sebastian.

"She'd done that already, hadn't she?"

"No," said David March slowly. "She had threatened other things, but she hadn't threatened to kill him."

"You said she had."

"I think not," said David. "I said she made threats, and you took it for granted. . . ."

"You wilfully misled us."

"Perhaps," said David imperturbably. It was not the only time he had wilfully misled them.

"How do you account for her excitement?" asked Garey Brennon. "I don't quite see why it was any worse."

"I've told you as well as I could," said David. "Outraged hospitality. The fact that Cornelia was a friend of mine. And then . . . well, she recognized Cornelia as belonging to a different class. It was more outside what was to be expected. It was as if Sebastian was putting on airs when he made advances to Miss Van Horn. Something like that. It was all very mixed up. I don't know that I can explain it any better than that. You have to know these people well in order to understand it. But the fact remains: Karen was angry enough to threaten Sebastian's life. I was alarmed about her. Her condition to me seemed close to mania. And yet you can imagine in what haste I was to return to Sascha, and get away from the place altogether. I did not stay any longer than I could help there in the sitting room. I took Karen with me again, though she was too much distraught to be of the least service, and went back again to Sascha."

When he returned, he said, Sascha was worse. In the excitement she had been left alone, and had made an effort to reach the window to find out who had screamed.

"Poor Sascha," he said. "She had an uneasy life. No doubt there had been screams before on the Como premises."

"I didn't ask you to preach a funeral sermon," said Pitt callously.

"Sorry," said David stiffly.

He found Sascha collapsed on the floor under the window. The exertion had brought on the bleeding again, and it looked rather serious. He carried her back to bed and laid her down. It seemed a long time before he could check the hemorrhage, but he did it finally. As soon as she was comfortable—and that in spite of his repeated warnings to be quiet—she persisted in asking questions. She had seen Sebastian getting out of the car and running away, and she made such a shrewd guess at what had happened that it was impossible to keep the truth from her.

"It wasn't anything," David tried to reassure her. "Miss Van Horn is waiting for me in my car, and Sebastian came up suddenly and startled her so that she screamed. That's all."

But Sascha was not convinced. "Oh, that Sebastian," she said. "He will bring shame and trouble on us all. I tell Luigi, over and over I tell Luigi, he should turn that Sebastian out." She struggled suddenly to sit up. "Let me go," she cried. "Let me go. I make him sorry with mine own hands."

"You don't have to," said Karen. "I'm going to do that."

David was at his wit's end between them.

At last, however, Sascha was quiet, and it seemed as if she would be all right if she did not move about. He went back to the sitting room, and Karen followed him.

"Now I don't want any trouble over this," he said to Luigi. "It was my own fault for bringing Miss Van Horn with me. You must remember that Sebastian isn't responsible tonight. By morning he won't remember what he has done."

"What did you mean by that?" cried Pitt.

"I meant: Sebastian is drunk; in the morning he will be sober; then he won't remember."

"You meant: in the morning he will be dead."

"I did not," said David March.

"And you told everybody to leave him alone, so you could have a chance at him yourself."

"I did not," repeated David.

He went on again presently. "I said: look after Sascha. She mustn't move around, or I won't answer for the consequences. And she is all ready to go out now and chase Sebastian. Luigi promised to sleep on the couch in the sitting room and go in every few minutes. He did, too. I'll take my oath he wasn't out of the house again that night."

"You don't need to," said Brennon dryly. "We don't think Luigi Como killed his brother."

It brought David up with a round turn. But again he went on. "When I said that, Karen slipped past me to the door. 'You tend to Sascha,' she said, 'and I'll tend to Sebastian.' The girl frightened me because she seemed to mean it. I didn't dare to leave her."

"You left the others. What were you, trying to build up an alibi? It didn't work, did it?"

"I wasn't thinking of that," said David. "I was thinking of Karen. Karen wasn't like the others, you see. She was more high-spirited and reckless; and she was not, like them, bound to Sebastian by ties of blood or marriage. She was not quite in a normal state, either. I have said that I thought her condition close to mania."

It was then, upon that impulse, that he had asked Karen to go with him to the drug store. The sleeping draught would be a good thing for Sascha, in case she was restless; and it solved the immediate difficulty about Karen. He took her firmly by the arm, though she struggled against him.

"Look out for Sascha," he said again. "And call me quick if she's worse." He said good night to Luigi and Matha, and went out.

He found everything all right when he got back to the car. Cornelia was curled up in one corner. She started nervously when he came, and he saw that her experience had left her upset; but he thought it had not done her any real harm. He was relieved by that. He explained briefly the situation inside and why he wanted to take Karen.

Cornelia moved over to make a place for her between them, and he unlocked the car door and helped Karen in. She fought against him like a cat, determined not to go, but he got her in finally. Cornelia put her arm round her and tried to soothe her; and he himself jumped in hastily and started the car, thinking that Karen would be quieter once they were under way. He drove out the Back Road.

"And you didn't see Sebastian?"

"No," said David shortly.

Karen was no better after they started. She tried to slip past Cornelia and get out of the car. She tried to beat her head against the windshield. Once she reached over and snapped off the ignition. He and Cornelia had an ado to keep her from injuring herself. He was afraid that she might hurt Cornelia too.

At last he stopped beside the road and gave Karen a hypodermic to quiet her. Half a tablet of hyoscine. That was how the hyoscine came to be in the syringe. He hadn't had any water to wash it with afterwards, and no chance to take it apart and put it away with Karen so violent. He had to hold her still for a little, until the hyoscine had time to work. He was afraid the syringe would be broken. So he passed it to Cornelia and asked her to put it in the bag the way it was. But he had dropped his bag over into the back seat, and Cornelia could not reach it—it was hard to move about with three in front. "Put it somewhere safe till we stop," he said to her, "then I'll take care of it. Look out for the needle. Don't let Karen get hold of it." She had dropped it into her own bag. Afterwards they had forgotten all about it; it was hardly strange that they had, with all the excitement. That was how the syringe with the trace of hyoscine still in it happened to be found in Cornelia's bag when she was searched.

"Clever!" muttered Brennon, with that wrench of un-willing admiration. "You can't beat that boy. He capitalizes his own drawbacks."

"He's telling about giving Karen the hypodermic and then putting the syringe in your bag," Angeline reported outside. "Brennon says he's clever. He says you can't beat him. Isn't that good?"

They drove around for a little until Karen had become passive under the influence of the drug, and then they went to Robbot's. Cornelia stayed with Karen in the car while he got the prescription. That was at one o'clock.

Again he knew that he should have taken Cornelia home, and again he didn't do it. She was still jumpy from her experiences of the evening—the trouble with Karen had not been very soothing on top of the trouble with Sebastian—and she did not want to be alone. In the end she rode back again with him to the Comos'. He was resolved this time not to leave her. She promised that if he had to go in, she would go with him.

He turned in the front drive, and stopped at the corner of the house, as he had said. He let Karen out there, and waited to make sure that she got in all right. She was heavy-footed and stupid from the medicine, but he knew that Luigi would look after her and take care of the prescription. The house was dark, so he judged that Sascha was sleeping and there was no further need of him. As soon as Karen shut the door, he drove past the house and out the Back Road toward town. That was when he saw Sebastian's body in the road.

He knew at once of course that he must stop and see what he could do. But he dreaded any further horrors for Cornelia. He drove the car a little past the spot, so that she could not see why it was that he got out.

"Good idea!" said Pitt, goading him. "You don't want too many looking on when you're going to do a murder."

"That was why I moved the body back," said David March imperturbably. "So that Cornelia should not see. That was why I did not use my flash light."

"I thought you were going to say that," muttered Brennon. "You would!"

3

Cornelia had to tell the story then—the same story. "If you can!" said Pitt.

Cornelia walked quickly into the wash room, as if she were in haste to have it over. Her step was firm and light. She met David in the doorway. They did not speak, but their look was like a handclasp, lingering. Cornelia flung up her head; she went in swiftly and shut the door behind her.

Cornelia told her story in a low, hurried voice, as if she could not wait. Short little sentences. Breathless. Jerky.

"It was all my fault," she said. "If I hadn't made him take me, it wouldn't have happened."

"You mean *you* wouldn't have killed Sebastian, or *he* wouldn't have killed him?"

"I don't mean either. I mean . . . all this."

She went on hastily. "It wasn't David's fault. I asked him to take me. I knew he didn't want me to go. But it was hot. I had had a hard day. I wanted to talk to him. He left me under the window where the light was. I could hear loud voices inside. I didn't know till afterwards what was the matter. I saw David come into the lighted room. He opened the window. I felt safe because he was so near . . ."

On and on, those short, brittle sentences. The same thing that David March had told, stripped of its details. It was like the synopsis of a longer story that she had learned by rote. It made it sound less plausible for her to tell it like that.

"Let's hear about Sebastian," Brennan suggested.

For the first time, Cornelia hesitated. "Sebastian was dreadful," she said, low. She caught her breath before she continued. "I was sitting there, still. I didn't hear Sebastian come up. I didn't see him until he had his head in the car window. He startled me. He said something about the weather. Then he said it was his sister who was sick, and the doctor had sent him to stay with me until he was ready. I thought it was queer. But I wasn't afraid then. I let him get into the car.

"After he was in the car, I was afraid of him. He had been drinking, and his breath smelled terribly. It wasn't very light and I couldn't see him plainly. But I could see his eyes shining, and they looked so—so big. It seemed as if he was all eyes. Eyes and breath. I tried to move away. But he moved closer. I tried to get out of the car. But he wouldn't let me. Then he—he put his hands on me. . . ." She stopped again, trying to control her voice. "His hands were hot and—and damp. He—he tried to kiss me. That was when I screamed. If I hadn't screamed, everything would have been all right. . . ."

"What do you mean by that?"

"They wouldn't all have been so angry, and then Sebastian wouldn't have been killed. Oh don't you see—somebody killed Sebastian because—because of me." There was stark horror in her voice.

"You mean Dr. March killed him because of you."

"Oh *no*," she pleaded. "I didn't mean that. . . ."

They made her go on with it again presently. And again she brought it out in those clipped, unnatural phrases. "Sebastian ran when he saw David. David stayed a little. Then he went back. He locked the car door and took the key. When he came again he brought Karen. He said she had threatened to kill Sebastian. He was afraid to leave her. She was very wild. David had to give her a hypodermic. He handed me the syringe. I put it in my bag. We got a prescription at the drug store. Then we took Karen home."

"And that was when you saw Sebastian?"

"I didn't see Sebastian. David stopped the car, and said there was something in the road and he wanted to find out what it was. He left the engine running, and went back."

"If you were so afraid to be left alone, why didn't you go with him?"

"I was tired," said Cornelia pitifully. "I was—very tired. I didn't want to move any more. I wanted to go home."

"You were too tired maybe to turn your head and look out the window?"

"No. I looked out, but I didn't see anything. The Back Road was very dark, and it was raining by then so that the windows were all streaked."

"You didn't see the body in the road?"

"I didn't see anything."

"What did Dr. March say when he came back?"

"He said there wasn't anything more we could do, and we might as well go."

"I'll say so! And then what?"

"Then? Then he took me home."

"When did you see him next?"

"The following night. He was waiting for me when I came out of the bank."

"And what did he say then?"

"He said . . ." She hesitated, marshaling her words. "He told me what had happened. About Sascha, you know, and Sebastian. And about Karen's being arrested. He said that he had seen Luigi, and they had agreed that it would be better not to say anything for a while. I felt terribly. I could see he took it awfully hard. And I—I knew that he was doing it for me."

"What do you mean?"

"Why, he wanted to keep me out of it."

"What did he need to keep you out of it for, if neither of you had done anything?"

"It wouldn't have been very pleasant, would it," said Cornelia impartially, "telling all this in court?"

"I guess you won't find it so," said Pitt cruelly. "And did he happen to mention what pressure he had brought to bear on Karen so that she was willing to do what she did?"

"Pressure?" repeated Cornelia. "Why Karen *wanted* to do it. Don't you see? She really meant to kill Sebastian, and David kept her from doing it."

"Oh I *see,*" said Pitt. "He took a dirty job off her hands."

4

After that they had in Luigi Como. They had in Mr. Vanguard, and Leo Rinschy, and Matha, and Rose, and even
François and Baptista and Valentine and Jesse and Eulie
and Sylvie, the twins, and Fabian and Germina. They had
David March back again. And Cornelia. It was like a shut-
tle. Angeline was all flushed and panting from her effort
not to miss anything.

"Karen?" said Luigi solemnly. "She is glad. She is proud.
Sebastian is her man. He do wrong. She make right. Doctor save her from kill Sebastian when she is mad. She save
Doctor from people say he kill him. You do not unnerstan'? It is too much honor for you? Yes?"

But gradually, out of the welter of conflicting evidence,
two facts emerged.

David March had had a chance to kill Sebastian, and
Cornelia knew it.

Cornelia had had a chance to kill Sebastian, and David
March knew that.

And then the corollary: the death of Sebastian Como
made necessary the death of Mrs. Vanguard.

They were questioning David March:

"You say you locked your car when you left Miss Van
Horn the second time, after Sebastian's attack?"

"Yes."

"How did you lock it?"

"With the key."

"The car had two doors, didn't it? Did they both lock
with a key?"

There was a breath's space of pause. "One of them
locked with a key."

"And how did the other lock?"

"With a catch."

"On the *inside?*"

"Yes. On the inside."

"Then Miss Van Horn was not locked in at all—as you tried to make us think?"

"Sebastian was locked out."

"I didn't ask you that. I said Miss Van Horn wasn't locked in. Was she?"

Again that almost imperceptible pause. "No."

"While you were gone, she could have got out if she'd wanted to."

"She didn't want to. She . . ."

"I didn't ask you that. I said she could have got out. Couldn't she?"

"Why, I suppose she could."

"That's what I wanted to know," said Pitt with satisfaction. He moistened the end of his fifth cigar and screwed it to that single tooth. "Now then. When you went back and found Sascha worse, how long were you gone?"

"I couldn't say exactly."

"How long do you think?"

"It's hard to judge, there was so much happening. I think it must have seemed longer than it was, because I was so anxious to get back."

"Oh come now! You can do better than that. Was it two minutes or ten?"

"Nearer ten, probably."

"Nearer fifteen?"

"Perhaps fifteen. I couldn't say."

"Anyway you had time to stop for some talk in the sitting room, put Sascha back to bed, stop the nosebleed, calm her down about what happened, give your directions to Luigi, persuade Karen to go with you, say good night all round, and come out. I guess fifteen minutes is pretty moderate. But we'll say fifteen for argument. In fifteen minutes Miss Van Horn could have walked down to the Back Road, done a little . . . errand, say, and walked back. Couldn't she?"

"She didn't go to the Back Road. She didn't get out of the car."

"I'm not asking you that. I'm asking you if anybody could walk from the house to the Back Road and return in fifteen minutes."

"Yes," said David curtly.

"That's what I wanted to know," said Pitt "Now when you got back to the car, how did Miss Van Horn seem?"

"Seem?"

"Did she seem anyhow queer?"

"No."

"I thought you just said she acted nervous. Kind of jumpy."

"I don't call that queer. I call that natural. She had had a trying experience."

"Some say murder's kind of trying," drawled Pitt. "I guess you ought to know."

". . . You can't remember yet seeing Sebastian's body in the road that first time you drove past?"

"No," said David sharply.

They understood now what that strange hesitation had meant the first time David had been questioned on this point. It would have been greatly to his own advantage if he could have said the body was in the road the first time he passed. But it would not have been to Cornelia's advantage. If the body was in the road then, it looked black indeed for Cornelia.

"You don't think you could have driven past it without noticing?"

"Certainly not," said David.

Oh yes, he knew that Cornelia could have done it. But he wasn't admitting it, not for a minute. Because she was Cornelia.

They were questioning Cornelia:

"Was Sebastian's body lying there the first time you went out the Back Road?"

"I don't know. I didn't see it."

"You would have seen it if it had been there, wouldn't you?"

"I don't believe so. I was on the other side of the car. I didn't even see it the second time, you know."

"But Dr. March would have seen it. He couldn't have got by without, could he?"

"Oh easily," said Cornelia glibly. "It was very dark. And it was already beginning to rain a little—not really rain, more of a mist—but it clouded the windshield. And then Karen was with us. She took all our attention. Dr. March was trying to drive with one hand and hold her quiet with the other. I don't believe he could possibly have noticed."

"Mm," said Brennon thoughtfully.

You could not tell a thing about it now, where the truth lay. They were trying as hard as they could to shield each other—with just enough truth in what they said to sweeten it. No, you couldn't tell. . . .

"When Dr. March left you alone in the car, that second time you drove out the Back Road, how long was he gone?"

"I don't know."

"You can guess. Did it seem long?"

"It seemed long because I was waiting. It wasn't long really."

"Five minutes?"

"Oh not more than that."

"Five minutes would have been enough," said Pitt. "Less would have been enough. You don't need much time for some things. Now you say you didn't see anything?"

"No. I didn't see anything "

"What was it you heard then?"

"I couldn't hear very well. The engine was running."

"Oh. Dr. March left the engine running so that you couldn't hear."

"Oh I didn't say that," pleaded Cornelia. "You twist everything I say right round. It's a very quiet car."

"I thought March said the other day," put in Brennon, "that it was a noisy one."

"It is an old car, and full of squeaks and rattles when it's going. But it has a good engine. The engine is quiet. . . ."

"Then you think you could have heard it if there had been any outcry?"

"Oh I know I could have." Cornelia was growing panicky. "I heard everything there was to hear and there wasn't any outcry. . . ."

"Just voices?"

"Not any voices. How could there be, when . . ."

"What did you hear then?"

"Why, just twigs snapping."

"Oh yes. Twigs. Was that before or after the sound of the fall?"

"Before . . ." Cornelia stopped, smothering an exclamation of dismay at what she had said. "The wind was coming up," she said frantically, and her voice was a plea for belief. "Really and truly it was. I thought a branch had fallen in the woods. And I was afraid David was hurt. . . ."

"What made you think that? Because of the groan?"

"It wasn't a groan, exactly. More a kind of grunt. But it frightened me, because I was afraid the branch had hit David. I called to him out the window. But he came running up in a minute and said he was all right. He said there wasn't anything more for us to do and we'd better get back home."

Oh, she knew he could have done it. . . .

Garey Brennon thrust his head out of the wash-room door.

"Will you step in here a moment too please, Dr. March?" he said gravely.

David March went in without a glance at anybody.

"Dr. March, can you explain the noise of snapping twigs while Miss Van Horn was waiting for you in the car beside the Back Road?"

"Why yes, I can explain that easily. I was walking round in the undergrowth in the dark. And then I moved the body back, and that made a noise too."

"Oh of course," said Brennon casually. "You would have to do that, wouldn't you? That was just after the noise of the body's falling."

There was not the least note of change in David March's even voice. "Right after," he agreed. "I was the one who fell. I stumbled backward over a root in the darkness, and went down flat."

"God!" breathed Garey Brennon. "Right to the end. You can't faze him.—And that," he said derisively, "was why you groaned."

"Why, yes," said David March.

There was silence in the wash room. David March and Cornelia Van Horn were still in there together. Angeline couldn't resist a little peep round the corner of the door. It was just a glimpse she had.

She saw David and Cornelia standing together. Hunted. Driven. Brought to bay at last. White lipped. Heavy with weariness. A dampness on their foreheads. . . .

She saw them facing Pitt and Brennan without flinching. Level-eyed. Prideful still. They two against the world.

"You killed Mrs. Vanguard together," challenged Pitt. "One of you killed Como. Come clean now. Which one did it?"

"David. . . ." gasped Cornelia. She plucked at his sleeve.

But David March laughed defiantly. "My dear man. Don't be fantastic. Cornelia couldn't have done it. She's too little. Sebastian was a big man."

"You're a pretty big man yourself," said Brennan.

"I am a tall man," said David March coolly. "You can't expect me to admit more than that."

X
Saturday (Continued)

Dr. David March and Cornelia Van Horn were arrested for murder at four that afternoon.

This was the way the matter stood, as summarized by Pitt:

Dr. March had taken Miss Van Horn with him to the Comos' on the night of August 18. While she was waiting for him in the car, Sebastian Como had assaulted her. Dr. March was furiously angry. He had intended then to kill Sebastian. He had dissembled his anger; he had warned every one else off, pretending to make light of it; he had taken good care that Karen should not have a chance to carry out her threats and cheat him of his vengeance. Probably he had meant to take Cornelia home, arrange some sort of alibi, and return by himself to do the job later. But as he was driving out the Back Road he saw Sebastian lurking in the bushes. Rage overrode judgment. He left the car, ran back, killed Sebastian, and hid the body. Miss Van Horn heard Sebastian's cry and the sound of his fall. Dr. March cleaned the knife he had used—probably some kind of surgeon's knife—placed Sebastian's knife beside him, wiped his hands, ran back to his car, and drove quickly away.

Nobody knew that he had been on the scene of the crime except Miss Van Horn, and he could count on her to keep silent. She was too much mixed up in it herself to want to say anything. Dr. March went home, removed the blood from his person, and immediately went out again on a convenient case in a remote part of town where there was no telephone. He stayed in hiding there until the next afternoon. But when he went home, he found Luigi Como waiting for him.

The news of Karen's arrest was undoubtedly a blow. Luigi Como knew that Karen had an alibi. He knew that everybody in the house had one. He was suspicious, if not certain, of Dr. March's guilt. Perhaps he had heard the car stopping in the Back Road; perhaps he had seen the flash light. But he was very heavily in the doctor's debt. Dr. March, by a clever combination of bribery and appeal to Luigi's loyalty and a mistaken sense of honor, made him promise to keep silent. In return, he promised that Karen should never be convicted. Luigi Como believed that in the event of a conviction, Dr. March meant to come forward with the truth. But Dr. March was already resolving different plans.

When Miss Van Horn was drawn on the Como-Garetti jury, it seemed as if all Dr. March's troubles were over. Miss Van Horn would, of course, stand for acquittal, and do all in her power to sway the jury. She was in the nature of a victim; she was under the influence of a man of enormously strong will, and one moreover to whom she was passionately devoted.

But Dr. March was taking no chances. Against the possibility of something's going wrong, and the truth about himself coming out, he equipped Miss Van Horn with a hypodermic syringe and a killing dose of hyoscine. He ascertained that there was a cup machine in the jury room, and taught her how to remove a screw from the case with a penknife, and how to prepare the hyoscine and inject it directly into the cup beneath. This of course was only in the event of an emergency. But Miss Van Horn understood now what the cry and the sound of a fall in the bushes by the Back Road had meant. And she was willing to do even murder to save the man she loved. Dr. March promised to await the outcome in the court room.

The emergency that Dr. March had feared presently arose. Mrs. Vanguard, who knew that her own husband had been present on the scene of the crime earlier in the evening, and was resolved to protect the Vanguard name from scandal at any price including corruption of jury and conviction of an innocent person, was unexpectedly adamant. In spite of Miss Van Horn's best efforts, she turned the jury to her side. Moreover it became increasingly evident that she knew something about the presence of Dr. March—and probably of Miss Van Horn also—that night at the Comos'. The fact that there was already bad blood between them, both between Mrs. Vanguard and Miss Van Horn, and between Mrs. Vanguard and Dr. March, made it possible that at any moment she might bring them into it. She had already made veiled threats to this effect.

Just before lunch, on Tuesday, therefore, Miss Van Horn went to the wash room and poisoned a cup according to the instructions that Dr. March had given her. There was no time to wash the syringe, and she put it back in her bag. Luck was with her, and she had an opportunity to pour the coffee. Otherwise she would have had to resort to some other device—perhaps a cup of water. As it was, she had only to make sure that Mrs. Vanguard received the coffee cup that contained the poison.

The plot failed of immediate fulfillment only because Mrs. Vanguard did not drink all her coffee. She was made ill, but not fatally so. Following her seizure, Mr. Gilley called for a doctor, and Miss Van Horn suggested Dr. March. He was brought in. Miss Van Horn found an opportunity to tell him that she thought Mrs. Vanguard knew the truth. Dr. March acted without hesitation. He administered a second dose of hyoscine, which caused Mrs. Vanguard's death three hours later.

David March and Cornelia Van Horn were both held as principals in the murder of Mrs. Vanguard; David for

the murder of Sebastian Como, with Cornelia as accessory
after the fact.

"Captain wants to see you down to the house," Pitt said.

It seemed to Angeline a curiously inadequate phrase to
stand for so much. Mr. Vanguard collapsed with a moan
of misery and impotence. But no one except Oliver Elding
paid him any attention.

Dr. David March and Cornelia Van Horn stood up at
Pitt's words, as if they stood to receive sentence. It wasn't
right, it wasn't reasonable; but Angeline had never felt so
proud of them as she felt at that moment.

The final blow had fallen. They had done bitterly
wrong. And fate had brought the wrong home to them.
But they did not bow to fate.

David March had never looked so tall. So tall and thin
and straight and strong. His face was ashy gray with the
gray pallor of a man mortally hurt. His eyes burned, with
the unnatural brightness of fever or long suffering, under
his straight brows; there was a dark hint of dampness in the
edges of his hair, where it swept back in those high points
from the temples. There were cruel lines about his mouth,
and his mouth itself was set to the bitter taste of shame.
But no, he did not bow to fate. Shame is in acknowledgment of wrong. And David acknowledged nothing.

Cornelia Van Horn stood close to him, as if she drew
strength from the mere physical nearness to his strength.
She looked dazed, like a child who wakes from a bad
dream, and finds her dream come true; and who waits still
for some one to rouse her and tell her it is not so. Her
face was pinched to a small white triangle, framing the
small pinched triangle of her lips. A white mask pulled
smooth over tortured spirit. Only through the brown eyes
the spirit looked out, full of dread and horror and bewilderment and incredulity. Her hands were crammed down
into the pockets of the brown jacket, dragging it forward
tight at the shoulders over the irregular beating of the
close, cream-colored blouse . . . and you saw that in the

shelter of those pockets her hands were locked in hard little fists, trying to hold onto reality in a disordered world.
But they held on. No, Cornelia did not bow to fate either.

They were so unthinkably young to have had this happen to them. There was so much warmth and life in the set
of their bodies. There should have been so much happiness
in a future that could have no happiness now.

David March turned suddenly and smiled down at Cornelia. The wrung smile of a man in mortal pain, who hides
his pain for the sake of one who is dear to him. A smile
of wrenching tenderness, of promise unfulfilled, of sorrow
and of heartbreak and . . . of love.

Cornelia Van Horn smiled back. There was not a sound
in the big room. Nobody dared to look at Cornelia, when
she smiled.

"Keep chipper," said David steadily. "We've got to see
it through."

"All ready," Pitt was saying, bustling about importantly.
He went to the door. "Got the taxi, Trollope?"

Angeline was whispering to Garey Brennon. She stood
on tiptoe, to bring herself close to his ear. "I can't help
wondering . . ." she began. The whispering flowed on,
with a soft swish of s's.

"You're crazy," said Brennon. But he listened. To Garey
Brennon's everlasting credit be it said that he listened.

Suddenly he began to whisper too. Urgently. Fast. "Do
just as I say. Give it a try anyhow. It can't do any harm. . . ."

"All ready," repeated Pitt. "The car's waiting."

"Be-before you go," said Angeline, and if her voice was
a little fluttery and uncertain it was not strange; there was
a tightness in more throats than one that afternoon. "Before you go, I—I'd like to get your address. I want to write
you and Cornelia a letter."

"That's nice of you," said David March. He was obviously touched. "I suppose we'll be held right here in town
for the present. Won't we, Pitt?"

"I want to write it down," insisted Angeline. She plumped her round person into the chair that Garey Brennan pushed forward. "May I borrow your pen, please?" she said, to Gideon Hawes, beside her.

"Take my pencil," said Gideon Hawes. He was inscribing final notes at the end of his manuscript, but he held the pencil out.

"I'd rather have a pen," said Angeline, with the soft stubbornness of very gentle people. "I don't like pencil writing; it gets all smudged up so I can't read it." She reached for the pen clipped to the edge of Mr. Hawes' pocket.

Gideon Hawes put his hand to his heart, in that familiar gesture. Any one in his feeble health, the gesture said, should not be argued with. His fingers were over the pen. "There isn't any ink in it," he said.

"Oh but there must be a little," persisted Angeline. "It wouldn't be a bit like such a careful man as you to have a pen without anything in it. I only need a drop." Her fingers burrowed under his, and she pulled the pen from his pocket.

She unscrewed the cap. "Oh there's plenty of ink after all. Isn't that lucky? But I wonder what makes it rattle?"

She held the cap beside her ear, shaking it; her head tipped a little to one side, so that she looked like an inquiring gray bird. She peeped inquisitively into the hole. "Why," she cried. "It looks like gum! Do you like gum, Mr. Hawes? I never noticed you chewing. But what a cute place to keep it!"

Gideon Hawes made a sudden clutch across the table at the cap of the pen. His face was oddly suffused for such a bloodless little man. "You let my gum alone!" he cried in a queer strangled voice. It must be very embarrassing to have one's secret vices, like gum-chewing, dragged out like that in public. It was grotesque, almost indecent, on top of tragedy. David March and Cornelia standing there waiting. . . .

But Angeline seemed unaware of incongruity. She held
the pen perversely out of reach. "I want to see," she insisted. "I wonder . . ." Before he could stop her, she had
unfastened Grandmother Hawthorne's real cameo brooch
from her tight little round bosom. She bent back the long
pin, and pried with it at the substance inside the pen cap.
A moment, and she was successful. A fat gray cud of gum
came out on the point of the pin. Angeline turned the cap
slowly upside down.

From the open space at the end of the cap, beyond
where the gum had been, there rolled out onto the table
. . . a hypodermic needle.

2

"Yes," Gideon Hawes was saying, "I killed Mrs. Vanguard."

He sat bolt upright in his chair at the end of the long
table, his manuscript, with the corners all meticulously
laid together, square before him, his feet square on the
floor: a little puttering, careful man, in a tidy gray suit
that matched his hair, and a dull blue tie that matched his
eyes, tied precisely in the middle. He took off his spectacles and wiped them composedly on a clean white handkerchief. He set them back with deliberation on the small
round nose that marked the centre of his small round face,
and glanced about benignly. He did not look confused by
guilt. He looked proud and rather pleased.

"In the taking off of Mrs. Vanguard," he said, folding
his hands before him on the table, as a thousand times he
had folded them before him on a class-room desk before he
began a lecture, "I consider that I have done a public service. I do not view this act in the light of a murder. I view
it as an execution. There are many in this town—I speak
without rancor, as without dissimulation—who would
have been glad to have Mrs. Vanguard removed. They did
not themselves remove her only because they shrank from
the onerous duty of removing any one. To me all such are
deeply indebted. I have performed that duty."

He paused. Not from any pressure of emotion, not
from any dearth of words to frame his speech, but only to
let the import of what he said be felt. There was a little
gasp about him . . . and quiet. Not even one of the young
Comos stirred or whispered.

Gideon Hawes was restored to the place to which he
felt he rightfully belonged. While he was teaching, he had
occupied the centre of the stage, without question or competition. Following his discharge from academic service,
he found himself swept away from this central position.
He was no longer one of the principals in the drama. He
was an unconsidered member of the mob scene. Less than
that even. A voice from the wings. Now he was back again,
well remarked by all, in the weighty role of villain.

No audience that Gideon Hawes had ever known had
paid him more close attention. Every face in that jury
room was turned toward him, rigid to catch his smallest
word. No one interrupted, not even Pitt. They looked at
him with awe. Awe and a tinge of fear. That doddering,
inconsiderable man to be a murderer. That absurd little
man, with his small round face and his big round forehead
. . . and his kidneys and his capsules and his drops . . .
and his terrible single-mindedness. There was something
of the fanatic about him. Something a little more than human or a little less. Something not quite sane. He nodded
at them pleasantly.

"Consider," he said, "this jury. It may, I think, be taken
as representative, brought together by the laws of choice
and chance. Yet with the possible exception of Mr. Gilley, who was, if I may say so, drawn to Mrs. Vanguard
by purely mercenary considerations, there was hardly one
here to whom Mrs. Vanguard had not done a wrong. That
these wrongs were done in an impersonal way, with a large,
unperceiving cruelty, made them the harder to bear. Let
us see them. She wrecked Mr. Apple's business. She de-
prived Miss Madras of a happy childhood. She poisoned
Miss Tredennick's cat. She took away from Rinschy's son

the labor upon which he depended to support his family. She tried to break up the friendship between her husband and Mr. Elding, which was the dearest thing that either of them had. She bribed Miss Lee's fiancé with a promise of gold, and rewarded him with a stupid wife. She discharged Miss Van Horn without reason, and attacked her character without justice. She quarreled with Dr. March, and did all in her power to injure a successful practice. I include Dr. March, though he was not a member of the jury, because he has been for so long associated with us. I include also Mr. Vanguard, whose life Mrs. Vanguard so completely ruined. How many of these would have been glad to see Mrs. Vanguard dead"—there was an uneasy licking of dry lips—"how many, it would perhaps be embarrassing to ask.

"Degrees of resentment felt against Mrs. Vanguard naturally varied. They varied from, let us say, the irritation of Mr. Kashaw, who had merely been insulted, to, let us say, the avowed hate of Miss Madras, the course of whose whole life had been altered. But none of these here present was prepared to kill her. They did not kill her because there were forces at work to prevent them. There were, as I have previously pointed out, inhibitions. There was too much risk. There was the possibility of losing more than could be gained. There were counter-motives of love, of business, of pleasure, of family, of friends, of life to be lived, duties to be performed and the future to be enjoyed.

"But now consider my position. No such inhibition swayed me. I had nothing to risk. Nothing to lose. I had no business, no pleasure, no friends, no future. I had, in short, no life before me. My life was teaching. When Mrs. Vanguard took away my teaching, she took away my life. So I took away her life. It was quite logical."

Gideon Hawes coughed delicately behind his hand. "If I might have a drink of water," he suggested. "Speaking always makes me a little hoarse. . . ."

It was Biggs who brought it. No one else seemed capable of motion. But Biggs was accustomed to unquestioning service under the most surprising conditions. He padded out like a useful shadow, and like a shadow brought the cup and set it at Hawes' elbow. Gideon Hawes took a small, composed sip, and wiped his mouth on his handkerchief.

"If you had listened," he said, "while I read you extracts from my book, you would have seen at once that I was the logical person to have executed Mrs. Vanguard."

Suddenly they saw that it was true. Gideon Hawes had told them over and over, with a polite insistence, that he was fitted in every way for the part of a murderer. He had pointed out that a murderer must of all things be careful of detail. And only a glance at Hawes' own trim person—with his belt and his galluses and his safety-pin, his two pairs of glasses, his two sets of teeth, his polished boots and his polished linen and the knot of his tie charted by rule and compass—would have shown them that no one could be more meticulous in detail than he.

He had pointed out that a murderer must drag red herrings across the path—must give those set to catch him something to take their attention—and he had flourished his drops and his capsules and his heart and his kidney trouble in their faces.

He had pointed out that a murderer must be trained to such command over his own emotions that he would not betray himself, and so intent had they been on the self-control demanded of a physician that they had passed unheeded the fact that no one needs to be so self-possessed, so impervious to surprise or embarrassment from unexpected situations, as he who sits daily before a class of sharp-eyed youngsters and undertakes to teach.

He had pointed out the matter of inhibition: that a murderer must have little to lose by murder. But they had forgotten that Dr. March had his practice to lose and his love to lose and the whole of his young life to lose also; and they had not remembered that Gideon Hawes had himself told them that he had no family, no friends, no occupation now that his book was done, no expectation of

a future limited by ill health. Oh, he had told them times
enough. And nobody had listened.

"If you ask me whether this execution was premeditated," he continued calmly—though no one had asked
him anything—"my answer would be in the affirmative.
I determined to kill Mrs. Vanguard two years ago, at the
time when she unjustly secured my discharge from my position in the Sheffield High School. Before reaching this
decision, I considered the case in all its ramifications. I
considered, that is, the general benefit to the community
of such a step, as well as my personal gratification; I collected a considerable amount of data, and I concluded that
the action was, from all points of view, desirable.

"Since that time, my leisure has been occupied with the
writing of my book: 'The Logic of Behavior.' I felt that I
owed it to humanity to leave behind me some record of my
theory and practice; by including a chapter on The Logic
of Crime, with reference particularly to murder, and most
particularly to the murder of Mrs. Vanguard, I had hoped
to contribute to the science of detection and perhaps
indeed to correct in some degree the present haphazard
practices of the police. But this book was merely by way
of avocation. My chief preoccupation was with the details
of the execution which I had in hand.

"I have spent two years," repeated Gideon Hawes complacently, looking about him as if he expected approbation
for his effort, "in planning a logical crime. And if I may
say so, no crime has ever been more completely logical. If
I may so far trespass upon your patience, I will describe it
to you in detail."

It was a tribute to the spell under which he held them
all that no one found anything absurd in the offer.

"Having once determined upon the method to be
used," he told them, "a matter you may be sure of no small
thought and care in construction, I looked about me for
an opportunity by which this method might be applied. I
had at first intended to employ the cup machine located

in the corridor of the Civics Building. Mrs. Vanguard was, as you know, president of the Civics Club; she presided at meetings in the club rooms there and not infrequently made speeches. It was not uncommon on such occasions for her to come to the water cooler in the hall for a cup of water before she assumed the chair. It was my intention to poison the cup from which she drank.

"In the practical application of my design, however, I encountered certain difficulties. There were often loiterers in the corridor of the Civics Building, so that I had no opportunity for approaching the cup machine. It was undesirable, of course, for me to be myself too frequently, or too long, seen in its vicinity. In particular I must not be seen by any one on the afternoon when my project was consummated. To be so seen automatically precluded any action for that day. I was in no great haste at first. But weeks dragged by, months dragged by, and nothing was accomplished. Under the nervous strain to which I was subjected, my health failed more rapidly. I began to fear that after all my care and labor, Mrs. Vanguard would outlive me.

"When Mrs. Vanguard and I were both drawn on the Como-Garetti jury, therefore, and I found that there was a water cooler and a cup machine in the wash room of the same general type as that situated in the Civics Building, I felt that fate had mysteriously intervened in my behalf. I came, of course, fully prepared. Indeed, I was never otherwise.

"I brought a hypodermic needle, as you have seen, concealed in the end of my fountain pen. I brought a medicine dropper, which I employed publicly in the measurement of my medicine. By removing the rubber bulb at the end of the dropper and fitting it to the hypodermic needle, a very creditable syringe could quickly be constructed. It is a simple device, and one not uncommon, I believe, among habitual users of drugs. I brought also a quantity of hyoscine—which, after lengthy and painstaking study I had determined was most convenient and practical for my purpose—sufficient for two fatal doses. I thus provided for the possibility that my first attempt might fail, but did not burden myself with a supply of poison which might later offer embarrassment in its disposal. The hyoscine was placed in large capsules like those which I was myself accustomed to take, and you must often have seen those identical capsules openly displayed before you. I believe that I overlooked nothing. It was all completely logical.

"Just before lunch on Tuesday, I decided that the time for action had arrived. Under the pretense of getting a drink of water—a thing to which by frequent repetition I had accustomed those present—I went into the wash room. By a hasty experiment I ascertained that the third cup in the rack would be the one containing the poison. I prepared my dose quickly—hyoscine, as you know, dissolves almost instantly in a minute quantity of water—and injected it through the case directly into the third cup.

"By this means you will see that I did not come into contact with the fatal cup at all, and thus avoided the possibility of betraying finger prints. The screw I removed from the case with the blade of my penknife without touching the case with my fingers. In my haste I had the misfortune to break a tiny nick out of the blade. This gave me a moment's uneasiness, and for the nonce I considered abandoning the project altogether. But an instant's reflection showed me that to one ill-attuned to the decrees of logic, a broken knife blade would have no meaning in a death from poisoning. In this I was, as usual, correct. The knives were not even examined, simply because Mrs. Vanguard was not stabbed. The screw, once removed, I folded in my handkerchief. When the injection was finished I replaced it, still holding it in my handkerchief so that again my fingers did not come in contact either with it or with the surface of the case.

"The logic of my scheme, further, precluded the necessity of giving Mrs. Vanguard the poisoned cup myself.

I had simply to make sure that she received it; from what hand it did not matter. I returned unostentatiously to the jury room, and let events take their course.

"Events, then, so developed that Miss Van Horn was the one chosen to pour the coffee; Biggs was the one who offered to bring the cups. As soon as he had done so, placing them on the table before Miss Van Horn, I started back again to the wash room after water. On the way I stopped for a moment to tell Miss Van Horn that I did not drink coffee, a fact already established by my procedure at breakfast. Standing over her I was enabled to see that Biggs had arranged the cups on the table in the order in which they had come from the machine; I could see the little dampness in the bottom of the third one, indicating the presence of the hyoscine which I had placed there. My problem, then, was simply how to make sure that Mrs. Vanguard received the third cup.

"For this, naturally, I had recourse to logic. Biggs was still absent from his place; I sat beside him, and I was absent also. I called to Elding who sat next to help me bring in water for everybody present. Elding's departure left a considerable gap at the lower end of the table. It left also three persons—Miss Lee, Mr. Kashaw and Mrs. Vanguard, in that order—at Miss Van Horn's right. It was logical to suppose that Miss Van Horn would pass the cups of coffee, as she filled them, to Mrs. Vanguard, and that Mrs. Vanguard in turn would pass them on. They would not go beyond Miss Lee, because of the space between her and Rinschy. Mrs. Vanguard then would retain the third cup in her possession. I stood in the washroom door, while Biggs and Elding filled their cups, and watched to see if my theory developed satisfactorily. Had it not done so, I should have had to resort to some method for shifting or destroying the poisoned cup; perhaps I should have had to feign awkwardness, and tip it over. But the need did not arise. There was no flaw in my reasoning. It was all too logical to fail.

"That the plan in its entirety did not immediately reach fulfillment was through no breach in the wall of my logic. It was due to a wholly illogical failure on the part of Mrs. Vanguard to drink all her coffee. She received, in consequence, less than half of the intended dose. She collapsed, yes. But I had no assurance that, with prompt and skilful medical attention, she would not recover.

"You can imagine, then, my dilemma." He paused to look about at them as if for sympathy in his unjust predicament. "Frustration at this point would be more than a mere temporary miscarriage of my plan. It would be impossible, having tried and failed, to repeat the technique which I had once employed. To have done so would have been to invite to myself the attention even of the most illogical. It would mean that two years' work had gone for nothing, and that I should have to begin again at the beginning and construct a new method of procedure. I doubted if the time left at my disposal by my frail health would allow for this repetition.

"Under these trying circumstances, there was logically only one thing to be done. The other dose of hyoscine with which I had provided myself must be administered, and the affair carried through at once to its conclusion. In the confusion following Mrs. Vanguard's collapse, therefore, I repaired again, unnoticed, to the wash room. There I repeated my former action. I removed the screw, prepared the poison, injected it into the cup, and replaced the screw. I then drew out the two bottom cups, which were harmless, and threw them in the waste, thus leaving the poisoned cup next in the machine. It seemed logical that, under the supposition that Mrs. Vanguard had fainted, some one would bring her a drink of water or give her medicine.

"Results again justified my expectations. Immediately upon his arrival, Dr. March hastened to the wash room to prepare Mrs. Vanguard a dose of aromatic. Watching him through the open door, I saw him pour it into the cup which I had made ready. I saw him hold this cup to Mrs. Vanguard's lips, and force her to drain the last of the poisoned draught.

"After that, events followed logically. Mrs. Vanguard grew rapidly worse. The rest you know. I need not here repeat it.

"The first capsule," he added, "I swallowed immediately upon emptying it. The second, because of my haste, and the danger of interruption, I kept by me. Following Mrs. Vanguard's removal, I swallowed it here, openly, in the sight of all of you, washing it down with my usual liberal drink of water. I commented on the fact that I was taking an extra one, saying that the excitement had put a dangerous strain upon me. And so indeed it had. The other capsules, when they were taken for analysis—as of course I had foreseen they would be—were found harmless. It was all quite logical."

He stopped, beaming around at them all, as if he expected applause. He peered at them over his spectacles, a little dry, unpretentious, kindly-seeming man, suddenly grown monstrous in his satisfaction at the monstrous thing he had done. He was outside reality. He was outside anything human.

There was no sound in the room—only the broken sound of Mr. Vanguard's shuddering breaths. Even Pitt did not speak. Even Damaris Lee, who prided herself on being hard-boiled, shrank from the horrid gloating of Gideon Hawes' look. They glanced at him obliquely, doing him the homage of fear. Garey Brennon patted Angeline's shoulder.

"The substance of what I have said," Gideon Hawes added his peroration, "is appended to the end of my manuscript. It seemed safer to write it down. With my heart and my kidneys in the condition that they are, it is hardly putting it too strongly to say that any moment may be my last. Naturally I did not wish any unpleasantness over this matter while I lived. But when I am gone, then the

statement might have been of value to others. Moreover, I
have added a careful survey of the Vanguard case from the
beginning. It was my idea that, by a careful study of the
points at which they have departed from logic in this case
and so built up an erroneous proposition, police officials
might prevent a recurrence of the same mistakes in other
cases. I should thus, as Mrs. Vanguard would have put it,
in a Larger Sense forwarded the Cause of Justice."

The malice of that last sentence seemed almost worse
than murder. More venomous. But it accorded with the
reasoned brutality of every word he had uttered.

"Throughout, my logic was impregnable. It could not
fail. It . . ."

He stopped—and for the first time it seemed to occur
to Gideon Hawes that it *had* failed. He was caught. The
pattern of his logic crashed about him. He whirled upon
Angeline.

"How did you know?" he cried. And his voice from
being low and smug was suddenly a shrill, unfocused cry.

"Well I guess I didn't exactly," admitted Angeline, looking at Garey Brennon. "All the time I kept kind of wondering how you could know so much about it all as you
said you did. But I didn't think so much of that at first.
But then afterwards I got to wondering how you made
the little nick in your knife that I borrowed to cut up the
chocolate bar for the children. And then I got to wondering why you wouldn't let me take your fountain pen that
time I asked you, when you let me take the knife without
any fuss. And then I remembered where Dr. March put his
stethoscope when he listened to Mrs. Vanguard's heart—
over almost to the middle it was—and I got to wondering
why, if your heart felt bad, you put your hand way round
by your pocket where the pen was. . . ."

Gideon Hawes made a lunge at her. He was not a pretty
sight. He was like a harmless, foolish little lap-dog that
goes suddenly berserk. His lip was drawn back in a snarl, so
that the artificial pink gums of his plate showed above his

teeth. His eyes were blood-shot, and his strangely crowded features were working in a frenzy of rage and hate. There was a thin slime on his lips.

"You . . . you *woman!*" he screamed at her. "You don't know what logic is. You just *blundered onto it.* . . ."

Garey Brennon pushed Hawes down again into his chair. He held him with hands that were like a pair of vises.

"Give him back his fountain pen, Miss Tredennick," he said, "so he can sign his statement."

3

"No," said Gideon Hawes dully. "I did not kill Sebastian Como."

He slumped forward against the table. The unnatural satisfaction in what he had done, the passion of achievement that had sustained him, had fallen away; he realized that after all he had failed. Not he himself had failed so much as logic. Logic had been defeated by the blundering inquisitiveness of a woman. He seemed shriveled, like a pricked rubber toy, so that his clothes hung on him laxly, bunched and wrinkled, and all the lines of his face sagged. He did not seem monstrous any more. Just a bad little man who had been caught.

The collapse of Gideon Hawes had restored the room to normalcy. William Apple and Mary Madras held hands under the edge of the table. Oliver Elding devoted himself to Mr. Vanguard, who sat with his head buried in his arms and his whole figure heaving and shuddering with the uncontrolled emotion of Hawes' recital. The others glanced from time to time at Cornelia and David March, waiting together so quietly for the final outcome. But their appetite was for Gideon Hawes. They pressed about him. They felt no more fear of him, no more awe; only a curious avidity, as if they would have liked to finger his person to see what a murderer felt like, as if they would have liked to snip a bit off his coat for a souvenir to carry away.

Pitt was restored to his usual bullying manner. "If you didn't kill him," he said sharply, "I guess likely you know who did."

"Yes," said Gideon Hawes apathetically. "I know that. I should think it would be plain to any one with an ounce of logic in him."

"You won't make out anything for yourself, not telling. We got you anyway."

"Oh I'll tell you," said Gideon Hawes. He rallied a little to the defense of logic. After all he could show these blunderers yet that there was something in his theory. After all, he still held the centre of the stage. After all they would think he killed Sebastian too, if he did not prove the contrary.

"The Como case," he said, in a flat voice unlike his former arrogance, "puzzled me from the beginning. You will remember that I voted for Karen Garetti's acquittal. I saw that it was not logical for her to have killed Sebastian. Nevertheless, I was quite honest in saying that I was ready to be convinced. I thought that there might be circumstances not previously brought out which might alter my conviction. Moreover, if she did not do it, I could not understand who did. No one else so far as I knew concerned in the matter fitted any better than she the demands of logical conclusion."

"Cut out the frills," commanded Pitt, "and tell us what you know if you know anything."

"I know that Karen Garetti did not do it," said Gideon Hawes, with a kind of weary scorn for Pitt's stupidity. "In the light of the evidence that has since been submitted, it must be evident even to you that she did not. Karen had an alibi.

"Rose had an alibi too. Luigi had an alibi. So, probably, had Matha. If not, it did not matter. Matha, as you should have noticed, is left-handed. It was no left-handed blow that killed Sebastian.

"To think that Dr. March was the murderer was absurd. The same inhibitions which, as I have already pointed out, would have functioned to prevent his killing Mrs. Vanguard would have been operative here also. He was young. His life was before him and his work and his love. More than that, he was totally unfitted, both by nature and occupation, for the working of violence. He would not kill in passion, because he is not a passionate man. He would not kill with deliberation, because, if I may put it so, he is too prone to pity. It would have been impossible for him not to see the other's point of view. . . .

"To think that Miss Van Horn killed Sebastian is doubly absurd. I will not take your time by going into that. Suffice it to say that she lacked the physical strength."

"I'm not asking you . . ." began Pitt.

"Of course," said Gideon Hawes, as if he did not hear him—as perhaps indeed he did not—"it is plain enough who the Comos thought to be guilty. Why they were so anxious to have the matter hushed up that they were willing to victimize Karen. It has all along been amazing to me that no one seemed to think of it. Sascha."

Luigi Como gave a strangled cry, but again Gideon Hawes went on as if he had not heard. "Sascha, as the doctor's statement has brought out, had always disliked Sebastian. On the night in question she was so angry at him for what he had done that she tried to leap out of bed, ill as she was, and follow after him. The doctor, he has himself told us, repeatedly warned Luigi to watch her to prevent this very thing.

"Now consider. Luigi Como, we will say, dropped asleep. When he awakened, he hurried into Sascha's room and found her dead. She had obviously been up, for she was lying half across the bed, as if she had fallen in the very act of getting back. Luigi's explanation that the baby cried and she had risen to attend him was a feeble effort and should have attracted attention. No woman, sick to death, rises to tend a crying child with a house full of people to do it. There was blood on Sascha's nightdress, but no one noticed that because it was known that she had had a nosebleed. No one noticed, that is, except Luigi—and Luigi loved Sascha. Sascha's bare feet were wet. Luigi wiped them dry and did not mention it, but he betrayed himself by that question about the water spilled on the floor.

"The supposition is then that Sascha, hating Sebastian for past wrongs and the insult of the evening, rose up while Luigi slept, climbed through the low window, sought out Sebastian, wetting her feet in the rain-soaked grass, killed him, returned to her room, and collapsed across the bed in the moment of reaching it."

Luigi Como's mighty hands were working at his sides. His face was all contorted. He made a strangely expressive gesture: rage, and hate of Gideon Hawes, and pleading, and compassion for Sascha. Then the great head drooped.

"But Sascha did not do it," said Gideon Hawes. "It was not logical. If she collapsed, merely by crossing the floor to look out of the window, is it likely that she climbed out that window, walked a considerable distance from the house, overpowered and killed so lusty a man as Sebastian, returned, climbed in the window . . . No, no, it is not possible. Dr. March, I think, will bear me out in this. The blood on her nightdress *did* come from her own nosebleed. The dampness on her feet *did* come from the spilled water on the floor. She started up for no darker reason than to summon Luigi in her extremity. . . ."

"Say!" bawled Pitt. "You're kidding us. You're filling up time. You don't know anything. . . ."

"I know who killed Sebastian Como," said Gideon Hawes stubbornly. "It is a marvel to me that all of you do not know. For there is one—and one only—who fits the demands of logic.

"The person of whom I speak had no inhibitions. He had nothing to lose, because he had already lost every-thing that he valued. He was a constant visitor at the

Comos'. For reasons abundantly evident he wished his presence there kept secret. Knowing this, Sebastian Como was probably blackmailing him, for that was Sebastian's way.

"On the night in question, he went to the Comos'. Fearing to be recognized, however, he turned back. But he did not go far. Perhaps he had an appointment with Sebastian that he did not dare to break; perhaps he simply wanted to buy liquor. He returned on foot. . . ."

"You mean . . ."

"Mr. Vanguard."

"Mr. Vanguard met Sebastian in the bushes at some time after his attack on Miss Van Horn. Sebastian was very drunk and excited by passion. Mr. Vanguard was a little drunk and obsessed by fear. They quarreled. Sebastian drew his knife. Perhaps Mr. Vanguard meant to kill him. Perhaps he did not mean to. . . ."

Angeline could not bear it one minute longer. She seized Mr. Vanguard's bowed shoulder and shook him urgently. *"Did* you mean to?" she begged.

DeQuincy Vanguard raised a face that was like a death's head. His eyes were sunken almost out of sight in their gaping sockets. His lips were drawn back in a dreadful grin. He was without reserves. There was no liquor in him and no strength.

"No," he whispered. "I didn't mean to do it."

Pitt set his sixth cigar at a rakish angle. "I always get a confession by the sixth," he boasted, swaggering.

But Garey Brennon cocked an amused eye at Angeline. "Do you?" he said. And he patted the tight little gray shoulder.

David and Cornelia did not hear. They did not hear anything. For them in that wide moment there were neither jury rooms nor court rooms, neither curious faces nor prying eyes nor questionings nor pain nor unbelief. Not even life and death. Only they two.

"David," she whispered softly.

"Cornelia . . ."

He put out his arms to her, and she came into them as simply, as naturally as breathing. With the touch it was as if all the darkness in the world vanished away, and all the suffering; the hard lines smoothed out of David's face, and the weariness fell from his shoulders. There was life in his look again, and a knowledge of life before him. Cornelia's eyes were brimming pools of light. The pinched white triangle of her lips was a full red curve when she lifted it to his.

David's hands were tender on her body. His kisses were on her face. And its brightness was an earnest of their future.

Angeline unwrapped a peppermint patty. "I can't help wondering," she said to Garey Brennon, "if they will be married right away."

MURDER ON THE *APHRODITE*

(1935)

For
Kenneth Payson Kempton
with thanks for help in boats and books

ONE

Bill Galleon picked up the bitstock and bored six holes in the bottom of the boat. The water came in briskly, washing round his shoes. Bill kicked the shoes off. He made sure that his gun was dry in its oiled wrapping, that Jane's handkerchief was safe in his inside pocket. The water slopped against the gunwales. Bill swung himself clear as the boat sank.

Bowsprit Island was not more than two hundred yards away, and Bill swam easily, lifting his big shoulders clear at the stroke. His hair was a flaming cap, and light winked on wet brown skin. Across his back the muscles bulged under his taut shirt. He put his feet down when he could touch bottom, walking strongly, rather fast, in spite of the pull of the water; his arms swung backward as if he tossed the sea behind him. Bill was six feet two.

Bill Galleon stood on the westward point of Bowsprit Island and shook himself lustily. Well then, here he was. The next thing was to stay. He examined the *Aphrodite* thoughtfully.

The house boat *Aphrodite* lay in a crescent-shaped cove at the upper end of the island, and Bill had only to walk across the point where he had landed to reach her. He had an impression of orange awnings on the after deck and ruffled gold taffeta curtains at the bow ports, of white paint and shining brass and the tall gilt letters of her name; on the upper deck a dinghy swung in davits, and he caught

the glint from the tilted lens of a searchlight; a Union Jack
flew on a jackstaff at the bow, a yacht ensign with its ring
of stars in the blue from another at the stern, and at the
masthead hung the owner's flag—a burgee, forked, with a
device of the foam-born goddess rising from curly waves.
A gaudy, extravagant craft; a shade too fanciful. . . . A shot
rang from the seaward side of the island. Bill made sure
again that his gun was dry, before he started toward the
Aphrodite.

The *Aphrodite* was beached in such a way in the crescent curve that at low tide her stern would lie almost clear
of the water; amidships a gangplank and an improvised
float made a passage to the shore. At the head of this plank
a rosy apple-dumpling of a woman stood watching Bill's
approach. She had a round, sweet-tempered face, and grey
curls wound up neatly on top of her head; her round little
bosom, her round little hips, were buttoned smoothly into
grey silk, and the fall of lace at her throat was held with a
cameo pin. She was eating a piece of jelly cake. Bill waved
a hand in greeting.

"I'm Bill Galleon," he explained, as he came up. "Shipwrecked mariner."

She bit another half-moon from the cake before she
answered. "I'm Angeline Tredennick," she said then. "I'm
the housekeeper when we're home, but I don't hardly know
what *to* call it on a boat—I just kind of look after everything. I'm not a servant, though, and don't you think it.
I'm a member of the family—if you can call it a family."

"What should you call it?" Bill asked casually.

"I'd call it a queer mixture," said Angeline. "It was
funny, wasn't it, that your boat should sink on such a calm
day? I wonder what made it."

"Funny things happen," Bill agreed.

"But what made it sink?" insisted Angeline curiously.
"Why didn't it sink before? How could you get as far as
this if it was sinking? I wonder . . ."

"Well, I'll tell you," said Bill frankly. "All of a sudden that boat got full of water. I've always heard that when boats get full of water, they sink. I'm beginning to believe it." He grinned. Bill had a beguiling grin, big and whole-hearted. "Trouble with this Maine coast water, it's so darn wet. If I had a place to dry myself . . ." He wrung out a dripping trouser leg suggestively.

"Well, I don't know," said Angeline, licking a finger as unself-consciously as a kitten licks a paw. "I don't hardly want to take the responsibility of asking you on board unless Mrs. Van Wycke says so. Mrs. Van Wycke might not like it. Mrs. Van Wycke is a holy terror when she doesn't like things." She was plainly filled with suspicion of Bill—but she thought he was nice. Bill was like that.

Several shots sounded close together, cutting across her speech. Bill raised an inquiring eyebrow. That eyebrow of Bill's had a little nick in the middle, relic of a flying hockey stick; it gave a slightly quizzical air to a face otherwise wholly downright.

"They're target shooting," Angeline explained. "Round at the point. Mrs. Van Wycke is there. Why don't we go over?"

Bill and Angeline walked across the eastern horn of the crescent and along the seaward shore; the ocean lay flat and grey, with that oily calm that heralds storm; there was a waiting breathlessness among the pines and birches of the wooded slopes inland. Bill walked with a loose-limbed casual ease that yet had a certain readiness behind it; Angeline bounced beside him like a ball, four steps to Bill's one.

"Who is this Mrs. . . . Van Wycke, did you call her?"

"Why, she's the owner of the house boat," said Angeline readily. She was always willing to talk. Gossip was meat and drink and breath and sunshine to Angeline Tredennick—and the worst thing about this place was that no matter what a lot of interesting things you found out, there was nobody much to talk them over with. "She's stunning looking, though I don't care much for that type myself; and I don't care much for *her* either, the way she'll snap your head off if you ask her the simplest question. She's got money, and I guess that makes up for a good deal. But I always *do* think it's funny when a woman doesn't have any women friends. She's having a house-boat party now, but all the guests are men. Of course there's Beulah Mullins, but she doesn't hardly count. She's Mrs. Van Wycke's cousin, and sort of a companion; an awfully nervous little thing, and I guess she has a right to be, the way Mrs. Van Wycke treats her. There are three men. Ewell Choate is a Southerner, and he's got a lot of that Southern charm you read about in love stories. Everybody likes him. I think myself he's too good for Mrs. Van Wycke, but it seems she's bound to have him. He's interested in the secretary though—I can see that. Then there's a man named Varro: kind of foreign-looking. I can't quite make him out. There wasn't ever anybody more polite; but I'd watch him if he was selling me bananas to see he didn't put in a rotten one. And there's the professor. Professor Dante Gabriel Burge, and just as odd as his name is. Maybe psychologists get that way on account of being so psychological. He kind of gives me the creeps. That man can see a thought in your mind before you know you've thought it. And I believe to goodness he'd push you off the top of the Washington Monument, if he could find out how you felt falling down.— Were you ever in Washington, Mr. Galleon? I was once. It . . ."

"Yes," said Bill gently, firmly. "Anybody else aboard?"

"That's all the party," Angeline said. "Just the servants. Toombs. He's Mrs. Van Wycke's butler when she's at her town house, and it makes him just about wild if you call him anything else. It would make you laugh though, wouldn't it, to think of having a butler on a boat? And then there's Annie Budd, the cook, and the maid, Catriona Cooley. I can't help wondering why any of them stay with

Mrs. Van Wycke, the way they're put upon. But I suppose she pays them well. . . ."

"How much of a crew?" said Bill.

"Just the three of them," Angeline told him. "Mr. Kember—Cephus Kember—he's the sailing master that Mrs. Van Wycke hired to take the boat out for her; and Joe Rumney and Charlie Gowen for deck-hands. They all came from the same place, up the river round Oleport way. We don't see much of them: they're a kind of a clannish lot, and they keep themselves *to* themselves mostly down in the forecastle, when they're not on duty. They and the servants don't get along any too well. Seems they don't think servants have any business on a boat anyhow; and the way they've always done before, they'd sail three and a master, and divide up all the work on the boat among them, cook and stewards and everything; and they had another friend of theirs that they wanted to get a job for. But Mrs. Van Wycke would have her own servants, or she wouldn't hire any of them. She's very opinionated. And after all, she *is* the owner. It made a little bit of friction, but nothing to amount to much. They're real pleasant, take it in general, only not very talkative. Mr. Kember isn't aboard right now. You see, we bent the propeller blades or something, getting here; and so they had to beach the boat, and take the damaged parts off as soon as the tide was down. Mr. Kember went over to Trusett to see if he could get a machinist to straighten them; if he can't, he'll have to telegraph to Portland for some new ones. He's going to wait to bring them back, so he might not get here till late, or even in the morning. He's going to spend the night with his cousin, if he has to. About all the people round here are related. Mr. Varro went over with him of an errand, with Joe and the other dinghy to come back, but he didn't wait to find out anything, so we don't know . . ."

"There are eleven aboard, then," Bill interrupted.

"Twelve," said Angeline. "Now who did I leave out? Oh—Jane. Funny, too; she's about the nicest one. . . ."

"*Jane?*" said Bill quickly. He was sensitive to the name of Jane. His hand went instinctively to the pocket that held the handkerchief. "Jane who?"

"Jane Bridge." Bill lost his enthusiasm then. "She's Mrs. Van Wycke's secretary. Mrs. Van Wycke has a collection of jewels, and Jane Bridge is cataloguing them and writing out a history of each one. She's up in the library—the wheelhouse, they call it—working. You'll be sure to like her. . . ."

Bill Galleon felt no interest whatever in Jane Bridge. But Angeline intrigued him. He saw already that Angeline Tredennick, with the deep well of her curiosity and the clear spouting stream of her talk, could be of advantage to him in his mission. . . . They came round a curve of shore within sight of the shooting party.

"There they are," said Angeline. "That's Mrs. Van Wycke in the middle—the tall one."

The dog Telemachus saw them first. Born of a runaway match between a Russian wolfhound (who was a great lady in her day) and a wild Irish terrier (son of a well-known prize-fighter and a woman of the streets), Telemachus had his mother's height and meager build, her long aristocratic nose, ending surprisingly in the bulldog jaw of his grand-father, the fighter. He came lolloping up to meet them, his one good ear aloft, his tail beating a welcome on his ribs. He planted a pair of tremendous muddy paws in Bill's stomach.

"Hello, feller," Bill said.

"Lemmy! Lemmy!" Beulah cried shrilly. Telemachus was her dog. Awkward and well-meaning and blundering, there was a curious kinship between them. Beulah lavished on the dog the affection that no one else had asked for.

The target was fastened to a pine that stood near the end of the point, and wild shots fell harmlessly offshore. The party was hilarious. Professor Burge, to everyone's astonishment, had proved the best marksman, and the others were rallying him.

"What did you say you taught—psychology or ballistics?"

"I'll bet he leads a double life—probably a gunman in disguise . . ."

Varro fired once just as Bill came up. He was unbelievably awkward. The shot went wide, and Varro dropped the gun—one of a magnificent pair of target revolvers—at Beulah's feet. Beulah was reloading, obviously terrified of the weapons, holding them at arm's length; a miracle, Bill thought, the way she handled them, that they weren't all killed. She finished the one she was doing and passed it to Mrs. Van Wycke.

Christine Van Wycke came forward as soon as she saw Bill. She was, as Angeline had said, stunning. And yet, oddly, her reputation as a beauty was founded on illusion; for Christine Van Wycke was not beautiful. Not beautiful; gorgeous. The thought crossed Bill's mind that she was like her boat: gaudy . . . a bit bedizened . . . wholly desirable. A tall woman, almost as tall as Bill, she moved with a broad compelling grace. A great mane of tawny hair, dead straight, was brushed flat, slick as paint and shining as varnish, framing abrupt, rather large features, a wide mouth with strong white teeth; her long, light-colored eyes, curiously gold-flecked, held insolence—and temptation. She wore a sports dress of an odd metallic green, like the patina on old copper; it emphasized the glory of her hair. Bill noticed the elaborate gold mesh bag on her wrist—incongruous with her costume.

"Shipwrecked?" she repeated. Her voice was full-toned and rich; creamy. "You are welcome. Why didn't you get him some dry things?" she said to Angeline sharply.

Bill met the others then. Ewell Choate was the complete Southerner; Dante Burge, the complete professor; Varro looked like a dancing master, small and neat, a shade too mannerly, a shade too careful in his spotless white, with sideburns and an exquisite little mustache. He fingered it self-consciously.

"D'do," Beulah jerked out. She had an abrupt way of speaking—as if she counted ten and let it fly. *"Lemmy!* Maybe the gentleman doesn't like dogs."

"I'm very fond of dogs," Bill said. "He has such an . . . interesting face, hasn't he?"

Christine Van Wycke laughed unkindly. She tolerated the dog Telemachus, not because she liked dogs, nor because she liked Beulah; because Beulah's unfocused love for her pet made her vulnerable; a blow at Telemachus was a blow across Beulah's raw emotions. At Bill's words an unaccustomed flame of pleasure kindled in Beulah's cheeks; the difficulty with which it came made it somehow shocking. Beulah resembled nothing so much as a figure made from cookie dough: pasty, with two bright black currants for eyes, wisps and strings of coconut for hair. Her plainness made her a perfect foil for Christine's flamboyant good looks. Perhaps that was why Christine liked to keep her, a dependent, half companion and half personal maid, a convenience for the odd jobs that no one wanted to do. She jumped when Christine spoke.

"But how did it *happen?"* Christine was saying.

"How?" said Bill. "Very suddenly. I was rowing along, and all of a sudden I noticed that the boat was gone. It made it bad, because there was nothing to rest the oars on. So I had to leave them there and swim."

Christine laughed appreciatively. She could always appreciate a nice young man.

Bill was nice. "All castaways," he said, "don't have my luck."

"We are lucky too," said Christine sweetly. She was observing that Bill Galleon, for all his impressive bulk, stepped lightly in his wet-stockinged feet, with a precision and economy of motion; that he had the biggest grin and the reddest hair this side of Ireland; that his dark blue eyes were not half so sleepy as you would have said at first blink; that the nick in his eyebrow gave a gamin quality to his expression—ridiculous and endearing with his size. Bill dawned on you slowly . . . but he dawned.

He took the target revolver that Christine still carried, and turned it over in his hands. "Beautiful," he said in honest awe. Christine was pleased. She liked to have her possessions admired. "May I?" he said—and plugged six shots, offhand, into the target. It wouldn't do any harm to let them know he could shoot. "I used to be pretty good," he admitted modestly, in answer to the general acclaim. "I haven't had much practice lately. That was just a fluke." He smiled at Beulah when he handed the weapon back to be reloaded, and was startled at the intensity of feeling—gratitude, pleading, dread; he could not be sure what—that flashed in her small bright eyes.

"I hate to be a nuisance," he was saying apologetically to Christine. "But if I could borrow a boat . . ."

"Oh, but we can't let you go," Christine said quickly. She could always use another personable young man. "We'll find something to amuse you, I promise. At least you must stay till morning, when Mr. Kember is back with the outboard dinghy. There's just the other dinghy now, and it's a long way to row. Besides, that will give us more time to persuade you to stay longer."

"But . . ." said Bill with becoming hesitation. "Really . . ." He laughed down his dripping length. "Do I look like a dinner guest?"

"Ewell Choate can lend you something. He's tall."

"Certainly," said Choate without enthusiasm.

"Come," said Christine. "I won't let you say no. We'll all go back with you to the boat. There's going to be a storm. And anyhow it's almost time to dress for dinner. See—they're taking down the flags. Don't they look pretty?"

It was a tribute to Christine Van Wycke's sheer power that Angeline Tredennick in all this time had not spoken once. She trotted back ahead of the rest of the party to the *Aphrodite*.

Professor Dante Gabriel Burge fell into step on Bill's other side. He was, again as Angeline had said, every bit as odd as his name. A small-featured man, with what could only be called a noble brow: high and broad and finely chiseled, the brow for a Greek god . . . betrayed by an inconsequential chin, half-concealed under a sparse beard; by mouse-colored hair, fine and soft and fuzzy; by close-set eyes that were bright without color, as glass is bright. His body had a forward cant at the hips, as if he were perpetually reaching toward an idea which eluded him. He canted himself suddenly at Bill.

"Tell me," he said without preamble, "what were your sensations as you were sinking?"

"I didn't sink," said Bill definitely. "I swam."

"Shall I call you Bill?" Christine was asking archly. The gold mesh bag on Christine's wrist was cold against his hand.

They filed across the narrow gangplank aboard the *Aphrodite*. A corridor lay before them, bisecting the boat from side to side. Beulah placed the target revolvers on a small table, as if glad to be rid of them.

"Another place," Angeline said to Catriona Cooley, a pretty, bold-eyed little maid with indiscreet black lashes, laying the table in the dining saloon.

"I'll send Toombs to make you comfortable," Christine said to Bill. The dog Telemachus cringed from her voice, and Christine laughed as if it pleased her to be feared.

"If you will come with me," said Ewell Choate, leading the way down a side corridor, "we'll see about clothes."

So Bill stayed.

2

When Bill entered the lounge that night, in Ewell Choate's second-best dinner coat—only slightly too short in the sleeves and too narrow across the shoulders—it was to find the party already assembled. The lounge was a remarkable room, doubly strange aboard a boat: oriental rugs and tapestries, carved Italian tables and sofas cushioned in India prints, Mexican wood painting and pottery from Brittany and colonial pewter; cathedral candles in seven-branched candlesticks, and a fish globe made like a map of the world with continents of silver. It was a hodge-podge of the curious and rare; and yet not utterly incongruous, because the vigor of Christine's personality united and bound it to a whole. Christine was seated, and Beulah was setting a card table before her. The others were clustered round, as if Christine were about to create for them some marvel of legerdemain.

Angeline bustled forward to meet Bill. Her concession to dinner dress was a change from grey silk to grey crêpe, a wider white frill across her shoulders, three inches of soft white throat showing above her best seed-pearl bosom pin. Pearl ear-drops were screwed to the plump lobes of her ears. Her two little round chins quivered to her step.

"I guess you've met everybody, haven't you?" she said. "Or no—there's Jane Bridge. Right over here. . . ."

Jane Bridge was standing apart from the others, her back to the room, staring out the open port at the glowering storm-pricked sea. The strange red animals of the Javanese curtains blew back across her shoulders, and between them a dark head was held high and proud on a slender neck. Her arms were lifted against the window frame, and the unconscious posture showed you the long free lines of her body, so small-boned and finely made; there was in her that beauty of movement, that perfection of quietude, that betrays breeding. She turned when Angeline spoke.

"Why J . . ." Bill burst out—and stopped. It was Jane, his Jane, whose handkerchief lay in his pocket . . . and it was not his Jane at all. It was a strange person named Jane Bridge, with a still, unrecognizing face, and red lips that did not smile, and no welcome in her eyes. She held out a small steady hand—that lay like ice in his.

"How do you do, Mr. Galleon?" she said formally.

"How do you do, Miss . . . Bridge," said Bill.

Angeline watched the meeting with frank curiosity. "I wonder if you've ever met Miss Bridge before?" she asked.

"I don't recall the name," said Bill carefully.

The dog Telemachus pottered up, a broad grin on his face, his tail thumping with waggish humor. Jane covered an awkward moment by pulling his good ear.

"There's a storm coming," she said. Punctiliously polite. No more than that.

"It looks like it," agreed Bill gravely.

Jane made no further attempt at conversation. Bending above the dog, her face was hidden. When he trotted away presently through the door to the after deck, she followed, leaving Bill with Angeline.

"Not very chatty," said Bill uncomfortably.

"I wouldn't mind, if I were you." Angeline was consoling. "Jane's an awfully nice girl, but a little bit . . . reserved. I think she acts as if she had something on her mind. I think . . ."

Angeline's further thoughts were lost in the entrance of Annie Budd, the cook. Annie Budd padded in heavily, her broad flat face, with its spread nostrils and ample mouth, as colorless as the apron she was smoothing over her stomach. She spoke to Christine in a low voice, with a kind of defiant meekness. "That mushroom soup you ordered for Mr. Choate had to go and curdle."

Christine Van Wycke looked up from the card table— just once and then away. But in that moment's glance there was something so merciless and razor-sharp that it was as if it sheared away all Annie Budd's apologies and left her without speech. "If I were you, I wouldn't make too many mistakes," Christine said.

Annie Budd went out again without speaking. She seemed somehow to have shrunk. Bill felt a cold discomfort. He was repelled by Christine's harshness over so trifling a matter. He was hurt and puzzled by Jane. When Angeline bounced away to confer with Annie Budd over the spoiled soup, Bill pretended not to see Christine's beckoning finger, and slipped through the door where Jane had disappeared.

On the after deck dusk had gathered. The furniture was ghostlike in the gloom, holding up the blank faces of its lemon-yellow cushions; the bright awnings cracked on their rods as if struggling to be free. The storm clouds hung heavy in the sky.

Jane Bridge stood against the port rail, facing the open door. Her hands, extended by her sides, were clutching the shining bar. The wind was in her hair. A curly forelock whipped across her eyes, but she did not push it away. It was strangely as if she stood with her back against a wall, without retreat; in the light from the lounge her face looked small and desperate—and brave. She did not move nor speak when Bill came.

Bill walked quickly across the deck and took Jane in his arms. He did it without conscious thought, as if it were the only thing possible to do; for a minute he held her so, still and close, feeling his own heart pounding, sending the hot blood pouring through his veins. Then his lips found hers. Jane's lips were sweet and cool, with a new freshness on them like spring gardens after rain. Her body went backward in his arms; his hand felt the short curls in her neck. The touch stirred him, ringing in his nerve ends, and he gathered her more closely. She neither resisted nor yielded; and yet it was curiously as if she held herself tight, using all her strength to accomplish exactly that— nothing. Her very quiet startled him, so that he raised his head. He saw the wide blankness of her eyes. "Don't," she said in a little broken voice. He let her go then.

"Jane," he said urgently. "Why did you run away? Why . . ."

"It was . . . time to go," said Jane.

"I was crazy. I thought I'd lost you. I couldn't find a trace . . . Jane, what are you doing here, changing your name. . . ."

"It's my own name, whatever you think." Her voice was low. "What are *you* doing? I didn't expect to see you . . . here. I didn't think even you could find us."

The words came short between his teeth, flung away in the wind. "Jane, don't you . . . love me . . . after all?"

"As much as I ever did," she said.

There was bitterness in her voice. Bill winced at the sharp meaning underneath. "But you said . . . you told me . . ."

"Exactly nothing. That was not Jane . . . Bridge. That was Jane Barron. It is over. Let it pass. Forget it ever happened."

"But it did happen. I don't want to forget. . . ."

"It didn't really," she insisted. "We were two different people then—playing a game. The game is over now, and we're ourselves. We might as well admit it."

"I don't know what you mean," Bill cried. "I . . ." He moved again toward her.

Jane stepped back from him, leaning once more against the rail. "Don't," she said wearily. "What's the use? But we can do this for each other still: pretend we never met. It's only fair." Her voice was small, without its natural roundness, drawn flat with the stretched threads of self-control. But when he touched her she began to tremble. She put up her hands against her lips, and a little shaken cry came from them—the first thing she had said without her will. "Oh, Bill, Bill, please go away. *You'll be sorry if you don't.*"

Angeline stuck her head a little farther out the door. Her eyes were two blue circles of amazement. She was to remember Jane's words afterwards. And so was Jane. And Bill.

"Don't you want to come in," she said, "and see Mrs. Van Wycke's jewels?"

3

When Jane and Bill returned to the lounge, Beulah was covering the card table in front of Christine with a black velvet cloth. Her hands shook as she spread it out, and she bumped awkwardly against the edge of the table, so that it nearly fell. Choate righted it neatly.

"You're so clumsy," Christine said. "What will you do next?"

For all the sharpness of the words, Bill was astonished by Beulah's reaction. She sprang away as if Christine had laid violent hands upon her. Her own hands flew upward, fingers spread, in a gesture of guarding herself. "I—I don't know," she said. Her voice was no more than a husky squeak. Professor Burge observed her closely.

But Christine paid no further attention to Beulah. She was undoing the gold mesh bag—the same that Bill had noticed on the beach. It was an unusual bag. Rather large for its type, firmly and intricately woven, it was held about her wrist by a strong band of flexible gold links, closed by an ornamental lock. Christine opened it slowly, enjoying her own deliberation; slowly she took out a jeweled snuff-box. From the box she turned out upon the cloth . . .

Bill whistled.

There must have been half a hundred of the gems, Bill thought, some of them very large, all of them very beautiful; emeralds and pearls and diamonds, star sapphires, topaz . . . fire and ice on the black cloth.

"I'm drunk," said Bill—and broke the tension. "I knew all that sea water would upset me."

"They're real," said Christine, with a startling, child-like pride.

"Real!" said Jane. There was a note of unguarded bitterness in her exclamation. Involuntarily she shuddered. "Jewels scare me," she confessed, apologizing. "People do such terrible things to get them."

"What do you mean?" said Beulah sharply.

"You'd know if you worked on the records," Jane said, turning the matter off. She pointed out a magnificent star sapphire. "Why, if I should tell you the story of that one, it would frighten you half to pieces."

"It doesn't take much to scare Beulah," said Christine, with fortuitous unkindness. "Their histories increase their value."

Beulah slicked her stringy locks nervously behind her ears. She was wearing an apple-green chiffon, obviously a hand-me-down of Christine's; it did shocking things to her complexion. But she did not resent Christine's words. It seemed even, in some subtle way, that Beulah was relieved.

The truth was that the appearance of the gems had set a constraint upon the whole company. It was as if the sight of so much beauty, so much wealth, gathered in a snuff-box, had unnerved them. Perhaps Christine's own attitude was to blame. She sat hunched over the table, her arms spread circle-fashion about her shining hoard; there was a gloating look on her face, as of hunger momentarily appeased; she licked her lips as if the taste of possession were sweet upon them. Her hands closed with a slow, grasping motion. Even Bill was uneasy as his glance went round the group.

Professor Burge was standing beside Beulah. His body was bent toward her, with a suggestion of shielding her— if only from herself. It would have been impossible to say whether his attitude were dictated by pity, or by scientific curiosity . . . for Dante Burge was at once the kindest and most ruthless of men. Painfully interested in people, probing their emotions with as much intuition as science, it had been his cross never to be liked. He might have been different, given friendship. He had been denied friendship, and he was . . . Professor Dante Gabriel Burge, head of the Department of Applied Psychology at Middlewestern. Before him lay the most exciting laboratory specimens that it had been his lot ever to examine.

Ewell Choate moved easily across the room to Jane's side. For the first time Bill noticed him explicitly. The sunny hair, the leaf-brown tender look, the willful wistful smile, the silken voice, the light caress—all the unthinking charm of the Old South, all the beauty that man may have and still remain manly . . . these things were Ewell

Choate's. Christine's smile up at him was pure invitation. Choate's smile back was half acceptance. And yet, even as he smiled, his fingers closed lightly round Jane's arm.

Abruptly Bill did not like it. He remembered something Angeline had said—about Choate and the secretary. He had paid no attention then. Now it was important. He sensed a connection between Jane's manner and the presence of this big young Southerner.

Varro was the only one, perhaps, who appreciated the jewels intrinsically. He himself wore diamond studs, too flashy but very fine; a great square diamond on his little finger. His comments were informed. He pointed out a stone that lay at the other side of the table.

"I would have sworn," he said, "that it was the Shah Truzi emerald. I did not know there was another like it."

"But it is the Truzi emerald," Christine cried, with her air of candid pride.

"It was found in a dead man's hand," said Jane somberly.

It was Bill again who created a diversion. He walked over to the table. His big figure, in the too-tight clothes, was saved from being ridiculous by the very unpretentiousness of his long stride. He picked up a great ruby.

"That's a splendid thing," he said—and turned it over in his palm. The jewel was set in a thin frame of platinum, with a loop to hold a chain; he could not see the back plainly. Two or three of the others were similarly set, but most of them were unmounted. It was not in wearing jewels that Christine Van Wycke found pleasure; it was in bare possession. She was restive while Bill held the gem; he saw that she did not like to have her treasure touched. He laid the ruby down.

"What's the story of that one?" Ewell Choate asked.

Christine's long light eyes moved over Choate in speculation. "I don't know. Why?"

"Mine looks like it," Choate said. "The one I came about. They'd make a good pair of earrings."

Christine was suddenly too eager; there was avidity in the set of her mouth. "We must compare them. It will be exciting."

"Very exciting," Choate agreed. Behind his back his fingers still held Jane's.

"I think you're crazy to keep them down here," Beulah burst out in her explosive way. She looked instantly as if she wished she had not spoken.

Christine smiled provokingly. "And why not here?" she wanted to know. "It's far safer than the city. There's no one else on the island. It's no fun to own jewels," she explained to the others, "if you keep them in safety deposit. I want them near where I can . . . feel them." There was something not quite healthy in the way her fingers crooked over her precious store. It made them all uncomfortable again.

"Why don't you wear one tonight?" Ewell Choate suggested with his ready tact.

Christine hesitated. "If *you* would like it," she agreed finally. Her manner made of it a personal, an intimate thing between them. "The emerald?"

"Too cold," said Choate definitely. "The ruby." He added: "Most women cannot wear rubies. They lack the inherent fire."

Christine glowed under the skillful flattery. "A chain," she commanded Beulah.

Beulah darted out and brought a thin chain of platinum. She was more breathless than the short errand demanded.

Christine threaded the chain through the loop on the ruby, and held it out to Choate. "You may fasten it round my neck," she said. Her air was that of a queen, rewarding a faithful subject. Yet there was no absurdity in it. Christine Van Wycke was above absurdities. Ewell Choate gave a little bow as he received the jewel from her hands. The gesture held no irony. It was a recognition of Christine's quality; of his own privilege. He made a graceful ceremony of clasping the chain round Christine's full white throat.

Jane turned away abruptly, and went to stand again at the port where Bill had first found her. She did not like the incident; he could see that. Bill's fists clenched in his pockets. He was upset because Jane cared.

"Dinner is served, Madam," announced Toombs, stiffer than any statue in the doorway.

Christine Van Wycke locked away the jewels and stood up. She was a splendid figure, in ivory satin, close-cut to noble lines, with the smoke and fire of her tawny hair, and the sparks in her gloating eyes; the ruby lay magnificent on her breast, round and full, a-quiver to her breath and the reflected lights, like a drop of blood, brimming and trembling to fall. She led the way to the dining saloon.

"Like a parade," Angeline said cheerfully.

She could not know—who could?—that it was the last time they should all walk together.

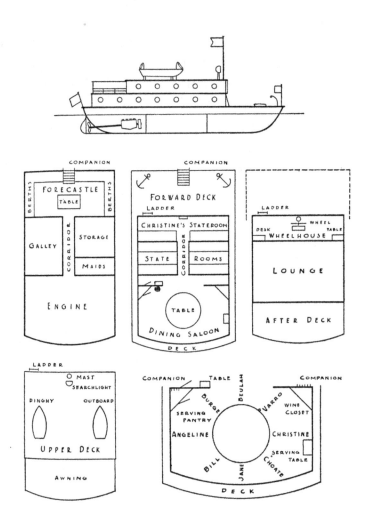

TWO

The *Aphrodite's* dining saloon was in the stern, square-built for space, with high portholes round three sides; the fourth side opened into the main corridor—a wide arch with no door. It was a very different room from the lounge: by day the cool sea-green of the walls, blending into the green of the sea, the simplicity of furnishing, gave an illusion of size. There were only the round table with its eight chairs, a small serving table. The cream and green chintz of the curtains bore a fancy of fishes and tropic islands. Toombs drew them across the open ports.

In the starboard corner of the dining saloon, next the corridor, was a wine closet, capable of being converted, by folding back the doors, into a small bar; in the corresponding corner, to port, a serving pantry was connected by a dumb waiter, as well as by a companionway, with the galley below. A door also led from the pantry into the main corridor. This corridor cut right across the boat, giving at each end amidships onto a narrow-railed deck, not more than three feet wide, extending round the after part of the boat and roofed by the after deck; to starboard was the gangway to the shore. Opposite the door of the dining saloon a side corridor branched forward, bisecting the midships section. The staterooms opened here on either side; Christine's was at the end, double the size of the others, occupying the boat's full width; the ports,

where the ruffled taffeta curtains had caught Bill's attention at his first approach, looked out on the forward deck.
In the middle of this deck a companionway with ladder
and booby hatch connected with the forecastle; a second
ladder led upward to the wheelhouse. The wheelhouse was,
roughly, over Christine's stateroom; the lounge over the
other staterooms and the corridors; the after deck over
the dining saloon. From the lounge, on the starboard side,
another companionway led down to the main corridor,
ending just outside the saloon door. Down this companionway now swept Christine with her party. The drums of
distant thunder ruffled a tune.

Christine took her place at the head of the table, with
Angeline at the foot. Varro, somewhat to Bill's surprise,
was at Christine's right hand, Ewell Choate on her left.
Next to Varro was Beulah Mullins, then Professor Burge,
then Angeline. Jane was on Ewell Choate's other side, then
Bill, then Angeline again.

Ewell Choate, forestalling Varro, seated Christine with
the same exaggerated courtliness with which he had fastened the ruby round her throat. Bill was quick with Jane's
chair, and she smiled as she moved forward. There was
something refreshing always in Jane's movement—like a
clean wind, vigorous and free, blowing life clear of com-
plications. But the smile was not right. It was too bright,
too fixed, too unamused; a smile drawn in scarlet lipstick
with a very steady hand. This was not the Jane Bill had
loved—and lost—one night beside a river. Not the desperate brave Jane of the after deck. This was a Jane gay, formal, untouchable, smiling at him out of an impenetrable
reserve. But it was Jane. The very untouched loveliness of
Jane set up in Bill a queer inward trembling.

Jane was not, exactly, beautiful; and yet one had the
feeling that beauty lurked behind her features, like a fire
laid, waiting to be kindled. The mouth was generous,
shaped wide for mirth, too sensitive to be spared pain.
The eyes were deep blue and very clear; they looked black

under tilted fringes. Her dark hair was brushed upward and backward, pinned tight away from her ears; from crown to nape the short ends tumbled out in witch curls that matched the curly forelock. The quaint mode of hair-dressing suited her; the quaint dress: against the shining brilliance of Christine's satin, Beulah's sick green and yellow, the pretty fussiness of Angeline, starkly simple. Black linen, cut low and straight, so that the hemstitched band which finished it made a shallow curve across her breast and arms and left the tips of her shoulders bare; the bodice tight, with a basque-like point, and below the skirt swelling and blooming like a black bell-flower to a glimpse of black linen slippers. . . . There was more gold in her skin than rose.

Bill, looking down on those bare shoulders, faintly golden under the lights, had an impression that they were very, very tired. Not because they drooped. Rather they were too rigidly erect, as if they would not have known how to bend without breaking.

Bill slipped into the chair beside hers. "You're tired," he said. "You've been working too hard."

"You have no tact," Jane said pleasantly. "You have no subtlety." She bent on him again that dazzling, formal smile, and turned abruptly to Ewell Choate on her other side.

There, Bill thought with sudden clean detachment, were tact and subtlety. Ewell Choate was devoting himself to Christine, attentive and charming; and yet he had time for a word to Jane—too quick a word to give Christine offence, too intimately low to be less than a word of endearment. Bill had again, more sharply, the impression that had come to him in the lounge; that there was more between Jane and Choate than a light flirtatious interlude—some perfection of understanding that lay deeper than the moment.

They were alike, Bill thought suddenly: they had some inner poise, some common graciousness of manner, as if

they might have fitted the same background and cared for
the same books. Jane was of the South too—he had known
that always from the warmth of her voice, that tilt in the
end of a sentence that no Northern tongue can master.
Perhaps that was it, then. They belonged together. And
he—where did he belong? A great blundering insurance
fellow, on a fool's errand about a ruby. He felt big and
uncertain. His uncertainty betrayed him.

"Jane," he said, calling her back by a touch on her arm.
"Jane, talk to me."

She lifted to him again that bright, impassive face.
"Talk?" she said. "Why of course." He did not know what
he had expected: not this uncompromising gaiety, not this
brittle veneer of small talk that turned his seriousness
back upon him and left him floundering. "You are going
to spend the night, Mrs. Van Wycke tells me. How very
pleasant! You must get her to show you over the boat.
The library where I work is well worth seeing. All the
books are rare editions. Mrs. Van Wycke's first husband
collected them. Jerome Grosvenor. He was very rich. Of
course it isn't a library really; it's the wheelhouse and the
chart room. It gives me a fine large feeling to be up there
alone, with the wheel and the binnacle and the charts in
the locker drawers . . . as if I were the captain bold and
the bo'sun tight and the midshipmite and everything. The
foreward bulkhead is all windows, so it makes the sky seem
nearer than the world. When we are under way, the men
stand tricks at the wheel there. They're rather sweet, really. Though you can see they have a hard time to keep their
faces straight when we're trying to be nautical and getting
our words all wrong. Mr. Kember is a dear uncle-y sort of
man. Joe and Charlie put up their pipes when they steer,
and stand there with their legs spread out, looking about
eight feet tall and growing all red behind the ears. . . ."

"Don't, Jane," Bill said unhappily.

"Don't what?"

"Talk. Like that."

"I thought you wanted me to talk. English is the only language I speak. Just a little boarding-school French: *C'est le livre de ma tante,* and things like that. . . ."

"You know what I mean," Bill said. "I wanted to talk . . . about something. About us."

"Us?" said Jane brightly. "How could we? What would there be to say?" She dropped her voice. "Please, Bill."

But Bill was stubborn. "What makes you act like this?" he demanded. And added, upon a growing suspicion: "Who is this Choate fellow, anyway? Is it because of him?"

"It's because of . . . everything," Jane said.

"I don't know what you mean," Bill insisted. "Where does he come into it? What has he to do with you? I . . . loved you first. Or didn't I?"

Bill was startled then. He had broken Jane's calm at last. Just for an instant the bright mask that she held up so proudly was all twisted; the painted smile awry. Her eyes were two black holes torn in laughter that looked into a wrenched spirit underneath. "Don't be mean, Bill," she said. Her voice, strangely with her words, was light and inconsequential. Then the mask was in place again, and she was laughing. "Ewell—Mr. Galleon wants to know who you are."

Choate's manner was as offhand as hers. "I?" he said. "I'm the Pretender to the Austrian throne. I thought everybody knew." It was all passed by on an easy round of laughter. But in the level look Choate gave him, Bill sensed a deep antagonism.

Bill stabbed a spoon into what he believed was soup. "Hang the feller!" he muttered. "He gives me a pain." And knew at once that he had been careless: Angeline was watching him.

Angeline was chewing bread sticks with a slow, contented fervor—and obviously trying to overhear. Bill considered, too late, how much she had overheard already. "A pain?" she said. "Dyspepsia, maybe. I've got some splendid dyspepsia tablets. You dissolve two in hot water. . . ."

She was interrupted by Beulah Mullins, straining toward Bill from across the table, a look akin to terror on her face. "Oh *don't!*" she begged him. "Don't have a pain. *Please* don't."

Bill shrugged. "All right," he said, humoring her. Professor Burge laid a hand on Beulah's arm. His touch gave her something new to think about; she clutched with swift, incredulous eagerness at his fingers. "What's the matter with *her?*" Bill asked impatiently of Angeline.

Angeline reached for another bread stick. "I wonder," she said thoughtfully. "She does act awfully nervous, doesn't she? I'll see if I can find out. . . ."

Bill's glance passed to the others. After all, he must not forget what he came for, just because Jane was here. Christine dominated the table. She was telling with a crude, compelling gusto the bloody story of the Shah Truzi emerald. Varro listened without comment, nodding now and then. Under his perfunctory attention he seemed preoccupied—perhaps with his table manners. There was something over-fastidious about Varro: the crook of his little finger as he lifted a fork, a too-nice care with his napkin. Seen in repose, his face was unprepossessing. The features were meager. It struck Bill that they were all set a trifle crooked: as if his face had been made in two sections and fitted together not quite true. It lifted one corner of his mouth, a nostril and an eyebrow, to a faint perpetual sneer.

Choate hung on Christine's words, spurring her with eager questions. His eyes hardly left her face. Jane bent her dark head above her plate. She did not like the story, nor Choate's absorption in it. Bill saw that she was not eating.

Directly opposite, Professor Dante Gabriel Burge saw it too. He saw everything. The materials of his human laboratory were spread before him, and he missed no least cadence of a voice, no least flicker of a passing mood. His curved fingers rested lightly on the table edge; they moved a little, like fingers on a ouija board. It was a characteristic gesture.

Afterwards they all agreed that it was Dante Burge who was responsible for the crisis.

It was a remark by Choate, however, that set the thing going. Christine had finished her story. "The other emerald . . ." he began.

"There isn't another," Christine corrected him. "Just the Truzi. I never found another to equal it. There is no pleasure in acquiring a stone less perfect than one you have. You must have been thinking of the pearls. There is a matched pair."

Ewell Choate shook his head. "Not the pearls." He said: "Have you more than one ruby?"

"Not yet," said Christine coyly. Her fingers played with the gem about her throat. "I hope to add yours to the collection, if it is as perfect as you say. Then I shall have a pair of rubies too."

It seemed a matter of no moment. But Professor Burge, the psychologist always, picked up the scrap of talk between them, giving it importance. "I cannot help being interested in your discussion," he explained, "because it shows how unreliable evidence may be. I venture to suggest that of the eight people gathered here, no one except Mrs. Van Wycke and myself could state accurately the number of gems which were shown us before dinner, nor give their names correctly."

"There must have been fifty," Bill guessed.

"Half that," said Varro.

"Twice that," said Ewell Choate.

Jane lifted her head. "Oh, but that isn't fair," she said. "Some of us had seen the jewels before. Some not. I could name them all, of course; I've been working on the list."

"It is the principle," Burge told her, "and not the specific instance, which is significant. In general I can formulate this axiom: Give me six honest witnesses, and I will give you back six totally different stories."

Christine took up the argument. "I think you exaggerate," she said decidedly. "Surely any normal person . . ."

"But there are no normal persons," Burge assured her. "The normal person is an illusion, like the average man; he is a composite of what we all think we are."

"I guess we're a pretty normal lot here," Bill remarked. He looked himself almost abnormally normal.

"Oh, no," said Burge positively. "Perhaps you have not noticed it. But there is an abnormal amount of fear and jealousy and anger seated round this table; there is one obsession, certainly, probably two; there is a split personality, at least three complexes, a dangerous inhibition. . . ."

"My goodness!" cried Angeline. "You make us sound like an insane asylum."

Burge leaned across the table toward Jane. He said a strange thing, softly. "Why are you afraid?" he said. "You are too young and pretty to be so frightened."

Jane met his look composedly. "I do not understand you," she said. Her face did not change by the least flicker of an eyelash. But Bill saw her straight back stiffen.

A silver spoon bent under Bill's fingers. But Christine did not notice. She came back to the original issue. "I still think you make people out worse than they are. I don't believe *we'd* tell different stories about the same thing."

"If you like," Burge said, "I will prove it."

2

"My suggestion," Burge was saying, "is this. I will leave the room presently to make a few simple preparations. I will then return and perform a series of actions, which you are to observe closely. As soon as I have finished what I came to do, I will again withdraw. Pencils and paper will be distributed, and you will each record, without consultation with any of the others, every detail which you observed during the entire period while I was in the room. These should include not only my actions, but my appearance, manner, remarks if any, etc., together with the comments and reactions of other members of the party, the time consumed, and such other items as may have presented themselves to your attention. A fixed interval will be allowed for the preparation of these lists—say fifteen minutes; they will then be signed, and I will myself collect and judge them. Judgment will be based on three points: the number of facts accurately given, the number omitted, and the number of false statements."

"You're wonderful," Christine cried. "Simply wonderful, Dante. It will be no end of fun. Didn't I tell you, Bill, that we should find something to amuse you?"

"Er—yes," said Bill hastily. "Yes, indeed." He muttered something to Angeline about a giddy garden goat.

Frankly, Bill did not like it. He could not have said just why. Perhaps it was the cold science in Dante Burge's eyes. Perhaps . . . it was Jane's hands.

Jane had nice hands, slim and steady, a little, faintly, browned. They were lying quiet in her lap. But in those still hands of Jane's Bill sensed the same conscious quietude, the same rigidity, that he had seen in her unbending shoulders. "I was never good at parlor games," she said.

"Well, I *do* think," said Angeline, "that you might have waited till we finished dinner." She beckoned Toombs back with more crackers and cheese.

"Anything *you* like," Ewell Choate was saying gallantly to Christine.

Varro shrugged noncommittally. Beulah had not spoken.

"Then it is settled, is it not?" said Dante Burge. "I will leave you now. Be on the watch. I might add that you have the advantage, in this test, of being prepared; most evidence is required without warning." He passed down the side corridor and entered his own stateroom.

As soon as Burge was gone, Ewell Choate made a further suggestion. "I'll tell you what," he said. "Let's play a trick on the old boy. Let's agree on some perfectly fool thing, and when we make out our lists, we'll all put it in. If it's in all of them, he'll have a time proving he didn't do it."

"Clever!" Christine applauded. She patted Choate's wrist fondly. "That will make it twice as exciting. What shall we say he did?"

"Something silly," Choate said, "that will be bound to embarrass him. After all, he's trying to embarrass us."

Bill was a little surprised at Choate's prankishness. But the idea appealed to the bright thread of cruelty that ran in Christine's nature. "We might say he had kissed Beulah," she suggested heartlessly, "and we all heard the smack."

"I don't call that silly," Bill said shortly. He was rewarded again by one of those brilliant flashes from Beulah's eyes, of gratitude . . . or dread. Her hand rested on the head of the dog Telemachus, lolling against her knee.

Christine was not pleased with Bill's championship. She passed the incident by. "Or," she said, "we could say he had snatched one of Angeline's false curls for a keepsake."

"They're natural," said Angeline sharply. She grew very pink, choking a little on a cracker. "All I have to do is wet a comb. . . ."

"Of course it is," said Jane soothingly. "I've seen you do it no end of times."

Toombs brought Angeline a glass of water, and stalked down the table length to refill Christine's wineglass. Toombs was so erect that he bent a trifle, rearwards. His large plain face had a barren look, the lightness of brows and lashes contributing to the absence of expression. He had no tolerance for this child's play.

"We'll have to hurry," Varro reminded them.

"Maybe," said Ewell Choate, hesitating, "if we pretended he'd taken something. . . ."

"I've got it," cried Christine. "I'll jump up and scream, and say he's stolen my bag. And *you* all say . . ."

Before she could finish, Burge returned. He was, after all, right there before they saw him.

Bill heard Jane draw in her breath sharply.

Professor Dante Gabriel Burge presented an appearance almost unbelievably grotesque. He was dressed in pajama trousers of a bright magenta, a green turtle-necked sweater, a coat with tails. He had borrowed someone's rouge and brightened his nose. He had blacked out a front tooth. He wore rubber boots, pigskin gloves, a Panama hat, and a pink Angora scarf; he carried a spread umbrella. He stood for an instant inside the door, surveying the company.

The room rocked with mirth. Even Bill laughed. Even Beulah. Even Angeline laid down her knife. Even Toombs paused, decanter in hand, to wipe away a curve of lip not quite seemly in a butler. Christine clapped her hands. "Dante, you're too simply superb. I adore you. I'll never forget you to my dying day. . . ."

Burge did not even smile. Bill saw suddenly that to Professor Dante Gabriel Burge there was nothing funny about it. It was . . . an experiment.

Burge lowered the umbrella and went over to the wine closet. He took down several bottles, examining each in turn; finally he poured himself a drink, tossed it off, wiped his lips on an embroidered guest towel that he drew from his pocket, hung his umbrella on a hook, walked across the open doorway, tying his muffler as he went, and . . . snapped off the lights. The switch controlled all the lights on that level except the staterooms; the darkness was complete.

"Oh, *not* in the dark!" Jane begged. Her voice was hardly more than a whisper—lost instantly in the murmur of pleasurable apprehension that unexpected darkness always brings. Beulah squeaked like a cornered mouse. "My goodness!" Angeline exclaimed, provoked. "Why couldn't you wait till I was ready?" Bill could hear her fumbling for her knife.

The gust of exclamation died away, and at once there descended on the silent room that lack of balance, of focus, that comes with darkness. One does not realize, till it is withdrawn, how much of his interpretation of life depends on sight. Without sight, sound becomes generalized; lacking meaning, it loses direction. There is a sense of unseen

presence, of impending touch. Far off the muffled roll
of thunder still further confused the moment, blurring
small sounds. The distant lightning winked against drawn
curtains, too faint for illumination. Bill's eyes smarted
from widening them against the solid dark. His ears were
strained with listening. He sat so tense that all at once his
muscles ached.

In that darkness, Dante Burge was moving. He walked
clumsily in his rubber boots. Bill thought he walked once
all round the table; yet he could not precisely follow his
movements. Then he stopped. He must be somewhere near
the head of the table, at Bill's right. Just about behind
Christine. . . .

The moments dragged insufferably. There are few things
harder to bear than waiting. A rustle of nervous movement
ran about, a half-hysterical titter from Beulah; it passed,
and the room was still again, and the distant thunder muttered, and the lightning winked, and Dante Burge did not
move. Bill tried to count the seconds, remembering the
estimate of time he was to make; he counted too fast, and
was aware of it, and stopped to divide by two, and lost
track altogether. The darkness burned on his eyeballs.

Suddenly Dante Burge was moving again. He was moving fast—running. There was a sound of bodies in colli-
sion. The slosh of wine in a shaken decanter.

"Uh!" Toombs' voice came explosively. At once, the
perfect butler always, he added: "I beg your pardon, sir,
I'm sure."

Dante Burge recoiled from the impact; Bill could hear
the thud of his boot heels on the bare floor at the edge of
the rug, irregular, as if he had barely saved himself from
falling. Immediately there was a second crash. He must
have staggered backward, Bill thought, right into the serving table placed against the bulkhead to starboard. The
silver fruit dish clattered. A ripe peach squished sicken-
ingly on the floor.

Bill recognized next the tiny scratch and rattle of claws on polished boards; a snuffling, as the dog Telemachus investigated the peach. Dante Burge moved again, and a yelp announced a trodden tail. Telemachus scuttled away, whimpering. *"Here,* Lemmy!"

Then it was still once more. And yet—not quite still either. There was a sound of footsteps, very soft, as if Dante Burge walked on tiptoe now and was at pains to hide his whereabouts. He was coming down Bill's side of the table. . . . He had had time to reach him. . . . He must be just behind. . . . In spite of himself the back of Bill's neck prickled.

Bill turned in his chair, staring over his shoulder—and could see nothing. The room was full of lurking shadows. A board creaked. Bill's eyes felt bursting; colored lights floated before them without substance. He could hear the blood pounding in his ears.

Bill was right. Dante Burge must have been behind him. For it was from behind him, but farther back in the stern, that the revolver spoke.

Several shots were fired—fairly close together, yet at ir-regular intervals. In that enclosed space, the reverberations seemed to shake the *Aphrodite* to her mooring lines. The spit of fire was in Bill's face; it came irregularly too—from the left, from the right . . . as if Dante Burge were running in circles like a madman and firing as he went. Maybe he *was* a madman. Maybe . . . The room was filled with the reek of powder. Somebody gave a frightened squeak; that must be Beulah. "My goodness!" cried Angeline in a muf-fled voice—and clutched at Bill's knee.

Bill whirled toward her at the touch. As he turned, a flash of lightning, brighter than the others, wiped a smear of light across the blank page of the dark—instantly gone. In that less than moment's space, Angeline's round pink face, her round astonished eyes, sprang at Bill out of noth-ing—and disappeared; with the foolish particularity that tension brings, he noticed that she was still eating crackers and cheese.

Bill's first conscious thought was for Jane. It was like Jane not to cry out at the shots. But she would be terrified. He stretched a reassuring hand. . . .

Bill's hand fell on cold and polished wood. Jane's chair was empty. *Jane was gone.*

The crash of revolver fire behind him seemed no louder than the crash of realization in Bill's mind.

It was at this supremely artistic moment that Christine Van Wycke screamed. She sprang up . . . and her chair smashed over behind her . . . and she screamed. "Stop!" she cried, with every seeming of frantic protest. "My bag. . . ." The scream rose, shattering, agonized, above the crack of the final shot. It was too horribly realistic.

"Say, she's good!" Varro remarked to Beulah, on a note of admiration. The fellow had steady nerves.

"You'd almost think . . ." began Angeline.

Christine's scream trailed off in a choking gurgle, bubbling into silence. There was a sound of something falling. . .

"The lights, Toombs!" Bill cried—and sprang for the switch himself. "Jane. . . ."

The switch was just inside the corridor door—between that and the pantry; Bill remembered seeing Dante Burge snap it off. He plunged toward it with both arms extended.

Fumbling and groping in the unfamiliar room, Bill Galleon ran hard into some person in desperate haste. He heard a faint outrush of held breath. Something thudded on the rug. He clutched at the dark before him, and the thing his fingers found was shocking; soft and faintly fuzzy, as if it were covered with short fine hair or down. At once it was wrenched away. Bill clutched again, and his hand closed on nothing. A breeze went by him, and he knew he was alone.

For just an instant, Bill stood still. Bill Galleon was a brave man. But in that instant he knew the feeling of cold fear. . . . Then his hand found the switch.

Christine Van Wycke lay fallen forward across the table. It was Varro who sprang to raise her—Varro suddenly cool and deft, his mannerisms discarded. Her head tipped backward across his arm.

On Christine's breast the color of the ruby swelled and gleamed. The ruby drop ran down slowly.

THREE

"She's dead," said Varro.

In the stricken silence that followed his words, they could hear the heavy footsteps of Annie Budd pounding up the companionway from the galley. Before she had time to reach the top, the swing door into the serving pantry flew open, and Catriona Cooley burst in. Catriona was a cocky young thing, pretty in a rather common way; but for once her rosy cheeks were pale, her pert black eyes emptied of their pertness. She cast one look at the grim spectacle of Christine Van Wycke, and with a cry that was half a sob and half a scream, flung herself upon the stately Toombs. She locked her hands about his unbending neck, and burrowed her snub nose in his lordly shirt front.

"*Gus!*" she cried. "Don't let her look at me like that! I wasn't even in here, was I, Gus?"

"Sh-h!" said Augustus Toombs austerely. It would have been hard to say whether the look of restrained horror on his long bare face was at the bad taste of his mistress in being shot at her own dinner table, or at the unseemly public manners of Catriona.

Ewell Choate sprang at once to Varro's assistance. Christine was a big woman, and Varro supported her weight with difficulty as it sagged against him; Choate put his hands under her knees, and they eased her body backward to the floor. Her head rolled a little. It came to rest on the great knot of tawny hair in her neck.

Immediately behind Catriona, Annie Budd in her turn flung back the pantry door. At the same instant there was the sound of running feet overhead, and Joe and Charlie swung themselves down the companionway from the lounge, and skidded to a stop under the corridor arch; the sight that met them rocked them back as abruptly on their heels as if they had collided with a physical barrier.

"Gosh!" Charlie muttered. "Look what they done now!"

Annie Budd for a moment stood still too, her bulk filling the whole space between the pantry door-jambs. She was red-faced and panting with her haste; her bulging eyes rolled like two prunes in a dish of cooked cereal. A crocheted bedspread was caught up under her arm, with the long wooden crochet-hook, still through the loop where she had been working, stuck into the ball of cotton in her hand. "Merciful heavens!" she gasped. "What's going on here?"

"She's dead," said Toombs in a hollow voice over Catriona's head.

"She's dead!" Joe repeated, and nudged Charlie. They stood, jaw-dropped and staring.

Annie Budd let the door flap shut behind her. She paddled past the table to the place at its head where Christine Van Wycke lay. A corner of the bed-cover dragged, getting under her feet. She stood looking down at her late mistress.

"God have mercy on her soul," she said. "She surely needs it."

She had not been a good mistress. But she was dead. Annie Budd was genuinely moved. She pulled back the chair that Ewell Choate had left, and sank into it, breathing hard, the quilt clutched up to her broad bosom. "How come she to get killed?" she said.

No one answered. Annie Budd's question was like a blast of icy air in their faces.

Bill's hand dropped from the switch. He did not know that he still held it there. It had all happened too quickly.

In the turmoil of sensation he was conscious at the moment of only two things. Christine Van Wycke was dead. And . . . Jane had been in her place when the lights came on.

Bill was sure of that. She had been half-standing, her hands on the table edge. As if she had risen when Christine screamed. Or as if . . . she were just sitting down. She sank slowly into her chair as the switch clicked. Her hands still gripped the table edge, holding it hard, as if it were needful to keep it steady. Her finger-tips were pressed white below the nails. Her face was white too, and very still. It seemed drained as empty of expression as of color. She moved when Annie Budd spoke. She took her hands off the table, rubbing them frantically together.

The others were all in their places too. Varro and Beulah and Angeline and Choate; Toombs in his accustomed station near the pantry door; all except Bill himself, beside the switch, and Dante Burge in the stern. Beulah burst into wild weeping, flinging her arms out on the table amid the clatter of dishes, burying her head in the angle of bony elbows. The dog Telemachus nuzzled her knee, whimpering in trouble and uncertainty.

Angeline let out a held breath with a little explosive pop. She bobbed up from her place and trotted round the table. "Here let me. . . . Maybe she isn't . . ."

Angeline was handy about sickness and . . . things like that. She knelt beside Christine's still form, feeling the wrist for the pulse she did not find, stroking back the hair from the white brow. "Bring me some water. . . . Get some wine. . . . Toombs, let me take your coat to put under her head. . . ."

Toombs extricated himself firmly from Catriona's clasp, and with a look of deep disapprobation removed his coat. He folded it neatly and slipped it under the head that Angeline lifted up. Toombs' coat was well padded; without it he was revealed as a high-shouldered, narrow-chested man with lean arms. There was something scandalous about Toombs in his shirt sleeves. One did not imagine

Toombs undressed. One thought of him sleeping, if he
slept at all, erect in a corner like a tailor's dummy, with
his trousers well in crease. He fetched a decanter and a
glass and poured a small measure of wine. Angeline tried,
without success, to force it between Christine's lips. She
set it aside then. Ewell Choate handed her a glass of water
from the table, and she bathed Christine's head. The diamond drops ran down beside her ears.

"Give it up," Varro said. "She's dead, I tell you." He
lighted a cigarette. The snap of the match made everybody
jump.

The others gathered in a hushed group, watching
Angeline's efforts. Only Joe and Charlie held back, uncertain in a situation so far outside their experience that they
had no wit to meet it; only they—and Professor Burge.
Burge remained by the stern ports where the lights had
found him, his motley apparel suddenly horrible, the
smoking gun hanging in his hand. He wore a curious look
of frustration and chagrin—as if, even in the face of death,
he could spare a regret that his experiment was spoiled.
There would be no lists now, no careful tabulations. "A
great pity!" he muttered.

Even so soon it occurred to Bill to question with how
much foresight a psychologist could control his own de-
meanor.

Psychologically speaking, however, the day was not
lost for Professor Burge. No more fruitful material can be
spread before the scientist's eye than the faces of eleven
human beings in the presence of violent death. After the
first quick glance, Burge did not look toward Christine
again. Christine, dead, held for him no further interest.
Her mind, her reactions, obsessions, coordinations, all her
fascinating abnormalities, were dead with her body. While
the others gazed at her dead face, Dante Burge was scanning the living faces round him.

So, for that matter, was Bill.

Varro was by all odds the most composed of the group. The hand that held the cigarette did not tremble; his voice, when he spoke to Angeline, was controlled. To most men the spectacle of sudden death will prove in some wise moving—unless indeed he is habited to sudden death. Yet for all his composure, the tragedy had wrought a certain change in Varro. He had cast aside his over-niceness of manner; he seemed more alert, more sure of himself, as if his faculties functioned best in an emergency. His eyes were bright and watchful under lowered lids. He smoothed his small mustache with a bent knuckle, his hand hiding his mouth. The mouth, next to the eyes, is the most betraying feature.

Ewell Choate reacted very differently. He was obviously distraught. It did not escape Bill that when he straightened after helping Varro lay Christine down, he was breathing heavily—as if from great exertion, or from an effort at self-control. Could Christine be so heavy? Choate's face had gone an ugly mottled red, so that his fair good looks were momentarily lost. That deep flush puzzled Bill. It was more the color of anger than of shock. Choate shook his shoulders, stepping back, as if he were shaking off . . . a thought. His look went instantly to Jane. As instantly away. Jane was still at the table then.

Beulah stood away from the others, constantly pressing a little forward, constantly shrinking a little back. She was still crying, her hands held across her face as if she could not bear to see Christine, her fingers spread as if she felt a compulsion to look. Christine Van Wycke had controlled and ordered Beulah. Without her, she was indecisive. For the moment she was even unmindful of the dog Telemachus, cowering against her ankles, sniffing the odor of death. The hair rippled along the dog's spine. He lifted his head, thrusting it forward, a low moaning rising in his throat.

Varro noticed it first. "Here," he said sharply. "Get out of here." He took the dog by the collar, pulling him toward

the door. But Telemachus dropped his haunches and spread
his legs with the complete immobility of a determined dog
who distrusts his captor. "Put him out," Varro said to Beulah. "The next thing we'll have him howling."

Beulah, accustomed to obedience, obeyed. "Come,
Lemmy," she said. Telemachus followed her to the hall
door, dragging his rear abjectly. "Run along. That's a good
dog." She gestured him away, and Joe helped him with a
friendly push. Telemachus slunk down the corridor, tail
low, with a reproachful look over his shoulder.

Bill became aware then for the first time of the deck-
hands, Joe and Charlie. He had not really seen them before: a glimpse of tousled head vanishing down the hatch
as he came aboard, a pair of long legs straddling up the
ladder to the upper deck—that was all. Now he saw two
big, raw-boned young men in dungarees, with strong red
hands hanging uneasily at their sides—completely different, those two, and yet oddly similar. Their hair, originally one of the indefinite browns native to the region, was
sun-scorched and wind-scorched to a shade lighter than
the smooth fawn leather of their skins. Their eyes were as
clear and grey as rain. But they both wore already those
straight marks between the brows that come with squinting against sun; that well-closed look about the mouth
of those whose pipes are their chief confidants. Joe's was
the heavier face, with more breadth in the jaw and less in
the forehead. There was more endurance in that face, and
more patience, and more plodding. Charlie's face was more
sensitive, with high, strongly marked cheek-bones and a
long thin nose. There was humor under his noncommit-
tal look, and shyness and will and temper. When he was
Cephus Kember's age, he would be a sailing master too,
taking parties of summer people out "yachting," treating
them with a kindly tolerance, noting their foibles without
comment, accepting their inept orders with a grave nod
. . . and doing exactly as he pleased about carrying them
out. But Joe would still be a deck-hand, and a good one;

dependable without imagination. Charlie was the first to redden under Bill's frank stare.

"What did you hear?" Bill said. "Where were you?"

"*Her* screaming was what brought us," Charlie said. He jerked his head sidewise at Christine. "We was on the upper deck. It was Joe's watch. But I went up to have a pipe with him after supper."

Bill nodded. "Stick around, will you?" he said. They lingered just outside the door, and Bill turned back to Jane.

Jane was the last to leave the table. She pushed herself stay to her feet, as if she could hardly trust her knees to bear her weight. It hurt Bill terribly to watch her.

She walked with her head carefully high and her wide eyes staring straight ahead—like one who walks a narrow ledge and does not dare look down for fear the height will make him dizzy. Bill saw that her breath came short and quick between clenched teeth. It sharpened poignantly the delicate bony structure of her face, pointed a desperately steady chin. She stopped short when she saw Christine. Ewell Choate sprang forward. He put his arm about her.

"Don't look, Jane," he said. "Don't think about it. It can't be helped now. . . ." But for once Jane made no response. She stood taut in the circle of his arm, not yielding by an inch. He tried to draw her closer, soothing her with soft words, his voice no more than a murmur. "Jane, honey. Don't take it so hard. I'm here. I'll look after you. . . ."

And with that she pulled herself away in a kind of unreasoning panic. "Don't *touch* me," she said. Her voice held such a still intensity that Choate, startled and perplexed, let his hands drop. "Why, honey!" he protested. But she turned wholly from him, leaning against the table. Her head drooped. Bill and Choate both sprang to help her, thinking she would faint. An untouched glass of wine stood on the table, and she caught it up in desperate haste and drank it at a draught; it rattled against her chattering teeth. The liquor warmed and strengthened her. She turned, staring again at Christine. And then, to Bill's horror and her own, she . . . laughed. That terrible, unmirthful laughter shook her, and she bit it back with white teeth caught in her lower lip. In shame and confusion she pressed her handkerchief to her mouth. . . . The next instant she was in Bill's arms.

The shocking thought crossed Bill's mind that it was worth it. Jane's lovely body, warm and slender against his; Jane turning from Ewell Choate to him, clinging, her face pressed hard into his shoulder till the dreadful laughter died. The touch of her wrung the strength right out of Bill. His lips were against her hair. Long tremors that she fought to still ran through and through her body, shaking it like a cold wind. They passed. She was quiet, gathering herself. She lifted her head. She commanded herself once more. Only the tightness of the small fist that held the crumpled handkerchief betrayed her.

"I'm sorry," she said—and she spoke now to Bill and Choate together. "I didn't mean to be so silly. I—I've never seen a person . . . die before."

She stood staring down at Christine as if she were bewitched. Bill's eyes followed hers.

Bill had known Christine only a few hours. He had not liked her. And yet he felt, even in her death, a power and a ruthless beauty. She lay with one arm bent under her, the other, round and firm and white, stretched on the rug. The hand lay palm upward. The head was turned a little, naturally, toward that outstretched left arm. There was a look on her face of angry astonishment. The tawny hair glowed in the lights. The satin gown that was her shroud molded a splendid body. The wound was the only flaw in her white beauty: a little round hole, faintly blue about the edges. It had not bled much externally. Only a few bright drops had trickled down in the hollow between the full breasts. They soaked the tight white satin with the color of ruby. . . .

A shock passed over Bill like that of an electric current. *The ruby was not there.*

Bill did not immediately announce his discovery. Looking more closely, he guessed what must have happened: the bullet which had killed Christine had cut the thin platinum chain and let the ruby fall. Bill searched the floor with his eyes. Presently he discovered the chain. One of the loose ends had caught in Christine's shoulder strap; the rest had slipped back, when they laid her down, into a shining puddle under the curve of her neck. Perhaps the ruby was there too. Perhaps it had fallen earlier. Bill moved to command the floor round Christine's place at table.

Bill wanted very much to find that ruby before anybody else did. The Verity Insurance Company would not be pleased if he lost trace of it again. But Bill did not find it.

Angeline sank back on her heels, wiping her plump fingers on a handkerchief. "Well, I guess you're right," she said to Varro. "I guess she's . . . I guess I can't do anything for her." She looked worried—and important. Angeline Tredennick was not one to lose her head. She was too anxious not to miss anything ever to waste time with introspection. She began to smooth Christine's dress.

"Why!" she said suddenly. "Look!" She held up the chain. "It's broken. What do you suppose . . ."

"The bullet cut it open," Choate said. He spoke so quickly that Bill knew at once that he had made the discovery before Angeline. And had not mentioned it. For that matter, neither had Bill. But Bill had a reason. Had Choate a reason too?

"The ruby must have dropped on the floor then," said Varro. "See if you can find it. Here, I'll help you."

"Let Angeline do it," said Bill suddenly. "We'll all watch." He did not trust Varro's agile fingers. Varro gave him a sharp unfriendly glance. Bill thought perhaps his caution had been wise.

Angeline was always thorough. She got down on her round little knees, and her round little back humped up in its tight grey crêpe, and her plump hands went smoothing and patting all over the cream and green and black pattern of the rug. She poked under Christine's shoulders, slipped a hand under her neck. "I don't seem to find it. . . ."

"Mightn't it have gone down inside her dress?" said Jane, in a husky voice that she tried to make natural.

"Why, I don't think so," said Angeline. Her hands moved over the white bodice. "If it had, I could feel it. It was quite big. Unless . . ." She plunged her hand suddenly into the hollow at the bosom.

The next instant she stood up, looking greenish and ill. She held her hand out stiffly, fingers spread, turning her head away. Jane smothered a faint cry. Bill snatched a napkin from the table and wiped Angeline's hand.

"I didn't think," she said unhappily. She added, biting her lips a little: "It wasn't there."

"You're sure?" said Bill gently.

"Oh, yes, I'm sure," said Angeline. "She—you see she's got on a . . . foundation, that's just as tight as her skin is. There couldn't anything get inside."

"Maybe it's under her," Choate suggested.

"We'll have to move her," said Varro.

The three men moved Christine. Bill put his hand behind her head to keep it from falling backward as they lifted her clear of the floor. Angeline shook out the white skirts. But the ruby was not found.

They laid Christine down again then, and Angeline replaced Toombs' coat under her head. Somehow she did not look so . . . dead, if she had a pillow. She composed the limbs decently, setting the white satin slippers upright on their heels, arranging the skirts about them. "Get something to lay over her," she said. "Then we can't see. . . ."

Varro and Ewell Choate sprang at once to do her bidding. But Bill was before them at the door. "I don't think anybody better go out," he said.

"What do you mean by that?" Choate demanded belligerently.

"Nothing personal." Bill's voice was mild. "Just an old custom."

Choate was inclined to make an issue of it. But Varro was more reasonable. He passed the matter off with a shrug. "We don't need to," he said. "Here's just the thing right here." He turned to Annie Budd, still sitting as if stunned by the enormity of what had happened, the crocheted bedspread clasped to her heaving bosom. "Let me take that."

Annie Budd hesitated. Her crocheted bed-covers were her pride. They were her works of art. This was a specially pretty pattern, too. The Repeal. It had a lot of work in it. She had begun it to celebrate Repeal Night, and it was all done now except the border. To Christine Van Wycke, living, she would have denied it fiercely. But Christine Van Wycke, dead, had claims that no living person could have. Her grasp slackened. "All right," she said reluctantly. "Take it." She snapped off the thread and tied it so that it would not ravel.

It occurred to Annie Budd then that she was sitting in the presence of her betters. She pulled herself to her feet and went to join Catriona and Toombs. "There, there!" she said, patting the girl's shoulder. "Don't take on so. I'm sure nobody blames you." She said to Toombs: "Who done it, anyway?"

"How would I know?" said Toombs crossly.

Varro spread the quilt over Christine, and helped Angeline arrange it. She drew Christine's lax hands together to fold them on her breast. . . .

They all saw it at the same time. Around Christine's right wrist—the one that had lain hidden under her—the flexible links of the chain to the gold mesh bag made a broad, closely woven bracelet. It was locked in place with a jeweled clasp, intricate and lovely. About an inch from the clasp, the chain had been cut off short. Something strong and sharp had done it. The ends stood stiff and empty on her wrist.

"Look!" gasped Angeline. "The bag! It . . . had all those jewels in it!"

Varro was again the first to recover himself. He stroked his slick mustache with a knuckle. He said composedly: "Now we know why he shot her."

With his words, Beulah went suddenly and terribly to pieces.

It was as if, for thirty-seven years, all Beulah's repressed emotions, all her inhibitions and fears and hates and indignities and unwanted loves, had been strung on a wire; and this wire had been twisted tighter and tighter till it knotted in loops and coils—and Christine's death had been added at the end. At Varro's speech the wire broke free at last, spinning and uncoiling, and all the emotions that it had held in check for thirty-seven years went crashing off in every direction. Beulah broke into violent hysterics. Her face was distorted. She pushed through the startled group, and threw herself upon Dante Burge.

Joe and Charlie exchanged glances. It was, the look said, about what you might expect of this crazy lot.

The truth was that in a life in which Christine Van Wycke had absorbed all masculine attention, Dante Burge was probably the first man to have shown an interest in Beulah. Whatever his motives, this interest had stirred her. His touch at the dinner table, wholly unaccustomed as it was, had excited her more than it had any right to. Her imagination, long unindulged, had dwelt upon it. So now it was Beulah's thwarted womanhood that was on the loose, acted upon by the emotional strain of tragedy. She snatched at the tag-ends of Burge's farcical raiment, locking her arms about his body. She pulled his head down and forced her open lips against his mouth. It was conduct of which shy, repressed Beulah, in her senses, would have been no more capable than of flight.

"You did it for me, Dante dear," she cried. "Didn't you? You shot her to set me free."

Dante Burge took the frantic woman by the shoulders, holding her away. For once in his life he had more psychology on his hands than he could manage. He shook her a little, trying to sober her.

"Control yourself," he said sternly. "You don't know what you're saying. I had nothing to do with it."

Varro flicked the ash from his cigarette with a jeweled little finger. "I wouldn't say that," he remarked coolly. "Of course you shot her. We all saw you do it."

2

"But I didn't shoot her," Burge reiterated.

"The bunk!" said Varro.

"Don't be funny," said Choate. "This has gone beyond a joke."

"Do you seriously mean," said Bill, "to stand there with that gun in your hand, and say you didn't fire it?"

"I said nothing of the sort," Burge retorted. "You should be more accurate. Of course I fired the revolver. I fired five shots into the wall above the wine closet. But I did not shoot Mrs. Van Wycke."

"I wonder how she got shot then," murmured Angeline.

Bill was upset. It was a shocking business, anyhow. Professor Burge was not a man to be trusted with a gun; he was too much preoccupied with science, too unconcerned with the rights of people. Bill could not understand how they had ever allowed him to proceed with his monstrous experiment. It would be an accident peculiarly hard to explain to the authorities. But that it was more than an accident had never once occurred to him. He had even felt a kind of angry pity for Burge. But now the disappearance of the jewels, Burge's resolute denial of responsibility, put a different look upon the matter. "I suppose you can explain," he said, "how you shot her without shooting her."

Burge plunged into an explanation—which explained nothing. "You will remember," he said in his precise voice, "that the two revolvers which were used this afternoon in target practice were placed on the table in the corridor by Miss Mullins when we returned to the boat. They had remained there ever since. When I left the dining saloon preparatory to the experiment which I proposed, I took one of the revolvers with me to my stateroom."

"I don't remember seeing you stop to pick it up," Bill said.

"I did not state that I stopped, young man," Burge corrected him. "You jump to conclusions. It is upon such false assumptions that many errors in evidence are based. The table, you will observe, is placed flush with the door-jamb on the corridor side, and by leaving the dining saloon at the left of the opening into the corridor, I passed directly beside it. I picked up the revolver without stopping, or even turning my head. I did not, naturally, wish you to observe me, as you would then be expecting shots, and much of the value of the surprise element would be lost."

"So?" said Bill.

"You will recall further," continued Burge, "that of the two revolvers, one was completely loaded, the other in five chambers only. The latter was fired once by Mr. Varro just as Mr. Galleon joined the party; he then laid it aside, and it was not used again. A little later, Mr. Galleon, using the other revolver, emptied it into the target. Miss Mullins reloaded it. Upon reaching my stateroom, I examined the revolver which I had picked up at random, and found it to be the one which contained five bullets only. At the point at which the progress of my experiment demanded it, I fired five shots into the wall."

"You had a nerve," Bill said, "to fire anything but blanks in a dark room full of people."

Professor Dante Gabriel Burge, in the interests of science, did have nerve. It was now a trifle shaken. He answered, however, with admirable composure. "I am, if I may say so, a good shot. The point was commented on this afternoon. I knew, of course, where everyone in the room was placed." (*Did you,* thought Bill.) "It is hardly possible, even for the most unskilled, to miss a wall. There was no danger."

"No danger at all," said Bill grimly. "Only one death."

Jane spoke urgently. "Anyone can make a mistake. You were moving about as you fired. . . ."

"That," Burge said, "is where you are again in error. Once I had taken up my position here, I did not stir from the place where you now see me. I moved my hand, yes. That only. By swinging it from side to side, I created an illusion of bodily movement which in your mind was translated into fact."

"Still," said Jane earnestly, "you might have miscalculated. . . ."

"I never miscalculate," said Dante Burge. "I fired five shots. You will find five bullets lodged in the wall above the closet."

"I wonder," said Angeline thoughtfully, "if there weren't six. It kind of seems to me as if there were."

Jane nodded.

"By Jove, that's right," Bill said. He could not say why he was so sure. Only it seemed that there was a memory of five shots stamped on his mind; a sixth when Christine screamed.

"I should be interested in an expression of opinion," Burge said primly.

"Six," said Varro.

"Five," said Choate.

"I don't know," said Beulah wretchedly. "Five. Six. I don't *know.*" The passing of her emotional attack had left her flaccid. She slumped sidewise in her chair, her head resting against the back.

"Did you hear the shots too?" Burge said, turning to Charlie and Joe.

Joe nodded, and Charle said: "Uh-huh. Didn't make out to count them though."

Burge muttered to himself, checking the answers on his fingers. "I thought it would be like that. A variation in the auditory memory. Interesting."

It did not interest Bill. "We'll soon settle it anyhow," he said. He moved a chair to the wine closet and climbed up, passing a hand over the wall. "Five," he said. "Here are the holes. But . . ."

"And what does that prove?" said Varro nastily. "It proves that you fired five shots at the wall—and one at Mrs. Van Wycke."

For the first time a troubled look crossed Professor Burge's face. It sat oddly on his comic countenance. For the first time he hesitated. "I can see now," he said slowly, "that I should have made this statement earlier. I had not, I confess, anticipated your . . . strange attitude. That I did not make this statement was due to a scientific curiosity as to whether anyone had noticed the detail which I am about to mention. I admit, of course, that six shots were fired. . . ."

"Noble of you," muttered Bill.

". . . six shots were fired," repeated Burge. "I fired only five. The sixth shot—the one which killed Mrs. Van Wycke—was fired from a point somewhat to my right, and by a taller person than I."

A little tremor ran over the group; that involuntary shudder that is said to shake the frame when a careless foot treads a grave.

"*Oh!*" breathed Jane. "Don't. . . ." And checked her speech.

"You know, it's funny, but I kind of think that's so," said Angeline. She puckered her round face, trying to recall that fleeting picture of blackness and flashing fire. "It does seem to me as if that last shot came from farther away, up that side. But I just thought Professor Burge had stepped along. . . ."

"Oh, come, come!" Ewell Choate broke in irritably. "If six shots were fired, you fired them, Burge. You can't get

out of that. The best you can say for yourself is that you
took the revolver that was fully loaded by mistake."

Professor Burge stiffened. His scientific accuracy was
touched. You may call a scientist a poltroon and a murderer; but you must not call his accuracy to question. "I do
not make mistakes," he said.

"All right," said Choate. "Then you took it . . . on purpose."

"But I didn't shoot her, I tell you." Burge's voice rose.
"Why should I? Will you tell me one reason why I, a scientist, in the midst of an experiment, should deliberately
sacrifice the value of my own findings. . . ."

"I should think the reason was plain enough," Varro
said. "The bag's gone, isn't it?"

Professor Dante Gabriel Burge was a brilliant man.
Within the scope of his own subject, he was acknowledged
an authority. But like many brilliant men, he sometimes
overlooked the obvious. He appeared to realize now for
the first time the full significance of his position. Or was
it only appearance? Was he clever enough for that too?
A curious flutter came in his voice, like that of a heart
patient.

"I don't know anything about the bag," he said. "I
didn't take it. How could I? I . . ."

"You could have taken it," said Bill deliberately, "that
time when you were quiet so long . . . behind Mrs. Van
Wycke's chair."

"Well, there," said Angeline. "That's so too. I wondered at the time what he was doing."

Dante Burge came toward them. His hands fumbled
with the pink scarf, tying knots in the fringe. A strange
greyness had overspread his face; the reddened nose, the
blackened tooth, gave it a comic horror like the masks
which children wear at Hallowe'en.

"I beg you to believe me," he said earnestly. "I—I was
taking Mrs. Van Wycke's handkerchief."

The very feebleness of the excuse half inclined Bill to
believe it true.

"Oh yeah?" said Varro.

"Whatever for?" said Angeline.

"It was part of the experiment," said Burge, pulling at the fringe till a bit came loose in his fingers. "I—I noticed before I went out that Mrs. Van Wycke's handkerchief had fallen to the floor. I planned to take it. Some time was required to find it in the dark. My purpose in taking the handkerchief was two-fold: to discover how many would notice that it was gone; to discover how many could say definitely when it had disappeared. If I could lead the company to think that it had vanished prior to my entrance or subsequent to the relighting of the lights, then I should automatically be cleared of the suspicion of taking it. I meant thus to demonstrate the unreliability of evidence. To show how easy it is to implicate the innocent; how easy to clear the guilty."

"A very pretty idea," said Bill evenly. "And one that would apply as well to jewels as to handkerchiefs."

Burge made a weak effort to smile. "It seems that I have proved my point," he said. "I did not do it, however, in the way I had intended." The smile was a failure.

Then a thought struck him. "Why, see," he said. "I can show you that what I say is true. I can show you the handkerchief." He rummaged through his pockets, his search growing more fevered as he met their skeptical gaze. Then, actually, he found it.

Burge laid the handkerchief on the table. It was a wisp of lace and linen, absurdly unimportant. There was a smear of lipstick in the corner. That gay splash of scarlet, from lips that were painted now with death, sent a coldness through them.

Varro tapped his cigarette. "And what does that prove?" he asked again. "It proves that while you were taking the bag and the ruby, you took the handkerchief too for an alibi. Afterwards, when Mrs. Van Wycke discovered her loss . . ."

"That's what tore it," Bill cried in a flash of illumination. "She found it out too soon. When she screamed, Burge lost his head. . . ."

"But I wonder if she *did* find it out," said Angeline. "She was going to scream anyway."

"Professor Burge didn't know that."

"What are you talking about?" cried Burge wildly. "The sixth shot killed her. I fired only five."

Bill struck his fist suddenly into his open palm. "Here we stand arguing, and the other gun right there. . . . Bring it in, Toombs."

But Toombs was fully occupied. ("I didn't steal it, did I, Gus? How could I? I wasn't even in here. I wouldn't steal anything, not if I could, would I, Gus?")

"I'll get it," Annie Budd said. Charlie moved to pick it up, but she was before him, hurrying to the table that stood just outside the door. "Why—I don't see it.—Oh, here it is. On the floor. It must have fallen off."

"Guns don't jump off tables by themselves," Varro remarked.

"I wonder how it got there," murmured Angeline.

Bill knew. The revolver had dropped from some one's hand, when he ran into . . . some one in the dark.

Annie Budd brought Bill the revolver, holding it out between a gingerly thumb and finger, as if she expected it to explode in her face. Bill broke it. Only five chambers were loaded.

If Professor Dante Gabriel Burge were not surprised by this development, then he gave an excellent imitation of surprise. His eyes widened and his jaw dropped. His features twisted into a perfect pattern of incredulity. But it occurred to Bill again that a psychologist would be the very man most completely to control his expression.

"But . . ." he gasped. "But . . . but . . ." And in that moment of stammering he found his explanation. "Some one else took that revolver," he cried. "He fired one shot.

That shot killed Mrs. Van Wycke. He returned the revolver before the lights came on. In his haste he missed the table, and it fell on the floor."

Angeline Tredennick stood staring down at the crocheted quilt that covered Christine's body. It was a pretty pattern: the raised circles that looked like foam were just as natural as could be. . . . She lifted round, distressed blue eyes to Dante Burge.

"Oh, don't say that," she begged him.

"Why not?" Burge demanded.

"But don't you see?" said Angeline softly. "If you took the wrong revolver and shot Mrs. Van Wycke, it was terrible, of course, and everything; but it—it must have been an accident. But if some one else took the revolver, on purpose, and shot her, and put it back, then . . . then it was *murder*."

FOUR

"Well, after all," said Angeline wearily, "Mrs. Van Wycke is dead, and the jewels are gone. You can't get away from that."

They had been trying to get away from it all night. The black wind blew cold against the ports that Toombs had closed. The height of the storm had passed, leaving rain and a rough sea. It seemed to Bill that the cold and mists outside had penetrated his own mind. Everything had seemed so clear at first. Now it did not seem clear at all.

As the long hours passed, it became increasingly evident to Bill that Christine Van Wycke's death had not been an accident. If Professor Burge had killed her, he had done so by intention. And this intention he knew how to hide in psychological entanglements. *Would* Burge have done it? Bill did not know. He knew he *could* have. He could have taken the gun that was completely loaded, and killed Mrs. Van Wycke with the last discharge. He was a good shot. That lightning flash would have given him the range. But . . .

As the talk went on, it became evident also that some one else might have done it. Some one who left the table in the darkness and fetched the gun remaining in the hall; some one who stood near Burge in the stern and fired the fatal shot so close to his that it seemed like a continuation of his own firing; some one who counted on the difference not being noted save by Burge—who would not be believed; some one who carried the gun back and resumed his seat before the lights came on. Some one . . . Further than that Bill would not let his thoughts go. Why—*any* of them might have done it.

They had carried Christine to her stateroom. Bill opposed that. "It isn't ethical," he said. "You're supposed to leave a body where it is. The authorities won't like it."

"What authorities?" Varro wanted to know.

"The police," said Angeline helpfully. "You always have police where there's a murder. I was on a murder jury once, and the police . . ."

"We don't need police mixed up in it," Varro said hurriedly. "Say it was a shooting accident. Target practice."

"Why, you can't say that," cried Angeline innocently, rounding her blue eyes. "It isn't so."

"We can't get the police till morning," Bill conceded. "Nor a doctor either. There's no use starting out in this storm before light. But if you want to know, I don't trust anybody out of this room with the body. How do I know he wouldn't carry the jewels with him?" His bluntness startled even himself.

"Want me and Joe should take her?" Charlie said suddenly. He wiped his hands on the seat of his dungarees, and examined the calloused palms as if to make sure that they were fit to handle Christine's satin.

Bill nodded slowly. "That would be best," he said. And to the others: "They haven't been in here at all—not really *in,* enough to touch anything. I'll agree to that, all right, if you're bound to have her moved."

It was Angeline who settled it. "Well, anyway," she said, "I can't think with her lying there peeking at me through the holes in that quilt. It mixes me all up. I can't tell *what* happened."

Bill saw that she was right. The mounting hysteria in the room would defeat inquiry. "All right," he said to Charlie. "Put her on the bed in her stateroom, and fix her up, and open all the ports. Shut the door when you come out. Better step down and turn the lights on, Joe, before you start."

Joe nodded without speaking, and went at once about his errand. He was back almost immediately, and he and Charlie picked up Christine Van Wycke. Angeline fussed about, arranging the limp arms so that they should not swing; Varro caught up a trailing corner of the crocheted quilt to tuck it into the crook of Joe's elbow, and moved a chair or two away to give them a free passage to the door. Joe performed his task as stolidly as if it were part of his routine to clear the bodies from the dining saloon after dinner; but Bill noticed that Charlie kept his eyes fixed with intention on the ceiling, as if to avoid the look of the tawny head rolling against his midriff. They shuffled slowly down the side corridor.

As if by common consent, the others clustered just inside the door of the saloon, watching their progress. At the far end of the corridor, the visible portion of Christine's gold and cream stateroom lay like a small brightly lighted stage. The bed stood against the foreward bulkhead, facing the door with an odd effect of watchfulness. The two men laid Christine there, and Joe straightened her limbs, and crossed her hands on her breast, and closed her eyes, before he smoothed Annie Budd's coverlid in place. Charlie moved about, appearing and disappearing as he opened the ports; the wet wind poured in, flapping the bright curtains. His hand went out to the wall switch, and the room dropped into darkness. The door closed behind them.

Charlie came at once to the saloon and spoke to Bill. "I'll be getting along back topside," he said, "if there's nothing more I can do. It's coming my watch. I don't hardly feel easy to leave her, take it in this wind."

"Is there a watch all night?" Bill asked.

Charlie nodded. "Watch and watch till morning," he agreed. "That's what Ceph told us before he went. Most times, take it at anchor, or mooring, or wharf, there wouldn't be need. But you could see there was weather brewing when Ceph left. Take it like this with a break-down and the ship beached, if you wouldn't keep an eye to the wind and the sea and her lines ashore, she might start pounding or go adrift."

"I see," Bill said. "All right."

Charlie scuffled his big feet, embarrassed. "I just as lief Joe would come up with me a while, if you got no call to keep him," he added.

Evidently they had it arranged between them, for Joe nodded quickly. "Sure," he said.

Bill didn't much blame them. It was not a gay night to be alone in the wind. "All right," he repeated. "I don't suppose either of you can tell us anything that we don't already know."

They shook their heads positively. "Figure not," Charlie said. "We heard some shots, but we didn't pay them much mind till *she* screamed. We was pretty well used to the doings."

Bill wondered what he meant. But it was no time to press the point. "Go ahead," he said. "I'll let you know if we need you."

Joe was already out of sight before he finished, and Charlie followed him quickly.

Already, in the dining saloon, there was confusion. If vindication were needed for Professor Burge's theory that a group of people, witnessing the same scene, will describe it in completely different terms, then here was that vin-dication. But no one was interested now in proving the Burge theory. A larger, more appalling proof confronted them.

". . . We'd better go over it from the beginning," An-geline was saying. "If we could get it straight, the way everything happened . . . Jane, why don't you take notes, as long as you're a secretary?" Burge handed her paper and a pencil from the supply he had brought for his lists.

"Wouldn't it help if we sat down at the table?" Bill sug-gested. "Make us remember how things were."

So they took their places again. Seven, where eight had been. But though Christine Van Wycke was lying in the stateroom at the end of the corridor, it seemed to Bill as if her presence were with them still, pitiless and beautiful, in that vacant place at the table's head. The other faces seemed hardly more real.

The faces moved in a kaleidoscope through Bill's mind. Choate, silent, half-sullen and half-defiant, his arm, now that Christine was gone, laid openly across the back of Jane's chair. Varro opposite, lighting one cigarette from another, flipping the ashes impudently, now that Christine was gone, onto the rug. Angeline smoothing down her dress importantly, her eyes round and her cheeks puffed out in a kind of pleasurable horror. Beulah, limp from emotional excitement, with her elbows on the table, her head resting in her hands. Beulah's mind was as unstable as a jelly. But it seemed to Bill that her body was quieter than he had ever seen it; she had lost that air of expecting a blow—now that Christine was gone. Burge was grey and watchful. He had laid aside as much of his costume as was possible: the Panama hat, the pink scarf, the gloves; he sat a figure of tragic fun, in his green turtle-necked sweater, his magenta pajama trousers, his tailed coat and his boots. His fingers, resting lightly on the table edge, moved a little. . . .

Bill saw them all. But it was Jane whose presence he felt inside him, vibrating like a chord of music.

Jane sat quiet, with a quiet face. Looking at her side-wise, Bill could see the clear upward sweep of lashes that matched the long sweet curve of throat lifting to a strong-ly tilted chin. The mouth was pressed straight—too thin for Jane's. Jane had sweet lips. . . . The lights from over-head made pools of shadow at the temples. He saw that she was shivering.

"You're cold," he said.

"Yes."

Bill fetched the wool scarf that Burge had discarded and wrapped it about her. (It was too big. The soft thing he had clutched in the dark was small.) His hands knew the strong straight shape of Jane's shoulders under the scarf, the good little bones under the firm flesh. The scarf was one of Christine's, with long silken fibers and deep fringes. (Not like short fine hair. Not like down.) He followed the length of it till his hands found Jane's in a reassuring pressure. Jane's hands were small and steady, with tender little thumbs. They gave back no answering clasp. "Thank you," she said. She turned on him the deep look of her eyes. Jane's eyes were the full unclouded blue of sea on a very clear day. Like the sea they held secret depths. There was no bottom to Jane's look.

"Do you know who did it?" she said.

Bill was startled by the stark simplicity of the question. He answered without thinking. "No. Do you?"

And at once her eyes were black, storm black, with the dilating of the pupils. "No," she said clearly. "Why should I?" She was gone from him as completely as if she had left the room.

". . . I'll tell it the way I remember it," Angeline was saying. "And if you think I'm getting it wrong, you stop me. I'll begin where Professor Burge came in, all dressed up. He had the revolver that he took off the table on the way out. . . ."

Choate interrupted immediately. "How do you know he took it on the way out? Why couldn't he have taken it on the way in?"

"As far as I know, he could," Bill said. "I was listening to Mrs. Van Wycke. I didn't see him until he was right in the door."

"Neither did I," Angeline admitted. "But I don't see what difference it makes."

"Why, if he took it on the way *in*," Choate explained, "he wouldn't have had time to look at it. It might have been the one fully loaded."

"That's so too," Angeline said. "You better write it down, Jane."

"But I *told* you . . ." began Burge.

"We're trying to find out what everyone knows to be facts," Bill said. "Not what one person tells us."

"Well, anyway," Angeline resumed, "Professor Burge came in, and he had his umbrella spread. He closed it and hung it on the hook in the wine closet where it is now. And then he took a drink. . . ."

"Four drinks," put in Varro.

"He took down four bottles," said Jane quietly. "But I believe he drank from only one."

"I wonder what that was," said Angeline.

"Gin," said Varro.

"I have no taste for gin," said Burge. "It was Bicardi." He added in explanation: "I was about to appear in a role which would inevitably appear to some of you absurd. One cocktail, I have found, tends to equalize self-consciousness."

Varro was handling the bottles. "Biccardee Chanticleer Cocktail," he read. "Pure lime and orange, rum and grenadine flavors. 50.4 Proof. . . . White Label Finest Scotch Whisky of Great Age. John Dewar & Sons, Ltd., Perth, Scotland. . . . Hildick Old Fashioned Applejack Brandy. 100 Proof. Aged in Charred Oak Casks. . . . Mexican Habano 11. . . . Quite a mixture. In sufficient quantities."

"Do you mean to suggest that I was drunk?" Burge demanded.

"Not very," said Varro. "Just enough so you didn't know what you were doing."

"That's a good idea too," said Angeline. "Better write it down, Jane.—So then he turned off the lights, and walked twice round the table. . . ."

Toombs gave a little deprecating cough. "If I may speak, please? Once, I think. I felt him pass."

"I don't see what difference . . ."

"All the difference in the world," said Choate. "Because it was right after that when he stopped behind Mrs. Van Wycke's chair. The less time he spent walking round, the more time he had. . . ."

"It wasn't less than two minutes," Bill said. "I started in to count seconds for those lists we were supposed to make. I lost track and gave it up. But I'm sure . . ."

"So he took the bag," said Varro.

"And the ruby," said Choate.

"And the handkerchief," said Angeline, always a stickler for detail. "And that was when he bumped into Toombs. . . ."

Beulah's thin voice rose like a picked fiddle string. ". . . All blaming poor Dante. What about Toombs? What was he doing?" Burge bent on Beulah a look that was queerly gentle.

"Sure enough," said Bill. "Toombs, what *were* you doing?"

"Filling Mrs. Van Wycke's wineglass, sir."

"All that time?"

"No, sir. Just as I finished, Professor Burge came in. I remained standing where I was. You understand, sir, the novelty. . . . When the lights were extinguished, I stepped back to be out of the way. I did not like to risk walking about in the darkness, sir, for fear of running into some one."

"Into the Professor, you mean?" said Angeline.

"Into anyone, Miss Angeline, who was walking about."

"Was anyone walking about besides the Professor?"

"I really could not say, Miss Angeline."

"Let's be getting along," said Bill quickly. His glance turned irresistibly to Jane. Jane met his look squarely. There was no acknowledgment in her eyes. And no denial.

"He could have taken it just as well as Dante could," Beulah insisted shrilly. "Better. He was right there. . . ."

Catriona broke away from Annie Budd's restraining hands. "Gus wouldn't steal anything. And I wouldn't either, would I, Gus?"

"There, there!" soothed Annie Budd.

It would have been impossible to tell from the expression on the wooden face of Toombs, whether he preferred the name of Thief, or Murderer, or Gus. "I should hardly have chosen," he said with dignity, "to undertake so delicate a task as cutting the bag from Mrs. Van Wycke's wrist with a full decanter in my hand."

"You could have set it down," said Beulah. "You had time enough."

"Better make a note of it, Jane," Angeline said. Instantly she went on; her gift was narrative. "So after Professor Burge ran into Toombs, he sort of staggered backwards into the serving table, and the fruit bowl tipped over, and a peach fell on the floor, and he stepped on Telemachus and made him yelp, and the peach went *squish.*"

They agreed that the peach went *squish*. It was not without a grim humor that of all the events of that eventful night, the only matter on which the company was completely in accord was that the peach went *squish*.

"And then," Angeline continued, "Professor Burge began to move around again, only he was very quiet and I couldn't be sure where he was; but I knew he was moving because I could sort of feel him move and once in a while his boots squeaked. And then he was right down here, shooting; and the shooting scared me, so I caught hold of Mr. Galleon; and that lightning flash came, the one that was brighter than the others, and I saw him. . . ."

"Who?"

"Why Mr. Galleon. And I saw somebody else, too, right over there. . . ."

"*Who?*"

"Well, I'm not quite sure who it was. But I can't help wondering. . . ."

"Burge, of course," said Bill quickly. He did not dare to look at Jane now. "Burge was behind me."

"And then Mrs. Van Wycke screamed, and the sixth shot was fired. . . ."

"You mean she was shot, and then she screamed."

"I wonder if it makes any difference?"

"But naturally," said Burge. "If she screamed first, the supposition is that she knew the bag was stolen, and probably by whom; the murderer shot her because she *knew.* But if she was shot first, and screamed because she was *shot,* then murder was the primary object, and the theft was secondary. A very nice point."

"You can't tell," said Jane firmly, "because she was going to scream anyway."

"Right," said Bill. "And the lightning flash and the shot and the scream all came practically together."

It seemed to Bill that they were all shouting their theories in one another's faces. Only . . . for one of them it was not theory. It was knowledge.

"I think Jane ought to write down something," Angeline said distractedly. "I wonder what."

2

"We're not getting anywhere this way," Bill said. It made it seem more horrible: their sitting there, discussing it together, accusing each other—and somewhere among them a thief and a murderer, bearing his part, directing suspicion elsewhere with all the craft he knew. "Until the law is in command, it would be better to appoint one person to take charge of the investigation."

"I suppose you'd appoint yourself," Choate suggested.

"I am willing to act, if you like."

Choate's voice was disagreeable. "Then you could ask all the right questions. And leave out the wrong ones." Something of the sort had certainly been not far from Bill's mind. He flushed uncomfortably. "Frankly," said Choate, "you would hardly be my choice. Why? We have all been here several days, at least; some for years. You come. And what happens? In four hours Mrs. Van Wycke is murdered and a fortune in jewels is stolen. What have you to say about that?"

"Do I understand that you have taken charge of the proceedings?" asked Bill coldly.

"I am the logical person to do so," said Burge. "I have, of course, had training. My psychological experience would stand us in good stead."

"Well, I guess I know how it's done all right myself," said Angeline, bridling. "I was on a jury in a murder case once. And that district attorney—my goodness, he could ask more questions in a minute. . . ."

"If I may be so bold as to make a suggestion, sir?" said Toombs tentatively. "It occurs to me that there are questions which particularly puzzle each one. Why not take turns?"

"That's a good idea," said Angeline, readily pleased. "Then that would be fair for everybody. I'll begin, if you want me to." She began forthwith. She asked instantly the question which Bill least wanted to hear. "I can't help wondering who it was that I saw standing over there when that lightning flash came."

"Burge," said Bill again.

"Well, that's the funny part of it," said Angeline. "I don't hardly think it was Professor Burge. I think Professor Burge was farther down this way. Of course I didn't exactly *see* him. Not in the lightning. But I saw where the flashes of his revolver came from, and of course that's where he was. It seems as if this person was farther along—nearer Mrs. Van Wycke's end of the table."

The movement of Burge's finger-tips accelerated nervously. "But my dear lady!" he cried. "This is of the utmost consequence. It is our first real clue. Also, you will observe, it corroborates my previous statement that the fatal shot was fired from my right. Miss Tredennick—of course I understand the difficulties—but could you in any wise describe this . . . person?"

Bill's breath caught in his constricted throat.

"Well—no," said Angeline. "You know how lightning is. Awful quick. But I did get a kind of an impression that he was tall."

Bill breathed again. Tall. A man, then. Not. . . . "You're tall, Choate," he said.

"Don't be silly," said Jane sharply. "It couldn't have been Ewell."

"I'm not as tall as you are, matter of fact," Choate drawled.

"But it wasn't I," said Bill, grinning. "I was right in this chair, and Miss Tredennick had hold of my knee." That was one in the eye for Choate, if it did make Angeline blush. He was puzzled and disturbed by Jane's instant defense. Did the fellow mean so much to her? Did that account for the strangeness of her manner? Could it have been Choate after all? Had he blundered, by accident, on the truth?

And at once an explanation occurred to Bill so exquisitely simple that no one had thought it. "Why, of course," he said. "Toombs. He's tall. He was in the room all the time. And that was near where he was standing when Burge hit him."

"Yes, sir, Mr. Galleon," said Toombs. "That was near where I was then, sir. But I wasn't there when the lightning flash came. When I—ah—collided with Professor Burge, I saw that I was in the way. I therefore returned as quickly as the darkness permitted to my usual place here. I did not leave this part of the room again, sir."

"Mm," said Bill thoughtfully. But was it true? "Did you see anyone when the lightning came?"

"No, sir."

"Think, Miss Tredennick," Burge was urging Angeline. "Search your subconscious mind. Try to reconstruct the visual image below the threshold of consciousness. Can you recall anything more?"

Angeline puckered her round face. "Well, it does seem," she said, hesitating, "as if this person—well—disappeared."

"The light went out," Bill said. "Lightning does."

"I don't mean that," said Angeline carefully. "Of course it did. But it does seem as if he—well, dropped down on the floor, sort of, as if he was hiding. But why should Toombs hide on the floor?"

"Mm," said Bill again. "That's what proves it wasn't Toombs. We all knew Toombs was here. He had a perfect right to be standing up. It would have been the height of folly to hide."

"Thank you very kindly, sir, I'm sure," said Toombs, gratified.

"Ah—yes. But consider this," said Burge. "If it *were* Toombs, and if he *did* hide, then it was tantamount to a confession of guilt. To Toombs, innocent, the thought of hiding would not have occurred." You could depend on Professor Burge to put the last psychological twist in the tail of every fact.

"But I *wasn't* there," protested Toombs. "And so I *didn't* hide, and so . . ." He stopped, baffled. "The durn academic fool," he muttered to Catriona.

"I haven't hardly asked my question yet," said Angeline. "What I started out to ask was: did anybody else see him?"

"Yes," said Varro promptly. "I did."

Burge whirled upon him. "You *did!* Why didn't you say so, man?"

"Nobody asked me," said Varro provokingly.

"Did you get a good look at him? What did he look like? What . . .?"

"Tall," said Varro laconically. "Might have been Choate."

"Might have been you, just as much," Choate retorted.

"I'm not tall," said Varro smugly.

It was true. Varro was not tall. But every inch of him there was, Bill distrusted. He did not like his bright eyes, nor his quick fingers. There was a slipperiness about him, like a fish. "We won't get ahead," he said, "by calling each other names."

Angeline must have been searching her subconscious again. "There's a little more to my question," she said now. "Really just part of the same one. I wonder if anybody besides me noticed an empty chair."

Every muscle in Bill's big body stiffened. It had come. He felt again the cold clutch at the pit of his stomach that had taken him when he put out his hand to Jane—and found her gone.

"Of course," he said evenly. "Burge's chair was empty."

"I know that," said Angeline, her smooth forehead knotted. "But it couldn't have been that one, could it? You see Burge's chair was on my left. And when the lightning came, I was turned the other way—toward the shots, and toward you. If I saw an empty chair, it must have been on that side."

"But you're not sure you did see one," Bill prompted her gently.

"It kind of seems that way," she insisted. "I thought if anybody else had seen it. . . ."

"I did," said Varro. "Choate's."

"You're good at seeing things, aren't you?" said Choate. "After somebody tells you what to see."

They all had to admit the justice of Choate's comment. It destroyed any weight Varro's testimony might have had. But the thought struck Bill then that Varro knew about Jane. He might be striking at Jane through Choate, goading her to self-betrayal. . . .

"Perhaps we can check this," Burge was saying. "We may take it for granted that Mr. Galleon and Miss Tredennick were in their places, since they say they saw each other. My chair was next. We know that was empty. Then— Beulah?" He spoke gently.

Beulah lifted a wan face of utter wretchedness. "I couldn't have got up if I'd wanted to," she said. "My knees wouldn't let me."

They were all sorry for her. "I guess she was there, all right." Angeline came to the rescue. "I heard a kind of a squeal, and I guess it must have been Beulah."

"Then Miss Bridge, opposite?"

It was again a comfort to Bill that it was to him that Jane had turned, and not to Choate, as Burge's questioning drew nearer. Her eyes looked into his, deep and clear. But there was no plea for mercy there. They were proud eyes, and brave eyes. Bill would have sworn that they were honest eyes. There was some simple explanation. She would tell him when they were alone. . . . She faced Burge, when he addressed her, as steadily as Bill. Bill answered for her before she could speak.

"It is impossible," he said, "that Miss Bridge could have left her place without my knowing it."

Under the table edge, Bill saw Jane's fingers twist at the lace cloth until it tore. But the look she lifted to Burge never faltered. "I can say the same for Ewell Choate," she said. "If he had not been there all the time, I should have known."

"Varro?"

"I was here," said Varro with a leer. "If I hadn't been, I couldn't have seen that Choate was gone."

"I did hear him say something," Angeline conceded. "Something about Mrs. Van Wycke's being good."

"I think you are our best observer," Burge said. He gave a resigned shrug. "I regret that we cannot answer your question conclusively. It has raised some interesting points for conjecture. But it comes down to this. If you saw a tall person, who concealed himself by dropping to the floor, he was the one who left the vacant chair. If you saw a vacant chair, it was the one left by the tall person. . . ."

About what you would expect of a psychologist, Bill thought. He did not dismiss it as easily as that. There was something between Choate and Varro that he did not understand—yet. But he put his trust in Jane. "Go ahead," he said to Burge. "It's your turn."

"My question," Burge said, "is a very simple one. What was meant by the statement that Mrs. Van Wycke was expected to scream? Who expected her to scream? The murderer?"

"Why, we all expected her to," said Angeline. "You see . . ." She flushed a little. It wasn't very easy to explain. "I guess maybe you'll think it's queer. But after you went out, we decided that it would be fun to play a little joke on you. We thought we would pick out some kind of foolish thing, and then we'd all put it in our lists and say you did it."

"Ah," said Burge sarcastically. "Very helpful, I'm sure."

Angeline squirmed uncomfortably. But she went on. "So then Mrs. Van Wycke suggested different things that we might say you did, and finally she suggested that she jump up and scream and say you'd stolen her bag. And that was what we decided on. And so when she *did* scream . . ."

"Rather a grim joke," said Burge.

It was a grim joke now. And grim as . . . death.

"And do I understand," he said, "that this was altogether Mrs. Van Wycke's idea?"

"About the bag and the scream and all, it was. Yes," said Angeline. "She didn't think of the plan in the first place."

"And who did?" said Burge softly.

"Why," said Angeline uneasily, "I—I guess Mr. Choate did."

"Ah!" said Dante Burge more softly still. "That was what I wanted to know." His fingers moved delicately on the table. "I recall that it was also Mr. Choate who suggested that Mrs. Van Wycke wear her ruby."

Beulah Mullins turned to Burge when her question came, as if he were the only person in the room. She lifted tortured eyes in a fixed bright stare, her poor helpless face quivering like raw flesh under a lash. "Did you do it?" she whispered.

"No," said Burge soothingly. He took her hot hands; they were as dry and bony as birds' claws, curling about his fingers. "You wouldn't have wanted me to. Would you?"

"No," said Beulah obediently.

"No," approved Burge, smiling. "Of course you wouldn't." He clinched his argument. "Any more than I should have wanted you to."

Beulah Mullins' husky whisper sounded round the table like a shout. "I couldn't. I would have if I could."

Professor Burge, psychologist though he was, had overreached himself. Beulah was completely unpredictable. He put an end to the scene quickly. "Varro?"

Varro threw away his question, as did Choate after him. "Where's the ruby, Choate?" he asked unpleasantly.

"Varro," Choate countered. "Where's the bag?"

And so it came at once to Jane.

Jane sat erect in her straight chair, leaning against the back without ease. Her head was high and her lips were firm and her hands were quiet in her lap. But Bill sensed a gathering of all her forces under that quietness. It took courage to command that quiet voice.

"I am not clever at things like this," she said, with a little wry smile. "But there is one thing that troubles me . . . very much. Suppose the fatal shot to have been fired from this side of the room—behind me. I should like to put it to the company if there would then have been time for the person who fired it to run round the table, place the revolver in the hall, and return to his seat before the lights came on. It seems to me that there would not. If this was not possible, then the whole theory breaks down."

It was a gallant effort. Bill wished he did not know . . . what he knew. He pretended that he didn't. He threw away his question also, and came to Jane's aid.

"That's what I want to ask too," he said. "It seems to me like too much to happen in such a short time."

"An excellent point," Burge approved Jane. "And naturally one to which I have given thought, since by it, as you suggest, my whole theory stands or falls. After the most careful analysis, I am convinced that there was time."

"But isn't that just a matter of personal opinion?" Bill asked.

"No," said Burge. "Of scientific analysis." He laid his findings before them. "Consider, then. The table on which the revolver lay, while nominally in the hall, is for our present purposes, within this room. That is, it would not be necessary to leave this room in order to reach it. This room is not large. After the shot was fired, it would have been necessary only to run to the door, and return. The fact

that the weapon fell to the floor indicates great haste. Of
the places at table, that occupied by Miss Mullins would
be nearest; Miss Bridge's most distant. Even allowing for
the place of least accessibility, I am convinced that one
minute would have been more than enough for the action.
We will test this supposition later. For the moment, let us
accept it. But more than a minute actually elapsed. For
think what happened in this interval. The scream—somewhat prolonged. The sound of a fall. A perceptible space
of silence, before Mr. Galleon called for lights. The sound
of Mr. Galleon himself hurrying toward the switch. And
. . . again an appreciable delay before the lights came on.

"It appeared to me at the time," Burge finished, turning to Bill, "that the reaction was very slow. Perhaps this
point requires elucidation. Perhaps, Mr. Galleon, you can
elucidate it."

"Well, of course," Bill admitted, "I was expecting Mrs.
Van Wycke to scream. You understand that now. That kept
me from seeing right off that anything was wrong. It was
when she—choked at the end, and I heard the fall, that
I realized." Bill knew that in explaining his slowness he
was confessing it. He knew that every word he spoke was
defeating his own interests—and Jane's. And he could not
help it.

"Precisely," said Burge. "You then called to Toombs for
lights, and yourself immediately went to turn them on.
But there was again a definite delay before they appeared.
Perhaps you can explain this too?"

"The room was unfamiliar," said Bill unwillingly. "I
was aware of the general location of the switch, since I had
seen you turn the lights off earlier. But in the darkness I
did not immediately find it."

Professor Burge's eyes bored into Bill's. There was no
hiding from that look. Burge was not a psychologist for
nothing. The very effort to conceal emotion was to him
emotional betrayal. "And what else delayed you?" he insisted.

Bill was forced to answer because of his doubt about how much Burge knew. It seemed as if he might know everything. "Toombs had started for the switch too," he said. "I ran into him." He hoped that it was true.

It was not true.

"But you didn't run into me, sir," Toombs said. "I was paralyzed, as you may say, sir, by Mrs. Van Wycke's scream. I did not move from beside the pantry door."

Burge spoke deliberately. His pale eyes were like glass. "Fortunate, if true," he said. "Because the person Mr. Galleon ran into *was the murderer.*"

The words rang in Bill's mind like a tolling bell. That moment in the darkness was upon him. The outrush of pent breathing was in his ears. Something hard thudded at his feet. Something soft and fuzzy was torn from his clutching fingers.

"You have no idea who it was?" Burge asked inexorably.

In his pocket Bill's fingers clenched hard over a torn scrap of pink fuzz. Like down. Like soft fine hair. . . . The sweat started on his temples. His mouth was dry. Jane's eyes were on him.

"*No,*" he said.

FIVE

"I was on a jury in a murder case once," said Angeline, "and everybody that was mixed up in it any way was searched." She took a bar of nuts and chocolate from a grey silk bag, and unwrapped the tinfoil carefully. It was her fourth since dinner, and there were only two left. She must be more saving. But you needed something to stand by you in an emergency. "I think it would be a good idea if we searched each other."

There was a storm of protest.

"I won't," said Beulah flatly.

"The man's not born can frisk me," said Varro.

Catriona began to whimper. "Holy Mary, Mother of God. . . ."

"Hush up," said Annie Budd. "What you got to worry about, a little thin thing like you? Lord sakes, I would a-changed my underwear this morning if I'd known. Do you s'pose I'll have to unhook my corsets?"

Toombs, under Bill's interested gaze, turned a furious brick red.

"I think it's a good idea," Bill said. "We've been working at this thing all the time from the murderer's end. But there's the jewel angle too. While we do not know that the person who killed Mrs. Van Wycke took the bag and the ruby, it is at least the natural assumption. The jewels must still be in this room, because there has been no chance to take them out. It would simplify everything if we could

353

find them. I don't see what valid objection there can be—from any innocent person."

"As you put it," said Jane with a strained smile, "we can hardly refuse. Can we?"

"But I wasn't even in here," wailed Catriona. "I wouldn't take any jewels if I was. . . ."

"That's so too," Angeline reminded Bill. "She and Annie Budd both came in after Mrs. Van Wycke was . . . killed. Just as much as Charlie and Joe did."

"Charlie and Joe didn't come in," Bill objected. "They stood back there in the doorway all the time except when they took Mrs. Van Wycke. We were all watching them then—they couldn't have touched anything else. But Catriona and Annie Budd have been all over the place. Suppose the jewels were hidden here—they've had plenty of chance to find them. No, we'd better make a clean sweep. Everybody. We'll search the room afterwards."

"Why not search the room first?" said Choate. "Then if we find them there'll be no need . . ."

They searched the room first. They stood in a row against the wall, while Toombs and Annie Budd and Catriona carried out their watchful instructions. They were thorough. They emptied the dishes on the table, and shook out the lace cloth, and turned the table on its side to peer round the cleats that held the legs. They rolled up the rug, and removed the bottles from the wine closet, and pried into the mechanism of the serving table, and upended the chairs. The time for concealment had been brief: the jewels could not be under the floor boards nor inside the paneling. But they examined even places that seemed impossible: the runs on the curtains, the balls at the ends of the rods, the bowl of the chandelier. . . .

They did not find anything.

Annie Budd put the room back to rights. She liked things tidy.

"Well," said Bill at last slowly, "if the jewels are here now, they're on one of us. I guess there's nothing for it. . . ."

Choate was the first to step forward. "All right. Come on," he said. "I haven't got any jewels."

Did Bill imagine it? Or did Jane look relieved?

They divided into two groups. Angeline's room and Bill's were the nearest, at the after end of the corridor where all the staterooms opened. They went there. Bill whispered a word of warning and instruction to Angeline, and led the men to his door. Choate, trying to drop behind the others, received a push from Varro that sent him staggering inside. Bill turned on the lights. In the split second before the switch clicked, he took a torn scrap of fuzz from his pocket and dropped it on the floor.

The room sprang at them out of darkness. It was a spectacular room, a shade flamboyant; rather blatantly a man's room. Christine Van Wycke's taste had run to scenic chintzes and pure color. Bill's chintz featured hunting scenes: wily foxes, and hounds in full cry, and the pride of the county in the pink riding at impossible barred gates. The walls were autumn yellow tipped with scarlet at the molding, and the rug was hunter's green. There were hunting prints on the wall. Red carnelian stags at eve drank their fill from crystal ash trays; a pen with a scarlet quill was stuck in a tankard of shot. But it seemed to Bill that the biggest thing in the room was a scrap of fuzz.

"Everybody stand back against the wall and put your hands up," he said. "Keep them up while we take turns being searched."

"You're a trusting cuss, aren't you?" said Choate. He did as Bill instructed.

"No," said Bill shortly. "Do you suppose I want the stuff planted in here?" (Choate was standing on the scrap of fuzz now.) Bill pulled out his revolver and threw it on the bed. "All right," he said. "There you are. Make what you can of it. It hasn't been fired." He stepped back and put up his hands like the others.

Varro examined the weapon. "It hasn't been fired," he admitted. "What do you pack a rod for anyway?" Varro's idiom interested Bill. His speech was like that of two people put together without editing.

"Carried it for years," Bill said carelessly. "I do a lot of night driving. Makes me feel safer."

"What's your business?" Varro asked.

"Insurance," said Bill candidly. "What's yours?"

"Importing."

"And what's yours?" he said to Choate.

Choate's hesitation was too slight to put a name to. "I don't suppose you'd call it a business. There's the family place in Virginia. I run that."

One of these country gentlemen. Always hard up, those chaps. Must be, if he'd come there to sell Mrs. Van Wycke a ruby. A family heirloom, presumably. Or had he come for that? "All ready?" Bill said. "I'll go first if you like."

Professor Burge searched Bill, and Bill searched Burge and Toombs. Afterwards Choate and Varro searched each other with a vindictive thoroughness. ("Try my ear!" Choate derided. "How do you know I haven't got a wad of jewels in each cheek like a squirrel?" The pinch of Varro's thumb and finger left red marks on his smooth boy's face.) The affair did not forward friendly relations. But when they finished, there was no chance that anything had been overlooked.

They did not find the jewels.

They laid their booty on the bed. There was the usual collection of handkerchiefs, of cigarette cases and lighters, a watch apiece, a few coins, a pigskin billfold from Varro's pocket and one of pin seal from Choate's. Dante Burge, in fancy dress, had nothing, except the embroidered guest towel with which he had wiped his lips after that ill-starred drink at the wine closet; a pad and some pencils for his lists; a penknife for pencil sharpening. They looked harmless. Bill nipped the hems of the towel and examined the pencils for false ends, feeling rather foolish.

No one had much, since they were all in dinner clothes. But there were certain items of interest. Conspicuous among these were the automatic strapped into Varro's armpit, and Jane's handkerchief in Bill's pocket.

Bill was embarrassed by the handkerchief. It was a plain linen one, hemstitched, with a white monogram in the corner: **B**. Choate examined it curiously. "Seems to have been an epidemic of handkerchief snatching tonight," he said.

Bill could feel himself flushing. Probably Jane bought those handkerchiefs by the dozen. Choate must have seen its like no end of times. . . . "She dropped it," he said shortly. "Don't worry, I'm going to give it back. It isn't a lethal weapon, is it?— All right, Toombs."

When Toombs was stripped, he was discovered to be wearing a corset. His ears were a pair of blazing torches when the thing came off. Bill understood then his confusion when the search was first mentioned. Varro sniggered. Dante Burge looked wistfully at his pad and pencils on the bed, as if he would have liked to make a note or two. But Bill knew what red ears felt like.

"A truss, Toombs?" he said kindly. "Too bad." After all, wearing a corset was not a criminal act. Maybe a butler's figure was important, like a dancer's feet.

"Yes, sir. Thank you, sir," said Toombs gratefully.

Bill examined the interlining. Nothing there. Toombs' pockets yielded a bunch of household keys, a folding corkscrew, a box of safety matches, a small pearl-handled knife with a nicked blade, and a square of pink cotton flannel.

Bill pounced on that. "What's it for?"

"For polishing silver, sir," said Toombs.

Bill tried not to look at the scrap of pink fuzz on the floor. Surreptitiously he pulled off a corner of the flannel.

Choate was obviously well pleased when he turned out Varro's automatic. Bill whistled. "So I'm not the only one!" he said. "Why didn't you come clean along with me?"

"Thought I'd leave you something to find," said Varro imperturbably.

"I suppose you do a lot of night driving *too*," said Choate.

"Who doesn't?" inquired Varro. "Matter of fact, I've been held up twice. After that I thought I'd play safe."

The automatic, like Bill's, had not been fired. It could have no bearing on Mrs. Van Wycke's death. His explanation was as plausible as Bill's. But Bill was disturbed by his manner of carrying the weapon, more than by the fact of possession.

The most exciting find was the last. Choate's knife.

They had all had knives—all except Bill, who had arrived without excess baggage. Burge's pencil sharpener; Toombs' unimpressive pearl-handled tool; a small gold penknife, of Varro's, such as is sometimes worn on a watch-chain. But now he drew from Choate's pocket a great horn-handled, brass-bound thing, bulging with corkscrews and pliers, its blade long enough and strong enough to stick a moose. Even Varro was taken aback.

"Well, that's a pretty thing!" Bill ejaculated.

"I think it's pretty too," Choate said. "That's why I carry it." His voice was elaborately casual. But he wet his lips before he spoke.

"But why *do* you carry it?" said Bill. "Deuced awkward thing. Must weigh a couple of pounds."

"I didn't want to leave it lying round," Choate said.

Bill shrugged. He took the knife from Varro and ran his thumb appraisingly down the blade. "There's a dull spot in it."

"I know," Choate said. He wet his lips again. "I was prying on a window catch that stuck, and turned the edge."

"Here?"

"Oh, no. Some time ago. I never got around to having it ground."

Varro took the knife back again. He held it, as for use, in his palm. "This dull spot comes more in the place for cutting than for prying window catches. . . ." He said deliberately: "You could cut . . . a gold chain with this."

Ewell Choate went white. The red marks of Varro's fingers stood out brightly on his cheeks. He sprang at Varro with his whole boy's body a tight white knot of anger. "You damned insinuating liar!" he cried—and struck at Varro hard. The blow went wild before Varro's neat retreat, and the empty force behind his fist sent Choate reeling. Varro turned and kicked him quickly and accurately in the stomach. It was not a pretty thing to see. Too coldly vicious. Choate doubled backward onto the edge of the bed.

". . . I'll tell you how it was," Choate said finally. The kick had taken the temper out of him. He looked shaken and a little sick. "I didn't want to tell you, because I know it sounds cock-eyed. But this was the way it was." He hesitated, gathering himself. Composing his thoughts, perhaps. "There was one of our Negros down home got mixed up in a cutting. I took the knife before they arrested him. He set store by that knife. But it looked bad. I'm convinced he didn't kill the fellow, but he was mixed up in it all right. He's on the road now. When he's done his time, he'll come back to the Place. I don't suppose I can explain to you up here how we feel about our boys. We have to look after them. They're just kids. He was a good boy. I couldn't let him die just because he had the knife. I told him I'd keep it for him till he got back. We're honest down there, even with our Negros." He tossed his head back and his lips showed whiter than white teeth. He flung his defiance in their faces like a hurled gauntlet.

"When I came up here," he said, "I brought the knife with me. It seemed safer. At first I left it in my stateroom. But that maid goes into our rooms to turn down our beds every night while we're at dinner. I have a hunch she pretty well goes through everything. I thought it might look funny. So lately I've carried it on me. Tonight I put it in my pocket same as usual. How did I know Mrs. Van Wycke was going to be killed?" His voice cracked on the edge of hysteria. Bill had not realized before how young he was.

"How did the blade get dulled?" he asked quietly.

"It was done in the fracas that night," Choate said. "Pelly hit it on an iron hitching-post." He added, wildly, his mouth working: "You don't believe me, do you?"

"I don't know," said Bill slowly.

It was a fantastic story. Too fantastic, perhaps, to have been improvised. For the first time, under the superficial charm of Choate's manner, under his young defiance, Bill sensed a flicker of something solid and unbending—something willful and reckless and wrong-headed perhaps, and yet oddly appealing, because it was sincere. He would be decent to his Negros, Bill thought. He thought, with sudden understanding, that this quality would appeal to Jane, because she was like that herself. He must not be unfair to Choate . . . because of Jane. But . . . that knife would cut a gold chain from a bag.

A suspicion washed over Bill's mind like a wave. *Was that what Jane knew?*

"No," he said more slowly still. "No, I don't believe you."

"I should like," said Burge meticulously, "to see the cutting power of that knife demonstrated."

They kept the knife and the two guns, emptied now, locking them away in Bill's desk. The small things were returned to their owners. Bill made the room tidy. He smoothed the bed-cover. He picked up some bits of lint and dust and threw them into the scarlet wastebasket.

One of the scraps that Bill picked up did not drop into the basket with the others. It remained lodged between Bill's fingers. It was a scrap of pink fuzz, no bigger than a lady's littlest nail. It had the texture of soft fine hair or down. It was still between Bill's fingers when he stuck his hands in his pockets.

It was just then that they heard the cry from Angeline's room.

2

"*Jane!*"

Bill could hardly have said whether it was his word, or Choate's, that went ringing through the echoes of that cry. He knew that he was running—out the door and across the corridor. Choate was beside him. The blood was knocking in his ears. Crazy thoughts swirled in his mind. He pounded at Angeline's door. He flung it open without waiting to be answered.

Annie Budd, in a form-fitting pink cotton union suit, uttered a shocked yelp and scampered for the bathroom, her scant grey hair and a pair of white stockings streaming. It seemed impossible that so heavy a woman could move so fleetly. She slammed the door behind her.

"Well, my goodness!" said Angeline, pinning her broach tidily into the lace at her throat. "Haven't you got any manners? Did you find them?"

"Did-you-who-screamed?" cried Bill. He was aware of Joe and Charlie once more, looming behind him.

"Jane," said Choate. "Are you all right?"

Jane was standing at the mirror, powdering her nose. She turned. She looked bitterly tired. There were pools of shadow underneath her eyes. But she was calm.

"Of course." She said urgently: "Are you?"

Beulah sat on the edge of a chair, completely dressed save for her shoes, which she held carefully in her hand. Her face had the blankness of a sleep-walker; the eyes were empty. Catriona was flung full length across the bed. The curves of her body were warm and tempting under the sleazy silk of a peach-colored slip. Toombs' marble eyes flickered and his palms grew moist. She was sobbing with complete abandon.

"No," Angeline was saying. "We didn't find them. We didn't find anything except Jane's bracelet that she lost yesterday. Catriona had it. She's the one that screamed."

Joe and Charlie backed out hastily when they found that they had burst into a ladies' dressing room. "It's all right, I guess," Bill said. "Just hysterics. Gave me a start, though."

"Us too," said Charlie, in his voice the expectation of further tragedy fading into relief. "Well . . . glad it's no worse. Come on, Joe; I guess they don't need us."

"I don't take to all this screaming," Joe complained mildly, following Charlie away.

Bill took time to watch them past the door of the dining saloon before he went back inside.

Jane crossed over to Catriona and laid a hand on the girl's shaking shoulder. "Don't cry," she said kindly. "It isn't worth it."

"I wouldn't of stole it, Miss," Catriona wailed. "I meant to give it back, so help me God. I only just found it on the floor. I only just wanted to try it on myself the night, the way I'd be giving it back to you tomorrow. I wouldn't steal anything. . . ."

"Do you care for it so much?" said Jane. "Keep it, if you like."

A very round black eye, looking rounder and blacker in its frame of wet black lashes, appeared in the crook of Catriona's arm. "You mean it, Miss?" she gasped.

"Of course," said Jane. "I would have given it to you in the first place, if you'd asked."

Catriona sat up. Bounced up. Her facile spirits soared as abruptly as they had fallen. "Say, you're a lady, Miss," she cried. "The good Saint Teresa of Lisieux bless and keep you! I wouldn't steal anything off you again, not if I had a chance to. I wouldn't steal anything anyway. I wasn't even in there, so how could I? She wouldn't give me anything, not that old hen-hawk. She'd about have the hide off me if I so much as looked crossways at her old jewels. . . ."

"Well, what do you think?" Angeline asked Bill in a worried way.

"I don't think it matters," Bill said. "Shows she'd steal, of course. But as long as the jewels weren't on her, it doesn't prove anything."

Annie Budd unlatched the bathroom door. "Catriona," she hissed through the crack, *pass me in my bloomers.*"

Choate gravitated to Jane's side, as if it were the place where he belonged. When they looked at each other there

were questions in their eyes, and answers, Bill thought.
Choate said: "They found the knife. They think I cut the
bag off her wrist."

"How perfectly absurd, Ewell," said Jane coolly. "You
couldn't have done it without pulling her arm half off."

Instantly Bill was shaken by doubt. Wasn't it true?
Wouldn't Christine have felt it? Wouldn't the chain have
been all hacked and twisted? Jane could do that to you just
by the tilt of her head and the set of her shoulders. (But
she *had* known, then, about the knife.) Just the free way
she walked dismissed the matter as beneath notice. "May I
take my lipstick now?" she said.

It had been pulled from the holder, and Jane pushed it
back again into the silver tube. She returned to the mirror.
She painted the scarlet curve of her lips with a hand as
steady as faith. Even the straight line of her back looked
intrepid. It looked incorruptible. Did Bill imagine that
her lips were white before her hand touched them? Was it
derision that she painted in the red tilt at the corners of
her mouth?

She tossed the lipstick back onto the bed. Bill was looking over the assortment. "What do you make of it?"

It wasn't much, certainly. Handkerchiefs and vanities,
Beulah's nose glasses with the round gold button and the
spring that reeled in the chain, Angeline's grey silk bag
turned wrong side out, a little heap of beads and pins and
earrings, two watches, and Jane's lost bracelet—a pretty
trifle, natural turquoises in silver, of no great intrinsic
value; a heap of thread, Annie Budd's crochet cotton, un-
wound to the last inch. Choate looked maliciously from
Bill to a white hemstitched handkerchief with a monogram
in the corner.

Bill took the mate to it with reluctance from his pocket. He hated to give it up. The faint smell of lavender had
faded, but when he laid it against his face it was fragrant
still with memory. He held it out to Jane.

"Yours," he said. "You dropped it."

Between them lay the knowledge of that night when she had . . . dropped it in his car. There had not been so much denial in the shape of her lips then. Bill glanced down at the monogram.

"Jane, what's your other name?"

"Bridge." She was instantly defiant: daring him to remember that she had called herself Jane Barron; daring him to remember . . . anything—or to make her remember.

"I mean your middle name—the one the T stands for."

"Oh," said Jane. "T-Talisman." She caught the handkerchief out of his hand and turned away abruptly.

Jane Talisman Bridge. Jane Bridge Galleon. "It's a good name," Bill said.

"Thanks," said Jane. Why need she be so bitter? He hadn't done anything to spoil . . . that night. It was she who had run away. "He likes my name, Ewell," she said with a little mocking laugh.

Angeline was straightening her bag, putting in a bottle of dyspepsia tablets and a handkerchief edged with tatting. "They cut my last two chocolate bars all to *pieces*," she complained. "My goodness, we might have eaten them. We'd know then what was inside. What shall we do with the things?"

"Might as well give them back," Bill said. "There's nothing there,"

"Well, let me tell you," said Angeline firmly, "that's all there *was*. My goodness! *Thorough!*"

Annie Budd came out of the bathroom, rather flushed, but fully dressed. She picked up her tangled cotton and began to wind it. Beulah put on her shoes. Catriona tied her pert little apron round her waist, and set her pert little cap over one ear; she placed her left hand at her hip where the new bracelet would show to the best advantage. The others gathered their belongings. Angeline salvaged a few crumbs of the chocolate bars. They filed out into the corridor.

"What we need," Angeline was saying, "is some good hot coffee and a bite to stay our stomachs. . . ."

In the corridor, before the door of the dining saloon where the lights fell full upon him, stood the dog Telemachus. He had been engaged in some doggish frolic, and his legs and ears were all at a loose end. He came to a stand when he saw them, his tail waving pleased half-circles of welcome.

"Urrumpfh?" he remarked in a muffled voice.

The dog Telemachus held the bag in his mouth.

3

Telemachus in that cold dawn received the shock of an eventful life.

He had been playing with a little shiny thing that had come into his possession in the most innocent way in the world. It was a good thing to play with. It didn't go all to pieces and stick to your teeth like the inside of a down pillow, and yet it wasn't really hard, either; when you bit it, it made a pleasant crunching sound like bones. It was fun to worry it between your paws and pretend it was a woodchuck; to throw it, and run after it and slide, till the back half of you fell down on the polished floor. That tall sly one, who knew how to pinch and had red-setter hair, wouldn't bother him this time; she was down in the room at the end of the hall, smelling bloody. The others were all with the little round smooth one, who smelled of candy and looked like a pug. It was about time for them to come out. The game lacked an audience. When the door to Angeline's room opened, Telemachus sprang to his feet, full of good fellowship.

"Urrumpfh?" he asked them pleasantly.

A lot of things had happened to the dog Telemachus. Once a fire-cracker exploded between his feet; and once he had a tin can tied to him and nearly bit off the end of his tail getting rid of it; and once he put his head through a hole in a chicken run and couldn't get it out again, and

a rooster pecked him on the nerve end in his nose. And
there was the time when he lost his head over a woman
(a cute little bitch she was, too, with a come-hither look
and black curls down her back); and had lost an eye also
and part of an ear in consequence. But he had never been
pursued by ten human beings, all baying like a pack in full
cry. Even his mistress, whom he trusted with reservations,
came at him yelping like a Peke. It was enough to upset
any dog. Telemachus pulled in his tail, pulled down his
ears, and ran.

Telemachus bolted straight down the corridor and out
the door on the starboard side that led to the gangplank
and the shore. They were all right behind him.

"Lemmy! Lemmy!"

"Come back here! Good dog!"

"Stop, you brute!"

"Drop it, I tell you!"

But Telemachus cleared the plank in one frightened
bound, and was off across the beach, his long whitish body
flung straight in flight like a wisp of fog in the whitish
dawn.

Bill was the first ashore. They all reached the narrow
plank together, and in the scuffle and confusion, with
everyone trying to cross at once, that precious moment
was lost which would have meant capture. Bill straddled
the rail and jumped. He landed among round stones, slippery from the tide, and came to his knees in shallow water.
He recovered himself and ran.

The beach curved in a white crescent round the cove
where the *Aphrodite* lay, but back from the shore the land
rose sharply, well-wooded: pine and white birch and oak.
Through the black and white of the trees, themselves half-
seen in the deceptive light, flickered the body of the dog
Telemachus, a very wraith of a dog, merging with the birch
bark and the mists. Behind him, alternately cursing and
cajoling, ran Bill.

It was hard running. The pitch grew steeper, inland. Wet leaf mold and pine needles made an unsteady footing. It was still almost dark in the more heavily wooded parts, and unseen tree trunks sprang at Bill out of nothing. A dozen times he slipped, and fell, and scrambled up again; he crashed into stumps and ploughed through thickets. Abruptly the dog Telemachus disappeared.

Bill ran on stubbornly, hoping to sight him again. The trees thinned presently, and the ground grew more solid underfoot. Bill came out on bare rock. He had run the whole length of the island. Before him the cliffs of Bowsprit Head stood to sea in a smother of foam.

Bill stopped then, getting his breath, listening. It was a wild and lonely spot to lie less than a mile from the peace of the *Aphrodite's* cove. Far off he could hear the shouts of the pursuit, but the surf drowned smaller, nearer sounds. A single boat lay off to the east, no more than a low black cloud. A pretty place, Bill thought irritably, to find yourself in a grisly dawn on the trail of a lost ruby. The salt needles of the spray pricked his face with cold.

Bill doubled back, keeping along the landward shore. On the other side the cliff fell sheer to the water; the dog must have gone this way. The rocks were ghostly in the thin light, jagged, with tossed boulders, and deep fissures between them; a tatter of kelp and sea moss marked the high-water line, and there were pools left by the tide. It was some time before he found any of the others.

Afterwards Bill was to know a number of things that had happened during that interval. How Angeline tried to step across a crevasse and got stuck there, one foot on one side and one on the other, and no way to get forward or back; how she screamed her head half off before Beulah found her. How Catriona slipped and would have fallen right into the water and drowned as like as not, if Toombs hadn't been so brave and caught her; she twisted her ankle pretty bad anyway, and Toombs had to help her when she

walked and put his arm right round her. They went back
and sat on the beach to wait for the others. How Professor
Burge, hot in pursuit of the dog Telemachus, had seen him
drop the bag into a standing pool; how he had lain on his
stomach and groped in the pool's cold depths, and finding
nothing had painstakingly bailed out all the water with a
shoe, because he dared not go for a dipper lest he never
find the same pool again; how he came to the bottom
finally and salvaged an aged beef bone. How Annie Budd
had got plumb tuckered, running, and sat down on a log
to rest, and while she was sitting there she had seen, just
as plain as the nose on your face . . .

But that was later. Bill rounded a boulder and came
upon Jane and Choate.

They were below him, in the angle that two rocks made.
Jane stood with her arms lifted, her palms flat against the
stone; her head bent down between her arms in an attitude
of complete abandonment to grief. Choate hovered uneasily, smoothing her brown hair.

"That's the only way I can see out of it," he said. "You
meet me where I said. I'll wait until you come. . . ."

A pebble rolled under Bill's foot. When he came down
to Jane, Choate had disappeared.

Jane turned, her head tilted against the rock, her chin
lifted, watching Bill's descent. It seemed impossible now
that this could be the figure of despair he had seen from
above; a teasing smile tipped the corners of her mouth.

"Nice exercise," she said. "I've taken my daily dozen
falls already. This is a grand place for it. Try one."

"Where's Choate?" Bill said.

"Somewhere on the island, I imagine. Why?"

"He was talking to you when I came in sight."

"This light is so deceptive, isn't it?"

Bill came close. At once he felt the spell that Jane
always put upon him. When he was away from her, reason
was cold and facts raised ugly heads. But when the clear
look of her eyes met his, even facts grew small. Now reason
told him that she was simply detaining him, teasing him

a little, keeping him amused, to give Choate time to get away. And . . . he knew that if Jane were in his arms he would not care.

Bill did not take Jane in his arms. He only came close, and he laid his hand over hers. "Jane," he said unhappily, "why are you like this?"

"A question I've often asked myself," Jane said cheerfully. "If I'd put in the order, I should have been a blonde."

"You know what I mean."

"Do you?"

"Jane—aren't you going to tell me?"

"Tell you what?"

It was no use. She was gone, the Jane he had held in his arms that night, whose lips he had kissed, who had kissed him back again. She was gone inside this cold bright shell of a Jane, who fended him off with a ready wit, and a painted smile, and unfathomable blue eyes.

"The truth!" Bill cried. He caught Jane by the shoulders, and held her, hard, till anger leaped in her eyes. "You can't treat me like this. I've got a right. . . . Of course I know you weren't in your place at the table."

"And so you think I killed Mrs. Van Wycke?" Her voice was mocking.

"You know I don't. I don't think you killed Mrs. Van Wycke. And I don't think you stole the bag. . . ."

"That's generous of you."

". . . I know there's some simple explanation. I thought you'd tell me when we were alone. It's only fair, if I'm to do anything. Where were you, Jane? What were you doing? What are you hiding? What are you afraid of? What is it that you know?— You can see how it would look to the others."

"Have you told them . . . yet?" said Jane deliberately.

Bill stepped back as if she had struck him. "You know I haven't."

For an instant it was as if her purpose wavered; as if she almost spoke to him frankly, meeting his desire. The line of her mouth softened, and her lashes fluttered down; her

whole body relaxed a little of its tautness where she held it
so straight against the rock. "I know you haven't," she said
more gently. And at once it was as if some memory flogged
her back again to defiance. "Say I was tired of the game,"
she told him, with a bitter flippancy. "Say I went to take
a walk. That's as good as the next thing. You wouldn't believe the truth."

"I would," Bill cried. "If you *said* it was the truth."

She flung the word back at him. "Truth? How can there
be any truth between us now? Of course I know why you're
here. Do you think I believe that story about your boat's
sinking? You came after the ruby. And you think I came
after it too."

Above them a pebble rolled and came tinkling down
the slope. Angeline's round inquisitive face rose like a full
moon over a boulder. But when she had clambered down
to Jane, Bill too was gone.

4

They assembled finally on the beach. Day had come, without sun. There was not much rain, but the fog was closing
in. It was clammy to their touch, gathering in beads on
hair and lashes. They were a sodden company.

The dog Telemachus was the last to join them. He
strolled nonchalantly round the point, wearing a pleased
grin. He saw now that he had taken offence where none
had been intended. They had given him a turn, all rushing
at him like that. But they hadn't meant any harm. It was
just their funny human way. As soon as he understood that
they wanted to play Chase, he had joined in heartily. Now
they had given it up, he might as well come in. He extended his paws before him and made them an obeisance.

There was mud on the dog Telemachus' paws. There
was mud on his chin. He had obviously been digging. The
bag was gone.

SIX

Joe fetched the clam rakes.

". . . I know just exactly where he's got it buried," Annie Budd was saying. "I got near about tuckered, running so far, so I set down on a log to rest myself; and while I was setting there, I saw the dog, just as plain as I see the nose on your face, digging a hole under a tree. I know right exactly where it was. I set there so long I got the whole place by heart. There was a tree same as here, and a tree here, and a tree *here,* and the tree where he was digging at was right over *here,* and I'm almost certain it was a white birch. It was up this way. I can take you right to it. . . ."

"You go too," Bill said to Charlie.

Charlie hesitated. "Figured I'd stay aboard. Look after things."

"You go," Bill repeated. He did not want anyone left aboard the *Aphrodite.* "I'll take the responsibility."

He saw Charlie's expression close, like a door swung shut in the draft of his suspicion. The mouth tightened as if it had been locked. But he pretended not to notice; and Charlie moved away without answering.

"Come on, Toombs," Angeline cried excitedly. "You got a rake too?"

"I was employed as a butler, m'am," said Toombs austerely. "Not as a ditch-digger."

"Gee, you're brave!" whispered Catriona. "Talking up to them like that. I wouldn't dare to. Say, am I hurting you, Gus, leaning onto you so hard?"

"Who, *me?*" inquired Toombs largely. "A little bit of a thing like you? Why don't you lean harder?"

They followed the others up the slope and disappeared.

"I thought it was about here," Annie Budd was saying, "but I guess it must be further along. The trees all look quite a lot alike, don't they? But I'll know the place all right when I see it. . . ."

Bill did not join the digging party. Numbers insured the safety of the jewels, if they were found. It had occurred to Bill that it would be more useful to know who, if anyone, tried to slip away from the others. There might be things on the boat that some one would like done. That was why he had sent Charlie away. If anyone tried to go aboard . . . He chose a place on the wooded slope overlooking the cove. When he sat down a fringe of bushes screened him from view. He folded his long legs into the circle of his arms, and rested his chin on his knees.

Before him the day was done in pallid hues, like a wash drawing. The sea was grey, rolling uneasily under its burden of fog; the sky was a feeling, more than sight, of grey above it. Ashore everything was water-laden. Bill's lightest movement brought a shower of drops off the weighted leaves. Even the *Aphrodite* had no luster. Its white was dead white. Its brass gave no reflection. Behind Christine Van Wycke's open ports, the curtains hung limp with dampness. Bill's thoughts were as grey as his surroundings.

The person you ran into was the murderer. Burge's words drummed in Bill's ears to the rhythm of the small waves on the beach. He went over that moment in the darkness—cautiously, for fear of what he might find. A thud of something falling. That would be the gun. A gasp of held breath, suddenly released. That proved nothing. But the scrap of pink fuzz. . . . Ah, *that* now.

Bill took the scrap from his pocket and examined it scrupulously. It was such a bit of fuzz as might have come from a wool scarf. Dante Burge had worn a wool scarf. But the scrap did not match. Bill had satisfied himself of that when he put the scarf round Jane's shoulders. No one else had worn a wrap of any kind; nothing woolly. Bill turned the thing over thoughtfully. It was grimy now from its stay on Bill's floor. But it had certainly been pink. He took out the corner of pink cotton flannel from Toombs' polishing cloth. That did not match either. The nap was thin and matted. But Bill's scrap was full-bodied: like plush or one of the short-haired furs, beaver or sealskin. Bill snorted. Pink fur! It didn't make sense.

It didn't make sense, either: what Jane had said to him down there by the rock. "You came after the ruby. *And you think I came after it too.*" What did she mean by that?

Bill's mind turned backward, searching for an explanation. Right back to that bright day when he had first met Jane. . . .

Bill worked for the Verity Insurance Company, and Jane—Jane Barron, strangely, she called herself then—had come to work there too. She was in the filing room, but Bill saw right away that she was no ordinary filing clerk. Just the way she stood showed that: quiet, not fussing with her hair. He had made himself some business at the files that very first morning; fixed it so the department head would have to introduce them.

Jane had been wearing a blue suit, he remembered. Bill had always supposed before that a blue suit was just a blue suit. It wasn't necessarily. It could have a white dickey with a high collar under the most delectable chin that ever tilted up to match the smoky tilt of lashes; it could have white leather buttons, and a big white leather belt round a waist that would just have fitted the circle of Bill's hands. The prim bang across her forehead gave a child's candor to her lifted gaze. Bill felt a trifle awed. It made her look so . . . innocent.

"If there's anything I can do for you . . ." he began. And when she smiled at him, not with her lips, but right out of the blue deeps of her eyes, he added eagerly: "I could show you a place to have lunch, if you wanted me to."

They had lunch together that day, and the day after;
it came to be understood that they should lunch together. Sometimes they went to Merrick's. Bill liked that best
because there were alcoves. But even when they had only
time for the drugstore round the corner, still it was worth
doing. They sat on high stools and swung their legs and
liked each other. Just the way Jane took a round little bite
out of her Swiss-on-rye, just the way her lashes flicked up
when she looked at him over the rim of her coffee mug, set
up a wild sweet jangling in Bill's nerves like the sound of
sleigh bells. It was like that from the beginning.

Looking back on it now, Bill could see that there were
things that would have made Angeline . . . wonder. But
at the time Bill was absorbed by the wonder of Jane's self.
They came back to him now—pictures and snatches of
talk, without connection.

Jane had never worked before. She asked the most in-
genuous questions. She did her work conscientiously, coming early and staying late, pouring over the files. But she
wasn't, ever, a girl you imagined in an office. You imagined her on horseback, riding through woods that were
scarlet and rust with autumn. You imagined her in a boat,
with her hair blowing. . . .

Bill took her to the shore the next Saturday. He never forgot Jane that day, with the sail of the boat behind
her: Jane in white flannel and a scarlet jersey, a white
beret with a feather. The beret blew off finally. Bill remembered, because it was the first time he had seen Jane
with her hair loose, whipping about her ears. Jane had the
nicest ears. . . .

Jane lived in a two-room apartment, way uptown. She
seemed startled the night Bill asked to go in with her, and
the pink came up in her face. Bill was profoundly moved.
Sweet, he thought. She wasn't used to having men there.
. . . Inside the tiny living room, she stood with her back
to him, fumbling for the lamp; a picture in a silver frame
fell down and she left it lying—tossed her gloves on top

of it as if she had not noticed. But she looked at him too quickly, Bill thought, judging if he had seen. Her look gave the picture importance. Bill had a fleeting impression of a young man, slender and fair. That was all. But he was startled at the cold stab of jealousy that racked him.

"Friend of yours?" he said—and hated himself because he had had to say it.

"Naturally," said Jane coolly. An edge showed in her voice, as if she were annoyed.

There was a fireplace in the room. Bill made a fire and they sat before it. But Jane remained big-eyed and breathless, answering him at random. And Bill was nagged by the presence of the picture, lying face down on the table. Who was the fellow, occupying a settled spot in a room that Bill had hardly seen? He burst out again at last, irrepressibly: "Look here, Jane. I . . . like you an awful lot. I guess you couldn't help knowing. I meant to tell you some time. Jane, who is he? What is he to you?"

"You're taking things for granted," Jane said.

The words left him in doubt of her meaning. Did she mean that the picture had no special significance? Or did she mean that he had no right to ask? It was easy to think the former . . . then.

But Bill guessed now, with a pang of understanding, that the picture must have been of Ewell Choate.

Afterwards Bill forgot about the picture. It was easy to forget, with Jane, the things you chose not to remember. He was often in her apartment. They had Sunday-night suppers there. They cooked over the grill and ate at the round table. There was no picture on it after that first night—no pictures anywhere; no ornaments. Of course it was a furnished apartment. But somehow you expected a girl like Jane to have things—books and cushions, pretty cups and saucers; things like that. The room was bare. It gave it an air of impermanence. . . . Bill realized that now.

At the time Bill did not even know that the room was bare. It wasn't bare with Jane in it. When Jane sat across

the table, they were in another room, somewhere else.
There would be sun in it, and flowers. Breakfast was the
nicest to imagine. Jane would sit opposite like that, pouring their coffee from a silver pot. She would have on one
of those pink things, with lace, such as you see in store
windows; a pair of slippers with toes and no heels. . . .

"You won't be here next year at this time," he said once.
He had been assigned to the Drake and Durgin case, and
it gave him confidence.

"I hope not," said Jane composedly.

Her composure startled him, so that he did not finish.
He remembered the picture then, but afterwards he forgot
it again.

Jane always took the deepest interest in Bill's work.
She led him to talk of it, asking a thousand questions—
more than he could answer. He had to be careful what he
said; the details of his work were secret. But it pleased
and encouraged him because Jane wanted to know. Under
the warm eagerness of Jane's look—red lips a little parted,
breath coming quickly—insurance seemed the most exciting business in the world, and Verity supreme among insurance companies; he saw himself rising from an obscure
investigator, doing routine work, to a position of dignity
and trust; passing from triumph to triumph, incapable of
failure, for Jane's sake. She asked him about the Drake and
Durgin ruby one night. It was not a thing he could discuss; he turned her question off. But he remembered now
that she had asked. . . . He remembered that a description
of the jewel had been in the files—it mentioned the mark
on the back. . . .

Drake and Durgin, the jewelers, had lost a valuable
ruby, insured with Verity. An employee named Sheel Tarrant was suspected of its theft. When he was accused, Tarrant practically confessed his guilt by committing suicide.
The ruby was not found among his effects, and all the
usual means of tracing it failed. But Verity never gave up
a case, no matter how hopeless. Bill was working on it,

under supervision. When by following a hunch of his own, he turned up what looked like a clue, he was jubilant.

The troublesome thing about the case was that there was so little to go on. Young Tarrant had been hired by Mr. Drake himself, on the recommendation of an old college classmate; the man was now on an ethnological expedition somewhere at the headwaters of an obscure African river—it would be months before communication could be established. Tarrant had no intimates among the other employees of Drake and Durgin—if so, they would not now admit it. He lived in a rooming house and took his meals here and there. The other tenants had with him no more than a nodding acquaintance. The landlady, close-mouthed over the only scandal that had ever touched her respectable establishment, could hardly remember him. There were no papers in his room: no letters, no addresses. His clothes were few, but good. He had a nice taste in ties and socks. That was all they knew about him.

Bill was telephoning to Jane, drawing curlicues on the pad at his elbow while he waited for his number, when the idea came to him.

Bill went that very night to the house where Sheel Tarrant had lived. He wanted to look at rooms, he told the landlady. Not for himself. He had a friend. . . . She showed him the two that were vacant. Neither was the one which Sheel Tarrant had occupied. That did not matter now; there was nothing more to be learned there. Bill examined the rooms, asking interested questions about hot water and the noise from the street. Was there a telephone on each floor? No, she told him; just the one downstairs. But there was a buzzer on each floor, and the maid buzzed your number when you were wanted. That would do nicely, Bill said.

"May I use the telephone before I go?" he asked, as if on an impulse, making ready to leave. "If I called my friend from here, I could tell him. . . ."

"Right this way," she said affably.

The telephone was in a small room under the stairs; a wall telephone; pay station. There was nothing else except an unshaded electric light, a stand for the directories, a pencil tied to the instrument, and a pad, long since worn down to the last page, nailed beside it. The walls were a rusty yellow, shading at the top to cigarette-smoke grey. On the pad, and on the painted wall around it, were the accumulated jottings of many months; scrolls and geometrical figures and impossible ladies' heads; names and addresses and telephone numbers, handsomely shaded.

Bill took down the receiver and dropped his nickel in the slot, for the landlady's benefit. He placed his elbow on the hook before the operator answered, and holding the receiver to his ear, carried on a long conversation with himself. While he described the two rooms to his hypothetical friend, while he listened to his friend's hypothetical answers, Bill copied all the names and addresses and telephone numbers into his notebook.

Bill thanked the landlady, and took his departure. There was nothing more he could do that night. So he went to see Jane. It was a great temptation to tell Jane all about it. But he didn't.

The next morning Bill sat at his desk in the Verity Insurance Company offices, with his telephone before him, and worked resolutely through his list.

"Excelsior Dry Cleaning Company," he said briskly to each new number. "Can you give me any information about Mr. Sheel Tarrant? Want to get his present address. I've got a suit here that he never called for."

No one had ever heard of Mr. Sheel Tarrant.

Late that afternoon, Bill was still stubbornly hard at it; names like Brown, without initials, have great possibilities. It was after four when he struck something.

It was a maid's voice, Bill thought. "No, sir," she said. "I wouldn't know. I'll get Mr. Toombs to speak to you if you'll hold the line."

Mr. Toombs, presently, spoke to Bill. "Mr. Sheel Tarrant?" he said. "I understand that he died some little time ago."

"Oh," said Bill. "Don't know what his address was, do you? Maybe I could deliver the suit to his family."

"No, I don't know."

"Nobody there that would?"

"Mrs. Van Wycke would know. I can ask her if you like."

"I wish you would," Bill said.

He waited a long time. "Mrs. Van Wycke does not remember the name," Toombs reported. "I must have been mistaken."

"Well, all right. Thanks," Bill said. "Have to let it go, I guess. Sorry to trouble you."

So the servants recognized the name, but their mistress did not even remember it.

Within the hour Bill knew that the telephone was listed under the name of Mrs. Christine Van Wycke, and that Mrs. Christine Van Wycke collected jewels. He stayed late at the office, writing his report.

When Æneas Verity read that report, he sent for Bill. He tapped a square white finger on the pages. "Not bad," he said. This was rare praise from old Mr. Verity, whose customary comment, when he had no fault to find, was "Hum." It was arranged finally that Bill should be allowed a free hand with the Drake and Durgin case, following a plan which he now roughly sketched. "See what you can do with it," Mr. Verity agreed. "Then I'll see what I can do with you."

Bill left that office treading on air. It was his first big opportunity. A rosy future opened before him. If he could make a go of this case . . . Why it meant about everything. Not just promotion: more responsibility; more money. It meant that now he could ask Jane to marry him.

Bill was excited that night. "It's a celebration," he told Jane. "Put on your clothes. We're going places." He took her to the most expensive hotel in the city. He ordered caviar and venison and champagne and hearts of palms— every crazy, extravagant thing he could think of. He spent a week's wages. More. It didn't matter. Jane's dress was fire and her eyes were sky. The closeness of the gown showed him the clear young lines of her body; from the shoulder the great gorgeous sleeves dropped to the hem. When she walked, the sleeves were wings behind her. Bill caught his breath.

"I want you to be as much excited as I am. I want it to mean as much to you as it does to me. . . ."

"But it does," she told him. "More. I *am* excited."

It was true. She was flushed, and her eyes were shining. Bill had never seen her like that. He had not thought that she would care so much.

They drove outside the city in Bill's car, and stopped on a bluff that looked down on the river. It lay below them pale and chaste under the touch of the moon. The trees were in new leaf. A sweet madness ran in Bill's blood like the stirring of the spring in the trees. He took Jane in his arms. After that first waiting moment, Jane gave herself to his embrace with a lovely frankness.

Bill slipped out from under the wheel and gathered Jane close. He held her hard, so that he felt the shape of her body against his, the warm young lift of breast under his hand. She began to tremble a little, and her head slipped back in the crook of his arm. He bent down and his lips found hers in a long rich fulfillment. Jane had sweet lips. He kissed her again and again; and Jane kissed him back. She put up her arms about his neck, and the great sleeves wrapped them round. . . .

She was still at last, with her head against his shoulder. Bill's lips were in her hair. "I can tell you now . . . ask you. . . ." he began eagerly. "I'll have something to offer you now. Why if I can crash through with this case . . ."

"The Drake and Durgin case, you mean?" Jane said.

He answered her, half-laughing: "Sweet, what do you know about the Drake and Durgin case?"

"I work in the filing room, don't I?" Jane said. "I filed your report."

"Did you *read* it?" Bill said.

"Why not?" said Jane calmly. "Naturally I'd be interested, wouldn't I?"

The admission of her interest took his mind, so that he lost sight of the issue. Surely it meant that she cared. . . . "You were wonderful," she was saying. "I never should have thought of that telephone pad in a thousand years." He warmed under her praise.

"You made me think of it," he said eagerly. He felt her awareness of him quicken, and added: "I was telephoning to you . . . writing your name on the pad while I was waiting. I realized it was what everybody did. . . ." He stopped in happy confusion. It had been *Jane Galleon* that he was writing.

"Perhaps I could do something more," she whispered. "Could I, Bill? What are you going to do next?"

"I don't know exactly."

He was conscious of the stiffening of her body, her almost imperceptible withdrawal. But her words struck him like a blow. "If you don't trust me . . ."

"But sweet, of course I trust you. You know it isn't that. It's . . ."

"If you trusted me, you'd tell me," Jane said.

He was surprised and hurt by her unreason; it wasn't like Jane. "But that hasn't a thing to do with it," he repeated. "It's just—well, one of the rules. Why if I went round chattering all the time, it would be as much as my job's worth. . . ."

"All right," said Jane. "If you care more for your job than you do for me. . . ."

"But Jane . . ." He was utterly wretched now; only half-coherent. "I don't. You know I don't. I love you. I always have. I meant to tell you tonight. . . . Besides, Jane, it's true—what I said. I *don't* know exactly. It depends on how things happen. . . ."

Bill did not guess then how true it was. For when he went to Christine Van Wycke's house, he found it closed. Bill had a bad time before he located her finally aboard the *Aphrodite*. When he arrived, it was to find Jane before him. *Why was that?*

". . . Let it go," she had said then, when Bill floundered into silence. "It doesn't matter. I only thought maybe I could help you."

"But you do help me," Bill cried. "You have, from the beginning. Why just looking at you helps me. . . ."

She lifted her head, and he saw that at last he had touched her. "What do you mean?" she said slowly.

He groped for the right words. "Just being you. You kind of . . . inspire me." That was true too, he thought. Jane did inspire him. He could do, for Jane, things that without her he could not have imagined. "Why I never would have got anywhere with this case if it hadn't been for you."

He saw her lashes flicker down, and he thought that he had won. But when he would have kissed her again, she drew more definitely away. "Not now," she said. "It isn't fair."

"All's fair in love . . ."

"And war." Jane's voice was somber. Bill didn't understand it then. He didn't now. She said, strangely: "It isn't finished."

"The case, you mean?"

"Yes."

Bill was puzzled. That wasn't like Jane either. To set a price on love. To make his success a condition. "I can't see what that has to do with it," he burst out.

"Everything," said Jane. It was the word she had used again last night at the dinner table. . . .

Suddenly Jane was not in his arms at all. She was in her own corner of the seat. Bill was under the wheel. He didn't know how it had happened. "Take me home," Jane said. "Please, Bill. I'm cold."

It all came back to Bill now—that bleak long ride. The moon went down in darkness, and the wind blew chill from the river. He did not see Jane again after that night. In the light of recent events, their whole acquaintance was shadowed with possible meanings. Why had Jane run away? *Why was Jane here?*

Jane did not come to work the next morning. Her department had no message. Bill telephoned, and there was no answer. He went tearing up to her apartment. He rang and rang. There was no click to the latch.

Bill sought out the landlady. "Miss Barron?" she said. "She's gone."

"Gone?" Bill cried. "Gone where?"

"How should I know? It's no business of mine. She paid up her rent." She softened when she saw Bill's staring grief. "You Mr. Galleon?" she said, more kindly. "I got a note for you then. She said give it to you if you came."

Bill tore the note open when he was alone.

> Dear Bill: It was a good celebration, wasn't it? Thank you for all you have done for me. I shall never forget it. I know you will agree that it is better for us not to see each other any more. It would be too much of a strain, wouldn't it, to try to keep it up? Don't hunt for me, Bill. It wouldn't do any good.
>
> Jane.

2

"Well!" said Angeline. "What are you doing?"

Bill raised his head. For an instant everything whirled about him. Then the *Aphrodite* was still again at her mooring; Angeline's round pink face and her round blue wondering eyes took solid shape before him.

"Thinking," Bill said. "I do it for the exercise."

Angeline plumped down on the wet leaves at his side. "There's plenty to think about," she agreed. "My goodness, the time we've had! Such a wild-goose chase as Annie Budd led us! I began to think she was doing it on purpose. But she found the place finally. Telemachus had something buried there all right, and we dug it up, and what do you think it was? A dead squirrel. You haven't got anything to eat, have you?"

"No," said Bill, "just cigarettes. What's the crowd doing now?"

"Oh, they're still digging. Upon my soul, I should think that dog was a kleptomaniac. They were on the twenty-first hole when I left. No, the twenty-second. The twenty-first was where they found the tea-strainer. . . ."

"All there, are they?"

"Oh, yes," said Angeline. "All but me. And you. That's why I came away. I couldn't help wondering where you were. And then I had a few questions I thought I'd like to ask you."

"Yes?" said Bill drily.

"Yes," said Angeline. "You see, I can't help wondering about you and Jane."

"I can't either," said Bill.

"What I was wondering was if you knew Jane before you came here. It did seem awfully kind of sudden for you to go right out on deck like that and, well, *hug* her, if you'd never even seen her before."

"Ever hear of a fast worker?" said Bill.

"Well, yes," said Angeline. "I was wondering about that, too. After all, as Mr. Choate says, you'd only been here about four hours when things began to happen. Of course you couldn't hardly have shot Mrs. Van Wycke, because I had hold of your knee all the time. But I guess you could have taken the jewels as well as the next one. And I couldn't help wondering about what Jane said down there by that rock. Why should she think you were after the ruby? And why should you think she was? And why . . ."

"I don't think so," said Bill shortly.

"Who do you think did it then?" said Angeline. "Do you think Mr. Choate was mixed up in it any way? Talk about fast workers. My goodness! Here this Mr. Choate showed up one afternoon—letting on he wanted to sell a ruby, and that shows he was interested in rubies, doesn't it?—and according to his story he didn't know anybody here on the boat. And in twenty-four hours, everybody was running after him, and butter wouldn't melt in Mrs. Van Wycke's mouth, if I do say so, as shouldn't now she's dead; and even Annie Budd was taking up his coffee of a morning, and saying how he put her in mind of her boy that was killed in the war, and sewing on his buttons; and he and Jane were as thick as thieves. . . ."

Bill fired up at that. "What do you mean?"

"Oh, I didn't mean anything," Angeline assured him. "You can't wonder if the word would come to mind. But all I meant was they seemed awful taken up with each other. I didn't hardly like it, the way he'd keep after Jane and Mrs. Van Wycke too. But I guess Jane was the one he liked all right. I don't suppose now there'll be anything to hinder. Seemed as if he didn't want Mrs. Van Wycke to notice anything. But the minute she'd be out of sight, he and Jane . . ."

"Do you think they're . . . engaged?"

"Well, I don't know," Angeline admitted. "If they're not, I guess they'd better be, the things I've seen. The way he'll be hanging round the library when Jane's working, making out he wants to see the books; and chasing off after her every time she goes to walk. I found them one day. . . . Of course I didn't mean to intrude. But I couldn't help wondering if he'd really gone after her. And sure enough, there they were, sitting on a rock, and she had her head on his shoulder, and he had his arm round her, and they were whispering. I couldn't hear what they said. But I know this for a fact—though maybe I ought not to say it, and I wouldn't to everybody—but last night, night before last I suppose it is now, he was in Jane's stateroom."

"*No!*"

"Oh, I don't mean there was any *harm* to it," Angeline said hastily. "I guess there wouldn't be so much talking going on if there, well, *had* been. Not that I mean they were quarrelling. Arguing, more; as if he wanted something she didn't or the other way round. He was in there two hours and forty-seven minutes. I couldn't help noticing. And when he left he kissed her good-night."

"Are you . . . sure?" said Bill. His voice was shaken.

"Of course I'm sure," said Angeline. "Didn't I open my door and put my head out—I'd stayed dressed on purpose, all but my shoes—and I said, 'Is there anything I can do for you, Mr. Choate?' and he asked me for a match. And I said I didn't have any matches, because I didn't smoke, and I wouldn't either, though they do say it keeps you from having colds, and I have a very delicate throat; and I said if it was a match he wanted in Jane's room, it certainly took a lot of talk to get it. And he said he hoped I'd meet my match some time, and that would take a lot of talk too. And then he went in his room and slammed the door. And it was five minutes past three."

She broke off. "What's the matter? You look as if you'd seen a ghost. I wonder . . . are you in love with Jane, *too?*"

Bill lifted harassed eyes. "Who wouldn't be?" he said incautiously.

Angeline was instantly all concern. Love in her own person had passed Angeline Tredennick by, but she had the elderly virgin's sensitive awareness of the affairs of other people. "Why, you poor boy!" she cried. "I upset you, didn't I? I wouldn't have said all that if I'd known. Why it's just like a novel, isn't it? One of those triangular ones. I wonder which will turn out to be the hero, and which will be the villain? I kind of hope you will. The hero, I mean. You and Jane would make a handsome pair. I wonder if that was what you meant when you spoke about changing her name? A ruby would make a nice engagement ring, wouldn't it . . . ?"

"Very nice," said Bill drily. "Was that all you wanted to know?"

Angeline missed the irony. "Oh, no," she cried eagerly. "I wonder if you came because Jane was here? And I wonder if that was why she was so upset last night? You know Professor Burge spoke of it before anything, well, *happened*. And I can't help wondering what made your boat sink on such a calm day. It doesn't seem hardly natural. What *did* make it sink, Mr. Galleon?"

"It sank," said Bill wearily, "because I bored holes in the bottom."

While Angeline talked, an idea had been forming in Bill's mind. Angeline was sufficiently irritating. But Lord, the things she knew! There were details Bill wanted to know too about the *Aphrodite* and its people. It had occurred to him already that Angeline might be a valuable ally. He realized now that she might be a formidable adversary. He could not have her wondering about him all over the place. . . . "All right," he said. "I'll tell you."

Bill told Angeline only so much as was absolutely necessary. "Jane has nothing to do with this," he began. "I knew her when we were both working in the city. That's all. I was with an insurance company, and I am now investigating the theft of a ruby that was insured with them. There was some reason to think that the stone had come into Mrs. Van Wycke's possession—though I don't mean she knew it was stolen. I wanted to have a look around. I did not know Mrs. Van Wycke, and when I found that she was spending the summer on a house boat I saw there was no possibility of meeting her in any conventional way. So I just rowed within swimming distance, sank the boat, and trusted to luck. Naturally I was interested in the ruby that Mrs. Van Wycke wore last night. I could not be sure whether it was the stone I was after or not. I thought so. But I couldn't get a good look because of the setting. And . . . now it's gone again. And . . . Mrs. Van Wycke is dead."

Angeline was seething with excitement. "Why, you're a real detective!" she cried. "Just like in a murder mystery!"

"Not just like that," Bill said with a wry grin. "I've never had any experience with . . . murders."

"Oh, but I have," cried Angeline eagerly. "I was on a jury in a murder trial once. I helped the district attorney a lot. I guess I can help you too."

"I hope so," said Bill thoughtfully. He must keep her from finding out that Jane Bridge had worked for Verity too, under the name of Jane Barron. That it was Jane's empty chair which she had seen in the lightning flash. That he had a scrap of fuzz. . . . "Look here," he said, "do ladies ever wear pink fur on their—underclothes?"

"Pink fur!" cried Angeline. "Are you crazy?"

"I guess so," Bill admitted.

3

Bill leaned over and placed his fingers firmly across Angeline's lips.

From the direction of the Point on the seaward side, a solitary figure had come into view. At first Bill could not make him out in the fog. Then he saw that it was Choate. He stood for a moment in the shelter of the trees, scanning the *Aphrodite* and its surroundings; his head cocked, listening. Apparently satisfied that no one was about, he stepped out of his hiding place and ran quickly across the beach.

Bill crouched on his heels, waiting. He wanted to give Choate time to go aboard the *Aphrodite*—surprise him at whatever he was about. If he arrived too soon, it would spoil everything. . . . But that delay was Bill's undoing.

The instant Choate had crossed the gangplank and disappeared on board, Bill came lightly to his feet and set off in pursuit. His long legs covered the ground with impressive speed. But the knoll where he had kept his vigil was some distance from the boat, and as he came near he had to be cautious. When he boarded the *Aphrodite,* there was no sign of Choate.

Bill went straight to the dining saloon and the pantry. He found no one. He made a quick round of all the staterooms before he ran up the companionway. There was no one in the lounge. No one on the after deck. No one in the wheelhouse. From the windows of the bulkhead, he looked down on the forward deck. It was empty. But the sight of the companionway in the middle reminded Bill that there was a region below that he had never visited. He swung quickly down the ladders.

Bill found himself in the forecastle. A long table extended fore and aft through the center, still littered with coffee cups; pipe berths lined the bulkheads. Bill followed a corridor leading to the after part of the boat: he looked in at the storage space in the starboard midships section; at a tiny stateroom beyond, evidently occupied by Catriona and Annie Budd; at the useless engine lodged in the stern. Then he turned back to port and entered the galley.

The galley was deserted like the rest. But as he glanced about, Bill was aware of a muffled bumping sound that seemed to come from outside. He knew at once then what was happening.

Choate was launching the dinghy.

Bill was quick about it. But Choate had a good start. By the time Bill reached the port rail outside the dining saloon, Choate already had the dinghy in the water and had loosed the fore and aft hooks. His only answer to Bill's shout was to toss the hooks and the fall ends up on deck and push hastily off.

"Stop!" Bill roared down at him. "You can't do that!"

"I've done it," Choate retorted, crazily triumphant. "I'm going for help."

Wherever Choate was going, he was going there fast. He crouched and pulled furiously, giving the oars a long sweep, putting his back into it. The space between a them widened.

"Come back here!" Bill shouted. "Or I'll bring you."

"You keep off!" Choate shouted back. "Or you'll darn well wish you had." He redoubled his efforts at the oars.

Bill kicked off his borrowed shoes and peeled off his borrowed coat. He vaulted to the rail and jumped, not daring to risk a dive. The shore fell away sharply at this point, and the water was deeper than he had thought it. When he regained the surface, Choate was already well away.

In answer to Angeline's frantic cries, the others came straggling in from the opposite side of the island. They gathered in a knot at the water's edge, watching and chattering. But no one came to Bill's assistance. Joe and Charlie, and that by no means uniquely among those who have lived always by the sea, could not swim. The outboard dinghy was ashore with Cephus Kember. There was no other boat. They consulted feverishly—and did nothing.

Above the voices of the others, Jane's clear call came to Bill's ears. "Quick! You can make it!"

Bill would have given a great deal to believe that that encouraging cry was for him. But Choate tossed back his head and grinned—and the boat leaped forward.

Bill was a powerful swimmer. His big shoulders lifted in a strong, sure rhythm, and his breath came easily and even. The grey water went spinning back. But his clothes hampered him. He took time presently to loosen his collar, but the tie held; it seemed to grow tighter. The shirt was too narrow in the shoulders, and the armholes galled him, shortening his reach. The group on the shore was already growing dim, but the distance between himself and Choate did not perceptibly lessen. Bill steadied his stroke for a long pull.

When Bill looked again, he was encouraged. Choate was no expert oarsman; his first wild burst of speed had told upon him. He was pulling more strongly on the right-hand oar, so that the dinghy veered from its course. There was a look of strain already in his face. His eyes were fixed and wide, and he was breathing heavily through the mouth.

Bill gained after that. Not fast, but steadily. When he thought the time had come, he taxed his strength with a spurt. But as he reached up to it, the boat swung, and his hand closed on emptiness. Instantly he repeated the maneuver. This time he was successful. He got a hand on the gunwale.

"Keep off!" Choate cried warningly.

Bill did not keep off. There was a ringing blow across his knuckles, and a shower of pain exploded in his arm. But he got his other hand up beside the first. The boat dipped under his weight. Above his head there was a flash of dripping silver. . . .

The blow of the oar knocked Bill backward, but he did not relax his hold. The boat went down with him into blackness.

The shock of cold in his face brought Bill to himself at once. There was the taste of blood and sea water in his mouth. The boat was gone. Choate was floundering beside him. He was swimming awkwardly, breast stroke, holding his chin too high; the slap of the waves in his face strangled him. He locked an arm round Bill's neck.

Bill was in no condition for a prolonged struggle. The water was bitter cold. He was giddy and half-blind from the blow on his head. Choate knotted his legs about Bill's, paralyzing motion. Bill was not sure how much of it was intent, how much the pure panic of a man drowning. As the water closed over them, Bill got an arm free. He drew it backward and downward. His fist came up hard behind Choate's ear.

Bill fought his way back to the surface, dragging Choate with him. He turned him over, holding his mouth and nose above water, and set off doggedly on his swim back to Bowsprit Island.

. . . It seemed to Bill that he had been swimming forever, in a circle of grey water capped with fog. His arm came up as stiff and heavy as an iron bar. Choate was an unbearable weight behind him. The cold had got into his bones and lodged there. The hand that held Choate had no feeling. Once he turned on his back to rest; but instantly the spreading numbness in his body warned him. There was a pain now at the bottom of every breath. Somewhere, far off, Jane would be waiting. He must take Choate back to Jane. Far off, Charlie was wading out, up to his armpits. Bill's head was bursting. He thought it had burst, in a spray of lights. Then it grew dark. Bill swam through darkness—toward Jane. . . .

Bill struggled to his knees, looking anxiously about. Jane was not there. Everybody else was there. Even Choate, beginning to sit up.

"Where's Jane?" Bill asked. He was surprised to find that his voice made no sound. Other people's voices made sounds. But they did not make sense. Jane must be on the boat. He must find Jane. . . . He staggered to his feet.

They were asking him questions that he could not understand. "I'm all right," he muttered. "Look after Choate. Dry clothes . . ."

The gangplank wavered before Bill's eyes, steep as a roof's pitch; but he got across it somehow. He stood in the corridor for a minute, steadying himself, before he climbed up to the lounge. His stockinged feet made no noise as he padded across the rug. He opened the door to the wheelhouse.

Jane was standing, her back to him, at the desk, tearing a piece of paper into very tiny scraps.

"Jane!" Bill said. His voice was hoarse, but it came this time. "Jane, what are you doing?"

She sprang away from the sound across the room, whirling to face him as furious and frightened as a little wild thing brought to bay. It was not until she turned that she saw Bill. Bill's dinner clothes were streaming with water, his face pinched and fierce with cold; Bill's red hair was tight with blood and he held his torn shirt together in a fist with bloody knuckles.

"Bill, you're hurt!" she cried. Her face was suddenly all broken. As suddenly, it was still. "You let Ewell go," she cried. "Let him go, I tell you. *He didn't do it.*"

She eluded Bill's reaching hands, and threw the torn paper out the port.

SEVEN

"What we need," Angeline was saying, "is a good hearty breakfast." Charlie had gone on ahead. She led the others back to the *Aphrodite*.

Ewell Choate walked between Joe and Toombs, leaning on their shoulders. His teeth were chattering. He looked sullen and frightened. But he was not seriously hurt.

"You go and get in a real hot bath," Angeline told him, "and put on some warm clothes—flannels, if you've got them. I'll fix you up a gin sling. By that time breakfast will be ready. There's nothing will keep a body from catching cold like plenty of good nourishing food."

Dante Burge held Beulah's arm, helping her over the rough places. Her gnome's brown face was wan, purified with weariness and cold, but it was suddenly and beautifully at peace. Her hair had come down; it was short and straight, and it clung in wisps from the dampness; its very disorder gave her a look somehow defenseless, with a child's uncalculated appeal. The look was intensified by the open forehead, like a child's a little bulging, the snub nose with its pale peppering of freckles. Her eyes had an unnerving trust. She lifted them to Dante Burge in unqualified worship. Dante Burge smiled down at her. There was no science in his smile.

"Don't be afraid," he said.

"I'm not afraid," said Beulah. "Not now." Her thin fingers were linked in his. She said calmly: "It's much nicer

like this. I'm glad now you didn't kill her. Of course you
didn't know, did you, how much I needed to have her die?"

"No," said Dante Burge gently.

He could have laid her soul bare at a touch. He could
have taken it all apart with the clever scalpel of science.
For the first time in his life he forbore. The closer pressure
of his hand was wholly human.

A strange thing had happened to Dante Burge. He had
been shocked and angry at Beulah's performance in the
dining saloon . . . but afterwards he was pleased. He had
always been regarded as a poor dry crust of a fellow, with
no heat in his blood; he had come to accept the world's
view, esteeming himself as a scientist, ignoring himself as
a man. But under the spark of Beulah's unconscious flattery, his manhood had flared up like a dry rick. He saw
himself suddenly a great roistering, deep-chested fellow,
inflammatory and invincible—one who might do murder
as a gallant gesture for a lady. He smiled again at the
author of this magnificent conception.

Catriona shrugged a pair of shapely shoulders. "Dis-
gusting, I call it. . . ."

But Annie Budd was more charitable. "You hush yourself, Catriona," she said. "I'm glad to see somebody taking up with her for once. The poor, chicken-hearted little
thing. Never had a chance, she hasn't. I'm glad if he's going to do something for her. It surely needed doing."

The dog Telemachus brought up the rear morosely, tail
at half-mast. A pretty mess they'd made of his island. He'd
have his work cut out for him, straightening it up. The
only thing they'd put back was the squirrel, and that was
in any old which-way. Besides, who wanted a squirrel all
smelled up with humans?

Aboard the *Aphrodite,* Bill came out of his stateroom.
He had changed back into the shirt and trousers in which
he had arrived at Bowsprit Island; they were dry, but stiff
and wrinkled with sea water. There was a bandage round

his head, cocked jauntily over one ear; above it a lock of fiery hair waved like a banner. Every inch of him ached, and his head was a roaring furnace. His eyes were red-rimmed with strain. But the big easy slouch of his body was debonair. He stepped across the corridor and tapped at Jane's door.

Bill had been craning his neck before the mirror, trying to make the sticking plaster stick, when Jane came in. She had a roll of gauze in her hand, and a bottle.

"Let me fix it," she said. "Sit down."

Bill sat on the edge of the bed. Jane came close, leaning against his shoulder, while her fingers parted the hair away from the long scalp cut. It was not deep, but it had bled freely. It made him a little giddy. Or maybe it was having Jane so near. "How did you ever do it?" she said.

"I . . . hit it on a piece of wood," said Bill. He was aware that there were questions that he ought to ask Jane. Why had Choate tried to leave the island? Had he intended to come back later after Jane? Was that what he meant when he told her to meet him? Why had he tried to kill Bill? What was the paper Jane had destroyed . . . ? The questions could wait. He felt her body against his arm. He heard the soft even thumping of her heart.

"I'm going to put on some disinfectant. . . . *Oh,* that hurts, doesn't it?" The sight of her own handiwork upset her; her fingers that had been so brisk and cool were suddenly all tenderness. She held his head between her palms, rocking it to and fro, pressing his forehead against her breast. "Oh, Bill, is it just *awful?*"

"No," said Bill, his voice pleasantly muffled in the front of Jane's dress. "It's nice. I like it. Do it again."

She stood away from him, laughing a little, not quite steadily. Just for an instant it was as if all the pain and confusion between them were wiped away, and it was again as it had been when they sat on high stools in the corner drugstore, and swung their legs . . . and liked each other.

Bill did not speak. The moment was too precious to touch with words. It was as if Jane felt it too. There was a breathing space of silence.

"I'll put a bandage on," she said then. "Here, hold still, why can't you? What do you think you're doing?"

"Hold still yourself," said Bill. "I think I'm kissing your wrist."

"Don't be silly."

"I'm not silly," said Bill. "I'm practical. The wrist, as a place to kiss, is much underestimated. It has a pulse in it. When the pulse is accelerated, indications are . . ."

She pulled her hand away and pinched his ear. "You're hopeless, Bill."

"I'm hopeful," Bill corrected her. "It's the first time I've been hopeful for months."

She finished winding the bandage round his head and pinned it with an enameled pin, black and silver, that she took from her belt. The pin, the cock of the bandage above one extravagant blue eye, gave Bill a raffish look. Jane stood back to view the effect. Bill grinned, his impudent, carefree grin. "You *do* like me," he accused her.

"Yes," she said. "I hate you, Bill . . . and I can't help liking you. Don't run your head into stone walls; you might hurt it. Good-bye, I'm going to change my dress."

. . . So Bill walked debonairly across the corridor, and knocked at Jane's door.

Jane came out to him. She was wearing the blue wool suit in which Bill had first seen her; the white dickey buttoned high under a tilted chin. Her hair was smoothed back so that it gave you more precisely the indomitable shape of her head. Under the midnight lashes the eyes were shadowed still. But there was a faint flush in her cheeks. A little secret smile, like triumph, hovered at the corners of her mouth. It was for him, Bill thought; the suit was for him, and the lifted look, in confession of their . . . liking.

They went down the corridor together to meet the others. "I don't want a gin sling," Choate was saying peevishly. "I don't want any breakfast. Let me alone, why can't you?"

It happened so quickly that at first Bill did not understand. Jane flashed about at him. The smile was set on her stiffened lips. But the triumph had gone out of it, and dread leaped again in her eyes. "That's Ewell's voice!"

"Why—yes," said Bill. "I brought him back. He's all right."

"What have you done?" she cried wildly. "He went for . . . help." She was running from him, down the corridor.

Bill understood then. She had not known before. She thought Choate had got away. That was why . . . The suit was not for him, then. It was a . . . travelling suit. Bill's face was as bleak as the white bandage round his head when he followed Jane.

Angeline was the first across the gangplank. "You come here, Annie Budd," she was saying. "I want to tell you about breakfast. . . ." Just in the niche at the end of the gangplank, where it met the deck, something crunched under her shoe. She stooped to pick the object up. It was the bag.

They took the bag into the dining saloon, where the light was better. They crowded about breathless, while Angeline opened it. Her plump fingers fumbled with excitement. She drew out the jeweled snuffbox. She pressed the spring and bent the cover back.

The box was empty.

2

"Of course," Bill was saying, "it's plain enough what happened. The dog was frightened by the rumpus we stirred up, and he dropped the bag when he ran off the boat. We went right over it."

"No one has been aboard since," Burge agreed. "Unless . . . wasn't there a chance at first, before we found the dog?"

"No, sir," said Toombs. "If I may interrupt, sir. Catriona hurt her ankle, so that she could not walk. We were sitting on the beach all the time."

"There you are," said Bill firmly. "No one came aboard." No one, the thought lay cold and still in Bill's mind, except Choate . . . *and Jane.*

"Then the jewels had already been taken out of the bag," Angeline murmured, "before Telemachus found it. I wonder where *that* was." She reached for another muffin.

They were at the breakfast table then. Angeline's views on breakfast were substantial. Cantaloupes. Dry cereal, toasted, with drawn butter. Mounds of scrambled eggs ringed with kidneys in bacon curls. Corn bread. Muffins. Doughnuts. Marmalade. Coffee with heavy cream. She beckoned Toombs to her side. "You go down and tell Annie Budd to flop up some hot cakes while we're eating. Hot cakes and honey would just make a nice topping-off. A body's got to keep her strength up, times like this." She spread her muffin thickly.

Bill was not eating. The warm little note of concern in Jane's voice when she spoke to Choate took away his appetite. "Drink some more coffee, Ewell," she urged him. "It will keep you from getting a chill." Bill's head ached intolerably.

It had been an awkward moment when they found that the jewel box was empty. They milled about the dining saloon uneasily, eyeing each other askance; Jane occupied herself with the dog Telemachus, feeding him bits of crackers and cheese from the littered dinner table, her look avoiding Bill's. Choate went off presently to take his hot bath. The others straggled after him, to change, Burge's magenta pajama legs twinkling beside Beulah, shivering in Christine's cold green dress.

Bill went at once to see Charlie about taking up the gangplank. It would be as well, he thought, if everyone stayed aboard. In spite of the fact that they had all been so long ashore, Bill felt certain that the jewels were still on the *Aphrodite.* At the time when they left the boat in pursuit of the dog Telemachus, they had just been searched;

no one could have had the jewels then. The only possibility . . . But Bill knew that Choate had not stopped
at the head of the gangplank when he came aboard; it
seemed improbable that Jane could have without being
seen. For a moment Bill was shaken by the thought that
Choate might have had the jewels on him when he made
off in the dinghy. But Choate, though he was morose and
irritable enough, still did not have the air of one who has
just dropped a fortune into the bottom of the sea. No, if
he had them when he went, they must have been safely
secured. Bill blamed himself sharply for not insisting on
another immediate search. But it was too late now.

When Bill returned from looking after the gangplank,
it was to find Angeline, in starched grey linen, bustling
in and out, giving a thousand orders to Annie Budd about
breakfast, while Toombs and Catriona cleared and reset
the table. Jane and Choate, in the corridor, were engaged
in earnest, low-voiced talk. Bill saw that Choate still wore
his soaking dinner clothes. He had not gone then to take
his hot bath. . . . He saw also the warning touch of Jane's
hand on his arm; Choate was instantly silent.

But as Bill approached, Choate came forward, grinning
disarmingly, his hand outstretched. "Reckon I owe you an
apology," he said smoothly. "I didn't mean to hit you so
hard. Sort of lost my head."

Bill responded to the friendly overture. "Darn near lost
mine," he said. "That's all right. Forget it. I didn't mean
to lay you out so cold either."

Bill took the proffered hand. In spite of himself, there
were moments when he almost liked Choate. The fellow
had a certain pleasant frankness that turned aside suspicion. But it didn't, Bill realized, change the facts the least
bit. Did it even, perhaps, give them an added importance?
At any rate there was no question now where Jane stood.
If she had just heard how Bill came by his injury, then she
believed that Choate was justified. Her look at Bill was

definitely hostile, as she tucked her hand through Choate's arm. Bill turned away abruptly. . . .

". . . So you and I together," he was saying to Choate now at the table, "sank the only boat there was."

Angeline bobbed her head, her mouth full of egg. "That's right," she said. "Mr. Kember's got the outboard dinghy, and that's the only other one. Still, it doesn't matter so *much*. Because he'll be back this morning with those new parts he's after, and then they can get the *Aphrodite* fixed so we can leave. And Joe can take the dinghy and go right back to Trusett for supplies. There are a lot of things we need. . . ."

"And a doctor," Bill reminded her.

"Oh, yes," Angeline agreed cheerfully. "And the police."

The others did not echo her enthusiasm. It was rather a quiet meal.

"I want to talk to you when we get a chance," Bill said to Angeline.

Angeline nodded importantly. "Why not right now?" she said. She bounced up and seized a plate of doughnuts and the coffee pot. "Come on. You bring some cups, Mr. Galleon. I can think better if I have a little something to quiet my nerves."

They went up to the wheelhouse and shut themselves in.

3

"Help yourself to doughnuts, Mr. Galleon," said Angeline. "Who do you think did it?"

"I don't know," said Bill. "I don't want to think anybody did it yet. What I do want is for you to tell me all the details you know about everybody here—even little things, that don't seem as if they could be important."

"Well, I guess I can do that all right," said Angeline contentedly. It was a request after her own heart. Angeline was not clever; she never arrived at any fixed conclusions. But she had a positive genius for collecting unrelated facts. She could never put two and two together and make more than three; but there was nothing she could not find out about one and one and one and one. It was as if now she opened the treasure box of her curiosity, and poured out before Bill the pieces of a puzzle from which he was, if he could, to make a picture.

"Where shall I begin?" she said.

"With Mrs. Van Wycke," said Bill promptly. "I didn't really know her. Tell me what she was like, and how she lived, and anything about her past, and who liked her and who didn't—things like that."

"Well, I guess there didn't anybody like her," said Angeline with devastating frankness. "I'm sure I didn't. She wasn't very likable."

"How do you mean?"

"Oh, she'd do horrid little things," Angeline explained, "so small you couldn't hardly put a name to them. The way she'd step on the dog's tail and pretend it was an accident. It's my opinion she just let Beulah keep that dog so she could torment her. Beulah was always afraid she'd poison it or something. It was a shame, I always said, the way she treated Beulah—her own cousin too; putting her down, and shaming her right before company, and making her do everything she took a fancy. . . ."

"What made her stay?"

"I asked her that myself," said Angeline. "When I very first came. But she just acted frightened half to pieces. She didn't have a cent, only what Mrs. Van Wycke gave her, and I guess she wouldn't hardly have known how to do for herself. She wasn't one that could get a job anywhere. The way I figure it, she'd been with her so long it got to be kind of a habit. It wasn't only her, either. Mrs. Van Wycke was always mean to the servants. You heard how she spoke to Annie Budd last night. She was always like that—they all acted scared of her. She tried it on me, too, at first. But I wouldn't take any of her back talk. And she tried it on Jane. I wish you could have been here that time. Jane didn't say a word. She just stood and *looked* at her. White,

she was, and her eyes as black as night. Mrs. Van Wycke
backed right down; she'd met her match for once. Honestly, if looks could have killed, I guess she'd have dropped
dead. . . ." She broke off, shocked at her own words. "You
don't think Jane did it, do you?"

"No," said Bill shortly. "You say Mrs. Van Wycke had
money?"

"Oh, yes, she had money. She didn't always have,
though. The way I make it out, she came of a real poor
family. But she was the kind that would get money wherever she was."

"How?"

"I don't rightly know," Angeline admitted. "Seems as
if she just looked as if she ought to have it. I didn't like
her, but I must say there was something *about* her—kind
of majestic. Seems as if there was a power in her that
men couldn't keep away from, like magic. Take young Mr.
Choate, now; for all he liked Jane so much, he couldn't
leave Mrs. Van Wycke alone. I guess men gave her things.
I never could make out where she found the money to buy
all the jewels she had. Of course her husbands left her
quite a fortune. . . ."

"She'd been married more than once, then?"

"Twice. Her first husband died of acute indigestion.
They hadn't been married long. It must have been a terrible shock; I don't think she was ever quite the same after.
But she couldn't get along without men, seemed like. She
always had a crowd around her. A queer lot, too, I thought.
Seems she was engaged to be married a third time a year
or so ago. The man fell off a cliff, mountain-climbing. It
was awful tragic. I tried to get Beulah to tell me about it
once, but she just went all to pieces. She was with them
when it happened. That biggest diamond—maybe you noticed?—that was their engagement ring. This house boat
was his too; but Mrs. Van Wycke had it all done over after
he gave it to her. You know I suppose I ought not to say it,
but sometimes I wonder if Mrs. Van Wycke wasn't a little

bit unbalanced, all the trouble she'd had. It always seemed kind of unhealthy to me, the store she set by those jewels: loving them up with her hands, and talking to them; I'd hear her alone in the dark sometimes, as if they were people. They say she'd do anything to get a new one she'd set her heart on. . . ."

"Choate came here to sell her a ruby?"

"He says so. I couldn't help wondering why he didn't bring it with him, if he wanted to sell it so bad. Mrs. Van Wycke was at him to send for it, but he kind of put her off. The way it looked to me, he wasn't ready to leave yet, and if the sale was finished up, there wouldn't be any reason for staying. I guess Mrs. Van Wycke kind of fascinated him; he'd look at her sometimes as if he could eat her up. But maybe he just wanted to find out if she could pay for it. He was always asking questions about her: how much money she had, and where she bought her jewels, and like that. I guess he was interested in jewels all right. Do you think he did it?"

"He could have," said Bill slowly. "He sat beside her. He had that knife. He could have got the gun as well as anybody. . . ."

"Better," said Angeline. "His chair was empty."

Bill was not so sure of that.

"I couldn't help wondering," Angeline added, "why he'd try to go away if he didn't have anything to do with it."

"It might have been like this. . . ." Bill mused. "He might have stolen the jewels under cover of the dark. Mrs. Van Wycke might have caught him. She screamed; and he lost his head and shot her to keep her from exposing him. When he realized what he'd done, he got the wind up and tried to skip out." (What did Jane know about it? Why had she planned to go too?)

"It did strike me," said Angeline, "he acted awful funny after Mrs. Van Wycke was killed. Mad, sort of, more than sorry. He had about the best chance to do it—only, of course, Varro was on her other side, and that was the side where the bag was; and Toombs *was* walking round all the time, and we don't know where he was only by his own say-so; and the Professor *was* right up there behind Mrs. Van Wycke plenty long enough. . . . Do you think the Professor did it?"

"I thought so at first," Bill said slowly. "Then I thought he didn't. It seems like such an obvious thing: he was bound to be suspected. But . . . well, he's a psychologist. He's got everybody's reactions all figured out. He'd be the very one to do it that way—because it was so obvious that no one would believe it."

"I think he'd rather steal an idea than a jewel," said Angeline, not without acumen. "My goodness, the things that man would do for an experiment! Why, one day he made Mr. Choate think he'd taken a dose of cleaning fluid out of a bottle marked *Poison,* and there was the worst hullabaloo: Beulah had hysterics, and Annie Budd talked terrible about blood and judgment—she was awful taken with Mr. Choate, on account of his reminding her of her son, and she'd always be doing for him, and never making a bit of fuss if Mrs. Van Wycke wanted her to cook something that he liked special. And then it turned out Mr. Choate hadn't drunk the cleaning fluid after all, and the Professor just made out he had to see what would happen, and he wrote a paper about it for a scientific journal. I guess he'd do anything for an experiment."

"Do you think he'd . . . kill for an experiment?" said Bill.

"Well, there," said Angeline cheerfully, "it wouldn't surprise me any." She poured herself another cup of coffee.

"What about Varro?"

"Do you think he did it?" cried Angeline eagerly.

"I think he ought to have done it," Bill said. "He's exactly the type. Small and sly. Typical asymmetrical features. Carried a concealed weapon. Talks like a dude one minute and a gutter puppy the next. Knows more about jewels than any honest man ought to. Never gives himself

away. Sat beside Mrs. Van Wycke. Certainly wasn't all broken up when we discovered she was dead. Oh, he's the
feller for it all right. Which leads me," finished Bill grimly, "to conclude that he is just as innocent as Telemachus.
It's the sweet old lady with white curls and a cap, or the
dear doddering old gentleman who wouldn't hurt a fly, not
your pure criminal type, that does the dirty work."

"I always wondered about him though," Angeline said,
"because he appeared so kind of sudden. And you could
see he wasn't quite a gentleman, because he'd act more like
a gentleman than any gentleman would. He was real nice
and helpful, though, after Mrs. Van Wycke was killed; and
he covered her up with Annie Budd's quilt. Did you notice
that quilt? Annie Budd sets great store by her crocheted
quilts, and she's got twenty-seven of them, all different.
She showed them to me once, and that's something she
doesn't do for everybody. This one is a real cute pattern.
The Repeal, it's called. It's got beer mugs and cocktail
glasses and highballs and I don't know what all over, and
the beer's got bubbles on it that stick right up. I want to
learn the stitch some time. Varro took quite a fancy to it,
and he offered to buy it; but Annie Budd didn't want to
sell, and I guess there wouldn't anybody want it now after
what's happened. Do you think Toombs would have done
it for Catriona?"

"Why should he?"

"Well, I just wondered," said Angeline. "I wouldn't say
a word against Catriona Cooley for anything, though she
is as pert an uppity piece of baggage as they make them.
I can't help thinking though that she's no better than she
should be. I know for a fact that she came to Mrs. Van
Wycke with no recommendation—it wasn't ever any too
easy for Mrs. Van Wycke to get servants, the way she'd
treat them, and these things *do* get around—and the way
it looked to me was if Catriona left her last place without a character, then there was probably a *reason*. That
business about Jane's bracelet shows what she'd do if she

got a chance; and you can't tell me she ever meant to return it. She's awful fond of pretty things. And she can
wind Toombs round her finger proper, for all he's so stiff
and stand-offish that if some people asked him a decent
question he'd hardly answer it decent. Of course Catriona
couldn't have done it herself, because she was downstairs
with Annie Budd. But Toombs was in the dining saloon
the whole time, walking round I don't know where, and he
might as well have been up by Mrs. Van Wycke as where he
says he was; and the pantry, where he was standing when
the lights came on, was nearer to the table in the hall than
anybody; and if he wasn't up to something, why didn't he
turn on the lights when you told him to?" Angeline paused
for breath and doughnuts.

"How long has Catriona been with Mrs. Van Wycke?"
Bill asked.

"Only about six months. But Toombs has been with her
two years come November. I don't think Mrs. Van Wycke
treated him as bad as she did the others. She was always
more pliable with men. Annie Budd had been with her a
long time. Years. As good a cook as she is could have got
a place anywhere; I never in my born days saw the like of
her puff pastry. I asked her once why she stayed, but she
kind of turned it off. I guess it got to be a habit, like with
Beulah. It's my opinion she pitied Beulah too, and hated
to leave her. She's awful kind-hearted. And conscientious,
my goodness! She'd always be doing more work than she
was paid for, and kind of looking after people, and whatever needed doing. I came last May, about the same time
Jane did. I didn't see her though until we were on the
boat, because I came on ahead to get it ready, while Mrs.
Van Wycke was engaging the crew and so on. Mrs. Van
Wycke's housekeeper left when she found she was going
on a cruise, not being a good sailor, and Garey Brennon
got me the place. Garey Brennon was the detective that
worked on the Como-Garetti murder case, the one I told

you about where I was on the jury. After being right in the
public eye so, and my name in all the papers, I hated to
go back to Marilla and the paying guests, and her always
harping on calories. . . ."

"Quite so," said Bill hastily. "And how long had Mrs.
Van Wycke known the three men—Varro and Choate and
Burge?"

"That's the funny part of it," said Angeline. "She hadn't
known any of them long. The way I understand it, Choate
wrote her a letter and said a friend of his had given him
her name as being interested in fine gems, and he had a
ruby he had to dispose of due to the depression; and Mrs.
Van Wycke just asked him to come down. She was like
that: impulsive. He lives in Virginia. The way I sense it,
he comes from one of these nice old families that used to
have a lot of money, and now it hasn't. I never could quite
make it out about Varro. I guess Mrs. Van Wycke liked
him because he told her stories about the Russian crown
jewels, and all like that. I asked him once where he met
her, and he said it was at the White House, and Mr. Roos-
evelt introduced them himself; but I kind of think he was
joking. Professor Burge teaches psychology at Middlewestern. I can't help wondering how it happened he was such
a good shot. . . ."

"Can Beulah shoot?" said Bill.

Angeline's eyes rounded. "Why, I don't suppose so. She
acted scared enough of those revolvers she was loading."

"And Varro acted as if he never fired one in his life,"
Bill remarked drily. "But all the time he had one on him."

"That's so too," cried Angeline. "Wasn't that clever of
him? But I don't think Beulah's clever, do you?"

"I don't know," said Bill.

"Do you really think she did it?" cried Angeline.

Bill sighed. It was heavy going, getting facts from
Angeline. Nevertheless their conversation had resulted in
the résumé of a case against every person present at the

time of the tragedy. Everyone but Jane. The case against
Jane needed no summarizing. It was burned too deeply
into Bill's mind for him to forget one least detail of it. . . .

"You haven't asked me anything about Joe and Charlie," Angeline said suddenly.

Bill was surprised. "I don't need to, do I?" he said.
"They were together on the upper deck when Mrs. Van
Wycke screamed. I guess that lets them out."

"Well, yes . . . if they were really there. But I can't help
wondering . . ."

"That's about the one thing I feel sure of," Bill told
her. "I don't believe either of those boys could lie without
turning purple. Besides, if Annie Budd's alibi is good, and
Catriona's, then theirs is good too, isn't it?"

"But we heard Annie Budd coming right straight up,"
Angeline reminded him. "So we know she was down in the
galley. And Catriona was right ahead of her."

"We heard the boys coming down too. Look here,
Angeline, what are you driving at? Did they have anything
against Mrs. Van Wycke?"

"Not specially," Angeline admitted. "Only about the
servants, and the way she wouldn't hire the friend of theirs
they wanted. I don't presume they'd even spoken to Mrs.
Van Wycke herself more than two-three times; she always
gave her orders to Mr. Kember. I only wondered. . . . If
it was Toombs now that was dead, I'd be positive they did
it. You know I told you the crew didn't hold with having
servants on a boat; and the servants didn't want to *be* on
the boat; and they never got along well. They were awful
independent—the crew, I mean. They'd kind of lord it over
the servants for not knowing about boats, for all they were
impressed with their city ways; and the servants would put
on airs because they said the crew was countrified and ate
peas with their knives. They all had to eat together in the
forecastle, you know. And Toombs had to sleep down there
with the crew. . . ."

"But Toombs hasn't been murdered," Bill checked Angeline firmly. "Just because they didn't like her butler, that's no reason for killing Mrs. Van Wycke. In fact, they had every reason not to. Now she's dead they'll all be out of a good soft job."

"I don't know about soft," Angeline said. "But if it's jobs you're talking about, you can say the same for Toombs, and Catriona, and Annie Budd, and Jane and me."

"You're rather narrowing it down, aren't you?" Bill said. "All the same, you'll have to give up the Joe and Charlie theory. It isn't just that they didn't have any reason. They didn't have any chance. They couldn't possibly have come down without being heard, got the gun, gone clear round the table without running into anybody, shot Mrs. Van Wycke, returned the gun, and got up to the lounge out of sight. . . . Besides, they were the only ones aboard who didn't know the revolver was on the table. That alone would be enough to clear them."

"Well . . . all right," Angeline conceded. She added, with one of her swift changes of subject: "Speaking of Jane reminds me. . . . You haven't asked me anything about Jane, either."

"Haven't I?" said Bill. He tried to push back the thoughts of Jane that came crowding down upon him. Jane . . . who had sought out Mrs. Van Wycke under a changed name. Jane . . . who had known about the ruby. Jane . . . whose place had been empty at the table. Jane . . . whom he loved. "Well," he said wearily. "What about Jane?"

"That's the queer part of it," said Angeline. "I don't know as much about her as I do any of the others. And it isn't for want of asking, either. Of course I think Jane is an awfully nice girl, and I'm sure I hope everything will come out all right. But she is kind of close-mouthed. Why, I don't even know where she comes from, nor who her people are. And I can't help thinking she's acted all along as if she had something on her mind. Why should she have

been frightened last night—you know the Professor spoke
of it—if she hadn't known something was going to happen? And how could she have known anything was going
to happen if she wasn't mixed up in it? And I can't help
wondering what she was digging in the flowerpot for. . . ."

"Flowerpot?" Bill cried. "What do you mean? What
flowerpot? Where? When?"

"The one in the hall," Angeline said. "That orange tree
near where you go down to the staterooms. It was right
after we found the bag, and the jewels weren't in it. Jane
was poking in the dirt. I asked her what she was doing, and she said the plant looked dry, and she got some
water and watered it. But all the same it kind of makes you
wonder . . ."

Bill bolted toward the door. His face was white.

Angeline drained the coffee pot. "It won't do any good
to look now," she said. "Because I pulled that orange tree
up myself and sifted all the dirt through the gravy strainer.
There wasn't anything in it."

4

They were interrupted by shouts from below.

"That must be Mr. Kember," Angeline cried, and went
scurrying away.

Bill found the others all gathered at the rail outside
the dining saloon, straining their eyes into the fog. The
muffled putt-putt-putt of an outboard motor came faintly
to his ears, and presently the boat itself appeared, nosing
through the water. A man was standing with his hand on
the tiller. That would be Cephus Kember, he supposed,
sailing master of the *Aphrodite*.

Joe and Charlie were already putting out the gangplank
again. Bill spoke to them as they were about to step ashore.
"I wouldn't," he said.

"Figured to tell Ceph," Charlie said, with a jerk of his
head toward Christine Van Wycke's stateroom. "He'll take it

hard. Ceph never had trouble on a boat he took out before."

"Better wait," Bill insisted. He was aware for the first
time as he spoke of a second figure in the boat with Kember—a man sprawled in the stern, long legs spread before
him and hands hanging between his knees. "Who's that
with him?"

Charlie was squinting across the water, drawing down
his brows and wrinkling his nose to bring the boat into
focus. "Can't rightly tell," he decided. "Looks some like
the constable from Trusett. I wouldn't say for certain."

"Who?" said Jane. She was standing beside Choate, and
Bill saw that her hands were gripping the rail. *"Who?"* she
repeated.

"Constable from Trusett, might be," Charlie said cautiously. "What you think, Joe?"

"Don't know," said Joe noncommittally.

Jane's hands were suddenly white across the knuckles.

Cephus Kember stepped aft to shut off the motor, and
returned to his place, easing the boat into the cove. As it
grounded he climbed up in the bow, scooping the coiled
line onto a bent wrist, and sprang ashore. His passenger,
sitting beside the engine, bent to it attentively a moment
before he rose to follow. Bill could not see what he was
about, but he noticed that when he straightened he thrust
his hand into his pocket. His long legs swung him easily
overside, and he stood beside Kember on the beach.

Cephus Kember hauled up the boat, and made the line
fast to a snag of rock, before he turned toward the *Aphrodite*. To the others he was already a familiar figure. But
to Bill he appeared with the sharp particularity of one
seen for the first time: a square-hewn, solid block of man,
like a chunk of his own New England granite; with strong
square fists, and a face built square in chin and forehead,
seasoned by life and weather, kindly and incorruptible.
His grizzled hair, grown harsh and brackish with years of
sun and salt wind, stood in curling uneven clumps, like

a rope half-frayed. A drooping mustache hid a wordless humor in the corners of his mouth, and his grey eyes were young. Bill knew at once that he should like him.

"Where's them parts?" Charlie shouted down to him.

Cephus Kember spat deliberately before he answered. "Had to send to Portland," he called back. "Just heard they didn't have the right size wheel in stock. Be twenty-four hours more. Mebbe longer."

Nobody paid much attention. It did not seem so important then as it did later. At the moment their eyes were riveted on the stranger, gangling awkwardly toward them across the beach. Bill found himself staring with the others. The newcomer was a sight to warrant staring.

A high-boned craggy face, all juts and promontories like the Maine coast that reared him, of such a bright bewildering red that it all but matched the lobster claw protruding from one corner of his tightly folded mouth . . . keen blue eyes deep-set under the scrub thickets of his brows . . . sandy hair, growing luxuriously in ears and nostrils, lifting in a tuft above his forehead like the high prow of a Viking vessel: this striking head crowned a long-limbed, raw-boned figure, so loose-jointed that it seemed as if all his parts had been placed separately in an empty suit of clothes, and only the toughness of the material held him together in the semblance of a human being. His person was set off by an old-fashioned blue policeman's coat, with magnificent brass buttons, topping a collarless shirt under a knitted waistcoat, and khaki trousers tucked into seaman's boots. A bright badge glittered among the buttons. At his hip he wore a policeman's billy, notched about the handle as if he followed the Indian custom of counting his scalps there. An antique six-shooter in a tremendous holster was buckled about his waist. From one big-knuckled hand, with the sandy hairs flourishing on the back, dangled a somewhat rusted but still serviceable pair of handcuffs.

He came to a stand at the foot of the gangplank, regarding the row of startled faces hung over the rail above him, giving them back their stare. A bony finger shot out, pointing at the spot where Choate still stood beside Jane, with Varro next beyond him beside the plank. Bill could not be sure at first which one was indicated. "Constable Amasa Loose of Trusett, Maine," he announced portentously. "I got you now. Red-handed. Y'coming quiet? Or do I have to take you?"

"*Oh!*" said Jane sharply. Her voice was thin and high. She put up her hands, clutching desperately, as if she sought support from something that was not there.

Bill caught her as she fell.

EIGHT

Constable Amasa Loose, of Trusett, Maine, was in fine fettle. He stood in the middle of the *Aphrodite's* lounge, legs spread, hand clapped to his pistol butt, his handcuffs jingling; he surveyed the company. A funny lot too, he figured. Pity a nice feller like Ceph would get mixed up with them. His mental comments would have startled their subjects.

That little bouncing one in grey, now, she'd sure make an armful. Nosey, though. And a hearty feeder by the look; awful expensive to keep her. . . . That holler-chested feller, all forehead and no face, must be one of them interlekchals; getting himself all riled up over the loony old maid; two of a kind, maybe. . . . The good-looking chap that could drag one word out to a fare-ye-well looked like he'd just swallered his first oyster. . . . Even the dog was funny; half calf, might be. . . . The tall red-headed boy took it hard about the girl. Pretty girl, too. Funny she'd faint just for pointing a finger. . . . He turned back to Varro.

"I'm quite a creaminologist, if I do say so. I got quite a creaminology liberry. And I don't never forget a face. When I seen you come over with Ceph yesterday morning and go in the telygraph office, I says to myself, Loose, I says, where've you seen that face before? So pretty soon I mosied over by the office and looked at your telygram. Code, wa'n't it? I figured so. And then I mosied round home and went over my liberry. And then I hunted Ceph

417

up and I says to him, Ceph, I says, when you get round to be going back, I guess I'll take a ride over with you. . . ."

Varro lighted a cigarette with admirable calm. "And so what?" His eyes were steel points in the flare of the match.

Amasa Loose fumbled with his buttons. "I got a paper here. . . ."

"Was that all you came for?" Angeline cried, disappointed. "I thought you came about the murder."

Constable Loose's hand jerked at his holster. *"Murder?"* he cried. "He murder somebody too, did he? Who'd he murder?"

"Well, I don't know as he murdered anybody," Angeline said. "But Mrs. Van Wycke is dead, and the jewels . . ." She poured a torrent of miscellaneous information upon the whirling head of Constable Amasa Loose.

Constable Loose looked about in agitation for Joe and Ceph and Charlie. They could talk plain talk, and a body could get some head and tail out of what they said. Not like this woman with her tongue hung in the middle and swinging like a clapper at each end. . . . The crew, however, was down in the forecastle, and Cephus Kember, master of the *Aphrodite*, was hearing for the first time the news of his owner's death. Constable Loose had to strike out for himself in Angeline's sea of facts and suppositions.

Still he got the right of it finally. More or less. There was a dead woman below. There were jewels lost. Constable Loose was excited when the full significance of the thing dawned upon him. But the rigors of the Maine coast do not lend themselves to open emotionalism; his excitement lay ice-locked under a bleak exterior. Only the lobster claw betrayed him. In moments of tension this claw moved from one corner of Loose's mouth to the other; travelling slowly, accompanied by a small chewing motion, along the straight and narrow path of his closed lips. It came to rest now in the right-hand corner, agitated slightly from within.

Constable Loose deserved to be excited. There wasn't much crime in Trusett—game violations sometimes, or a quarrel over a boundary fence, and sometimes the boys would lug off a hitching post and burn it come Hallowe'en. Mostly he played pinochle down back of Berry's store, keeping the peace and the like of that; adding to the sunburn from his summer lobster pots the airtight stove-burn of winter. There had been The Shootin', of course; 1909, that was. Things had been pretty quiet since. But Amasa Loose wasn't a man to let himself go. He kept up with his profession. There wasn't a day he didn't read the Boston paper, and he subscribed to *Crime* regular. He had the files in his library back over thirty years. And two packing cases full of clippings. Now perseverance was rewarded. Fate had sent a gangster to Trusett. Fate, finding Amasa Loose ready, had tossed a murder and a jewel robbery right into his open hands.

"Thought you was smart, didn't you?" he said to Varro. "Thought you'd be safe down here in the seaweed, where the natives wouldn't know a gangster from a horse thief. Well, I got you with the goods. Maybe this'll teach them smart city *po*lice a thing or two."

Bill heard hardly a word of it. He was kneeling at Jane's side, where he had laid her on a divan. He stroked the short curls back from her forehead, while Choate rubbed her cold fingers. Bill was frightened. She was so still. So white. It wasn't like Jane to faint. For all her fine frail look there was a strength of fiber in her, a will that informed the body. Now unconsciousness had broken her defenses. It was as if the spirit lay bare in her drawn face. The brave eyes that hid fear under laughter were closed. The red lips that defied suspicion with the bright tilt of courage were relaxed, drooping pitifully at the corners. The proud head that she carried so high rolled helplessly in the curve of Bill's arm. The lids were blue. There were smudges under her eyes; shadows at the blue-veined temples. It was as if the whole lovely fabric of her flesh were drawn tight over the bare bones of her fear. Bill put his head down against her breast.

Jane stirred a little then. Her eyelids flickered up. At once it was as if her eyes possessed her face: enormous, searching, dark with pain. "Where is he?"

"I'm here," Bill said. "I won't leave you." But he saw the restless eyes pass by him, searching still.

"Here. . . ." Choate said. The single word brought her peace, and a cold pain tightened in Bill's chest.

"He didn't . . . get you?"

"It was Varro," Choate said unwillingly.

Bill knew then what he had to do. It was cruel. But he owed his best to Verity. His throat went dry. When he spoke his voice was unsteady.

"You thought the policeman came for Ewell?"

"Yes."

"Why?"

"*Jane!*" said Choate warningly.

With that full knowledge came to her. She knew what Bill had tried to do, and she despised him for it. There was black scorn in her look. But her face, though pale, was quiet. It was as if she wore once more the well-wrought mask which she was accustomed to hold high for the public view. She struggled to sit up.

"How silly of me to faint!" she said almost gaily. "I guess I didn't eat enough breakfast."

Angeline came bouncing over. Her round eyes seemed bursting from her head, and the words burst from her lips in explosive pops. "You better, Jane? He's a gangster. Did you hear? Varro. Mr. Loose says so. From Chicago. He read it in the paper. He's got his picture. His name's Max Varro, and it's Maximilian Varrowisky, and it's Gem Varry, and he's mixed up in I don't know what-all, and the police want him. And he killed Mrs. Van Wycke and stole her jewels. Mr. Loose says so. . . ."

"Thank God," said Jane strangely.

They were all standing up then, in a broken circle round Varro and Constable Loose. Varro seemed to have drawn himself together, so that his body looked smaller and more compact; his eyes glinted unpleasantly under slit lids, but his narrow face was merely derisive. He flicked an ash from his cigarette.

"You got nothing on me," he said. "I didn't even jump my income tax."

"Oh, no," said Loose sardonically. "I got nothing on you. You're a gangster, that's all. You're a member of the most notor'ous gang of jool thieves in Americy, that's all. You done so good at it they call you Big Gem Varry, that's all. You was mixed up in the Cosgrove jool robb'ry. They had you up for questioning that time Mrs. Macarrom-Smythe's dinner party was held up at Newport and the jools was taken off'n all the guests; but they couldn't prove nothing because your crooked lawyers was too smart for them. You was driving the car the time Asher, Drew and Burwin's joolry store in Chicago was held up, and fifty thousand dollars' worth of jools was taken, and a policeman shot, and two clerks, and a innocent bystander. They got you, and you turned state's evidence and let the other fellers stand the racket; and so they left you go till they could catch you again. And now I got you with the goods right on you, and a murdered woman besides. And I got your picture here to prove it. That's all." He tapped a heavy red finger on a wad of newspaper clippings.

Bill peered at them over the constable's shoulder. The top one bore the likeness of a foxy-faced youth, with an oiled pompadour, and narrow eyes that looked past the camera. He had a high-bridged crooked nose, not at all like Varro's. And yet, through the smudges of printer's ink and thumb prints, Bill had an instantaneous impression that half the face was higher than the other, as if it had been made in two complete section's and fitted together not quite evenly.

"Not my map," said Varro coolly.

"You tell that to somebody ain't got no memory for faces," Constable Loose advised him. "I see you got your hair parted down different, and you grew yourself one *mus*tache on your lip and a couple more front of your ears. I allow you got your nose fixed. One of them plaster surgeons likely. But there couldn't no surgeon root out that high eyebrow and plant it over down where it belongs, nor pull your sneaking mouth out and set it in plumb."

Varro teetered on his toes. His voice was sneering. "What are you, trying to frame me?"

"No," said Constable Loose. "I'm aiming to arrest you. Gem Varry, or Max Varro, or whatever you call yourself and it don't make a cent's worth of difference to me, I arrest you in the name of the law for the wilful and p'meditated murder of Christine Van Wycke, and I hold you . . ."

Constable Amasa Loose, to his astonishment, found himself holding his prisoner in literal truth. Varro, rising with his insolent teetering, sprang from the balls of his feet, head down, arms close to the body, like a blunt-nosed bullet. The top of his head took Loose in the soft spot just above the holster. A deep-rooted grunt came out of him, and he flung his arms round Varro. The next instant Loose was holding Varro's empty coat. Varro, shedding coat and grasp alike with an inspired contortion, covered the length of the lounge in three bounds, and whisked down the companion.

"Hey you, Ceph!" shouted Loose in hot pursuit. "Hey you, Joe! Come on, Charlie! Quick!"

It was unfortunate for Varro that the demonstration attending Loose's arrival, and Toombs' later report that Miss Bridge had fainted and they were calling on for wine and aromatic, should have roused so much interest below. At the moment when Varro broke free, Catriona Cooley was crouching in the companionway, a rosy ear laid flush with the lounge floor. Able thus to hear but not to see, Varro's arrival took her by surprise. Varro, trying to avoid her, lost his balance and crashed full tilt into Annie Budd, posted for the reception of news items at the foot.

The others from the lounge, and Joe and Charlie and Cephus Kember swarming up through the galley from the forecastle, arrived to find Varro spread-eagled on the floor, with Annie Budd sitting in the small of his back. "Mercy on us!" she gasped. "Help me up. He knocked the legs clean out from under me."

Before anyone could comply, Varro jackknifed suddenly, squirmed out from under Annie Budd, and broke for the starboard rail. He found Cephus Kember before him. Cephus Kember, hot-eyed and square-fisted, crowned with the righteous wrath of a sailing master who has never had trouble on a boat of his before, was a grim sight to the fleeing Varro. He doubled back to port—and met Bill. That was the end of it. Varro was fleet, and he was slippery. Put a gun in his hand and he could shoot himself out of the tightest corner. But he was no match for the coiled strength behind Bill's fist. Bill took a twist in the slack of his shirt and swung him about to face Amasa Loose.

"Much obliged," Loose said. And to Varro: "Thought you was smart, didn't you? Thought you could take a ride in that bo-at. Wall—you see you can't."

"You're trying to frame me," Varro repeated sullenly. "I didn't do anything."

"I don't want to interfere," said Bill diffidently. "And I'm glad you've got him, if he's the right one. But . . . what evidence have you that he killed Mrs. Van Wycke?"

"I told you," said Constable Loose. He fumbled again for his papers. "He's a gangster."

"If he is," said Bill diplomatically, "it was smart of you to get onto him, all right. But . . . well, it wouldn't stand, you know, in court."

"And why wouldn't it?" Loose wanted to know. "He's a jool thief. He belongs to a gang of jool thieves. I find him on the scene of a jool robb'ry. And a woman dead to boot. What d'you want more'n that?"

"It isn't what I want," Bill said. "It's what the law wants." He was beginning to feel a trifle warm about the collar band. Still, it was no way to advance himself with the Verity Insurance Company to bring back the wrong man and let the ruby go. "That's circumstantial evidence," he insisted. "Unless you've got tangible proof, applicable to this particular case, and capable of being presented in a court of law, you really can't arrest him. . . ."

"That's the talk," said Varro.

"And why can't I?" said Loose. "Who be you to tell me?"

"Well, I guess he ought to know," cried Angeline excitedly. "He's a detective . . ." Too late she clapped her hand across her mouth. It was as impossible for Angeline to hold a secret as it would have been to hold her breath.

In the moment following her speech, Bill had all the sensations of a purveyor of bogus oil stock, meeting a delegation of his dupes on the morning the bubble burst. In the faces about him there was every degree of hostility. Beulah and Catriona and Annie Budd viewed him with the open distrust they would have felt for anything connected with the law. Toombs' face was a closed trap-door over a dark cellar. Professor Burge studied him with the air of one observing an unpleasant smallish bug whose bite is virulent. Choate's expression conveyed the thought that next time he hit Bill over the head he should make a clean job of it. Joe and Charlie nudged each other. . . . It was Jane's look that upset Bill most. There was no surprise in it. But there was such deep and bitter and concentrated reproach that it blacked out all the lesser faces.

"So you're one of them smart city dicks, be you?" Constable Loose said. The lobster claw travelled slowly across his sanguine face. "Mebbe I was a mite hasty," he admitted finally. "I know that gangster took them jools as well as if I'd seen him, and nobody'll make me believe different. But I got some questions mebbe I better ask about Mrs. Van Wycke."

"You can't arrest me then," Varro reminded him.

"Can't I jest?" said Constable Loose. "I arrest you for 'sault and batt'ry, and contempt, and resisting arrest, and breaking and entering and . . ."

"I didn't break and enter anything."

A gleam appeared in Constable Loose's deep blue eye that might have been a twinkle if it had been nearer the surface; it included Cephus Kember and Charlie and Joe, shutting out the foreigners. "You put your head in my stomick," he said, "and broke the top button off my pants." Instantly, as if regretting his levity, he added: "And now I'll sweat it out of you."

"I didn't do it," said Varro.

"No?" said Loose thoughtfully. "Wall, we'll see. I s'pose you think they know all the tricks down to the city. I tell you we got tricks up here they haven't even heard tell of. Hose? I wouldn't bother with it. Too gormin'. Take some good tarred rope now. . . ." He turned to Joe. "You got new ratline? Fetch me it, will you?"

Varro licked his lips uneasily.

"Now where," Loose inquired, as Joe disappeared on his errand, "would be a good place to go to? 'Tain't anything a lady'd ought to see. Mebbe we better go out on the island some place, out of earshot. You come along, Charlie; might be I'd need a little help. You want to come too, Ceph?" The twinkle showed in his eyes again as he considered Varro. "You got just the figure for it," he said. And he smiled.

Varro did not see the twinkle. But it was that smile which undid him. Twist Macgeegan used to smile before he lighted the slow matches for informers. Not with mirth. With a kind of relish, more the way one smiles at food which has such an appetizing odor that it makes the mouth water. That smile now struck cold to Varro's spine. He was a physical coward. His crimes were the crimes of cowardice—against those who had the means to hurt him: weapons or knowledge. Above all things he feared bodily pain. Cornered, he was merciless. But that was because he did not dare to let anyone escape who could bring him pain afterwards. His face turned a sick, moist grey. He swallowed repeatedly.

"I'll tell you," he promised. "I didn't do it. That isn't my picture. . . ." He added hurriedly, as Joe appeared with a coil of three-strand tarred rope: "Suppose it was my picture. That doesn't prove anything. I haven't done any harm. The police aren't after me. They had me and they let me go. That shows I'm innocent, doesn't it? I never heard the name of Cosgrove. I never heard of Mrs. Macarrom-Smythe. I never been to Newport even. I never saw Asher, Drew and Burwin's jewelry store. I . . ."

"You got a good memory for names then," Constable Loose said drily. "Don't bother. I'm not ready." He took the rope from Joe and began to measure rough yard lengths, flexing it between his fingers. "It'll do," he decided.

Varro's eyes showed a rim of white encircling the pupil. The pinched greyness round his nose revealed suddenly the scars of clever surgery. He tried to take the rope from Loose's iron grip. The futility of the effort frightened him still more. His voice was hoarse. "I'll come clean, so help me," he said hastily. "I was in the car that night they held up Asher, Drew and Burwin. They hired me to drive for them. I didn't know what they were going to do. When the shootin' started, I took it on the lam. The cops got me. I told them where to find the fellers, and they let me go. I had to leave Chi then. Them fellers burned all right, but they had friends. I wanted to get where they couldn't find me. I met Mrs. Van Wycke in a night club and we got talking. She asked me down here. I see it would be a quiet place to lay up till things blew over. . . ."

"And in the mean time," said Loose, looping the rope over his arm, "you could get her jools."

It came hard. But it came this time. "I meant to, all right," Varro said. "That's what I came for. But somebody beat me to it."

2

"Figure I better go down and view the body," Constable Loose was saying.

Bill went with him. It was not a duty that he craved. A chill struck through him when he opened the door of the bow stateroom; the cold and damp of the fog, seeping through the room, were like the chill of death itself that had taken its abode there.

Bill looked about uncomfortably. The room was as Christine Van Wycke had left it when she went out to her last dinner; the small details of her personal life took now an importance out of proportion to their value. The gold tops were off the crystal bottles on the dressing table; in a pot of cream was the dent of Christine's finger. A chaise longue stood under a reading lamp, the shape of her body still in the soft cushions; beside it a low table, gold lacquer inlaid with mother-of-pearl, held smoking things and an open box of candy; in the ash tray half-a-dozen cigarette stubs bore each the scarlet bloom of Christine's lipstick. A detective novel lay face downward: *A Foot Has Trod My Grave.* Bill turned away hastily. The green knit dress that Christine had worn the afternoon before was flung carelessly across a chair. Why had not Catriona put it away when she tidied the rooms? A thought struck Bill sharply. Choate had said that Catriona turned down the beds every night while they were at dinner. But no beds had been turned down that night. Not Mrs. Van Wycke's. And not his. And not Angeline's. . . . Why had not Catriona attended to her accustomed duties?

On the bench before the dressing table lay a negligée trimmed with pink maribou. Bill stiffened as the significance of pink maribou fuzz touched his consciousness. He idled across the room and slyly pulled off a bit of the soft stuff. But it was not Christine whom he had run into in the darkness by the dining-room door. Christine was already dead. . . .

He walked over to the bed a little unsteadily. "This thing is more complicated than it looks," he said.

Constable Loose was turning back Annie Budd's crocheted bedspread. Christine Van Wycke looked like a queen,

Bill thought, in the cold majesty of death. Even Loose was impressed.

"Handsome woman, wa'n't she?" he said. Bill's hands tightened on the footrail. Constable Loose was examining the wound. . . . "Who had a gun?"

"I had one," Bill said. "And Varro. There were two target revolvers on the table in the hall, where everyone had access to them. Professor Burge fired five shots in the dining saloon. It was the sixth shot that killed her."

"Don't be funny," said Constable Loose.

"I couldn't be as funny as that," said Bill grimly.

"How come you to have a gun?"

Bill explained about the gun. He explained briefly about the Verity Insurance Company and the ruby. He did not mention Jane.

"You'll find Varro done it," Loose said when he had finished. "You said he had a gun."

"It hadn't been fired. The shot came from one of the target revolvers."

"Why should it be fired?" argued Loose illogically. "What would he use his own gun for, and another right by handy?"

"All right," Bill said. "I hope he did. I'm willing to be shown."

"And I'm willing to show you," said Loose. "Don't think there can't anybody learn you anything, just because you come from the city."

Bill turned away to keep from answering; he stared, unseeing, out the open ports onto the forward deck. The trouble with Loose was that he was starting with a preconceived theory, and he wanted to bend all the facts to fit it. Bill had a theory, too, he realized, and the trouble with him was that he didn't want the facts to fit. . . . He conquered his antagonism. After all, Loose was the Law. "You want me to tell you what I know?" he said slowly.

Bill told him—part of it. Loose received his statement without comment. "You touched anything in here?" he asked finally.

"No," said Bill.

"See you don't then," said Loose. "I got plenty to do when I get round to it, and I don't want things all muxed up." He patted bulging pockets. "I got a fingerprint set here, and some magnifying glasses. Always carry them. Never know when they might come handy. We'll know something when I get to work round here. I got all the 'quipment. You got to keep right up in this creaminology business. There's no barnacles grows on our backs in Trusett if we do live on tidewater. I got a set of fingerprints in my liberry . . . everybody in Trusett, I got, and a lot of summer people. . . ." All that kept Constable Loose from closing his case summarily against Varro was the rare opportunity of investigating a major crime. He went on, half to himself: "I better go now and fetch Doc Rogers. Medical examiner. And the coroner. Doc'll get us the bullet out, and we'll know what gun it come from. And arrange to move the body. Might be I better take that gangster along with me. Shut him up on a 'sault and batt'ry charge, I'll know where he is when I want him. You give me all them guns. I don't want no accidents whilst I'm gone."

Bill led the way to his stateroom. He took the key from his pocket and unlocked the desk drawer. His gun and Varro's lay inside and the two target revolvers. He saw at once that Choate's knife was missing. . . .

Loose gathered the weapons with care into a huge pictorial handkerchief. He rounded on Bill sharply. "What'd the girl faint for?"

"Miss Bridge?" said Bill formally. "Miss Bridge has had a shock, naturally. She had no sleep last night. She ate no breakfast. It is hardly strange, I think, that she reached the end of her endurance."

"Funny thing though," mused Constable Loose. "All I done was point my finger." The look of his eyes was shrewd and bright from the ambush of his brows. "What you covering her up for?"

"Miss Bridge had nothing to do with it," said Bill loudly.

Constable Amasa Loose, he saw, was going to make trouble.

3

Bill stepped outside while Constable Loose went to fetch Varro. He paced slowly along the narrow deck, letting the wind blow through his hair. It felt cold and clean on his hot face.

Bill saw Jane almost at once. She was on the beach that fringed the cove, crouching at the water's edge, peering into the fog. Bill started down to join her. He saw her figure stiffen when she heard the crunch of his footsteps, and she stood up hastily. As she rose her hand flashed out, and something curved from it through the air and fell with a distant splash. She turned instantly to meet him.

It was not till then that Bill saw what had happened. The outboard dinghy had lain just there, its bow drawn clear of the water. It did not lie there now. The line with which Cephus Kember had made it fast was still tied about the snag of rock with a shipshape seaman's knot. But the long end hung slack, trailing on the stones. It was cut off clean and short . . . like the chain of Christine's bag. Bill knew in that moment, as well as he was ever to know afterwards, that it was Choate's knife which Jane had thrown away. Jane faced him with a white defiant smile.

"You caught me, didn't you?" she said. "I might have known you would. You're such a good . . . detective."

Bill was frightened then. He had not been really frightened before. Everything, he had persuaded himself, he could explain away. Everything . . . but this. The hard little note of recklessness in Jane's voice frightened him the more.

"Jane," he cried in shocked protest. "You don't realize what you've done."

"Oh, yes I do," said Jane brightly. "I've cut the line and pushed the boat off. It's outside now and the tide's got it. You'll never find it in this fog."

She would have passed him, leaving him like that, if Bill had not caught her wrists. He held her so, and she flung her head back, staring up at him in bitter, quick resistance. "That's right," she taunted him. "Hold me. You're stronger than I am, and I can't get away. You can do anything you like with me. You can kiss me, and say you love me. . . ."

Bill was angry then, the way he had never been angry before, because there had never been such hurt behind his angers. His fingers bit hard into Jane's shoulders. "You shan't say that," he cried. "You shan't make fun of our love. That was real. Whatever happens, you can't take that away."

She laughed. It was low laughter, fiercely controlled, and the more terrible for that. "Love!" she cried. "It would make you laugh, wouldn't it, to remember our love scenes. I making love to you to find out about Mrs. Van Wycke. And you making love to me to find out about Sheel. You were cleverer than I though with the love parts. I suppose you'd had more practice. You'll laugh when I tell you that at first I believed you. But you over-played it in the end. When you told me how much I'd helped you on the Tarrant case. . . . You thought you'd catch me with that monogram, didn't you? Pretending you didn't know what the big T stood for. . . ."

"And what does it stand for?" Bill said.

She pulled herself away.

"Oh, *don't* pretend any more," she cried. "It's carrying artistry too far. Of course you've known all along that I'm Sheel Tarrant's sister."

NINE

That afternoon Constable Amasa Loose held a formal inquiry.

Bill went to it in the attitude of mind of one already sentenced for life to slow, unresting punishment. For Bill was condemned to carry with him always the weight of Jane's words.

Jane Bridge Tarrant was Sheel Tarrant's sister. That new piece of the puzzle Jane had unwittingly placed in his hands. He did not know yet where the piece fitted. But it fitted somewhere. . . .

Suppose then that Sheel Tarrant, when he stole the ruby, had already contracted to sell it to Mrs. Van Wycke. He delivered it at once, to get it out of his possession, but had not been paid. The theft was discovered prematurely, and Tarrant died, leaving Jane without full instructions to collect his debt or recover the gem. Plainly Jane had known something about the ruby; as plainly, there was more that she needed to know. She had come then to the place, next to Drake and Durgin's itself, most certain to have the information—the Verity Insurance Company. From there she went straight to Mrs. Van Wycke. Failing to secure the ruby, or its equivalent, she had sent for Ewell Choate to help her. Before their plans were perfected, Bill's unexpected arrival forced their hand. In the darkness they—*he*—had taken the ruby. Mrs. Van Wycke had detected him in the act, and he had killed her. In desperation, he had taken the other jewels and tried to escape, having arranged to come back later after Jane. . . . Bill's suppositions crashed into nothing. This was Jane. One did not suppose things like that about Jane. . . .

Bill confessed to himself now that he loved Jane in spite of everything. If Jane had loved him in return, deeply and fully, the way he knew Jane could love, then he would have explained the facts away. Jane was young, he would have said; she had not realized. Mrs. Van Wycke's death had been an accident. Choate had forced her. Choate had done it without her knowledge. She was protecting Choate. . . .

But Jane had never loved him. Bill saw that now. She had come to Verity's with one end in view: and to that end she had sought his friendship, and taken an interest in his work, and asked him a thousand questions. The thought tore into Bill's memories, scattering the pieces. Why when they sat on high stools in the corner drugstore, swinging their legs and drinking their mugs of coffee . . . when they faced each other over their Sunday night waffles at Jane's table and Bill dreamed dreams of breakfasts in a Dutch colonial . . . even that night when she had lain in his arms and lifted her lips to his, and their breath had come together like one person's . . . even then Bill had no place in her heart. Ewell Choate was in Jane's heart, and Sheel Tarrant, and the knowledge of the ruby. She had offered Bill only the show of love that she thought needful to bring the information that she lacked. But when she had read his report to Mr. Verity, and found that Bill would talk of the case no more . . . then she had disappeared.

That was what Bill's reason told him. But he did not really believe a word of it. Jane looked so innocent in her little blue suit. . . .

Even when Jane had met the red anger of Constable Loose, after the discovery that she had freed the boat which was their one means of communication with the shore, it was with such a look of innocent distress that Bill found it hard to believe that she grasped the significance of what she had done. She neither denied nor explained her action. "Yes," she said. "I did it. Was it a very bad thing to do?"

Constable Loose snorted. "You were trying to get away," he charged her.

"It was the boat that got away," Jane said mildly.

Bill did not understand it . . . then. If Jane had tried to escape in the boat, or if Choate had . . . but in cutting it loose she had imprisoned herself as securely as she had the rest of them. For the moment, however, Jane got off with little questioning; for there was still hope at first that the boat could be recovered. There was a great scampering up and down, and much peering into the fog, and one or two false alarms. But they never saw the *Aphrodite's* outboard dinghy again.

"So we're really stranded now," Bill said thoughtfully.

Angeline uttered a horrified little scream. "Supplies!" she cried. "My goodness! There's no way to get anything to *eat!*"

Bill could hardly help laughing at Angeline's preoccupation. But he answered grimly enough. "And no way to get the coroner. And no way to take Mrs. Van Wycke's body ashore."

"And no way to get them new parts," Cephus Kember muttered.

There was a gloomy silence. It was not a pleasant situation that confronted them: beached on a deserted island, some distance off the coast, with a disabled boat, a dead woman lying in the stateroom below, and her murderer moving freely about among them. . . . Angeline was the first to recover. There was the same lightness in her spirits that there was in her quick plump body.

"Of course we can't really be stranded though, so near land," she said brightly. "All we've got to do is hail somebody."

"Who?" asked Varro trenchantly.

The question was not without basis. Bowsprit Island lay too far inshore for any considerable craft to pass close, too far out for picnic parties. "What about fishermen?" asked Burge. "Aren't there any lobster traps?"

"Not many so fur out," said Cephus Kember. "They won't be hauling them anyhow in this weather."

"There was a boat lying off the Head this morning . . ." Bill began.

"It's gone now," said Varro quickly. "I saw it too. But it put about and left while I was watching."

"There might be another," Bill said. "If we got up a signal . . ."

"There are those horns we had the Fourth of July," said Angeline doubtfully. "And a big bell . . ."

Constable Loose, bustling up, put an end to the discussion. Now the fact was definitely established that the boat was gone, that there was no way to get it back, that he was in effect a prisoner along with his prisoners, he rose magnificently to the occasion. Perhaps he was not sorry to assume full responsibility. The opportunity to solve single-handed the great Van Wycke Jewel Murder Mystery is such a thing as happens only once to the constable of Trusett, Maine.

"We'll get took off some time, I guess," he said philosophically. "Till we do, I'm the boss here, and I want you should all understand it. What I say goes, and no fooling. I don't want no more monkey business." He began at once to give his orders. "You got flags, ain't you, Ceph? Better get a signal up aloft there right away. Come night, we'll have the searchlight working; that ought to fetch somebody. Might be a good idea to put a signal on the Head too, where 'twould show from Outside. You look after that, Ceph? Now then, Joe. . . ." He roped off the gangplank and posted Joe beside it to see that no one went ashore. On the upper deck he stationed Charlie: watching out for signs of a boat; watching the rails of the decks below to see that no one tried to make a jump for it and swim. It was evident to all of them that Charlie and Joe and Cephus Kember were the only ones aboard whom the Constable trusted.

"Rest of you get along up to the lounge," he ordered them without ceremony. "Servants in the galley. Stay there till I come. I want to see you all before you scatter."

They obeyed reluctantly. This was no informal suggestion; no gentleman's agreement. This was an order, with the weight of the law behind it. They loitered uneasily about the lounge, eyeing one another with a mounting suspicion that was harder to bear than knowledge. Even Angeline was bad-tempered, after ordering a lunch of lamb hash from yesterday's roast; it couldn't have happened a worse time, she said—this was Joe's regular day for the supplies, and they were just about run down on everything. The truth was that while they were alone they had half-persuaded themselves that it was all some dreadful accident. Now Constable Loose's manner had given it reality. Theft had been committed here. Murder done. By one of them. They were no longer individuals. They were a Case. They were in the hands of the Law. They would become presently a matter of Court Record. . . .

"'Nother thing we got to do right off," Constable Loose was saying to Bill. "And that's get that knife back."

"What knife?" said Bill hardily.

"Knife that girl you're covering up threw away—Miss Bridge," said Loose sharply. "You know well enough what I mean."

"Did she throw a knife away?" said Bill. "What knife was that? How do you know?"

"Well, she threw something away," said Loose tartly. "Miss Tredennick see her. Stands to reason it was a knife, don't it, if she jest cut the bo-at free? Figure it was the same she took out of your desk drawer—the one you didn't say nothing about, time you give me the guns."

Bill was startled at the thoroughness with which Constable Loose had already reviewed the situation. Angeline's unfocused helpfulness was proving an embarrassment. He changed his tactics a little. "Even if it's so," he said, "and I don't know that it is—honestly, I don't see what difference

it makes. After all, Mrs. Van Wycke was shot. She wasn't
stabbed."

"And the chain on that bag wa'n't cut off with no fingernail scissors neither," Loose assured him. "I'm going
to get that knife up out of there if it takes me till come
Christmas. Dive, don't you?"

"Some," Bill admitted.

"All right," Loose said. "Go get your suit on."

"But look here," Bill protested. "I can dive; yes. But
I can't dive all over every inch of that cove. I don't know
where the thing went—if it's there at all."

"Miss Tredennick knows," Loose told him. "She says
she can point out jest the place. Be you going to get that
suit on now, or be'n't you?"

"I haven't any suit," said Bill.

"That stiff feller in the collar—Toombs—he'll hunt
you up one."

Bill hesitated. But he saw that if he refused outright
it would not help Jane. Even his further objection would
only emphasize the importance that he attached to the
matter. "Is it an order?" he said, grinning.

"It's an order," Loose said—and he did not smile back.

Five minutes later, in the bathing suit that Toombs had
produced, Bill followed Constable Loose ashore. Angeline
bounced before them, her grey linen slatting in the wind
against her legs. "Right down this way. . . ."

Above him, at the rail of the after deck, Bill was aware
of Jane . . . watching. Her face was still. It looked very
small and white. . . . Bill sent her a glance of mute con-
trition, because he was the one who had to do this. He
tried to make her a little sign, as who should say: you can
lead a diver to the water, but you can't make him bring up
knives. . . . Jane gave no evidence of seeing him at all.

"Hurry up," Loose called.

"Now you stand right here," said Angeline, "and I'll
show you the place. You see that rock? And then you see
the way my finger's pointing. Well now about as far from

the rock as I am from that piece of seaweed . . . there, right where that whitecap's breaking. Did you see it? Well, anyway, you swim out, and I'll holler when you get there."

Bill waded into the cold water and began to swim. It wasn't far, of course. "Right *there!*" Angeline called urgently. And Bill took a big breath and went under.

The water was comparatively shallow. Bill touched bottom, and came up, without opening his eyes. "Didn't see it," he called back.

"Go ahead," said Loose.

"Try a little farther out," said Angeline.

Bill tried a little farther out, and a little farther in, and a little farther to the left, and to the right, and in a circle round about. "Guess it's no use," he called back.

"Go ahead," said Loose.

Bill went on diving. It was beginning to grow chilly. Just to vary the monotony, he opened his eyes when he went down. When he had been down a few more times, he saw the knife.

"Nothing doing," he called back.

"Go ahead," said Loose.

Bill dived about a dozen times more, and every time he saw the knife, lying blatantly on a smooth white stone. It seemed to Bill presently as if it filled the whole ocean floor. Whichever way he looked, he simply could not get down without seeing that darned knife.

"Guess I'll have to give it up," he called back. "Growing cold."

"Go ahead," said Loose. "I got as much time as you have."

Bill knew then that Constable Loose had a very shrewd idea of the truth. If Bill did not choose to bring the knife up, he would keep him diving there until, as he said, come Christmas. Bill took a big breath and went down . . . and saw the knife once more . . . and did not touch it.

In the course of the next twenty dives or so, however, Bill did a lot of thinking. Constable Loose, it appeared, knew how to be stubborn. But Bill could be stubborn too. He could dive all day and all night and all the next day, until he got cramps and drowned . . . but Constable Amasa Loose could not make him bring up the knife unless he so elected. It wasn't the sight of Constable Loose, then, squatting on his heels and looking as if he had months and years at his disposal, that moved Bill finally. It wasn't Angeline's shrill repeated cry: "That's right *exactly* the place. I don't see how you can miss it." It wasn't even the thought of the Verity Insurance Company, though that was a very teasing thought indeed. It was the sudden perception that he was afraid of that knife. But if he had honestly believed in Jane's innocence . . . then he wouldn't have been afraid. In defiance of his own suspicion, Bill's fingers closed on the knife.

"I've got it," he said to Constable Loose, staggering a little as he waded out.

"Much obliged," said Loose laconically—and put the knife in his pocket.

Jane was still on the after deck when they went back. "You got it, didn't you?" she said.

"Uh-huh," said Loose.

Bill glanced up at Jane once—and fell again to regarding the sand sticking between his toes. How could he hope to say to Jane with a look the things that even with words he could hardly have explained? But he thought he saw a flicker of hope dying in Jane's eyes—and he was the one who had killed it. The cold east wind on his wet skin felt no sharper than Jane's reproach. But her words were easy enough.

"Sorry to make you so much trouble," she said.

"You'll be sorrier," Loose told her grimly.

He saw Bill and Angeline through the ropes, and stopped for a word with Joe before he bustled off. Bill went down to his stateroom to dress.

2

Constable Loose was very busy all the rest of the morning. He went about his investigations with a fine untrammeled gusto, reveling in the situation. He was everywhere at once, it seemed, with his magnifying glasses and his folding rule and his fingerprint powder and his endless questions. But his results were hardly in proportion to his efforts.

Constable Loose examined every inch of the dining saloon under the magnifying glass—and found nothing. He examined Mrs. Van Wycke's lipstick, and the stains on the stubs in her ash tray—and decided that she had smoked the cigarettes herself. He examined the bag—and decided that the chain had been cut by some sharp instrument. In the absence of the medical examiner, he recovered the fatal bullet and examined that; he decided that it came from one of the two target revolvers. He took the revolvers outside and fired a shot from each into a tree; he and Toombs—muttering that he was employed as a butler and not as a wood carver—pried them out again. Loose compared both bullets with the bullet that had killed Mrs. Van Wycke, searching for those minute, identifying marks dear to the heart of the expert in ballistics—and he decided that all three really looked very much alike.

Constable Loose then made a complete set of fingerprints for everyone aboard. There was a little trouble over this: notably from Varro, who had scruples; and Beulah, who threatened to become hysterical; and Annie Budd, who had her hands in the pie-crust dough and said that another time would be more convenient. He got them all finally, and marked and filed them in a box belonging to Jane. After that he examined Mrs. Van Wycke's stateroom—and found a great many of Mrs. Van Wycke's fingerprints. He examined doorknobs and light switches, and Bill's gun, and Varro's. He examined both target revolvers, and found the prints of practically everybody, albeit much confused.

He examined the bag, and found no fingerprints whatever, because the woven links kept no record. He found no fingerprints on the knife, because it had been washed. . . .

Bill was busy too that morning. While Constable Loose was occupied with his fingerprints and his magnifying glasses, he found an opportunity to examine the boat with more care than had thus far been possible. Illogically enough, perhaps, he felt that in doing this he was helping Jane. He was trying to prove that Jane was not . . . guilty.

Bill's first thought was for the jewels. But he searched also for something that would match his scrap of pink fuzz. The fuzz was important; he was sure of that. The maribou from Christine's negligée had not proved, after all, exactly right. It was too soft; too impalpable; too pink.

Bill began on the upper deck. There was not much there: the searchlight; the ensign, reversed, at the mast head, invisible at any distance in the fog; the empty davits speaking eloquently of the two lost dinghys. The boatfalls had been recoiled and secured to the perpendicular cleats on the shaft of the davits; the davits themselves swung back in the deck casings to their original position, and secured with the pins at the base. The tarpaulin was neatly folded. Everything was tidy—and useless. Charlie tramped morosely back and forth, by turns staring out to sea and peering down at the deck rails below. He nodded at Bill without speaking.

Bill tried to engage him in conversation, without much success. "Look here, Charlie," he said, "what did you mean last night when you said you and Joe were pretty well used to the doings on this boat?"

"Nothing special," Charlie said.

"But you must have meant something," Bill persisted. "Had there ever been any shooting before? Any trouble of any kind? Any . . ."

"No trouble," said Charlie. "Ceph never had no trouble on a bo-at of his before. I told you he'd take it hard."

Bill gave that up and tried again. "You and Joe heard the shots, didn't you?"

"Uh-huh."

"Didn't you think that was queer?"

"No," said Charlie. He added, after consideration: "They been shootin' half the afternoon."

"But that was outside. At a target. Didn't you wonder what they were shooting at aboard?"

"No," said Charlie. He turned his back to the wind—and to Bill—while he relighted his pipe.

"Tell me this then," said Bill. "How did the people aboard get along together? Were there any hard feelings? Any quarrels . . ."

"I wouldn't know."

"You never heard anyone below mention the jewels? Toombs, say—or Catriona?"

"I never paid them much mind."

"You knew the jewels were on board, didn't you?"

"Uh-huh."

"But it never occurred to you that anything might happen? That . . ."

"No notion," said Charlie. "If we'd had any notion, Ceph wouldn't a-went."

Bill gave it up then. Charlie's natural taciturnity had undergone a marked increase. Perhaps Loose had told him not to talk. . . . "Well, so long," Bill said, and climbed down the ladder.

The company was still gathered in the lounge, where Loose was detaining them until he had finished with their fingerprints; but Bill saw that the wheelhouse was empty and the door into the lounge was closed. He entered quietly.

The room was, as Bill already knew, at once the library, the wheelhouse and the chart-room. Books lined the after bulkhead, and charts were laid flat in the drawers of a locker under a broad table in the after starboard corner; the forward bulkhead was all windows, broken only by the door giving on the ladder; the big wheel, with its white rubber mat, and the brass binnacle occupied the forward center of the room. Jane's desk was in the port corner, opposite the table.

Bill went about his search methodically. He took the books down and examined the shelves behind them; he took the charts from their drawers and the drawers from their runners; he rolled up the rubber mat, and studied the way the compass was fixed in its brass stanchion. Finally, feeling like a thief himself, he turned to Jane's desk. Everything was in order. Mrs. Van Wycke's correspondence was filed in one of the deep lower drawers; the catalogue of gems, in the drawer opposite. The other drawers held paper and supplies, and material for the unfinished catalogue. She had evidently been working on the Shah Truzi emerald. Papers dealing with it lay on top of the desk, held by a paperweight—a sea of quicksilver, under glass, sailing a white jade ship. Bill found no material about a ruby. . . . He stood for a moment looking down onto the forward deck, before he descended.

The forward deck, where the crew lounged in fair weather, was hardly more revealing than the upper deck had been. One of the anchors was cleated there, and its hawser coiled down; the other was out; catheads sprouted like ants' feelers. In the middle was the companionway, with ladder and booby hatch, which Bill had used earlier that morning. After a brief examination, he went on down to the forecastle.

In the forecastle Bill found Cephus Kember, sitting on the edge of one of the berths that lined the bulkheads in a double rank. He was sucking a cold pipe, and he nodded, as Charlie had, without speaking.

"Wanted to have a look around," Bill explained. "That be all right?"

The movement of Kember's hand gave him permission, but he remained silent. Bill did not press him. After some time Kember said slowly: "Won't find nothing likely."

"Probably not," Bill agreed. And risked a question: "Toombs slept in here, didn't he?"

"Yeh," said Kember, and closed his mouth like a snap-trap.

"You didn't like him, did you?" Bill said softly.

"High-falutin'," said Kember—and closed his mouth again. But he considered his own remark, and at last he added justly: "That's not to say he's a murderer."

"No," said Bill. He watched Cephus Kember covertly as he moved about the room. He was, as Charlie had said, taking it hard. The seamed leather of his face looked strangely puckered, as if it had shrunk in an ill-considered washing; the young eyes, that Bill had noticed at once on their first meeting, were clouded. Bill had suddenly a perception of what this thing meant to Cephus Kember. He was not young. In a full life of hard work he had accumulated little of value save his reputation as a sailing master. And now this, the most treasured of his possessions, he conceived to be tarnished by what had happened. "Look here," Bill said impulsively, "I wouldn't worry about this if I were you."

"Never had trouble on a bo-at of mine before," Kember said. He lifted those clouded eyes to Bill, full of dignity and a mute sorrow.

Bill felt a quick embarrassment, as if he had come prying in a house of grief. "Why, you weren't even aboard," he said. "Nobody could blame you."

"It was my bo-at," said Kember flatly. And he added: "The b'ys are good b'ys."

"Why, sure they are," said Bill heartily. "Nobody blames them either."

Cephus Kember's look lightened a little, and Bill saw that he had said the right thing. "You think that?" he asked him.

"Why, sure," said Bill. "Which was Toombs' berth?"

"There," Kember told him briefly. But he watched Bill's movements after that, and presently he knocked out his

pipe on his boot heel and came to help him. They stripped
the berths together, and Kember showed him the men's
lockers. None of them was fastened, and Bill expected, as
he found, nothing.

"You want to come with me?" he said to Kember, when
he was ready to leave. "I don't know my way round down
here very well." And Kember went with him readily enough.

They stopped first at the starboard midship section,
where Bill had looked in hastily that morning, and Kember
showed him in detail the big tanks for storing gasoline and
water, the refrigerating system, and the dynamo for the
lights. The storage space for supplies was just beyond; and
Bill saw that the chief items of food on hand were tinned
tuna, dried apricots and canned pears—no wonder that
Angeline was perturbed. They passed by the small stateroom occupied by Catriona and Annie Budd, and came to
the engine room, aft, under the dining saloon. The engine
was rather old and cumbersome, powerful without speed,
but Kember picked up a piece of oily waste and touched it
here and there fondly.

"What is it?" Bill asked.

"Heavy-duty Knox," said Kember. "Trusty. They don't
make 'em now. No bird, she isn't, but she gets there." He
laid a hand against the bulkhead, sliding his rough palm
along the wood. "She's a good bo-at," he said soberly—and
Bill saw that he was thinking again that he had never had
trouble on a boat of his before.

"Just what was the accident to her?" Bill asked.

"Bent propeller blades and shaft," said Kember promptly. "We picked up a lobster buoy on the way out. It wa'n't
a day to move anyhow. Roding."

"Roding?" Bill repeated.

"Choppy sea," Kember explained. "Sun so bright on it
you couldn't see nothing. I tol' her how 'twould be. But
she was set on coming." He spoke of Mrs. Van Wycke with
the kindly tolerance shown a child who has always been
humored.

"I see," Bill said. "Then it wasn't anybody's fault?"

"I was standin' a trick at the wheel myself when it happened," Kember said with dignity—and Bill was abashed, seeing he had gone too far. But after a moment Kember continued: "We got her in here best way we could, and beached her; and then we got the mooring lines out, and an anchor, in case the wind would change. But it was dark before the tide was right so we could have the wheel and the shaft off her. That's why I waited till morning to take 'em to Trusett. We'd been all right if they'd had the size wheel in stock at Portland." He laid down his oily waste and turned away abruptly.

Cephus Kember left Bill at the door of the galley, and went back to the forecastle. Bill walked in unannounced on Annie Budd. She was standing with her back to the door, and she jumped when Bill spoke.

"Land o' love!" she cried. "You give me a start, busting in onto me like that. I'm all of a dither today, the goings-on we've had. What you after down here?"

"Jewels," said Bill, grinning. "You got any?"

"You're welcome to hunt, I'm sure," said Annie Budd. She looked up at Bill over a broad shoulder, softening to his grin; she couldn't help liking the boy, if he was a detective. Then she went on rolling out her pie-crust. "And it won't be any the better either," she assured him, "for standing while I had a picture took of my fingers. Here, set down, why don't you, and I'll bring you some hot tea. I always keep some good hot tea brewed by me. It's a comfort."

Bill sat in the chair beside Annie Budd's molding board and drank his strong, hot tea. He looked about the clean bright galley, with its floor scrubbed white. What a place to hide jewels a lump of dough would make. . . .

"Did you have any dough last night?" he asked suddenly.

"*Dough?*" repeated Annie Budd, in such blank bewilderment that he knew it was genuine. "There, I believe all this trouble's gone to your head."

"But did you?" Bill persisted.

"No," she said, humoring him.

An idea was working in Bill's mind. He tried to seem casual. "This Choate fellow," he said, "what's he like? You've talked with him some, haven't you?"

"Oh, yes," said Annie Budd readily. "And a finer, politer young gentleman I'd never ask to see the like of. I always admired to have him coming in. He's got that kind of kidding way with him, awful pleasant."

Bill saw that it was not going to be easy to find out anything to Choate's disadvantage. "Did he talk with you often?" he said. "Ask you questions, and so on?"

"Oh, yes," said Annie Budd. "He was real folksy. Always seemed to take an interest in what I told him."

"And what was that?" said Bill. "Do you suppose I could have another cup of tea?"

"Sure," said Annie Budd affably. "Oh, we talked about this and that. I wouldn't hardly remember all. Sugar?"

She folded the round of crust and fitted it over a pie plate; began to crimp the edges. "I guess the reason I fancied him so much," she said, "was he reminded me of my boy. Killed in the war, he was. Chatoo-Teery. I had a letter from his capting about him. Seems he went out alone to mop up a machine-gun nest. That's what the letter said. He was killed doing it. I guess he took after me some: he couldn't stand a thing that would need cleaning up, without he'd take hold himself and do it. Mr. Choate favors him. Both light-complected. My boy's name was Lucas. His hair kind of stood up on top like the way Mr. Choate's does."

Bill tried to say it casually when the time came. "Has Mr. Choate been down since last night?"

"Early this morning," said Annie Budd. "Before breakfast. Right after he fell in the water, that was. I fixed him up a hot drink, and made him put his feet in mustard. Boys are careless about taking cold. My own boy was just the same."

So the first time Choate had been alone following the tragedy, he had come straight to that galley. Was that after he saw Jane . . . ?

"Thanks for the tea," Bill said. "It's great stuff. Care if I take a look around?"

"Go ahead," Annie Budd invited him. It was plain to Bill that if there were jewels there, Annie Budd did not know it.

A galley is a troublesome place to search. There are things like flour sacks and sugar buckets. Luckily for Bill's purposes, if not for Angeline's, the stores were low. Annie Budd was bothered, but tolerant. Boys were always up to tricks. Her own boy was just the same. "Here, empty the coffee in this bowl, if you've got to. . . ."

Afterwards, at his request, Annie Budd took Bill across the corridor into the maids' room which she shared with Catriona. It was very tiny, and their things were crowded. Catriona was lying in the upper berth, looking sulky and rather frightened. She stared at Bill resentfully; but when he asked if he could look about, she scrambled down and began to whimper, protesting that she never stole anything in her life.

"There, hush up, do," said Annie Budd. "What makes you act so, Catriona? Mr. Galleon will think you've got something to cover up."

Bill was puzzled by Catriona's manner. He would not have thought her sufficiently sensitive to take the affair so much to heart. But Annie Budd spread out her effects amiably enough for his inspection. She even dragged out the box that held her twenty-seven crocheted bedspreads, and unfolded them in turn. This was the Pop Corn and Peanut Pattern; the Si'mese Twins; the Rock of Gibyralter. . . . Bill praised them warmly, sensing her pride; and Annie Budd expanded under his praise like some large thick-petaled blossom touched with sun. They parted in friendly fashion, and Bill climbed up the steps that led to the serving pantry.

Later, he decided, he would go over the dining saloon
again. But at the time it seemed better to proceed at once
with the staterooms; when Loose had finished with his
fingerprinting in the lounge, there might not be so good
an opportunity. He set about it methodically, working
down one side of the corridor and back the other. It was a
pity that Jane should have been the one to find him.

Bill was stirring Jane's jar of cold cream with a tea-
spoon, when he looked up to find her watching in the
doorway. She did not mention the knife specifically, but
the knowledge of it was instantly as cold and sharp as the
blade itself between them.

"Bill," she said, "must you always be the one to do me
harm?"

Bill blundered awkwardly into speech. "I didn't mean
to, Jane," he said. "Don't you see I had to do it when he
told me? Don't you see it would have looked queer if I
hadn't?" He floundered helplessly and added the prepos-
terous thing that was the truth: "Jane, I had to get that
knife to show I wasn't afraid to. I had to do it to show that
I trusted you."

She laughed, an unwonted edge of bitterness showing
in her voice. "Trust me?" she said. "Why should you?—Of
course a very natural way to show your trust. As natural,
perhaps, as . . . this." Her gesture indicated the jar and the
spoon that Bill still held. "Can I help you?"

"I . . . don't know," Bill said slowly. "Can you?"

"Perhaps if I knew what you were looking for this time . . ."

"A . . . ruby," said Bill flatly.

She laughed again, with that unnatural bitterness.
"'Why of course," she said. "Such a trustful thing to look
for. Well then, it isn't here."

He believed her. When Jane looked at him like that,
clearly and directly, then he would have believed anything
she told him. That was the devastating part of it. For if
he believed the things that he wanted to be true, then he
should have to believe also the hard words she had flung

at him in that unguarded moment by the shore. . . . He set the jar of cold cream back on the dressing table, and his hands dropped to his sides. "Shall I stop?" he said.

"Oh, no," said Jane. "By all means satisfy your craving for perfect trust. Show your absolute confidence by hunting through my things for stolen jewels. I'll help you. Probably I can think of a lot of places that wouldn't even occur to you." She came in and closed the door.

It seemed to Bill that nothing he had ever done was quite so hard as that search of Jane's room—with Jane, white-lipped and steady and defiant, helping him. There was in her manner now no trace of the wild antagonism she had shown him earlier. As little of the half-tender friendliness of those moments when she had bandaged his head. Now she forced herself to be completely matter-of-fact; as impersonal as if they searched together the room of a stranger. The very simplicity of her manner made Bill's errand the more monstrous.

"You'd better take off the pillow cases," she said quietly. "It would make rather a mess to empty the pillows. Perhaps if you squeeze them carefully you can tell. I'll turn out the bureau drawers for you."

She turned the drawers out on the bed before him, and he saw the pile of white linen handkerchiefs, each with its ℬ in the corner; the gloves and scarfs and stockings. The sight of all Jane's little intimacies unnerved him. She tumbled out a heap of white silk underthings, and shook them composedly, one by one. There was a smell of lavender in them. There was no . . . pink fur. Bill reached out a big shy forefinger, and laid it on one of the garments. It was soft and smooth like Jane's skin, but not so warm.

"Was there something you wanted to see about this one?" Jane said politely.

She brought her dresses from the closet, and invited him to pinch the seams; she brought her shoes, and warned him against false heels. There was a pair of blue mules with silver straps, and the shape of Jane's slim toes in the satin.

There was a sea-blue monk's robe with a silver cord. Was it in this that she had received Choate two nights ago . . . ?

"Would you care to rip the lining out?" said Jane.

"No," said Bill violently. He couldn't bear any more of it. Jane, with her cool, helpful little questions, tearing him all to pieces. "That's all," he said.

"You're sure you're quite satisfied?"

Bill stopped with his hand on the door. Turned. With the width of the room between them, he held out his heart to Jane. Jane could not really believe—could she?—that this love of his that ached in his bones and ran fire in his blood was anything but true. "You don't believe them, do you, Jane?" he said humbly. "The things you said—down there. It was real—all of it. I . . . didn't know who you were."

Jane put the blue velvet robe back on its hanger and flapped up the silver cord so that it should not drag. "You ought to be on the stage, Bill," she said. "You do it to perfection."

Bill could not see the door when he stumbled out.

Nevertheless, presently, Bill forced himself to go on with his search. He finished the staterooms and the corridors, and went back to the dining saloon. That was where he found the wire cutters.

It was such a pair of cutters as is commonly used to clip the wire seals from the tops of bottles; but it might have been used to cut any metal substance. It was hanging on a hook in the wine closet. Bill took it down carefully on the tip of a fork, and carried it to Constable Amasa Loose. He was suddenly excited.

"Looks to me," he said, "as if this was what cut the chain off that bag instead of the knife."

Constable Loose seized upon Bill's find with open eagerness. "Say, you done something now, young feller," he admitted. In the heat of his enthusiasm he added confidentially: "Jest between you and I, that knife didn't do it. I took it and I cut a bit off'n that chain that's still round the wrist on the body. Got it off too, finally. But say—that thing plumb mashed and hacked it all to pieces, doing it. The first cut was clean's a wink.—Thing I can't figure out: if that ain't how the knife was used, how's it come into this business anyhow?"

"It doesn't," said Bill cheerfully. "I guess Jane just threw it away because she had finished with it."

"Folks don't do the likes of that," Loose objected shrewdly. "No, young feller, you mark my words. That knife's important. And the girl knows it too, or else she would a-kept it." He laid out his fingerprint powder, and nodded to Bill to indicate that the interview was ended. "But you'll find Varro's prints is what's on this," he added confidently.

Bill left him to his task. When he had finished, Constable Loose summoned them all to his inquiry.

3

The inquiry was held in the dining saloon. Constable Amasa Loose made them take again the seats at the table which they had occupied when Mrs. Van Wycke was killed. Toombs stood by the pantry door, Annie Budd and Catriona Cooley beside him. The dog Telemachus lay by Beulah's chair, head on his extended paws. Cephus Kember and Charlie and Joe were stationed in the doorway. Material witnesses, Loose said. It struck Bill that they looked rather more like guards. They stood uneasily, trying to find a place to keep their hands; Kember brooded over his cold pipe, packing and repacking it with a fumbling thumb. Catriona was sniffling.

"I didn't take anything," she kept repeating.

Jane looked at Catriona Cooley with a kind of impatient astonishment. Not for Jane was the facile relief of tears. For her were the high head and the steady hands, the lips that smiled upon demand, the quiet voice that answered to her will.

"You look kind of peeked, Jane," Angeline said. "I don't believe you eat enough. You didn't hardly touch the hash this noon. Don't you like hash?"

"It was very nice hash," said Jane politely.

"Well, it's no joke," said Angeline, "trying to cater for fourteen people, and nothing to cater *with*. . . . Toombs, just step down and bring me up that jar of peanut butter, will you?"

"I'm sure it must be hard," said Jane. Her manner was that of one making small talk at a rather formal tea. "Did you have better success after you left me?" she asked Bill.

"Loose says I found a clue," Bill told her—and he saw her lips straighten over the question she would not ask. "A pair of wire cutters."

She said instantly: "Then Ewell's knife had nothing to do with it."

"I wouldn't know," said Bill slowly. She was too ready. The thought had lain too near the surface of her mind.

The wire cutters were on the serving table, along with the knife, the target revolvers, the empty bag, the empty jewel box, the chain that had held the ruby, and some scraps of gold chain matching that on the bag. Bill's attention was held by those severed bits of chain. One of them was clean-cut; the other all twisted and misshapen. But . . . the fragile links of the platinum chain that had held the ruby were crushed and broken too. The break came only a few inches from the clasp; that should have been nearer to Mrs. Van Wycke's shoulder than to the breast. Of course the chain might have slipped around through the jewel's loop. But . . . had it? They had taken it for granted that the bullet had done the mischief. But . . . had it happened like that? Bill did not call attention to his discovery.

Constable Loose moved the table forward so that it stood at the empty place where Mrs. Van Wycke had been. He took his station behind it, looking longer and leaner and looser-jointed and redder-faced than ever in the fervor of his great moment. The lobster claw twitched spasmodically. His manner was judicial.

Some time was lost while Constable Loose again went over ground which had already been covered. He turned to the crew for corroboration of testimony, embarrassing them no less than the principals. There were points, however, which he did not understand—and never would. Why, for instance, able-bodied people should sit still in a dark room while a crazy man in pajama pants ran amuck with a gun and shot up the whole place, was a thing that Loose's practical, unscientific mind could never grasp. And all Burge's explanations, and all Angeline's, never made it one whit clearer.

They came finally to the exhibits on the serving table. "I got a mort of questions to ask you yet," Loose promised them. Although he was convinced in his own mind that Varro had not only stolen the jewels, but had killed Mrs. Van Wycke, still he was not the man to forego the exquisite pleasure of questioning everyone in detail. The truth would come out all right, give it time. All the quicker for throwing Varro off his guard. But some of the facts which came to light astonished and troubled him. A fact is a stubborn thing, when you try to bend it to a theory.

"Now here," began Constable Loose, "we got some clues." His hand hovered for an instant over the knife; over the mangled scrap of gold chain. Then he decided not to mention them. He took a pair of sugar tongs and picked up the wire cutters carefully. "This here," he said, "is the clippers that cut the bag off'n Mrs. Van Wycke's wrist. I took this clippers in a han'kychief, and I cut a piece off'n the chain that was still on the body. I put the piece I cut off, and the piece here on the bag under the magnifying glasses, and the cut edges is jest the same. And now whose fingerprints do you s'pose I found on the clippers?"

Not one of the faces lifted to Loose's scrutiny showed any just picture of the emotions back of it. Jane's wore a look of polite, but purely academic interest. Only Angeline displayed an impersonal curiosity. She held her spoon suspended, a blob of peanut butter dropping off the end.

"*Whose?*" she cried.

"Nobody's," said Constable Loose triumphantly.

They did not understand him at first. But Bill nodded. "I see," he said slowly. "If it had been used for any innocent purpose, the prints of the last user would be on it. Toombs', probably. It has been wiped."

"That's right," Loose admitted grudgingly. He whirled suddenly on Varro. "What'd you wipe it with?"

"Wipe your eye," said Varro. "I never even saw it." Of Amasa Loose, armed with a tarred rope, Varro had a wholesome fear; but for Loose's words he felt only the contempt of one who had been questioned by the police of two great cities—and released.

Constable Loose let it rest there. He was so sure of Varro's guilt that he could afford to wait. "Way I understand it," he said, "you searched this room last night. Who done the searching?"

"Why, we all did," said Angeline. "That is, Toombs and Catriona and Annie Budd. But we all watched and told them what to do."

"And why didn't you find this clippers then?"

"I did, sir," said Toombs. "It was hanging on the hook in plain sight."

"But you didn't mention it?"

"No, sir. I understood"—there was a shade of wounded dignity in Toombs' voice—"that what we were searching for was Mrs. Van Wycke's bag."

"Then you're sure it was there all the time?"

"Oh, yes, sir."

"Then tell me this. You say you searched the room, and the bag wa'n't in it, nor the jools. Then you left the room all together, and searched each other. And didn't find anything? That right?"

"Yes," said Angeline.

"But when you come back, you met the dog in the hall, and he had the bag in his mouth. Where'd he get it? Tell me that."

"I've thought about it a lot," Bill said. "You realize that a good deal of time had passed, and at first we did not know that the bag was gone. There was no opportunity to leave the room. But I judge that during that interval some one could have stepped to the door and simply thrown the bag outside. While we were in our staterooms, the dog found it."

"And who d'you cal'late had a chance to do this throwing?"

"Why, I guess we all did," Angeline put in. "Toombs was standing there by the door where he is now, and Catriona was right beside him. Annie Budd went out in the hall to get the second revolver off the table. The rest of us were moving round a good deal, back and forth. And we all kind of crowded up here in the door to watch Joe and Charlie carry Mrs. Van Wycke to her stateroom. I don't know as there'd have been a chance to *throw* the bag then, exactly, but I guess anybody could have dropped it down and given it a push with his foot. I wonder . . ."

"You figure the bag was empty then?" Loose said to Bill.

"Yes," said Bill slowly. He saw too late where this point was leading him, and he wished he had not raised it.

"And where you figure the jools was?"

"I don't know," Bill said. "But some one might have taken them out, disposed of the bag, kept the jewels till the room was searched, then left them here while we went to search each other. Afterwards of course he got them again."

"Then the thing is, who come in first?"

"But we didn't come in," said Angeline. "We all went ashore when we saw the dog with the bag."

"And who came back first?"

"Why Mr. Choate did—that time he started off in the boat."

"If you think I had time to do anything but launch that boat . . ." Choate burst out violently.

"I was pretty close behind him," Bill admitted. "And I do know he wasn't in the dining saloon when I came aboard, because I looked here first. I don't know what he did afterwards. I lost track of him completely, and went about all over the boat looking for him."

"And who come aboard next after that?"

"We all came back together then," Angeline said. "That is—Miss Bridge and Mr. Galleon did come a little ahead of the rest of us, but . . ."

"Miss Bridge and I were together all the time," Bill said firmly.

"Why, the idea!" cried Angeline, staring at him with shocked round eyes. "You both had your clothes changed when we got here."

"Then while you was changing, mebbe Miss Bridge could have stepped in here a minute, and you not notice," Loose suggested.

"Impossible," said Bill positively. "She would have had to pass my door, and I should have heard her." But . . . he was not so sure. For that matter, Jane could have stopped in the dining saloon on her way to the library, before ever he came aboard.

Unluckily Bill had reawakened Loose's early suspicion that he was shielding Jane. Constable Loose had a certain awe of Bill, as one of those smart city dicks he affected to despise—but he wouldn't put it past him for a minute to double-cross him and take all the credit.

"Then who come in next?" he persisted.

"Why, we all did," said Angeline again. "And looked in the bag. Then we went to change our clothes. And then we had breakfast. I just slipped into some dry things myself and went right down to the galley to see Annie Budd, and Choate was there . . ."

"Oh, *Choate* was there, was he? And what was *he* doing?"

"I was having a hot drink," said Choate, flushing uncomfortably.

"I made him put his feet in mustard," said Annie Budd. "Boys are so careless."

"And how'd you get down there?"

"Walked," said Choate sulkily. His attitude, whether of temper or of guilt, did not make a good impression.

"You had to walk through here then," said Loose drily. "Who'd you see on the way?"

"Nobody."

Jane flung out her words without an instant's hesitation. With no thought of what it meant to herself. Her quick championship was a turn of the screw in Bill's private rack. "Why, yes, you did, Ewell. You saw me."

"Oh, yes," Choate mumbled. "I forgot."

Loose turned on Jane. "And what were *you* doing?"

"Watering the plants," said Jane composedly.

There it was. Had Jane arranged with Choate what to do? Had he returned, as soon as the coast was clear, to reclaim the jewels from the flower pot where Angeline had seen Jane digging, and find a safer hiding place in the galley? Bill saw that something of the same idea was working in Loose's crafty mind. But to his relief he left the matter for the moment, and picked up the two target revolvers.

"Now here's a funny thing," he said. "These have got the fingerprints of everybody on 'em, excepting Miss Tredennick and Miss Bridge."

"That's right," Angeline assured him. "They were target-shooting. And everybody was there except me. And Jane. Jane was up in the library working."

"Toombs was there, I figure," said Loose drily. "And Annie Budd and Catriona? Their prints is all over this one, the whole of 'em. Awful mess."

"Well . . . no." Angeline considered, licking peanut butter slowly off a spoon. "Annie Budd brought the second revolver in when we sent her after it. So it's all right about her. But . . ."

Catriona burst into ready tears, hiding her face in Toombs' sleeve. "I wouldn't steal any old pistol," she cried.

"I wouldn't want any old pistol anyhow. I wouldn't know what to do with a pistol if I had one."

"You could shoot somebody with it, mebbe."

"I *didn't,*" screamed Catriona. "I wasn't even in here. . . ."

"How'd your prints get onto it, then?"

"Tell the gentleman what he asks you," Toombs said severely. "About before dinner."

"Oh, yes," sobbed Catriona. "Before dinner. I was setting the table. I saw the pistols, where Miss Beulah laid them down, and I didn't ever see a pistol near to, so I went over and picked one up. And I asked Gus—Mr. Toombs—how it worked."

Catriona was visibly shaking. Her neat, pretty features were blurred with tears, her look fugitive and uncertain under swollen lids. But Toombs was betrayed by no least flicker of emotion. His large plain face was as frank and open as a closed barn door.

"I handled the revolver while I was explaining it to Catriona," he said. "That is how my fingerprints were on it, sir."

"And that's how mine were on it, too," Catriona cried triumphantly.

"Got your story down pat, ain't you?" said Loose. He bent the pin-prick look of his bright blue eyes on Toombs. "You know how to use a gun, then?"

"Yes, sir."

"Ever have any trouble with Mrs. Van Wycke?"

"Oh, yes, sir. You couldn't work for Mrs. Van Wycke and not have trouble, sir."

"So when you see there was shootin' going on, and it was a good chance like, you took that gun off'n the table and stepped round the other side . . ."

"I didn't go round there, sir. After I ran into Professor Burge early in the evening, I came back here."

"You mean to tell me you fired the shot from where you're standing?"

Toombs kept his head admirably. "I mean to say, sir, that since I was standing here, I could not have fired the shot."

"'Course he didn't," said Catriona.

"How do *you* know?"

Catriona hesitated, fearing a trap. "He told me so," she said finally.

"Then you don't know it of your own knowledge?"

"I know it of my own knowledge if he told me, don't I?"

"Leave me put it another way," said Loose. "Did Toombs fire the shot before you come in, or after?"

"He didn't fire any shot," said Catriona desperately.

"That's what I'm asking you. How do you know?"

"I'd have seen him if he had, wouldn't I?"

"Then the shots were fired *after* you come in?"

"Oh, no, sir. No, sir," cried Catriona in sudden panic. She twisted Jane's bracelet on her wrist till the band bit into the rosy flesh. "I wasn't ever in here till after it was all over, and the lights were on. I was downstairs with Annie Budd. When I heard Mrs. Van Wycke scream, then I run up quick. . . ."

"That right?" said Loose, turning to Annie Budd.

"Yes, sir," said Annie Budd placidly.

"And what were *you* doing?"

"Crocheting. After I'd dished up, and the last course was gone, I took my crocheting and set down to cool off."

"You heard the shots?"

"Oh, yes, sir. There couldn't anybody help hearing *them*. They fair shook the boat."

"And what did you do then?"

"I was crocheting."

"You mean to tell me you kept right on crocheting with all that shootin' over your head? Weren't you frightened? Didn't you try to find out what it was about?"

"I would have been frightened, yes, sir; only when Toombs found out there was going to be shootin', he called down the dumbwaiter and told us, so we wouldn't be."

Loose whirled again on Toombs. "So you knew there was going to be shootin'?"

"I judged so, sir," said Toombs frostily, "when I saw Professor Burge take the revolver from the table as he left the room."

Dante Burge nodded. He made a note on his pad. He had found a real observer.

"And all this time you was crocheting, Catriona was right with you?"

"Yes, sir."

"She couldn't have got out without you'd know it?"

"No, sir. I'd have missed her sure."

Bill interrupted. "Didn't Catriona usually put the staterooms in order at that time, and turn down the beds?"

"Oh, yes, sir," said Annie Budd. "She did go up for that, the same as usual. But that was earlier, so I didn't think. Maybe I'd ought to mentioned it. Had I?"

"She didn't turn them down," said Bill slowly.

Annie Budd bent a look of dire reproach on Catriona's flushed face. "Why, Catriona Cooley! And after all the times I've spoke to you about it!" She turned apologetically back to Bill. "I hope you'll overlook it, sir. Catriona's young, and kind of flighty. But she means real well. I guess it's my fault as much as hers. I'd ought to looked after it. You got to look after things yourself, or you don't ever get them done. . . ."

"My point was not a criticism of the housekeeping," said Bill soberly. "It was that Catriona came up to do the rooms—and didn't do them. Why didn't you, Catriona?"

"I forgot," said Catriona sulkily.

"And what made you forget?"

"There was so much going on, I guess. It put it clean out of my mind."

"What was going on? Shooting?"

"Oh, no, sir. No, no!" cried Catriona. She pressed her hands beside her face, as if trying to hold her teeth from chattering. "It was *long* before that. Honest. I don't know anything about the shootin'. I wasn't here, honest to God, I wasn't, sir. The Professor was out in the hall. All dressed up, he was. I thought you were having a show or something, and I'd be in the way. So I just went back downstairs with Annie Budd."

"And what was Annie Budd doing when you went down?"

"Crocheting. Yes, sir. And I just hung round, talking with her and like that, till Mrs. Van Wycke screamed. And then I run up quick."

"I came right behind her," Annie Budd said in corroboration. "The door was still swinging from her coming in when I got here."

"That right?" Loose turned again to Joe and Charlie.

"Figure so," Charlie agreed. "Joe and I come right down, and the others was all here before us."

"There's no doubt about that anyway," Angeline remarked. She explained to Loose: "It was awful quiet, just a minute after the lights went on. And we heard Annie Budd starting right off up the stairs. We could hear every step she took."

"Why didn't you hear Catriona then?"

"Catriona's real light-footed," Annie Budd said. "Might be you wouldn't."

Bill was not quite satisfied. But Loose appeared to be. "Did Mrs. Van Wycke leave a will?" he asked suddenly.

"No," said Angeline.

"How do you know?"

"Well, I just wondered," Angeline explained. "So I made some inquiries. I guess she didn't, all right. She didn't like to think about dying."

"Then there wouldn't a-been any bequests to servants," Loose mused. "Who's the next o' kin?"

"I am," said Beulah. She startled all of them. They had forgotten she was there; Beulah had a knack of being forgotten. Now her voice came to them meditative, serene, without the nervous jerkiness that had characterized it . . .

yesterday; the knots and tangles were all smoothed away from the little ugly face she lifted to Constable Loose. Bill was more shocked by her relaxed calm than he had been by the fears and angers of the others. It seemed hardly fair to ask Beulah anything. She was so incapable of concealing her . . . relief.

"You knew she didn't leave any will?" said Loose.

"Yes."

"And did you ever think what you'd do, if she'd die and leave you all her money?"

"Oh, *yes,*" said Beulah with a long, ecstatic breath. "I'd take it and *go away.*"

Bill was relieved when Loose left it like that. "There's another funny thing about them revolvers," he said. He spoke to Burge now. "That second one, the one on the hall table that you say you didn't touch, had your fingerprints on it."

"That must be the one I used in shooting at the target," Professor Burge replied. "My prints would be on that. Naturally."

"But the one you had in your hand, 'cording to everybody's tell, that one didn't have any."

Varro sniggered. "He had on gloves," he said with a leer.

"Gloves!" Loose cried. "You had on *gloves?*"

"Yes," said Burge. "They were part of my costume."

"You mean your costume was so's you could wear gloves without anybody thinking it was funny."

"It was all, as I have explained, part of my experiment."

"He had gloves on," Varro reminded them. "So his prints wouldn't show on the clippers either."

And Bill was suddenly sure for the first time that Burge had not taken the jewels. That probably, then, he had not committed the murder. He waited for Burge to make the obvious retort. He did not make it.

"The clippers were wiped." Bill said it himself finally. "It would not have been necessary for Professor Burge to wipe them, when he was wearing gloves. Therefore, they were used by somebody else."

"Well, that's so too," said Angeline delightedly. "It's real smart of you to think of that, Mr. Galleon."

"Why didn't you say it yourself?" Bill asked Burge curiously.

"I was interested to note," said Burge, "to whom this evident fact would occur."

Bill marveled again at the self-control of a man who could let a point against him be made without protest, while he observed the working of human minds. Could he, after all, have done the murder with no motive save a scientific curiosity?

But Constable Loose was not pleased at hearing his rival praised. His displeasure brought about the crisis Bill had feared. Loose turned to Jane.

They had all, in the beginning, underestimated Constable Loose. He had his absurdities. His unindulged enthusiasm for crime carried him too far; his lack of experience held him back on the brink of discovery. But behind those small bright eyes, shining through their scrub brows, there lurked a native shrewdness, a keen judgment of human nature, that under better auspices would have carried him very far. He showed an uncanny wit now in asking those questions which Bill most especially did not want asked.

"What'd you cut the bo-at loose for?" he began.

Jane steadied herself by a visible effort for her ordeal. "I guess it was a foolish thing to do," she admitted.

"That wa'n't what I asked you. I asked you what you did it *for*. Your boy friend put you up to it, didn't he?"

Jane was instantly on her guard. "If you mean Ewell Choate, he didn't even know it. It was my own idea entirely."

"Kind of funny idea to have, wa'n't it? How'd you happen to think of it?"

"It just came to me—all of a sudden," Jane said. "So I did it."

"It come to you all of a sudden," said Loose craftily, *"when you found you couldn't use the bo-at yourself?"*

Jane hesitated. "Yes," she said, low.

"You know what this is?" Constable Loose took something from his pocket and held it up triumphantly.

"Yes," said Jane, lower still.

"Well, I don't," said Bill, puzzled. "What is it?"

"It's the knob of the flywheel to that dinghy's engine," Constable Loose stated with unction. He was simply boiling with triumph, and his face flamed redder than the twitching lobster claw. He'd put one over on the city dick this time—showed him they knew a thing or two in Trusett. "I took it off while Ceph was tying up the bo-at," he explained with a certain condescension. "Figured I wouldn't be wanting anybody to use that bo-at excepting me. When Miss Bridge found out she couldn't escape in it, she turned it loose. Same way her boy friend sunk the other dinghy, when he found out he couldn't escape in *that*."

Bill's eyes met Jane's. It was true, then.

"I didn't sink it," Choate cried. He was nervous and his young mouth twitched. "Mr. Galleon did that. I was going for help."

"And not coming back."

Loose's words touched Choate on a spot unexpectedly raw. His voice rose raggedly. "I was too. Do you think I'd leave Jane alone with a lot like you? Do you think . . ."

"What'd you try to kill Mr. Galleon for, time he tried to stop you?"

"I didn't. I . . ."

"You hit him over the head with an oar, didn't you?"

"Yes, but . . ."

"You wanted to get rid of him because he knew something he might tell, didn't you?"

Jane's voice cut cool and clean across Choate's hot speech. "Mr. Galleon didn't know anything about Ewell."

"Something about you, then?"

"I didn't even know about the knob to the flywheel," Bill said quickly.

Constable Loose had begun now to perceive dimly what had all along been apparent to Bill: that Jane, at whatever cost to herself of danger and suspicion, meant to protect Choate. It was a gallant, high-hearted gesture. It recognized herself as the stronger of the two, paying the price in her own strength to save Choate's weakness and so holding him the dearer. Severe as was the blow of Jane's admission that she had actually tried to escape, bitter as was her championship of Choate, still Bill would have saved her, if he could, from the consequences of her own magnificent folly. But Constable Loose, stimulated by his success in the matter of the flywheel knob, and his triumph over Bill, pressed his advantage. The hammer strokes of his questions fell and fell.

"What'd you throw the knife away for, Miss Bridge?"

"Mr. Galleon startled me, and I did it on an impulse."

"Where'd you get it?"

"Out of Mr. Galleon's room."

"It was locked up in a drawer, wa'n't it?"

"Yes. I took some keys from my room and found one that fitted."

"What made you do that? Why didn't you get a knife from the galley?"

"The galley was farther away. I didn't have much time."

"Mr. Choate told you to get rid of it, didn't he?"

"No. Why should he?"

"It was his knife, wa'n't it?"

"No. It was mine."

"You pretty fond of this Choate, ain't you? Your fainting this morning have anything to do with him?"

"Of course not. It was excitement, I suppose. Loss of sleep. And then I hadn't eaten any breakfast."

"Did you know I was an officer when you fainted?"

"Yes. Charlie said he thought you were. And then I saw your badge before you spoke."

"Think I'd come after you?"

"No."

"Who then?"

"Varro, of course. You pointed at him."

"Didn't think I was pointing at Choate, did you?"

"Why should you? Ewell hadn't done anything."

"Sure of that, be you? What'd he sneak back in here for then, first chance he got? You say you see him. Take anything, did he, as he went through?"

"He wasn't sneaking. . . . No, he didn't take anything."

"*Give* him anything then, did you?"

"No. Yes, I did."

"*What was that?*"

"A pair of wool socks."

Constable Loose's look was crafty. "And was there anything *in the socks?*"

"There were two holes in them," said Jane with a little weary sigh. "But Annie Budd mended them."

Then the question came that Bill had been dreading all along. It made no difference that it was addressed to Choate. "What'd you leave your place for when the lights was off? What was you up to?"

The question was ringing in Bill's ears. And Choate was answering, the blood running red in his face, and his eyes hunted and suffused: "I wasn't up to anything. You can't prove it. You haven't any evidence . . ."

And Jane was answering too, white-lipped and tight-lipped, and as steady as all faith: "It isn't possible."

"Why not?"

"I should have known," said Jane. She laid the words quite simply down before her. The moment was too large for small concealments. No color touched her face. "Ewell and I were holding hands," she said.

In his pockets Bill's fists were hard against his thighs.

"All the time?" Loose barked at her.

"P-practically."

"You couldn't been. Miss Tredennick says his chair was empty."

"You can't be sure," said Jane. "The lightning was . . . so quick." It was a statement. But the look she turned to Angeline was pleading.

"Maybe I might have made a mistake," Angeline admitted, troubled. She had hardly understood, when she made the charge, that it was a charge of . . . murder. The knowledge frightened her. "Maybe it might have been another chair. But I saw an empty chair somewhere. I'm pretty sure of that."

"If it wasn't Choate's, it was yours," Loose charged Jane.

Bill's joints ached with tension. He felt his mouth go dry. He repeated his former statement, aware of its futility: "Jane's chair could not have been empty without my knowing it."

"And why couldn't it?" Loose demanded instantly. "You holding hands too? 'Cording to your own tell, you was turned toward Miss Tredennick. You said you see her when the lightning come. Now did you, or didn't you?"

"I did," Bill admitted.

"Then you couldn't seen Miss Bridge too. She was gone; or Choate was gone; or maybe both. Which should you say it was you run into over by the door: man or woman?"

"A man," said Bill quickly.

"If I may be permitted a word, sir?" said Toombs discreetly. "The person who ran into me . . ."

Bill turned on him, furious. "You told me I didn't run into you."

"No, sir. Quite right, sir," Toombs agreed. "I heard you go past me, sir, toward the switch; and I heard you hit somebody, and I heard the gun drop on the floor. But when this . . . person you hit sprang back, she ran into me. And if I may say so, sir, she was a . . . lady."

"How d'you know?" Loose bellowed.

Toombs coughed delicately behind his hand. "She was too . . . soft for a man, sir. And then there was a . . . scent."

"What d'you mean cent?"

"A . . . perfume, sir."

"Oh! And should you know it if you smelt it again?"

"I am not an authority on . . . ladies' perfume, sir," said Toombs austerely. He coughed again, very gently. "But my mother had a garden. . . . It smelled like that. Violet, I should say, sir, or lavender."

TEN

They buried Christine Van Wycke at the hour of sunset, with cold rain pelting unforgivingly into the open grave.

"I hate like all possessed to do it before Doc Rogers and the coroner have a chance to view the body," Constable Loose said. "Don't hardly see what else we can do, though. No telling now when we'll be out of here."

Bill helped to wrap the body in a tarpaulin, and secured it awkwardly. Joe and Charlie dug the grave at the foot of the big pine where, only yesterday, the target had been fastened. They took a door from its hinges and carried Christine Van Wycke to her grave. Bill went down with them. She was heavy, and they handled her ineptly, without grace or dignity. It was not so that Christine Van Wycke had moved—only yesterday.

Constable Amasa Loose insisted that there be a service, and that they all attend. Bill knew why, of course. Loose hoped that in that portentous moment, when the murderer stood in the sight of God and man with his victim at his feet, some stretched thread of endurance, of terror or remorse, would snap and grant betrayal. Bill could not have said whether he more hoped or feared that this would happen. They stood in a circle round the grave, with the rain on their bent heads.

Cephus Kember read the service for the Burial of the Dead in a voice of honest awe and honest grief. He read from a Prayer Book that Jane had found in the library: a

471

beautiful book, bound in white vellum, creamy with age
and heavy with gold leaf; it looked small and fragile in
Kember's big red hands, and he followed the lines with
a blunt forefinger to keep his place in the failing light.
Loose stood beside him; under the shield of overhanging
brows, his eyes went probing. . . . The solemn words fell
heavy in the silence.

> Man, that is born of woman, hath but a short
> time to live, and is full of misery. He cometh
> up, and is cut down, like a flower; he fleeth
> as it were a shadow, and never continueth in
> one stay. . . .

Bill himself was profoundly moved. Twenty-four hours
ago in this place they had stood with Christine Van Wycke,
gorgeous and taunting in her beauty, with vital laughter
in her throat and the sheen of life on her skin; a fortune
in jewels hanging at her wrist, and in her hands the very
revolver that was marked to bring her death. Today she
lay at their feet. Her empty wrists were crossed upon her
breast, and under her empty hands the jewel of her own
blood, dried from ruby to carnelian, was her only orna-
ment. Dead, she lay. And one of them had laid her there.

> . . . Deliver us not into the bitter pains of
> death . . . suffer us not, at our last hour, for
> any pains of death, to fall from Thee. . . .

Beulah and Catriona wept openly. But it was nerves,
Bill knew, more than sorrow, which caused their emotion.
Annie Budd, though she shed no tears, was more truly affected. She had been long with Christine Van Wycke, Bill
remembered. Habits, as well as persons, may be precious.
Or was it the memory of other, dearer graves that moved
her? She stood with her lips folded firmly together, breathing rather loudly through her nose. Beside her Toombs was

as completely immobile as a stage butler in a play—a contrast to Joe and Charlie, next beyond him, troubled and
fearful in the imminent presence of death, their Adam's
apples bobbing. Angeline stood with her hands devoutly
folded, her eyes, unquestioning, fixed afar on a tangible
heaven in the sky. Beside her, rather grotesquely, Professor Burge, scientist and skeptic, marked what he would
have called the emotional reactions of superstition. Varro
slouched, aloof and defiant, as if daring even death itself
to accuse him. Bill saw, with a feeling of shock, that in
Ewell Choate's face the same dark flush had risen, more
the color of anger than of grief, that had come with their
first discovery of Christine Van Wycke's murder. He saw
that Jane, standing opposite, had remarked it too. He saw
that she was biting her lip on the inside to keep it from
trembling. It gave her face a set expression. The little
muscle looked tight at the angle of her jaw. She blinked.
Behind the curtain of her lashes, he saw the shine of the
proud tears that she would not let fall. Tears for whom?
For Christine Van Wycke? For Ewell? For . . . herself?

> . . . and we commit his body to the ground;
> earth to earth, ashes to ashes, dust to dust. . . .

It was at the end that a rather dreadful thing happened;
during the prayer. Cephus Kember clasped his hands about
the Book, and lifted his kind worn face to the falling rain.
His voice broke over the solemn plea.

> Lord, have mercy upon us.
> *Christ, have mercy upon us.*
> Lord, have mercy upon us.

Bill opened his eyes. Across the circle, Ewell Choate
and Jane were staring at each other aghast. Wide-eyed,
dry-lipped, over Christine Van Wycke's dead body. Their

mouths open to a silent cry, their bare souls in their faces. As if . . . they were afraid to pray.

"Amen," said Cephus Kember.

Joe and Charlie heaped the mound and covered it with stones. Walking slowly back to the boat behind the others, Bill heard the dog Telemachus howling at the grave, his voice lost and eerie in the rain.

2

It would not have been so bad, Bill thought, if he could have talked to Jane. No matter how hard the truth was, if she could have told him freely . . . how it happened . . . what they had to do. But Jane eluded him. It was not until late that night . . .

It was black dark in the lounge when Bill crept stiffly from the after deck. Only the needle point of flame from a cigarette lighter glowed on the mantel. In the tiny pool of light stood Jane.

Jane's lifted face was white against the darkness of the room, as clean and fine of line as a mask in ivory. The crowding shadows gave it a startling clarity, almost unearthly, like the vividness of white fire. Her hair was loose, a cloud upon her shoulders, bound in a silver fillet. The monk's robe was cobalt at the throat, where the light touched it, dropping into black. She was utterly absorbed. Her look had the remote and selfless purpose of a young nun's. She reached up and set a tall white taper in the middle socket of the seven-branched candlestick. The antique brass gleamed dully under her fingers. The great blue sleeves slipped backward to the shoulder, rippling to the floor, like folded wings. Her lifted arms were bare. Bill remembered the feel of them, warm and slim. So her sleeves had slipped back that night. . . . There was a muffled drum beating in Bill's ears. He strained forward to see more clearly. A board creaked under his feet.

Instantly Jane extinguished the lighter. The silver cord that bound her waist flashed once like a sword. The darkness was a palpable thing in the throbbing stillness.

Bill did not hear Jane's going. Her bare feet were noiseless on the deep-piled rug. There was not even a rustle. Only a feeling of nearness. Bill's senses were brushed by a whisper of robes too soft to hear, a breath of lavender too faint to name. Then a chill fell on him. And he knew that Jane was gone.

Bill did not follow Jane at once. He came quietly across the lounge to the tall mantelpiece; as his match flared up, the seven candles in their lofty sconce rose in majesty. He took down the middle one.

When Bill turned the candle over, he found the bottom smudged and blackened, as if it had once been softened above flame. In the bottom was a hole, smooth and empty. Something small and round and hard had once been pressed there into hiding.

Bill put the candle back. He groped his way silently down the companion. At the foot he turned toward the corridor that led to the staterooms. He must see Jane now. Whatever came, he must.

Just beyond his own door, Bill stopped. He was not conscious of having heard anything. But the unnamed sixth sense that is largely premonition warned him that he was not alone in that dark corridor. He held himself rigid, every sense strung snapping tight, breath caught, eyes and ears straining. Presently, so, he became aware of sound.

There was first the sound of friction. Cloth against cloth, perhaps, as if two bodies were locked tight in silent struggle. The faintest possible thud like a hand against flesh. At once, then, breathing. Hard quick little breaths, through the nostril; a choke like a cry smothered under a palm. A hoarser breathing, growing loud with anger.

Bill moved forward. And was still again. Voices came to him. Words. Varro's voice was rough, all the careful smoothness gone in unguarded brutality.

"Damn you. Give it to me. You've got it. I saw you. . . .
Give it to me, or I'll tell what I know about Choate. . . ."

And Bill was wrung in cold sweat, and his knees buckled under him, at the voice that came back. Jane's voice.

"You wouldn't . . . dare."

"*Dare!* Don't you dare me. Give it to me, or I'll send
you where you sent Mrs. Van Wycke. . . . I can handle
Choate then. . . . They'd never pin it on me. I've got ways
and ways . . ."

Jane gave a soft little cry, a breath of pain bitten short.
And Bill sprang.

Bill's thumbs found the soft spot at the base of Varro's
throat. The breath lay behind it. Bill's thumbs bored in,
and he shook Varro till he went limp between his hands
like an old rag. He flung him to the floor. . . .

Afterwards Bill stood in Jane's stateroom, with Jane's
quiet body in his arms. He could feel the frightened flutter of her heart against the tempest of his own; the warmth
and richness of her youth through the soft robe. It set up
a crawling in his flesh to think of Varro's predatory hands
touching Jane. He groped across to the bedside stand and
found the lamp.

"He hurt you," he said fiercely.

"It's nothing," Jane said. "He bent my arm back. . . ."
There was a bruise on her slim wrist. The marks of fingers were red and angry. The hurt hand was still against
his chest. She gave a little broken sigh, lying inert against
him, for the moment worn with bearing beyond the knowledge of the need to bear still more.

Bill sat down on the edge of the bed, and gathered Jane
close. He offered her no endearment. That was past. He
could only hold her hard and quiet, giving her the comfort and protection that were all he could openly give. He
pressed her head into the curve of his shoulder. He laid his
face down against her hair. A long, dry shuddering racked
her; sobs without tears. She clung to him suddenly.

It seemed to Bill at first that he could not bear it: the impersonality of Jane's clinging. She clung to him because he was strong and steady, and she needed a strength and steadiness now beyond Ewell Choate's power to give. So one clings to an oak in a storm of wind, not because he loves the oak, but because it is not easily uprooted. And Bill, knowing this fully, was strong—because Jane needed his strength.

"Jane," he said very quietly, "you must tell me now. The things you know. Before it is too late. No matter . . . how bad it is, I—will try to help you. I—I'll make it easy for you, Jane. . . ."

He felt her fingers lock in the back of his neck, drawing his head down. The unconsciousness of the gesture twisted him like physical pain. "I wish I could tell you, Bill," she said then in a little shattered voice. "I wish I could. Sometimes it seems as if I must. As if I couldn't stand it any longer all alone. . . ." She took a deep breath, steadying herself. *"I can't,"* she said.

He brought it out at last. That too. "You mustn't think about . . . what has passed between us," he said. "I understand that now. I . . . just want to help you, Jane. . . ." He said abruptly: "You're shielding Ewell Choate."

Instantly she stiffened. "Make no mistake, Bill," she said. "Whatever was done, I did alone. He had no part in it."

She took her hands away, clasping them against her breast, as if so she could hold her secret fast. Bill felt her slipping from him, without his power to save her, as things slip from us in our most evil dreams. The words were torn from deep inside him. "Do you . . . love Choate very much?"

"I love him . . . very much," Jane repeated gravely. "Enough . . . for anything." She struggled suddenly to be free. "Bill, let me go. Don't touch me, Bill. You don't know. There is blood on my hands."

ELEVEN

The next morning the sun rose bright. The sea danced blue. The white clouds and the white gulls flew together. On Bowsprit Island the trees wore their water drops in diamond twinkles. It was a gay day outside. Aboard the *Aphrodite* it was a day of horror.

Bill had not slept that night. He flung himself, fully dressed, on his bed, not knowing how tired he was. The hours marched heavily, weighted with crazy plans. Jane's words burned across his mind. *There is blood on my hands. . . .*

He sprang up instantly when he heard the crash.

Jane's picture fell down at five o'clock. It was a big picture, representing one of Christine Van Wycke's flights of artistic fancy: Power, it was called; it portrayed a hairy man prying up a waterfall with a thunderbolt. Jane had laughed about that picture. It hung over the head of her bed, and she said it was well placed, because the only way it made sense was to see it upside down. It had a heavy frame, after the modernistic manner, with sharp corners. One of the corners made a great gouge in Jane's pillow.

Jane had not slept either. She rose early. She was at the window, watching the new sun paint the sky, when the picture fell. That was why her head was not lying on the pillow where the gouge was.

Bill came running. He found Jane standing in the middle of the floor, her little fists clenched up hard in the front of her childish white pajamas. There was a look of puzzled unbelief in her great eyes. "It—it fell down," she said faintly. "Didn't it?"

Bill leaned against the closed door, feeling sick. He had known pain since he came to that place. He had known fear. But he had never known before stark crawling horror. The horror of things that creep by night. That send messengers of death ahead and leave death behind them in the dark.

He said: "How did he do it?"

"It—just happened, I guess," said Jane valiantly. "The cord—wore out."

Bill examined the broken cord. It had been cut through very neatly, save for a single strand. "Did you lock your door last night?" he said. And knew, even as she answered him, how little a common lock would matter. "Did you hear anything?"

"There were noises," Jane said. "I thought it was the wind." Her eyes stretched wide over her own words. "Once I thought there was a . . . draft. That way: as if the door were open. And after that . . . Bill, *I didn't feel alone.* I felt . . . *watched.* I spoke, but no one answered. I thought it was just nerves. . . ."

"It was Varro," Bill said harshly. He felt the skin of his scalp prickle, and every nerve-end in his body tingled as if with cold. He imagined Jane, lying in the white bed, her hair tossed on the pillow, all the lovely length of limb outlined under the cover; Jane, lying so, in the dark, alone and helpless, feeling *watched.* . . . His voice was broken. "He tried to kill you," he said. He turned quickly toward the door.

Jane called after him. "Where are you going?"

"To tell Loose," said Bill violently. "He was right. The man's a murderer."

But Jane was beside him then, her hands urgent on his arm. "No, Bill. You mustn't do that. Maybe I just dreamed it. Maybe it *was* the wind. Maybe the cord *did* break. . . ."

"He threatened you," Bill said. "I heard him."

"Loose mustn't know that," she begged. She came close, laid her hands flat against his chest in a little unnerving gesture of supplication. "Don't you see? If he knows, he'll . . . find out why. Varro will tell him . . . everything." She said gallantly: "Please, Bill. I'm not afraid." And he saw, incredibly, that she was less afraid of . . . death than she was of Varro's knowledge.

"I won't gamble with your life, Jane," he said stubbornly.

But she pleaded still. "I'll be careful, Bill. Truly. I won't stay alone. I . . . Give me till tomorrow, Bill . . . to think what I shall do." Her head drooped down against him.

That was when Bill yielded. "I won't let you out of my sight," he said grimly.

The smile on her trembling lips twisted the heart in him. "Let me out of sight ten minutes so I can get dressed?"

Bill waited in the corridor outside her door till Jane came. She wore a snug little dress of cherry-red wool. She looked pale—and undaunted. The damp curls beside her ears shone with brushing. The tight cuffs hid the bruise on her wrist. . . . She walked lightly beside Bill, flaunting the red badge of her courage. They went in to a breakfast of canned pears and oatmeal with condensed milk.

"Did you sleep well?" said Varro, grinning crookedly.

"Not very," Jane said. "The wind was noisy, wasn't it?"

"Fierce," said Varro. "I thought it would blow the boat over. What was that smash I heard?"

"I got up early," Jane said. "I dropped a hair brush. Perhaps that was it."

"Toombs," said Bill. "Take these pears back, and ask Annie Budd to open a fresh can for Miss Bridge."

2

Afterwards Bill saw that day in a series of pictures, without continuity. An idea was stirring in Bill's mind. He pursued it relentlessly, aware that time was short. Bill never gave up. Even in the face of Jane's own words, he did not give up now. Jane was . . . Jane. She could not have done this thing. There was no reason back of Bill's conviction. Only faith.

As the day passed, the tension on the *Aphrodite* increased—as if they all sensed a crisis impending. Bill felt it in Choate's hunted look, his nervous, unfocused movements. He felt it in the attentiveness of Burge, sitting on the edge of his chair, pad and pencil ready, Beulah like a shrunken brown shadow beside him; in the unwonted silence of Angeline. There was an anxious pucker between Angeline's smooth brows; she licked a square of bitter cooking chocolate without relish. Catriona went tearfully about her half-done tasks. Toombs' wooden visage wore a complete absence of expression that was in itself expressive. Even Annie Budd, cooking with chicken fat instead of butter, was short-tempered; she turned Varro out of the galley. Even the dog Telemachus was uneasy, snuffling in corners.

Only Constable Amasa Loose was busy and cheerful. His cheerfulness worried Bill.

Varro glided about the boat like an evil shadow. It seemed to Bill now that there was something furtive and unclean in all his movements. Try as he would, he could not detect Varro in any questionable act. But when he was near Jane, Bill's nerves were jumping. Varro did not speak to Jane often. But he watched her. He watched her, unblinking, with a kind of anticipation. Once, watching her, Bill saw him lick his lips with a slow ardor, as a creature will run out its tongue at sight of food. It wrung Bill with nausea.

Jane was perhaps the most natural of them all. Her face had the conscious composure of one whom habit has taught to bear pain without flinching. But she went about quietly. She kept her promise: staying near the others, advising Angeline on the best menu from canned tuna and dried apricots. She did not shrink from Varro's presence. She did not start—much—at sudden noises. If she felt fear, she hid it.

Bill was afraid. Fear for himself he did not know. But fear for Jane stifled him. A tangible danger, that he could have grasped between his hands and broken, he would have sprung to meet gladly. But this shapeless threat that cast its shadow over Jane unnerved him. An unexplained creak, a movement of curtains, and he was on his feet with every muscle tight. He suspected the food Jane ate, the water that she drank. His eyes searched the air above her head, the floor beneath her feet, in endless dread.

It was not an easy time to work out the vague idea that lodged in Bill's mind. But he went about it stubbornly. As he worked, there was never a moment when he did not know where Jane was. Never . . . except that once.

3

Jane was whispering earnestly with Choate at the foot of the companionway. Bill lingered, out of earshot. It was so that he met Toombs in the corridor. Toombs was carrying an assortment of objects that Constable Loose had ordered from the staterooms, and he was muttering to himself that he had been hired as a butler, not as an R. F. D. man. He was silent when he saw Bill, turning to him a face as innocent of expression as a fresh-wiped slate.

"Toombs," said Bill, "were there any chairs in the dining saloon the night Mrs. Van Wycke was killed? Any chairs, I mean, that were not at the table?"

"No, sir," said Toombs woodenly.

"Any in the corridor?"

"No, sir."

"Where would the nearest chairs have been?"

"There were chairs in all the staterooms, sir; wicker in some, and leather; and there was a chaise longue. . . ."

"That isn't what I want," Bill said. "What I'm after is a small, straight-backed chair, with a hard bottom."

"There weren't many chairs like that aboard, sir. Mrs. Van Wycke did not fancy them. There was one at the writing desk in the lounge, and in the library. . . ."

"That would have been the nearest?"

"Yes, sir."

"Thank you, Toombs," said Bill. "That will be all. Where are you going, Jane?"

"Constable Loose wants me in the wheelhouse."

"I'll go up with you," Bill said.

4

"May I take that platinum chain a few minutes?" Bill asked Constable Loose. "The one that had the ruby on it?"

He watched the wheelhouse door close behind Jane's straight back. He did not like to think of her alone in there with Loose, being bullied perhaps . . . but she would be physically safe. He went down quickly to Mrs. Van Wycke's stateroom.

Angeline was just coming out. She was chewing, and her round face grew pink with embarrassment. "Well, there," she said. "I don't know as it's very nice to take Mrs. Van Wycke's candy. I thought I wouldn't. And I didn't either till this morning. But after all it won't do her any good now. It seems a pity to waste it. We're awfully short of sweetening, only just molasses . . ."

Bill paid scant heed to Angeline's frank greediness. "Have you a tape measure?" he asked.

"Why, yes," said Angeline. "Right in my work box. I'll get it for you." She was back almost at once. "I wonder what you're going to do with it?"

"Measure," said Bill noncommittally. "Would you mind letting me begin with you? If you'd just hold out your arm. . . ."

"Thirty-eight bust, thirty-four waist, and forty-four hip," said Angeline instantly. "And I *do* not pull in my corsets."

"I should have guessed a thirty-six," said Bill tactfully. "There, that's right. I just want to measure from your fingers to the floor. . . . Four, one." He made a note of the number on a scrap of paper and put it away in his pocket.

"I wonder what good that's going to do," Angeline murmured.

"I don't know," said Bill. "Maybe not any." He hesitated. He ought to have done this part before Christine was buried. But he hadn't had the idea then. . . . "Do you know how tall Mrs. Van Wycke was?" he asked Angeline.

"Not exactly," Angeline admitted. "She was real tall for a woman. Pretty near as tall as you. . . ."

Bill shook his head. It wasn't good enough. He said thoughtfully: "Those slippers she wore had high heels. . . . Did she have any more just like them?"

"Oh, yes," said Angeline readily. "Several pairs. There were some silver ones. . . ." She dived into Christine's closet and brought them out—silver brocade, with emerald clasps and high green heels.

"That's fine," Bill said. "Now did she have another dress the same length as that white one, and with the same neck line in front?"

"Any of her dinner dresses would be the same length," Angeline told him. "She always wore them long. The orange one would be the best about the neck: I remember noticing they were both as low as they *could* be." She brought him a gorgeous thing of flaming velvet. He caught himself imagining Christine . . .

"Now one more thing," he said. "Something with a high collar—that buttoned right up tight."

"There were the silk shirts she wore with her travelling suit," Angeline said. "I'm not sure where they are. . ." She began to go efficiently through drawers. "Oh, good— here's one. I wonder . . ."

"Thanks a lot," Bill said quickly. "You've helped me no end. And now would you do something else for me? Inquire round and see what you can find out about Mrs. Van Wycke's husbands, and that man she was engaged to last year—the one that fell off the cliff."

"Why, yes," Angeline promised. "I'd be glad to, I'm sure. Now, did you mean?"

"Right now," agreed Bill.

Angeline lingered, watching his preparations curiously. "Well, all right," she said with reluctance. "I can't help wondering though what you want to know for. They couldn't have anything to do with this. *They* didn't kill her."

"I only wish they had," Bill said.

Bill closed the door firmly upon Angeline's wonderment. When he was alone, he set the silver slippers side by side in the middle of the floor. He buttoned the shirt collar, pinned the bottom together, and stuffed it out with handfuls of silk underthings to the semblance of a person. He placed the garment on a hanger, and over it he draped the orange velvet gown. He fetched a cord, and holding the bottom of the skirt just clear of the slippers, as the satin had barely cleared the white ones two nights before, he attached the hanger to the chandelier. From his pocket he took out the platinum chain and hung it about the figure's neck, the broken ends dangling.

Bill stood back and examined his arrangements thoughtfully. If that was right . . . his suspicion about the bullet was confirmed. He checked it all carefully. It was right. Just here the bullet had entered. . . . He placed the end of Angeline's tape measure on the spot, and extended it to the floor.

After that Bill measured everyone aboard as he had measured Angeline: downward from the hand, held at right angles to the body. Individuals complied with his request according to their natures: Annie Budd, tolerant; Catriona, tearful; Toombs as stiff and disapproving as a lead soldier. Choate was unwilling, but afraid to object openly. Beulah submitted without resentment; almost, it seemed, without full consciousness. She moved in a kind of pleasant daze, where Christine Van Wycke never came any more with orders. She smiled at Bill vaguely. Bill noted all the measurements on his crumpled scrap of paper. Varro was the only one who gave him any real trouble.

"You don't come any of your shines on me," Varro assured him, backing away until he reached the wall. When Bill put out his hand, he seemed to melt from under it. Varro was an adept at not being where you thought him. He had had early training, when he collected the family living from the food stalls in the streets.

But Bill had marked precisely the place where Varro's shoulder rested against the wall. He placed the tape measure on the spot. . . .

"You watch your step," Varro warned him. Things that he did not understand, made him uneasy.

Burge, though he held forth his arm without argument, surveyed Bill quizzically from bright, colorless eyes. "I'm not tall enough," he said finally.

Bill, bending to read the figure under his thumb, looked up startled. It is always disconcerting when another reaches into your mind and grasps your thought. "That's the deuce of it," he said. "Nobody is."

"I think you're on the wrong track," said Burge.

"It wouldn't surprise me," agreed Bill.

Jane was coming out of the wheelhouse then. She looked tired and driven. But Bill judged from Loose's expression that she had not told him much. She sank into a long chair beside Choate, her head resting against the back. Angeline hovered about, asking a few questions. Bill stepped into the wheelhouse and perched on the corner of the desk where Loose was sitting. He could watch Jane through the door. . . .

"Constable," he said, "I'd like to ask you something. About the angle of entry of that bullet. Looked to me as if it didn't go right in straight. General direction downward, wasn't it, and a little to one side?"

The shop-worn lobster claw twitched once. "That's right," Loose admitted then. "I d'know these fancy names for what it went through. Take Doc Rogers to tell you that." He added proudly: "I got it out the back. Nigh down to the waistline." He sat silent, ruminating, peering shrewdly at Bill. "Now I'll ask you one," he said finally. "Got a case on the girl there?"

Bill, to his annoyance, felt himself flushing. "Why, yes," he said awkwardly. "No. That is . . ."

"Look here," said Loose. He laid his big red hands out on the desk before him. "Us repersentytives of law and order, we got to stick together. I tell you what I know; and you tell me what you know. Ain't only right. You figure she done it, don't you?"

Bill saw then that he had mistaken Loose's intention. He said quickly: "There is no case against Miss Bridge. I think you're right. Varro did it."

"Shaugh! Do you now?" cried Loose delightedly.

"I wish you'd keep an eye on him," Bill said earnestly. "He'll bear watching."

He climbed wearily down from the desk and went out to measure Jane.

"Four, four," muttered Bill. "It doesn't make sense."

5

Jane was with Angeline in her stateroom, and Bill was patrolling the corridor. He stopped Varro when he saw him coming out of Mrs. Van Wycke's room, with Annie Budd's crocheted quilt hanging over his arm. "Where you going with that?" Bill demanded.

"I'm going to buy it," said Varro hardily. "For a souvenir. I got a swell collection of souvenirs. I got the pruning shears that killed Fenian Geluso, and the torn shirt . . ."

Bill felt a sick distaste. But if he spoke more harshly than the episode warranted, that was because of what had gone before. Varro's very existence threatened Jane. Yet he could not catch him in any overt act. Now, upon the least excuse, he flung out all his accumulated anger. "Put it back," he said roughly.

"What's it to you?"

"It's what I make it. Put it back, I tell you." In another minute Bill would have struck him. Perhaps it would have been better if he had.

But Constable Loose, hearing raised voices, was already gangling down the companion. Angeline was opening her door. Annie Budd was coming from the pantry. There wasn't much cooking on hand now; Annie Budd had come up in search of news. She walked heavily, her wide hips swaying.

"What's all this about my quilt?" she said. "I told you once today already, Mr. Varro, you couldn't buy it, and no more you can't."

Varro's eyes evaded all of them. "I want it for my collection," he urged Annie Budd. "I'll pay you good money. . . ."

"Mercy, I couldn't take money for it now," Annie Budd protested. "But I d'know's I'd hardly care to keep it, either, after what it's been used for. If you have a fancy to it, you can have it and welcome when it's finished."

Varro's clasp tightened on the quilt. "Looks like it's finished already."

"Well, it isn't," said Annie Budd. "There's another scallop goes all the way around. Kind of a shell pattern. Real tasty."

"Looks all right to me the way it is," Varro insisted. "If I'm satisfied, you ought to be."

"Well, I'm not," said Annie Budd sharply. "I wouldn't want anybody should think I'd leave a piece of work like that all at a loose end. When a thing wants doing, I like it done right. That quilt wants another scallop, and it's going to get it. I'd have done it before, only it was over *her;* and afterwards I didn't hardly feel like going in after it." She turned to Constable Loose. "It'll be all right if I take it now, won't it, sir?"

"Shaugh, I guess so," said Loose uncertainly.

Annie Budd marched off victorious, the spread tucked under her fat arm. But Varro, turning away, bent on Bill a look of concentrated venom.

"Didn't you tell me, Angeline," said Bill slowly, "that Varro tried to buy that quilt *before* Mrs. Van Wycke was killed?"

"Well there, I did, didn't I?" said Angeline. "Annie Budd said so. I wonder . . . ."

"I wonder too," Bill mused.

6

"Please, keeper," Jane said with a whimsical little smile, "may I go and take a bath?"

It was only midafternoon, but already the day seemed ages long. Bill felt an unreasoning panic at Jane's simple request. He could not brook the thought of having her alone. Why, it was right in her own room . . . "I wish you wouldn't, Jane," he said soberly.

"All right," Jane agreed. But she sighed. "I only thought a hot bath would be nice and restful."

Bill could not bear the shade of wistfulness in Jane's voice. She looked so tired. . . . "Go ahead then," he said. "Only—you won't lock the door, will you? I'm going to stay right outside in the corridor."

Bill leaned against Jane's door and smoked his cigarette down until it burned his fingers. He was rummaging through his pockets for another when he heard the explosion. It sounded like a shot, slightly muffled. It was followed instantly by a splintering crash and Jane's sharp cry.

Bill was halfway across Jane's room in the first bound. There was a loud roaring from the bathroom. Before he could reach the door, Jane pulled it open. She had a white rubber cap over her curls, and the white bathrobe that she had caught about her was soaked through and clinging. She held the back of her hand across her mouth. There was a trickle of blood down her cheek. She did not speak. She pointed a shaking finger toward the door.

Jane had drawn the shower curtain, and turned on the tap. The instant the pressure touched the nozzle, the whole fixture blew out. Jane was just bending for the soap. The metal wheel with its heavy socket grazed her face, tore through the curtain, and struck the beveled mirror set into the door. The room was a welter of water and shattered glass. But Bill, in a whirling blackness, saw only the thin red trickle down Jane's white cheek.

There was immediately an uproar. Everyone came running. There were all the customary useless questions about how it happened, and the futile suggestions for mopping it up and shutting it off. Catriona wept more copiously than ever, and Annie Budd tried to hush her. The dog Telemachus howled. Cephus Kember sent Joe for a wrench. Varro stood alone, leaning against the wall, arms folded; he was laughing silently to himself, and his laughter drew back his lips until the gums showed.

When Bill saw that look on Varro's face, then he *knew*. As clearly as if he had seen Varro taking out screws. . . . Bill realized now that he could not wait till morning. Morning might be too late. . . .

Joe brought the wrench, and he and Charlie went into the bathroom with Kember, holding up their arms to shield their faces. Bill followed them to the door. He did not go in. His back was to the room for only a moment. But when he turned around again, Jane had disappeared. He pushed everyone aside and rushed frantically into the corridor.

Angeline could not help wondering where Jane had gone to all so sudden. Running round in those wet things. She'd catch her death. . . . When she went out she saw that Mrs. Van Wycke's stateroom door was ajar. The excitement had made her hungry again. The thought of Christine's box of candy teased her. It wouldn't take a minute . . .

Jane was standing by Mrs. Van Wycke's table when Angeline went in. Her head was bent above the candy box, and she was just stretching out a hand. She drew it back hastily.

"*Oh!*" she said.

"Well, there," said Angeline, soothing. "You needn't be embarrassed. It's exactly what I came for myself." She stooped, drawing a deep luxurious breath of the sweet chocolate. "These in the gold wrappers are real good. I had one this morning. See, there are just two left. You take one, and I'll take the other." She held one out to Jane.

"Thanks," said Jane in a small voice. But to Angeline's astonishment, she reached past her extended hand and took the other from the box. "Well!" Angeline exclaimed.

"They're just alike, I'm sure. In fact, I think the one you took is a little bit smaller. Aren't you going to eat it?"

"N-not just now," said Jane. She stood holding the gold ball in her fingers, smoothing the paper round it. It was so that Bill found her, the white wrapper slipping off one shoulder, and the bright drop on her cheek.

In the first instant of realization that Jane was still . . . alive, Bill knew nothing else. Then he saw that at last fear had caught her. She was shaking so terribly in every limb that she could barely stand. She put a hand against Christine's chair to save herself from falling.

"There!" said Angeline. "Now you've gone and caught a chill. I was afraid you would, in those wet things. Better eat your candy. It's a brandied cherry; it'll do you good. Here, I'll undo it for you."

She took the ball of goldfoil and unwrapped it. Constable Loose came in just as the cover dropped. In the palm of Angeline's hand, round and red and shining like a great drop of blood, lay the ruby that Christine Van Wycke had worn about her neck that fatal night.

Bill hardly saw it. He saw only the unfathomed suffering in Jane's eyes. They widened and widened. Her lips twisted in a dreadful little smile. But her voice was quiet.

"You watched me too well, didn't you, Bill?" she said. "Yes, I stole it."

TWELVE

Constable Loose had no mercy on Jane this time.

He had again assembled them all in the dining saloon—as if their presence in that fatal spot would wrench out truth. But he had not seated them as before about the table. Jane sat alone.

Jane's chair was turned toward the open ports, and the slanting light of afternoon lay on her like a blade. Outside the sea tossed purple, wearing its whitecaps rakishly; bright wind blew free, riffling the curtains. Jane sat quiet, facing her tormentor. She had put the red dress back on; its color was mocked by the flash of the great ruby in Loose's palm. Loose had not given her much time. Her hair was caught up at the crown with one big pin, as she had fastened it for her bath. The severity of line sharpened her features to a finer edge. There was no color in her face; only the burning mark on her cheek. Even her lips were white, pinched to the shape of desperate valor. Even from her eyes the blue seemed gone; black pools, ringed with shadow.

"Steady, Jane," Bill whispered. And he saw her fingers lock in her lap till white dents came under their tips.

Choate hovered uncertainly, twisting his hands in wretched impotence. It seemed impossible that he was the dashing boy of two nights back. His face looked hot and puffy; almost, Bill thought, as if he had been crying. Bill felt pity for Choate, because he was so unhappy

493

about Jane. And he felt scorn for him, because, innocent or guilty, he did not stand up to it and take the blame. Bill would have done it. If he could. No one ever so roundly cursed his own blatant innocence. He put his hand on Jane's taut shoulder.

Others, Bill saw, felt sympathy too. They liked Jane. Whatever they believed of her, they were sorry. Charlie and Joe scuffled the rug, studying their boots, keeping their eyes away from Jane with an innate delicacy; Cephus Kember frankly turned his back. Beulah's beady eyes held a vicarious misery, its cause only half-comprehended. Angeline, systematically eating her way through Christine Van Wycke's candy box in search of further jewels, munched without gusto. Annie Budd's broad, placid face, bent over the last row of scallops round the Repeal Pattern quilt, had a shrunken, eggy appearance like an over-baked custard; she punched her crochet-hook in fiercely, as if even so much action were a relief for pent-up feelings. Catriona mopped her eyes with a sodden handkerchief. "She doesn't look like a . . . murderer," she whispered to Toombs. "Poor young lady! She gave me this bracelet too. . . ." Even Toombs' wooden visage trembled on the brink of human expression. Even Professor Dante Gabriel Burge looked . . . unscientific. Only Varro, in the chair beside Annie Budd, watching her deft fingers move over the crocheted quilt, bent on Jane from time to time a look of bright, unmitigated hatred.

Bill stood steadfast by Jane's chair. He could not save her now. But he could . . . stand by. He could whisper "Steady, Jane," and put his hand on her shoulder. . . .

Bill was astonished at Constable Loose's frank brutality. But to Loose, Jane was no longer a person. She was a criminal. It was his duty, as it was his pride, to detect her in her crime. He pounded and pounded at her story. Remorselessly. Endlessly. Giving her no rest. Beating down her defenses with reiterated questions. They came fast and short and hard. Bludgeon blows against that white uplifted face.

"Yes," said Jane wearily. "I took it. I told you that."

"And you stole the other jools too."

"No, not the others."

"And then Mrs. Van Wycke found it out, and you killed her."

"No, I did not kill Mrs. Van Wycke. Mrs. Van Wycke was dead when I took the ruby."

He made her go all over it again, searching out the weak places. Her voice was low, but very clear. It was—almost—steady.

"My name is Jane Bridge Tarrant. I had . . . a brother. His name was Sheel. We did not have much money after the crash. Sheel went to New York. He worked for Drake and Durgin, the jewelers. I don't know how he met Christine Van Wycke. . . ." Her breath caught, and she paused, gathering herself. "Sheel fell in love with Christine. He was young; and Christine was . . . dazzling. Sheel loved Christine . . . very much." Jane's chin lifted in a pitiful catch at pride. "That is the way the Tarrants love. . . .

"Sheel did not mean to steal the ruby," Jane said. "He . . . borrowed it to show Christine, because . . . she told him to. He meant to return it that night. Christine . . . would not give it back. She . . . made a joke of it. She told him to see . . . how good his credit was. The next morning the stone was missed. Sheel was accused. He appealed to Christine again. Christine . . . laughed. Sheel was a high-strung boy. He . . . shot himself.

"Sheel did not take his life," Jane said quickly, "because he was accused of theft. He would have faced that. He did it because he knew then that Christine had never loved him. She had been *using* him to get the ruby." Jane's tormented look lifted to Bill—and turned away. "The Tarrants love only once. . . . Before Sheel died, he wrote us— he wrote me a letter. He had not wanted me to think that my brother died a thief. He told me all about it—but he did not tell me Christine Van Wycke's name.

"When I had the letter," Jane said, "then I went to New York. Sheel was weak, perhaps. Foolish, perhaps. But he was not criminal. We—I felt that I must clear his name. I thought if I could find out who the woman was . . . if I could get back the ruby. . . . I had to work very slowly. I did not dare to go to Drake and Durgin—the people Sheel had known. Sheel was fair and I was dark, but our features were . . . very like. I was afraid someone would recognize me. I called myself Jane Barron. I took a place in . . . an insurance office. After a long time I found out . . . what I needed to know." Unconsciously Bill's fingers tightened on Jane's shoulder, and he felt her muscles quiver.

"Who Mrs. Van Wycke was, you mean?"

"That, yes. And that she collected jewels. And what the Drake and Durgin ruby looked like."

"What did it look like?"

"It looked like that," Jane said. She pointed to the stone in Loose's palm. "It has a tiny mark on the back. Mrs. Van Wycke had it set, and the setting shields the mark. But if you hold it to the light, you can see."

"How'd you find out all this?"

"In the office where I worked."

"What'd they know about it?"

"I told you it was an insurance office. The Verity Insurance Company. The ruby was insured with them. There was information in the files. There was a man working on the case."

"Oh-*hoh!*" The lobster claw travelled once the full width of Loose's mouth. His eyes snapped in Bill's direction. "So you worked in the same place, did you?"

There was no help for it now. "Yes," Bill said.

"So you was on her trail the whole time. You come here after her. And you didn't let on to me. You covered up her doings, so you could take her yourself and get the credit. There's no co'peration for you. No wonder so many criminals escapes."

"I didn't come after Jane," said Bill. "I came after the ruby. I didn't know Jane was here."

"And I s'pose next you'll be telling me you didn't know her name was Tarrant."

"No," said Bill. "I didn't know." He felt the muscle jerk again in Jane's shoulder, but her quiet face gave no sign.

Constable Loose dismissed Bill's statement with a gesture which placed it beneath contempt. "Go ahead," he said to Jane. "Begin back where you left off." After a moment, Jane went on.

"As soon as I . . . found out, I left the insurance office. I was fortunate. When I found Mrs. Van Wycke, she did not connect me with Sheel. I changed the shape of my mouth with lipstick—made it wider. I cut a bang to hide my forehead. My mouth and the way my hair grew back were . . . most like Sheel's. Mrs. Van Wycke was not very observing about people. Perhaps she had forgotten already how Sheel looked. But I was . . . nervous when I went to see her. When she asked my name, I began to give my own. Jane Bridge . . . I said. Then I stopped. So she hired me under the name of Jane Bridge. I was to catalogue her gems."

"Then you admit you went to work for her a-purpose to steal the ruby?"

"Oh, yes," said Jane frankly. "If you call it that. I meant to return the ruby to Drake and Durgin. I can see now that I began the wrong way. I should have told Drake and Durgin first. I did not. I knew they would not believe me. No more than they believed Sheel. I thought if I could take it in such a way that Mrs. Van Wycke would never report its loss, then the fact that she did not would prove what I said was true. . . . I worked hard on the histories of the jewels. Some of them were . . . dreadful. None was as bad as . . . Sheel's. I wrote it all out. Everything I've told you. I meant to put it in the catalogue with the other histories when I . . . went away. I did not think, when she had read it, that Mrs. Van Wycke would enter a complaint. . . ."

"And what were you waiting for?"

"It wasn't easy to take the ruby," Jane said simply. "She kept it with her. I did not know at first that she was going to spend the summer on a boat. That made it bad about . . . getting away."

"I'll say so," agreed Loose. "When this Mr. Galleon come, then you knew he was on your trail, and you see the time was short." He said suddenly: "Charlie, go get that paper she talks about. We'll see how well it fits on what she says."

Jane swallowed. "It isn't there now," she said. Loose's look was triumphant. "No. I figured not. And never was."

"It was there," said Jane steadfastly. "After all this happened, I . . . destroyed it."

"She did," cried Bill. His voice was loud in the still room. "I saw her do it."

Loose said shortly: "I'm not asking you. I'm asking her. And what'd you destroy it for—if you did?"

"Don't you see?" said Jane. "After Mrs. Van Wycke was killed, the paper made it look as if . . . I did it."

"You're darn right," agreed Loose. "That's how it looks. Now d'you say you killed her *before* you took the ruby?"

"I didn't kill her. I said she was dead . . . when I took it. I did it on an impulse."

"Then you claim you didn't p'meditate the killing?"

"I didn't kill her," Jane repeated patiently. "I meant I took the ruby on an impulse. I'd waited for a chance so long, you see. I didn't stop to realize . . ."

He made her go all over it again—how it was she took the ruby. Short, bare little sentences. Hard and hurtful.

"They laid Mrs. Van Wycke on the floor. We all gathered round her. I saw that the chain was broken and the ruby must have fallen. In a minute I saw where it was. It had dropped into her wine glass and the color hid it. I took up the glass and drank the wine. It did not seem a strange thing to do. Everyone was upset. They thought I was faint. I got the ruby into my mouth. I was hysterical,

I guess. I thought of a terrible joke—about ruby lips—and it made me want to laugh. I hid my face . . ."

The dull ache in Bill's mind tightened to the sharp pain of memory. It was in the curve of his shoulder that Jane had hidden her face. Her body had lain against his, and he had felt its shuddering. He had known an instant's happiness because it was to him she turned and not to Choate. And now. . . . Why it wasn't to *him* she had turned at all; not to Bill Galleon. Just to any convenient place where she could hide. And yet knowing that, that too, still it was hurt that Bill felt, and not anger. Whatever Jane had done, she was still . . . Jane.

". . . I got the ruby into my handkerchief," Jane was saying. "It was there when the room was searched. When we went to be searched ourselves, I hid it . . ."

"*Where?*"

"There was a piece of Camembert left on my plate. I put it into that. Afterwards I got it back. . . ."

"*When?*"

"When we all came in here, after the bag was found. I meant to get the ruby when I first came aboard, but I had to destroy the paper about Sheel. Mr. Galleon came while I was doing it. I didn't have a chance after that. When we came in here to open the bag, I fed the dog with scraps from the table. I fed him some of the Camembert and got the ruby back. I hid it in the flowerpot. Angeline saw me. I told her that I was watering the plants. She wondered why it occurred to me to do it, and I did not dare to leave the ruby there. I took it out again . . ."

"And give it to Choate?"

For the first time Jane's fixed expression changed. It broke a little. "*No!*" she cried. "He had nothing to do with it. I hid it myself . . .

"With the search always going on," Jane said, "I had to keep changing it. I hid it in the end of a candle, and among the bright stones at the bottom of the aquarium. But when the lights were on, it *shone* so. . . . I had it in my pocket when I tried to take the boat. But that was very dangerous. At last I thought of Mrs. Van Wycke's candy. People did not go into her room much. I got up early this morning, and wrapped the ruby in goldfoil, and put it in the box. It looked like a chocolate cherry. Then I found that Angeline was . . . eating the candy. I expected that every piece . . . I had to leave it there all day, because I was being . . . watched. When the waterpipe burst, I tried to get it. So you caught me."

"You say you hid the ruby this morning? Where was it last night?"

"I took it out of the candle about twelve. After that, all night I held it in my hand."

Varro made a sudden spasmodic movement. He had stood over Jane, alone, in the dark . . . and the ruby had been in her hand. . . . He leaned forward abruptly and pinched together one of the raised bubbles that crowned the beakers of beer recurring every four blocks in the Repeal Pattern quilt; the threads had stretched, and a tiny hole was showing.

"It's kind of come loose, hasn't it?" said Annie Budd, bending to examine it. "I'll have to take my hook and catch it down."

"It's all right," said Varro quickly.

"Why, look," said Angeline. "There are quite a number that are just the same way." She popped a nougat in her mouth and came trotting over. "They sort of stick up. Isn't that funny? I wonder . . ."

"Here, let it alone, can't you?" said Varro sharply. "That quilt's mine. Do you suppose I want everybody pawing it over?"

"Well, my hands are clean, I'm sure," said Angeline. "I washed them just before I came in. I was only going to fix these places together."

She seized a bubble firmly between thumb and finger. Varro thrust her hand aside. Annie Budd jerked the quilt impatiently—they bothered her with her work, and she was in a hurry. Somehow, among them, it happened. The pulled threads spread; the small hole gaped wider. From it there rolled out . . . an emerald.

Bill was on Varro before he could draw breath; he bore him backward to the floor. He pinned Varro's wrists with his own weight, holding the writhing body between his knees. "So that's where you hid them!" he cried. "So that's why you wanted the quilt!— Get them, Angeline. Quick! They're all in there. Here, Charlie! Here, Joe. . . ."

Constable Amasa Loose sprang forward with a loud, exultant shout. He jerked Varro to his feet. "I told you all the time he stole 'em," he cried triumphantly. "I *told* you he was a gangster."

Angeline was industriously pinching bubbles. Up and down the rows; back and forth. Jewels spurted from under her fingers. Opal, diamond, star sapphire, topaz, pearl . . . ice and fire and snow.

2

Varro sat huddled in a chair, his shackled wrists jammed between his knees. Constable Amasa Loose, left hand on his billy, and right on his antique six-shooter, stood straddle-legged, magnificently, beside him. Constable Loose had brought the handcuffs for Varro, and Varro was wearing them. He had said Varro was a jewel thief, and he was a jewel thief. Constable Loose was a great criminologist. He had put one over on the city dicks. He was happy. . . . He had forgotten, momentarily, about Jane. Bill had not forgotten. He saw that Jane, who had held herself tight under the long grilling, was at the breaking-point. Her breath came short and uneven. She pressed a knuckle against her mouth. There were tooth marks in the flesh. . . . "Steady, Jane. It's all right. I knew you didn't do it. We'll have it out of him. . . ."

For once he and Constable Loose were in accord. They were resolved to wring a confession from Varro. A confession of *Christine Van Wycke's murder.*

Varro was desperate and defiant under questioning. Now that he no longer controlled them, his true self looked out of his scanted, crooked features. The corner of his mouth lifted, showing the teeth; it was something like a snarl that twisted it so, pinning back thin lips. From that crooked lifted corner slid out words they hardly knew. Gutter words; the words of slum and dive and brothel. But Varro's physical cowardice reasserted itself. He felt fear of Loose's bludgeon, deeper fear of Bill's big body. He answered what they asked . . . because he must.

". . . Sure, I took the shiners. Why not? That's what I came for. Nobody ever pinned anything on me before. They wouldn't now, if *she* hadn't double-crossed me, damn her eyes. . . .

". . . Sure, I cut the chain with the wire clippers. The old fool didn't even feel it. *No,* I didn't bump her too. Why would I? She didn't know I did it. . . .

". . . Do with the bag? Yah. You make me laugh. I broke the lock and put the rocks in my pocket. When the dog started to howl I gave him a yank to the door. I stuck the bag in his collar underneath where the hair was long. He carried it out for me. . . .

". . . Sure, I put the jewels into the quilt. What'd you think I wanted it for? To lay over the pianner? Right in front of your eyes I did it. I could've sewed them in at that, and you not notice. Too busy being smart, you were. . . ." Dante Burge nodded. But he looked troubled too; for he had not observed it either. "The last ones I put in when Joe and Charlie carried off the stiff, and I tucked up the corner of the quilt where it was dragging. Makes me laugh. . . .

". . . Sure, I had an out. Thought you were smart about the telegram, didn't you? Not so smart you'd hitch it up to that boat off the Head. Signal, would you? Yah, that's a laugh. I had my signaling all done while you were off chasing the dog. . . .

". . . Sure, I'd been gone before now if I'd had the ruby. I wanted that too. *She* double-crossed me. *She'll be sorry.* . . ."

Varro lifted his manacled hands, turning on Jane such a look of coldly evil hate that Bill's muscles flexed for a spring. But the hurt Varro had for Jane was to be administered in words.

Bill realized, too late, that Jane's state was not simply reaction. It was stark terror. She moved her lips, as if she would have spoken, but no words came. What was Jane afraid of? She had been afraid that Varro would reveal that she had the ruby. Yes. But she had no need to fear that now. There could not be anything more. But there was more.

"I wiped the wire cutters and hung them back," Varro said deliberately. "On the way to my chair, I ran into Ewell Choate."

They were on him in an instant. "How do you know it was Choate?"

"I felt his studs. Square. Not any others like them. I gave him a hard push, and ducked back. When I pushed him, I felt the studs."

"Then it *was* his chair . . ."

"Sure it was empty. I saw it when the lightning flashed, and he dropped down on the floor. I told you that all along."

It was true. He had told them. And Choate had discounted his testimony neatly.

"You didn't say you run into him. Why didn't you tell that too?"

"You're asking me? Why would I? If I had, you'd known I wasn't in my chair either. Well, you know why now. I was putting the clippers back. But what was Choate doing? *He was after the gun.*"

Bill was beside Jane. His place was there. His hands were strong and pitiful when he touched her. Varro's voice rose shrill, cracking on an uncontrolled high note. He brandished his shackles in their faces. "Oh, I stole the jewels all right. You can send me up for that. But I'll never burn for Mrs. Van Wycke. Ewell Choate killed her. He and his Jane. They were in it together."

3

Ewell Choate held out well at first under the storm of questions. His fair hair lay in damp wisps on his forehead, his face was feverish with high red spots on the cheek-bones. His eyes stared straight at nothing under lids pinned back tight with apprehension. His words came too high, too fast, stumbling over one another. But he kept his head—at first.

"I didn't shoot her," he kept repeating. "I didn't have the revolver."

"But you run into Varro?"

"Yes," Choate admitted finally. "I ran into Varro. I didn't know who it was at the time. . . ."

"But you knew afterwards?"

"Yes."

"How'd you know?"

He broke a little then, answering too quickly. "He told Jane. He was blackmailing Jane. Trying to get the ruby. Trying . . ." He said wildly: "God, I wish she'd given it to him. Jane's too brave. . . ."

"Ewell, please!" Jane cried.

"Oh-*hoh!* So you knew she had the ruby?"

"Yes, I did," said Choate defiantly. "And I knew why too. I knew everything she's told you. . . ."

"Oh, you did, did you? Then you knew what Mrs. Van Wycke done to her brother?"

"Yes."

"Ewell," Jane begged. *"Look out . . ."*

But Choate did not see, or would not, where it was leading him.

"You knew she'd be glad to see Mrs. Van Wycke dead. You left your place and got the revolver, and you shot . . . ."

"I didn't shoot her," Choate shouted again. "I left my chair to get the ruby. . . ."

"You told me you knew she had it."

"That was afterwards. Jane didn't have it then. She told you that."

"So *you* wanted the ruby too. What'd you want it for?"

"I wanted it for Jane," Choate said more quietly. "When the lights were off, I was afraid she'd try to get it—and be caught. I thought if I took it, it would save her the risk."

"And why didn't you get it?"

"I almost did," Choate said. "I cut the neck chain with my knife. But Mrs. Van Wycke felt me doing it, and the ruby fell and I lost it. She tried to catch me, and I sprang back and ran into Varro. He gave me a push. I ran toward my chair. The lightning flashed before I reached it, and I dropped down on the floor so that I should not be seen. Mrs. Van Wycke knew that some one had tried to take the ruby; she must have felt for her bag then, and found it gone. That was when she screamed. The shot came at the same moment. I didn't fire it. I barely got into my place before the lights came on. . . ."

"What were you doing? You had time . . . ."

"I was on the floor, I tell you. Sort of stunned. The shot sounded right over my head. And Mrs. Van Wycke's scream . . . ."

"You had plenty time to take the gun back. Wouldn't you?"

"I don't know. I didn't have the gun. I didn't shoot her. . . ."

"Then it was Jane shot her?"

"No!" cried Choate frantically. "No! Stop! You're mixing me all up. You're trying to make me say things that aren't so. . . ."

Pressed, cornered, pounded by Loose's rapid questions, Choate rushed on from one damaging admission to another.

"How did you meet Mrs. Van Wycke?"

"I wrote her a letter. She asked me to come down."

"What did the letter say?"

"It said I understood she collected jewels. It said I had a very fine ruby that I wished to sell."

"Did you have a fine ruby?"

"No. Yes. I had a ruby. It wasn't a very big one—not a collector's item."

"Did you bring it with you?"

"How could I? She wouldn't have been interested. I should have had to go away . . ."

"Then the ruby was just an excuse. You come here under false p'tenses?"

"I . . . suppose so."

"How'd you know Mrs. Van Wycke collected jools?"

". . . Jane told me."

"Then you knew Jane before you come here?"

"Of course."

"She tell you to come down?"

"No. She didn't know I was coming. I came to help her."

"Help her . . . get the ruby?"

"Yes."

"Help her . . . kill Mrs. Van Wycke?"

"No. No, I tell you. No."

". . . When you tried to get away in the bo-at, you meant to come back after Jane . . . and the ruby?"

"I . . . I guess so. Yes."

"Where was she going to meet you?"

"At the cove below the Point."

"When that didn't work, you was going to try again with the other bo-at? You was the one found out the knob was gone off the flywheel, wasn't you?"

"Yes."

"So you told Jane to cut it loose?"

"He didn't," said Jane swiftly. "I did it myself. I thought if you went ashore, everyone would be here. More police. And reporters. And it would all come out . . ."

"All what?"

"All that has come out now. I did it to give us time."

"You'll get time all right. Choate, what'd you tell her to throw the knife away for?"

"He didn't tell me. When he cut the chain on the ruby, it made a nick in the blade. I thought you'd find that out. You'd think he cut the chain on the bag too. The wire clippers hadn't been found then."

". . . When you tried to kill Mr. Galleon with the oar, was it because he knew about Jane?"

"I didn't try to kill him."

"But you knew then who he was? That he was investigating the ruby case?"

"Yes."

"Who told you?"

". . . Jane."

It was not a pretty thing to watch. Bill felt a little sick. The pieces of the puzzle clicked into place. . . . Jane was Sheel Tarrant's sister. She had cause to hate Mrs. Van Wycke. She had turned to Ewell Choate, the man she loved, for help. Neither she nor Choate had been in their places when Mrs. Van Wycke was killed. . . . His eyes sought Jane for reassurance.

Jane was sitting forward, her palms pressed flat against her knees, her eyes never leaving Choate. It was as if she tried by the power of her own will to save him from further blundering. But nothing could save Choate now. It was already too late.

". . . You tried to take the ruby *to save Jane the risk*. You shot Mrs. Van Wycke *to save Jane the risk*. You put the gun back on the table, and run into Mr. Galleon. . . ."

"I didn't shoot her."

"Jane shot her. She give you the gun to put back. . . ."

And then at last Ewell Choate went to pieces. "Leave Jane out of it," he cried in a piping quaver. "You say I did it. All right. I did it. Let it rest. I had reason enough of my own to kill Christine Van Wycke. She brought shame to my name, too. And death. Oh, I meant to kill her right enough. That's why I had the knife. . . ."

Jane uttered a little stricken cry. Beads of moisture gathered in the shadowed hollows of her temples. She thrust her hand into her bosom, groping for a handkerchief. But it was her powder puff that she drew out. She scrubbed it frantically across her forehead, as if thus she could rub out the knowledge of Choate's words.

Bill moved without conscious volition. He was still standing by Jane's chair. He bent down and took the powder puff from her hand. The edge of the puff was torn. The scrap of pink fuzz was lying in Bill's palm. They . . . fitted together exactly.

Constable Loose was sharp with Bill. He wasn't going to have his case ruined by any city dick. "What you got there?"

"A powder puff," said Bill.

"What's that tore place in it? What's that other piece? Where'd you get it? What's the point?"

"I . . . don't know," Bill said.

Jane moved her hands in a little gesture of utter, final defeat. But she lifted her head to one last gallantry. "Don't lie for me, Bill," she said softly. "It was I that you ran into by the door. I . . . had the revolver in my hand."

The world broke in roaring darkness round Bill's head. The last piece of the puzzle crashed into place.

THIRTEEN

Bill Galleon was the world's most stubborn young man. He never gave up. Also it was characteristic of Bill that he was never at his brilliant best until every last, single, living thing was against him: when the Varsity was seven down and half a minute to play; when he sank with a drowning child and caught his foot in a root; when his plane motor stalled two hundred feet above the rocks in the dead end of a canyon; when . . . Jane Tarrant admitted that she had the revolver in her hand.

"Don't be frightened, Jane," he said. "I know you didn't do it."

Crazily, against all reason, it was true. It was not true of the others. Bill, looking about at the circle of stricken faces, saw pity there, and horror; no belief. "I can't help wondering," Angeline said brokenly, "how such a nice girl could do such a thing." It did not occur to her to wonder *if* she had.

Bill did not wonder either. Without cause, Bill knew. Jane had deceived him. She had laid a plot. She had stolen a ruby. She had destroyed evidence. She had thwarted justice. *She had the revolver in her hand.* And yet stubbornly, irrationally, ridiculously, Bill did not believe that Jane had killed Mrs. Van Wycke.

Bill loved Jane, that was why. It did no good for Bill to love Jane, because she was in love with Ewell Choate. Bill loved her just the same. He loved her whether she killed

Mrs. Van Wycke or not. Jane did not kill Mrs. Van Wycke
because Bill loved her. She could not have killed Mrs. Van
Wycke because she was Jane. This was Bill's fallacious reasoning—and he knew it. But knowing did not stop him.
Bill was stubborn.

"Jane couldn't have killed her," Bill said. "There wasn't
any chair."

"Chair!" snorted Constable Loose. He had no patience
with Bill's vagaries. All he regretted was that he had not
brought more handcuffs.

But Bill went on in spite of him. He took from his
pocket the crumpled paper over which he had poured for
weary hours; he went stubbornly over it again. "Christine
Van Wycke was a tall woman," he said. "Almost as tall
as I. The point at which the bullet entered was at least
four feet, eight inches from the floor. Jane's hand, held
straight out, is only four feet, four inches from the floor.
Christine Van Wycke was already standing when she was
shot. In order to have shot her, Jane would have had to
fire upward. But the angle of entrance of the bullet was
definitely down. Professor Burge says also that the fatal
shot came from above the level where he was firing, and
must therefore have been fired by a tall person. Jane is not
a tall person. If Jane fired the shot, it would have come
from lower than Burge was firing. If it had been directed
downward, it would have struck Mrs. Van Wycke in the
abdomen. . . ."

"What's all this tomfoolery?" demanded Loose pettishly.
"She could a-held the gun up above her head, if she'd wanted, couldn't she? She confessed. What more d'you want?"

"She didn't confess," Bill insisted stubbornly. "She never said she killed Mrs. Van Wycke. She said she had the
revolver . . ."

"What's the difference?"

"That's what I'm trying to find out. (Hush, Jane. I'm
doing this.)"

"She could a-held the gun up," Loose insisted.

"All right," Bill admitted. "She could have. No sense to it. But suppose she did. Then not Jane—not the best marksman in the world—could have fired so accurately . . . by a lightning flash. No, if Jane did it, she had to stand on something. A chair would be the logical thing. And there wasn't any chair."

"What you talking about? The room was full of chairs."

"But Jane wasn't standing on them," Bill insisted. "We know where they all were. See, now. Jane's own chair was in its place. I know, because I had my hand on it. Choate's chair was in its place, because Varro saw it. Varro was in his chair after he put the clippers back. I was in my chair until I went to turn on the lights. Beulah and Angeline say they were in their chairs all the time; I saw Angeline myself in the lightning flash. Christine's chair tipped over behind her when she stood up and screamed. . . ."

"Professor Burge's chair was empty the whole time."

"I thought of that," Bill said. "But his chair was on the other side of the table. The shot was fired from this side. Jane could not have taken that chair, because there was not time to put it back. There were no extra chairs in the dining saloon. Toombs is sure of that. There was no other furniture light enough to move. Even the serving table was unwieldy. There would not have been time to bring any-thing from outside . . .

"There just wasn't any chair," repeated Bill.

Bill stood staring stubbornly at the place below the ports where the chair, however absurdly, should have been. And suddenly . . . he gave a shout. There were no words to it; just a big formless cry, incredulous and triumphant. He turned and rushed like a madman out the door. They heard him thumping along the corridor to the narrow deck outside.

In the room that Bill had left, there was a queer taut silence. They exchanged uneasy, pitiful glances. Poor young man, it had gone to his head; you could see he was fond of Jane. . . . Jane came slowly to her feet. Her hands were pressed hard against her breast. Her eyes were lifted, tranced, like one in a bewitchment.

They all jumped when they heard Bill's voice. It seemed to fall on them from the sky. Bill was standing on the rail outside the dining saloon, and his haggard face looked down from an open port between the curtain frills.

"You made one mistake," said Bill hoarsely. "There are powder marks on the outside of the curtains . . . Annie Budd."

Annie Budd looked up at Bill apologetically. "I knew they needed tending to," she said. "But I thought it might look funny if I washed them."

2

Annie Budd snipped off her thread. She pulled it through the last scallop and fastened it. She folded the Repeal Pattern quilt neatly, squaring the corners. "It's done," she said. "I was hurrying to finish before I said anything. The time was coming right along when I'd got to speak up. I never thought you'd lay it on Miss Jane." She folded her scarred fingers in her lap and faced Bill calmly. "I'm kind of glad you found it out natural, sir. I guess it makes it easier."

Bill shook his high red head. "What I can't make out," he said, "is how you put that revolver back on the table and got down to the galley before the lights came on. We certainly heard you coming up. That's what threw me off."

"I didn't go down," said Annie Budd tranquilly. "There are fourteen steps, you know, and I went down one step and came up it fourteen times."

Annie Budd told her strange story very quietly. Her broad, rather flat face, with its mild pale eyes, lost the shrunken yellow look it had worn during Loose's questioning, and regained its gentle placidity. There were no heroics in her manner. She spoke without bravado, as without regret. What she had done was done of her just consideration. She had gone about the killing of Mrs. Van Wycke

as she would have put her hand to the day's baking, in sin-
gleness of purpose and simplicity of heart. Now she felt no
shame. She felt no fear. "I'd known for a long time," she
said, "that I should have to kill her. I could see it needed
doing." So she explained to them how it was. They did not
interrupt her.

"Mrs. Van Wycke," she said mildly, "wasn't . . . quite
right. You said that too," she reminded Burge; and Burge
nodded, murmuring something about an obsession. "That's
the word," Annie Budd said eagerly. "I never could remember. It was the jewels, you see. They went to her head, like.
It was a craving in her, like the craving for strong drink;
and it worked like the drink, too, so that after a while the
effect of a new one would wear off, and she'd have to have
another. She wasn't so bad at first, but she grew worse,
the way a drunkard will, and she'd have to have new ones
oftener. When she'd seen one that was rare and fine, and
bigger than what she'd got, then she'd be possessed almost.
She'd do anything to get it, once the fit was on her. That
was what made her a killer, sir.

"The first one I knew about was Mr. Jerome Grosvenor. He was her first husband. I didn't get onto it right
off. He was a great big hearty man, fond of his victuals,
and pleasant and open-handed; he'd give you a dollar if he
liked an omelet as easy as tip-your-hat. He come in hot
one night, and he et some crabs. They were good crabs,
and I fixed them myself the way he liked them, and I put
a sauce to them that he was partial to, so I'd always keep
it by me in the ice box and nobody et it but him. He was
took sick that night, and he died sudden. 'Cute indigestion, the doctor said. He said he expected it some time.
Mr. Grosvenor left a sight of money. The day after the
funeral, Mrs. Van Wycke got lief to draw on some of it
somehow, and she bought that pair of matched pearls. It
seemed a heartless thing to do, and him barely cold, but I
didn't think no more of it than that.

"Mr. Van Wycke died of a heart attack. He was an old-
ish man and real frail-appearing, but he had a lot of hang-
on to him. Seemed like he took a new lease of life after
he married Mrs. Van Wycke. He kind of doted on her,
she was so handsome and full-blooded, the way a body
does that's ailing. He made his will over, all in her favor,
though he had children by his first wife. The doctor said
afterwards maybe the excitement was too much. He had
one of his heart attacks that night. Mrs. Van Wycke run
for the telephone to get the doctor, and she called to Beulah for her to fix him some drops out of his bottle. Beulah
fixed it for him, the way she'd done a dozen times, and
he drunk it right off. He was dead before the doctor got
there. It looked kind of funny, somehow. But they do say
you can't never tell with heart trouble. There was other
things looked funny too, afterwards. I'll tell you about
them. But we weren't never sure till Mr. Freehold fell off
the cliff.

"Mr. Freehold was a young man, and he enjoyed good
health. I guess Mrs. Van Wycke couldn't think of any natural reason why he'd die for years to come. He didn't have
much money, but he had a beautiful di'mond. It was that
one you see there. It had been in his fam'ly most forever,
and before that they say a Dodge in Venice used to wear
it on his thumb. The minute she see it, the fit was on her.
She didn't have money to hand to buy it, for all she'd in-
herited two fortunes; buying jewels kind of gnaws fortunes
away. Pretty soon they got engaged. I always thought she
magicked him. She had the power, take it with a man. He
give her the di'mond for an engagement ring. But I don't
think she ever meant to marry him. They went rock-climb-
ing one day up in the Franconias. He was very athaletic.
Beulah went with them. Beulah never could remember afterwards how she happened to trip and fall against him. . . ."

Beulah set up a high, thin keening that trembled on the
air like a shaken lash. "I didn't mean to," she moaned. "I
couldn't help it. . . ."

"There, there," said Annie Budd soothingly. "Of course you didn't do it a-purpose. Nobody's blaming you." She turned back to Bill. "After that we knew, sir. Mrs. Van Wycke was using Beulah and me to do her murders.

"We *knew,*" Annie Budd said, "but we couldn't prove it. That was how she had us. At first we thought she'd kill us too when she found out we knew. But it didn't work like that. It was worse, really. She used our knowing to keep us by her, ready to kill again. You see, she hadn't done anything her own self—not as you could put a proof to. It would've been our word against hers, and nobody would believed us. I'd have struck out myself, and chanced it. But I couldn't leave Beulah. Beulah didn't dare to go away. She always took it harder than me. I guess I was more used to standing things. Times I thought it'd drive Beulah crazy.

"It was the never knowing made it bad," Annie Budd said simply. "Always expecting it. We'd get up in the morning, and we'd wonder if we'd kill somebody before night, and who 'twould be, and how we'd come to do it. We'd try to ferret out what it was she meant to make us do, and try to get around it. Sometimes we would. Not always. It was the watchin' and the watchin' wore us out.

"When Mr. Choate come," Annie Budd said, "then we knew right away he was the next one. I don't s'pose you'd notice anything special. But Beulah and I got so we'd notice little signs. There was that way she'd shut her hands up, like taking hold of something. And then she was so affectionate to him. Mrs. Van Wycke was always awful affectionate to anybody just before she killed him. That was how Beulah and I didn't think she meant to kill us yet. She never was nice enough. We didn't know then that Mr. Choate didn't have his ruby with him. We only knew the fit was on her when she thought he had one would match hers. I'd hear her walking in her room all night. . . .

"Seemed like I couldn't stand for Mr. Choate to die," Annie Budd said in her quiet voice. "He was such a nice young man. He put me in mind of my son Lucas, him that was killed in the war. Lucas heired it after me; he couldn't bear for things not to be tended to, once they needed doing. That was how come he to get killed. Mr. Choate had the same way of laughing. And no airs to him. He'd come in my kitchen and talk to me just like I was anybody. I'd look at him sitting there with so much life to him, and I'd wonder if I'd be the one to kill him. That was how it come I couldn't stand it. I hope you'll pardon me, sir, Mr. Choate," she said humbly.

Ewell Choate made no answer. Only a little dry sound in his throat. He did not look up. His eyes were fixed on Jane's bent head. Jane was clinging and clinging to Ewell Choate as if she never meant to let him leave her. . . .

"Go on," said Bill thickly.

"When Professor Burge played his trick with the cleaning fluid, and made Mr. Choate believe he'd drank it, then Beulah and I thought the time had come sure. It hadn't come then. I thought it had come again that night you got here, sir. Mrs. Van Wycke ordered mushroom soup made special for Mr. Choate, and she was into the galley when I stepped out a minute to the bathroom. 'Peared to me that soup had a funny look; I let it curdle a-purpose. The time hadn't come then either. But Beulah and I could feel it coming. . . .

"That was when I fair made up my mind to kill Mrs. Van Wycke. It needed doing if anything ever did. I couldn't look to Beulah to help me any. She hadn't the nerve for killing. I had to do it myself. I figured on it quite a lot, but I couldn't make out a way. It isn't very easy," said Annie Budd, "to figure a good way to kill a body.

"When Toombs called down the dumbwaiter that night, and told Catriona and me what you were up to, then I see the chance had been put right in my hand. It seemed like a leading, almost. It was hard making up my mind to it, though, it come on me so sudden. You see I never killed anybody before, knowing. But it wasn't bad once I got about it. When Catriona come upstairs . . ."

Loose spoke sharply. "I thought she wasn't up here."

"Well there," said Annie Budd, gently deprecating. "I had to lie about that a little bit. I promised Catriona I wouldn't let on. But I guess it won't do any harm now. Catriona come up that night to do the rooms, same as always. When she see it was dark, and nobody would know, she stayed to watch. She slipped in the pantry door and she didn't stir from right beside it; Toombs came, and she stayed with him. She said it seemed like she was parylized, almost, the way things happened, and she couldn't moved if she'd wanted. When Mrs. Van Wycke screamed, and Mr. Galleon called out for the lights, then she slipped back in the pantry. She didn't ever go downstairs, so she didn't know I wasn't there. She waited till the lights come on, and then she run back in. Catriona's a good girl. But she's young. She had a little trouble to her last place. It didn't amount to much. But—well, you can see yourself, sir, how it would've looked, and the jewels gone, and her with no rightful business in the room. . . ."

Catriona began to cry again, with the slow heaviness of one who has already wept her tears away. Toombs' face was wooden; but his hand stroked the soft flesh of her arm. No one else paid her any heed. They were wound in the coils of Annie Budd's sober speech.

"I come quiet up the stairs," Annie Budd was saying. "I laid my crocheting on the top step to be ready. It was dark in the pantry and in the hall too, and I took the revolver off the table where I'd seen it before dinner, and I went out and around that little deck under the dining-saloon ports. They were open, and I stepped up on the rail and looked in. When the lightning come I fired by that. My father used to set us children to shoot woodchucks when I was just a tike; I was always steady-handed. But it didn't seem to me that night as though I could a-missed if I'd never had a shooting-iron in my hand. Seemed like the lightning was sent to guide me, and the bullet was bound to be carried true. I never doubted I'd killed her. I got

down and went back the way I come, and put the revolver
on the table. I felt somebody reaching for it when I laid it
down, and I slipped easy through the pantry door. I near
about run into Catriona there. She would a-caught me
sure, if she hadn't been to the crack of the dining-room
door. I got by her in the dark and picked up my crocheting. Then I went down one step and come up it fourteen
times. . . . I didn't think of fingerprints till afterwards.
But when you asked for the revolver, I went for it quick,
and that give me a chance to touch it."

"That's what I noticed first." Bill spoke gravely into
the silence. "You brought it to me between your thumb
and finger, as if you were afraid to touch it. But your fingerprints were all over it."

Annie Budd nodded solemnly. "That's right," she said.
"Well—a body don't think of everything. I'd do it over if
I had to. It surely needed doing."

3

Bill was rushing out the door when Jane stopped him. Jane
and Ewell Choate were hand in hand, like two children.
Jane said shakily: "Bill. Wait. We want to thank you. Ewell
and I . . ."

"That's all right," said Bill gruffly. He had to go through
with it now that they had caught him. The muscles of his
face felt stiff when he tried to smile. "I hope you'll be happy. I guess you've got it coming to you."

"Thanks," said Choate awkwardly. "I'll be happy, all
right, if Jane is. We owe it to you, you know. I . . . look
here, Galleon, I want to say I think you're a pretty decent
feller . . ."

"Don't mention it," said Bill. "Glad to do it."

"We want to tell you . . ." Jane began.

Bill pushed by them then and got away. He stumbled a
little going down the corridor because his eyes were blind.
He couldn't stand any more of it. He couldn't stand that
way Jane's fingers clung to Choate's. He couldn't stand

that *shining* in her eyes. He shut his stateroom door behind him. He sat down on the edge of the bed. He put his head in his hands.

It was all over. He had saved Jane . . . for Choate. He would return the ruby to Drake and Durgin. Verity would give him his promotion. What of it?

He did not hear the tapping on his door.

Jane was right in the room before Bill saw her. She was alone. She looked worn—and yet invincible, as if she were borne up by some secret strength. There was a white transparency in her face, a kind of radiance, such as is seen in the faces of those long ill, who feel, with an incredulous joy, the stir of life again. Her hair had come down in a cloud upon her shoulders. She put up her hands to Bill, standing to meet her, shame-faced at being caught like that, and the entreaty of her hands stilled him, so that she spoke. Her voice was muted.

"I thought Ewell killed her," she said. "I blamed myself for letting him know her name. Ewell is so young—and hot-headed. And he was so fond of Sheel. . . . When I missed Ewell from his chair, I thought he had—gone to do it. I couldn't find him in the dark. I tried to take the revolver so that Ewell couldn't get it. I reached for it with my powder puff. I felt it move and I knew somebody was putting it back. I thought it was Ewell. . . . I thought her blood would be on my hands forever, because I hadn't stopped him. . . ." Bill hardly heard. What did explanations matter? Her voice came to him across vast windy spaces, cold and empty. But he caught the clear note of her marveling. "You never believed I did it, did you, Bill? You know that was . . . sort of magnificent. Everybody else did. Even Ewell. Why didn't you believe it, Bill?"

He spoke roughly. He could not be gentle with Jane now. It would tear him all to pieces. "Because I love you," he cried fiercely. "Jane—go away. Please. Don't torment me any more. Don't you see I can't stand it—and not touch you?"

Jane did not go away. She came closer, and her hands were tremulous, like her lips. She was generous, as always, in her yielding. "It wasn't true, was it, Bill?" she whispered. "You see . . . I thought you knew. I thought you recognized Sheel's picture on my table. I thought . . . you were just pretending." She said quickly: "It wasn't true about me, either, Bill. That was why I went way—for fear I'd give it up and let you know. I tried to go through with it at first, the way I'd planned. Sheel's name was my name too, you see. I couldn't offer you a name that wasn't clean. But afterwards I was ashamed, because I thought you didn't want the love I gave you. I tried not to love you, Bill. I tried hard. But I couldn't help it. Ever. From the beginning."

He said hoarsely: "You told me you loved Ewell."

"Of course. I do," said Jane. "That's different. I loved Sheel, too."

"But . . . Sheel was your brother."

Her chin lifted in the little prideful gesture that Bill knew. "A Tarrant," said Jane, "may have two brothers. But only one . . . love."

Her head went back when he took her in his arms, and her eyes were wide and shining. Bill looked into their far, clear depths. It was love that lay down there, too deep to fathom. Beauty flamed in her face, a fire, long laid, that is kindled.

4

Professor Dante Gabriel Burge was writing an article for a learned scientific journal, entitled "The Will to Love." Beulah was curled in a big chair at his side, holding an offering of freshly sharpened pencils. The dog Telemachus lay at her feet, looking skeptical. Constable Amasa Loose was standing guard over his gangster. Toombs and Catriona had gone for a nice long walk. Ewell Choate Tarrant with a whetstone was repairing the damage to Pelly's knife. Down in the forecastle Cephus Kember and Joe and

Charlie were playing rummy. In the galley Annie Budd was frying cornmeal mush. Mr. Choate and Mr. Galleon said there wasn't ever a jury would convict her. She wouldn't know about that. But the supper needed fixing.

Angeline came pattering along the corridor; a package of dry cereal under her arm left a trail of kernels behind her. She bounced into Bill's stateroom.

"Come quick!" she called. "There's a boat. I wonder if they've got any sugar. . . . *Oh, I beg your pardon!*"

THE TRAIL OF THE CHITIGAU

(1923)

THE TRAIL OF THE CHITIGAU

Mrs. Lyman's boarding-house was not only respectable, it was of the elect. Strictly speaking, indeed, we should not have called it a boarding-house at all—Mrs. Lyman would not have liked that. It was, rather, a refined and cultivated home where a few guests of impeccable antecedents were allowed, for a weekly consideration, to establish themselves, and to take each unto himself a room and three meals daily. It was Mrs. Lyman's boast that those who came, came well recommended. Decayed gentlewomen, not too much decayed; professional men, not yet able to maintain bachelor quarters; business women, living inexpensively so that they might save their money for travel; from such respectable ranks was Mrs. Lyman's personnel collected. Mrs. Lyman was fond of saying that they were all like a little family together.

Mrs. Lyman herself was an ideal person to keep a boarding-house that yet was not a boarding-house. She wore black or plain dark blue always, and rubber heels and a net over her hair. She spoke, moreover, in a soft Southern drawl that she had inexplicably brought with her from the middle west, and which could never rasp the nerves of even her most sensitive guests. Her round, slightly freckled face and turned-up nose were the outward and visible signs of a good nature that could not be shaken.

Under such circumstances it was only natural that the personnel of Mrs. Lyman's house should seldom change.

It was therefore something in the way of an event when
Mr. Allyn Piper moved in and settled in the back parlor.
Mr. Allyn Piper was an anthropologist. It was only when
Mrs. Lyman had made sure, by reference to the dictio-
nary, that anthropology was a respectable pursuit having
nothing to do with vivisection, and at Miss Webster's special request had ascertained that he was related, though
distantly, to the Allyn-Pipers of Philadelphia, that she
considered him at all. For Mrs. Lyman's normally accom-
modated only five; Mr. Piper would be a sixth. It was a
tribute to the excellence of his references and the charm of
his manner, as well as to the price which he was willing to
pay, that the back parlor was finally placed at his disposal.

On the first night of Mr. Allyn Piper's residence, Mrs.
Lyman's guests arrived rather early for dinner. To be more
exact, Miss Webster and Miss Laura Pennell came early.
They were not curious to see Mr. Piper, but they wanted
to be there when he came in.

Miss Webster and Miss Laura Pennell were cousins and
lived in the two second fronts with the connecting doors.
Miss Webster was a tall thin lady with angles, who gave
always the impression of having concealed somewhere
about her person a very long and very inflexible ramrod.

Miss Laura Pennell, on the other hand, was a little fluttering person with thin gray hair which only Miss Webster's influence kept her from doing in curls. It was characteristic of both of them that people would as soon have
thought of calling her Miss Pennell, as they would have
thought of calling her cousin Miss Abigail Webster. Miss
Laura was always hovering about Miss Webster with little
twitterings of agreement, and little futile twistings of her
fingers. There was about her an atmosphere of perpetual
apology.

Miss Laura's one passion was for Literature as represented by the current magazines and the latest novels. Her
favorite authors were Dunstan Murray, John Barton King,
Richard Dean Frothingham, and Ethelyn Saunders.

Miss Webster and Miss Laura Pennell seated themselves at the large round table where Mrs. Lyman's little family dined, and fixed an expectant gaze on the door. They waited for five minutes. Then Mrs. Lyman begged to be excused, and herself went to fetch in Miss Ames.

To the other ladies at Mrs. Lyman's, Elizabeth Ames typified romance. She was young; she was attractive; Miss Laura, who was wise in the appearance of heroines, said that she was beautiful. Elizabeth Ames was a merry little person; there was a kind of breeziness about her that shocked, but also pleased, them. She had dark rebellious hair, always somehow slipping loose and curling up about her face in a manner which Miss Webster said was inherently untidy, but—well—not unbecoming. There was bright color in her cheeks, and laughter in her eyes, and she jested on all subjects with a freedom that Miss Webster would not for anything have admitted that she liked.

During the day Elizabeth Ames was confidential secretary to the president of the Hammerford Manufacturing Company. Miss Laura used to say sometimes that she didn't see how Mr. Hammerford had ever managed to be president before Elizabeth went there. In the evenings she was the pride of Mrs. Lyman's household.

Probably no unmarried woman has ever reached the age of fifty, and no married woman the age of thirty-five, without wishing to make a match between somebody and somebody else. The secret bond that drew together Mrs. Lyman and the cousins in the two second floor fronts was their desire to marry off Elizabeth Ames. At first, naturally, they thought of Mr. King, but Mr. King had proved himself unworthy.

"Well," said Elizabeth, appearing suddenly through the door, as was the way with Elizabeth, "I hear there's a new bird in the cage to-night."

Miss Laura giggled.

"Sh-h!" said Miss Webster. "He'll hear you."

Elizabeth Ames dropped lightly into her chair. She seemed singularly unwearied by seven hours of presidential confidences.

"Well, that's all right," she said. "I didn't say anything bad about him, did I?"

It was almost at this precise moment that Mr. Allyn Piper appeared, hesitating becomingly on the threshold. Mrs. Lyman flew to meet him, to bring him in and present him, to make him feel at home. And this Mr. Piper presently did.

Mr. Allyn Piper was rather a small man—slight without being actually thin, light without being actually fair. He had a small mustache above sensitive lips, and quick bright eyes under rather negligible brows. Mr. Piper talked easily and well, and Mrs. Lyman's little family listened with undisguised enthusiasm.

They hardly noticed when Mr. King came in and slid into the extra seat between Miss Laura and Mr. Allyn Piper. Mrs. Lyman made the introduction in a perfunctory sort of way. Only Elizabeth Ames, from Mr. Piper's right, really addressed him.

"Oh, Mr. King!" she said. "You ought to have got here quicker. Mr. Piper's been telling us all about himself. He's an anthropologist, and he's been most everywhere on earth. Haven't you, Mr. Piper?"

Mr. Piper smiled, his flashing, brilliant smile.

"Oh, perhaps I shouldn't say *that* exactly," he laughed.

Mr. King gazed back at him over the edge of his soup-spoon out of very round, very innocent blue eyes.

"Say what you like," he invited. "Right now I'm so hungry that I'd believe anything."

Mr. Allyn Piper stopped laughing. It seemed, just for a moment, as if he and Mr. King were not going to like each other very well. Then Mr. Piper went on again with what he had been saying when the interruption occurred.

After dinner, at Mrs. Lyman's suggestion, the party moved into the parlor to listen further to the revelations of Mr. Piper. The parlor was a stiff, respectable room, with dark red hangings which were supposed to look cheerful, but which in reality had somewhat the air of a bunch of red carnations at a funeral. It was furnished with a great many not very comfortable chairs, and at one end a large table for the magazines. Every one at Mrs. Lyman's subscribed for two magazines a year for the general good.

"Now you sit down here on the divan, Miss Ames," said Mrs. Lyman, "and Mr. Piper can sit beside you where we can all see him."

She glanced over her shoulder at Miss Webster and Miss Laura Pennell as she spoke, to see if they had taken note of this clever strategic movement. Miss Laura giggled a little, and fussed self-consciously with the pins in her hair, but Miss Webster would not for anything have betrayed the satisfaction that she felt.

"We'll sit here," she said, and drew up three chairs in a line just opposite—one for herself, one for Laura, one for Mrs. Lyman.

Elizabeth, bouncing irrepressibly up and down among the pillows, dimpled with suppressed glee.

"I guess you can all see from there," she said.

Then she looked at Mr. Allyn Piper, and they both laughed. Mr. Piper, Elizabeth discovered, had a perfectly delightful sense of humor, and already they understood one another very well.

Mr. King hesitated for a moment on the threshold.

"Shall I disturb you if I come in and read?" he asked.

A little wave of annoyance swept the group. Miss Webster straightened. Only Elizabeth Ames seemed not to mind.

"Of course not," she said. "Why don't you come over here and listen to Mr. Piper?"

Mr. King looked gravely at Elizabeth Ames, and at Mr. Piper already making arrangements to occupy the middle seat if there were to be three on the divan.

"Thank you," he said. "Don't move. I guess I can hear anyway."

And he sat down in the rocking chair at the end of the magazine table. It was rather a special rocking chair, and squeaked unless properly used, but Mr. King knew how to manage it.

Mr. King picked up the *Universal Magazine* and turned to Dunstan Murray's new serial, "Moth Wings and Candle Light," which Miss Laura Pennell had recommended. Mr. King also read much of the current fiction. Now and then he looked at the little group round the divan over the top of his magazine; at Elizabeth, vivid in coloring and manner, among the dark cushions; at Mr. Piper with his quick smile and easy speech; at the prim observant row opposite.

Mr. King had been a great disappointment at Mrs. Lyman's. He had come, of course, irreproachably recommended, and yet he had proved somehow not all that he should have been; Miss Laura, who was not above reading an occasional detective story, if the victim were killed in some quite nice way, had suggested tentatively once that perhaps his references were forged. Mr. King had never actually been seen to take up his soup from the wrong side of his plate—the trouble was deeper rooted than that. Miss Webster and Miss Laura had talked it over and decided that he had something in his past to hide—a plumber, perhaps, or a butcher, in his ancestry. He admitted openly that John Barton King was no relative of his, and that he had almost never heard of Mr. and Mrs. Pinkham King, who spent their summers at Newport and got their pictures in the papers.

The most suspicious thing about Mr. King was that he was so unnecessarily reticent. He did not vouchsafe information about himself; he did not invite questions. When questions were asked he answered them pleasantly and frankly, but afterward the questioner was likely to discover that he had really told nothing. Miss Webster still burned at the recollection of one encounter.

It had been at dinner, during the second week.

"Who are your people?" Miss Webster had begun.

"I haven't any," said Mr. King. "My father and mother are both dead."

"Oh!" murmured Miss Webster perfunctorily. "That's too bad. I don't suppose your father was Mr. Egerton King of Philadelphia?"

"No," said Mr. King.

"Oh!" said Miss Webster again. "Then perhaps—"

Mr. King looked up at Miss Webster with the air of one who is about to reveal all.

"I come," he said, "of poor but honest parents. My father's name was B. L. King. He and my mother spent a great deal of time in New York."

"Indeed! And would it be too great an impertinence to ask what he did?" Miss Webster went on.

Miss Webster was not curious, but no man ought to be ashamed to talk about his family.

"Father?" said Mr. King slowly. "Why, I—I suppose you'd call father a business man."

Miss Webster trembled on the verge of discovery. She leaned forward ever so slightly and lowered her voice.

"And what," she asked, "should *you* call him?"

"Oh, I?" said Mr. King. "Why, I suppose I'd call him a business man too. You see, in a way, he was a business man."

Mr. King hesitated for an instant. Then he made about himself the first voluntary statement in two weeks.

"I was always more like mother, though," he said. "She was very quiet."

He turned on Miss Webster a look of frank straight-forwardness impossible to associate with guile, but Miss Webster straightened as if she had suddenly found and swallowed the sword concealed in the evening spinach.

It was at this point that Elizabeth Ames had done the one unladylike thing of her life at Mrs. Lyman's. She had choked and been obliged to leave the table.

Mr. King had a rather round serious face, intensified by the roundness and seriousness of his blue eyes. He was very fair. Nevertheless his face was pleasantly browned, as if from a summer out of doors, and its very brown emphasized the blondness of the shock of hair that rose from his forehead. He was not a handsome man, but he was relieved of the necessity for being handsome by the niceness of his smile.

Elizabeth Ames, sitting in the corner of the divan beside Mr. Allyn Piper, was not at all unconscious of the difference between the two men. And she knew perfectly that Mr. King was watching her over the top of "Moth Wings and Candle Light."

Elizabeth Ames did not like Mr. King. She was not interested in him. But no one can help noticing a man who says so little and looks so much.

There was no possible doubt that Mr. Piper had a great many interesting things to talk about, and that he knew how to talk about them to advantage. He was an anthropologist specializing in the African field, and had made two stays of six months each with the Yao of Nyassaland. He was making a comparative study of Chitigau all over the world and had been to Spain, Persia, Norway, and Iceland to investigate possible clues. During his college course he had been on a summer field trip to Arizona and the Great Southwest, and since then he had spent almost an entire year there among the cliff dwellings. He had taken a two months' cruise among the South Sea Islands. During the war he had been in France for eleven months as an ambulance driver, and had seen all the worst of the fighting. It seemed almost incredible that so young a man could have done so much.

Mr. Piper spoke brilliantly. Elizabeth's color came and went in her excitement as he described the gaudy coloring of the buttes and mesas of Arizona; the Shire highlands of Nyassaland, and the time when he had witnessed the Salapa dance among the Yao; the Allied advance round Vierzy in 1918; the five-day festival of Tebureimoa. He said that the beautiful native girls with lotus blossoms in their hair who danced in the moonlight on the shores of Tahiti were no dream of fiction because he had seen them with his own eyes. He said that he had taken natural mummies out of the caves of New Mexico that still had sandals on their feet after a thousand years. He said that the study of the Chitigau was fascinating. He meant to give his life to a thorough investigation of the subject.

Miss Webster said that she liked to see young people who were interested in doing some kind of serious creative work.

Mr. Allyn Piper made a deprecating movement of slim, sensitive fingers.

"Oh, of course," he said, "I may not prove a thing, really. But in my own mind there is no doubt that there is a basic similarity in line form between the Chitigau of the American Indians of the Southwest and of the Yao of Nyassaland which points to the possibility of a common origin. If—*if,* I say, such a thing could be satisfactorily proved, it would revolutionize science."

"Squeak," said Mr. King's rocking chair suddenly.

Mr. Allyn Piper, lest he might seem boastful, changed the subject.

"I wish I could show you the Black Mesa above Mayence at daybreak," he said.

He spoke in general terms, but his glance included only Elizabeth.

Elizabeth clasped her hands together in unaffected delight.

"Oh-h!" she said. "I'd love to see it!"

"There'd be more colors than any one ever imagined," Mr. Piper went on, "and Pinnacle Rock in the distance— It was just the other side of Pinnacle that I took out the arthritic skeleton that's here in the Claymore Museum now. Sometime I'd like to take you down and show it to you."

"Squeak," said Mr. King's chair.

Half an hour later a nudge was passed from elbow to elbow down the line facing the divan, and Miss Webster, Mrs. Lyman, and Miss Laura Pennell rose simultaneously. It was plain that Mr. Allyn Piper was to be given a free hand with Elizabeth.

"We'll have to go now," said Miss Webster.

"M-hm," Mrs. Lyman agreed. "Ye-us."

She moved slowly toward the door, and as she moved she fixed on Mr. King over her shoulder a glance that said more plainly than words that if he had any tact at all he would join her.

Mr. King apparently had no tact. He looked at Mrs. Lyman blandly over the top of his magazine, and his chair squeaked.

It was, after all, Elizabeth Ames who followed the three ladies from the room. She said that she had some letters to write, and just simply must go. Mr. Allyn Piper went, too. And presently Mr. King was left alone with "Moth Wings and Candle Light."

The next night Elizabeth Ames was out for dinner. At nine o'clock, however, it happened that Elizabeth coming down to mail a letter, and Mr. King coming down to see if the new *National* had been delivered, met in the front parlor.

"Hello," said Mr. King.

He smiled his wide friendly smile, and lingered as if for conversation.

"Hello," said Elizabeth.

Mr. King held out his hand for her letter.

"Let me," he said, and slipped it into his pocket as if a little later would do quite as well for mailing it.

At precisely that instant, the door leading from Mr. Allyn Piper's room into the hall was opened and Mr. Piper came out. The folding doors which connected the front and back parlors—now locked and chastely concealed by red curtains—had a wide crack between them through which sounds were easily heard.

Mr. Allyn Piper did not exactly come running, but he came with utter promptness. He was plainly glad to see Elizabeth again, and indifferent to the continued presence of Mr. King.

"We missed you at dinner," he said.

"Thank you," said Elizabeth demurely.

She was standing, leaning back against the table, with her hands outstretched against its edge, and neither of the men was unaware of her loveliness. She was wearing a dinner dress of clinging gray, and its complete simplicity suited the fly-away splendor of her hair.

Mr. Allyn Piper looked suggestively in the direction of the divan where they had sat the night before.

"Shall we?" he asked.

"All right," said Elizabeth.

She crossed the room suddenly, as she did everything, in a little swirl of graceful floating gray.

Mr. King's progress was in no way remarkable save for its efficiency. Mr. Piper, arriving just behind Elizabeth Ames, found Mr. King already there. Elizabeth sat between them.

Mr. Piper looked at Mr. King without cordiality.

"Have you plenty of room?" he asked Elizabeth, not very subtly.

Elizabeth looked up at him, and unbridled mischief flashed in her dark eyes.

"Oh, Mr. Piper!" she said. "Am I crowding you? I'm *so* sorry."

And she moved over a little in the direction of Mr. King. Mr. Piper's sensitive face flushed hotly.

"Oh, Miss Ames!" he protested. "You know—"

Elizabeth laughed.

"Yes," she said. "I know a lot more than you'd think, just to look at me!"

The same thing, perhaps, might have been said of Mr. King.

Mr. King, however, made no direct effort to join in the conversation. He seemed content to accept his role as an outsider, and a comfortable seat on Miss Ames's very immediate left.

"We all liked your stories last night very much," said Elizabeth politely, doing penance.

Mr. Piper's face cleared.

"Did you enjoy it?" he said. "I'm glad you like to hear me talk as well as I like to do it. It's a funny thing, though, I remembered afterward that I never told you a word about the time when we were caught in a freshet when we were crossing Roaring Creek. Of course you've heard of brooks that grew into rivers in the night, but this one did it all in a minute, and we were in the middle of the ford. It carried all our wagons downstream, and I was half drowned."

"Oh-h-h!" breathed Elizabeth. "How exciting!"

"It's a terrible sensation, though, to feel the water closing over your head." He turned to the silent Mr. King. "You can imagine what it would be like."

"Yes," said Mr. King.

"I don't suppose you've gone in much for the dangers of the camp and trail?"

"No," said Mr. King.

"Ever traveled much in Arizona?"

"No," said Mr. King.

"Don't you ever regret having lived in one place so much?"

"No," said Mr. King.

Mr. Piper smiled with a rather studied kindliness.

"Rather an office sort of man, I take it," he said.

"Yes, sir," said Mr. King.

For just an instant Mr. Piper looked at him with the merest shade of suspicion, but Mr. King's innocence was too obvious to cause alarm.

"Well—it's certainly nice to be satisfied," Mr. Piper said.

Then he was swept away again on the flood of his own reminiscences. He repeated his statement of the night before that the Chitigau was fascinating.

"You know I've had some of the most amazing experiences," he said, "following the Chitigau round the world. If I could only write, now, I'd do an account of it all, and call it 'The Trail of the Chitigau' or something like that. That's a bang-up good title, now, isn't it—'The Trail of the Chitigau'?"

"Yes," said Mr. King.

'"Wonderful," said Elizabeth.

Then she laid her fingers lightly on Mr. Piper's coat sleeve and checked him as he was going on.

"I hate to seem stupid," she said, "but I'm afraid I don't really understand what a Chitigau is."

Mr. Allyn Piper was naturally surprised.

"You don't?" he said. "Why, it's a string figure. The word itself is from the Yao language and means spider's web. I use it—and am recommending that other scientists follow my example—in a universal sense as applying to similar figures all over the world. If I had a piece of string, I could show you—"

Mr. King produced one from a rather boyishly well-filled pocket, and Mr. Piper took it eagerly. His clever fingers twisted the strands with almost incredible swiftness; then he held out, stretched between his hands, a complicated geometrical figure.

"Oh," said Mr. King. "Cat's cradle."

"Well—yes," said Mr. Piper. "Of course that is the nearest modern equivalent. It's an ancient form, naturally, of great importance."

Elizabeth held out her hand for the string.

"Let me try," she said.

Mr. Allyn Piper placed the string in the proper position on her fingers, and taking hold of her wrists, guided her through the complicated movements. Elizabeth had firm, capable-looking hands, and yet hands that were small and soft and utterly feminine. The silver wrist watch on its narrow gray ribbon emphasized the precision and grace of every motion.

When she had finished, Mr. King held out his hands too.

"Now teach me, Miss Ames," he said.

And Elizabeth obligingly took him by his wrists and taught him all she knew.

Mr. King, however, was not quick at cat's cradle, and Mr. Piper presently grew restless.

"Of course," he said, "that's only one of thousands of designs."

He recaptured the string, and dazzled them by the multiplicity of his accomplishments.

"The Chitigau differs more or less," he told them, "both geographically and chronologically."

He broke off.

"I'll tell you what," he said. "You ask me questions, and then I'll be sure that I'm telling you the things that you want to know."

"All right," said Elizabeth.

Then she struck her hands suddenly together with the quick characteristic gesture that accompanied a new idea.

"Oh, I know!" she cried. "Let's take turns asking questions. First you and Mr. King can ask me questions, and then I'll ask you and Mr. King questions, and then—"

"Well," agreed Mr. Piper doubtfully. "I'll begin. What are your chief interests—scientific—or—"

"Personal," said Elizabeth promptly.

"Are you fond of science?" asked Mr. Piper.

"Some kinds," said Elizabeth. "Now you ask something, Mr. King. You missed your turn; you'll have to ask two."

Mr. King raised grave blue eyes.

"Are you fond of pets?" he asked.

"Some kinds," Elizabeth repeated.

"What kinds of pets have you had?"

Elizabeth checked them on her fingers.

"Horses," she said, "cows, sheep, cats, dogs—"

Mr. Piper had brightened at the mention of horses.

"Saddle or driving horses?" he asked.

"Saddle."

"Describe your favorite horse."

Elizabeth obeyed.

"He kicked," she said.

"Describe your favorite cow," said Mr. King promptly.

"She hooked," said Elizabeth.

Mr. King looked at Elizabeth Ames and suddenly he grinned, widely, irrepressibly, delightfully. Elizabeth laughed aloud.

Then she followed suit.

"What is your favorite bird?" she asked Mr. Piper.

Mr. Piper's face was rather red.

"Goose," he jerked out with a meaning more obvious than delicate.

"Mine's turkey on Thanksgiving," said Elizabeth. "What's yours, Mr. King?"

"Sandpipers," murmured Mr. King. "Along about October I like to shoot them."

Mr. Allyn Piper straightened in his seat.

"I guess it's my turn to ask Mr. King some questions," he said. "Do you hunt much, Mr. King?"

"No," said Mr. King.

"Do you know how to shoot?"

"A little," said Mr. King.

"What gun do you use?"

"Machine guns," said Mr. King.

Elizabeth thrilled with excitement.

"Oh, Mr. King!" she cried. "You were in the war too!"

Mr. King joined Mr. Piper in looking rather red and uncomfortable.

"Well—yes," he admitted.

"How long were you in?" Elizabeth demanded. "What branch?"

Mr. King looked even more uncomfortable.

"Oh—I don't know—about four years, I guess. Aviation. French Escadrille before America came in," he said.

Elizabeth leaned forward, her eyes shining with excitement.

"How perfectly splendid!" she said. "Why didn't you ever tell me about it?"

Mr. King shuffled his feet on Mrs. Lyman's dark red art square.

"Oh, I don't know," he said. "There wasn't anything very interesting to tell about."

"Goodness!" said Elizabeth. "I should think there would be. Shouldn't you, Mr. Piper?"

"Uh," said Mr. Piper.

"Mr. Piper," said Elizabeth, "was only in the war eleven months, and he told me lots of interesting things about it last night. Didn't you, Mr. Piper?"

"Uh," said Mr. Piper.

There was a brief silence.

Then Mr. Piper suddenly brightened.

"You know," he said, "there was one mighty interesting thing that happened toward the end. I was at Laon when they brought in a bunch of German prisoners. One of them had shell shock and wouldn't do a thing but sit and twist his fingers. When I saw him I gave him a piece of string just to see what he would do with it. And if you'll believe it, he twisted it up into a figure—of course it was different in lots of ways—but in its basic outlines it was strongly suggestive of a Middle Period Adamanese Chitigau. . . ."

It was quite by accident that Elizabeth Ames and Mr. King met the next night in the front parlor. Elizabeth had just come in to see if she had left her gloves there. Mr. King had just come in. He smiled at Elizabeth, and the smile revealed pleasant humorous lines about his mouth and an unsuspected twinkle in the grave blue eyes.

"Hello," he greeted her, just as he had the night before.

"Hello," said Elizabeth back again. "I've lost my gloves."

"Are you going out?" asked Mr. King.

"No," said Elizabeth.

For some reason this brief conversation seemed to them amusing, and they both laughed. And then abruptly they both stopped—listened. Mr. Allyn Piper's door had opened, and Mr. Allyn Piper's step sounded in the hall.

Mr. King was close at Elizabeth's side in two long strides.

"Let's go out on the piazza," he whispered. "Will you? I couldn't stand playing cat's cradle again tonight."

His smile was irresistible; and Elizabeth, greatly to her own surprise, heard herself saying that she would.

On the threshold they met Mr. Piper, not exactly running, but coming promptly. There was a look of expectation on his face, a suggestion, too, of certainty in his welcome. He stopped abruptly.

"Good evening," he said. Then, "Oh—you're going."

"Good evening," said Elizabeth.

"Yes," said Mr. King. "We're going."

And somehow the door had opened and closed between them. Outside soft June air stirred the decorous vines round Mrs. Lyman's porch. The porch chairs were uncomfortable, but even discomfort could not spoil the last of the June sunset that showed through an open space between the houses opposite.

For a while they were rather silent; they spoke in a desultory way of the day's newspaper gossip.

"What do you do?" Mr. King asked suddenly. "Are you a secretary?"

"Yes," said Elizabeth. "Mr. Hammerford's."

"You know, that isn't good enough for you," said Mr. King. "A person like you ought to be doing something different."

Elizabeth Ames was half annoyed, half amused. She thought this a strange, abrupt, young man, who did not like to talk about himself, and yet tried to interfere in affairs distinctly not his own. She opened her lips to say something which should discourage him at the beginning, but Mr. King did not wait for her to say it. It was a way that he had.

"What I mean," he said, "is that you ought to do something more original—creative. You could, you know. I don't believe you're a wonderful secretary—just a good one. Lots of people can be good secretaries. You ought to do something that nobody can do but you."

"Yes," murmured Elizabeth. "Easy. Discover the fourth dimension."

She did not want to be pleased, but she could not help being interested. No one could, because Mr. King so obviously meant exactly what he said. There was utter seriousness in the straightforward look of his blue eyes, in the little emphatic gesture with which he now and then ended his sentences.

"Don't you know a lot about it?" she teased.

Mr. King smiled again.

"You're making fun of me," he said, "and I don't blame you. But I know more about it than you think. I notice people more than you think. It's—it's a habit of mine."

Elizabeth laughed a little shakily.

"And out of your wisdom and experience," she said, "what should you suggest?"

Mr. King was embarrassed, but he was not a man to give up easily.

"Oh, I don't know," he said. "That's for you to say. You could be—a lady detective, or a diplomat's wife, or the heroine of the Great American Novel, or—or anything you wanted to be."

"That shows how little you know about it," said Elizabeth.

"It shows how little *you* know about it," Mr. King contradicted her—and smiled.

Afterward Elizabeth was shocked at the intimacy of their conversation; she did not see how she had ever let it happen. It was, obviously, Mr. King's fault.

During the summer Elizabeth Ames saw Mr. King perhaps one evening a week. She saw Mr. Piper, on an average, four evenings a week. On the other two evenings she was out. Mr. Piper took her about a great deal, but Mr. King never asked her to go anywhere with him. He was working very hard at the office, he said. Mr. Piper said that he was working hard too, at the Claymore Museum, where he was supervising the arrangement of the Chitigau Room. The most fascinating things were always happening to him there—he used to tell Elizabeth about them every evening. Mr. King did not talk about himself much. He seemed, oddly enough, to prefer to talk about Elizabeth Ames.

Miss Webster and Miss Laura Pennell were excellently well pleased with the way things were going. They used to whisper their surmises to Mrs. Lyman whenever they met, and Mrs. Lyman quite agreed with them.

"M-hm," she would say. "Ye-us."

And then in September three things happened all at once.

The first thing happened on Sunday, the sixth, at a quarter past ten; Miss Webster could have told you the exact minute. Sunday morning breakfast was over, and it still lacked five minutes of time to start for church. It is regrettable to have to record, however, that Miss Webster and Miss Laura Pennell missed church that morning for the first time in seventeen years.

At a quarter past ten, Miss Laura Pennell in the black silk with the white collar, and Miss Webster in the black silk, were sitting by the front window in Miss Webster's room watching the passing of the ungodly who were not

going to church when a car swept up in front of Mrs. Lyman's door.

It was no ordinary car; so much they could see by even
the most genteel Sabbath day craning of their necks round
the casing. There was an air about it at once dignified
and ostentatious. In color it was dark blue—later, indeed, there was argument as to whether it was not, after
all, black. A similar discussion attached to the matter of
whether the mountings were silver or only nickel. Miss
Laura Pennell, usually so meek in matters of disagreement
with Miss Webster, squared her shoulders and said that if
those fittings were not sterling silver she had never seen
any on any car.

As soon as the car stopped, a negro chauffeur in dark
blue (or black) livery with silver buttons climbed down
from the outside seat and opened the door. He spoke briefly with the person, or personage, inside and came up to
Mrs. Lyman's door. An instant later, Mrs. Lyman, for the
first time in history, was heard running up the stairs.

Miss Webster rose quietly and opened the door of her
room about three inches. She did this to see if Mrs. Lyman
was coming up to look for her. She was not; she was coming up to look for Mr. King. Nevertheless, Miss Webster
left the door slightly open. She was not curious, but she
hated a mystery.

"Mr. King," called Mrs. Lyman. "Are you here? Mr.
King!"

Mr. King came out and joined her, and they went down
together.

The chauffeur meantime had returned to the car at the
curb, and held the door while the man within stepped
down. He was, as the ladies in the second floor front had
suspected, not a person, but a personage. He was tall and
very straight, with gray hair round a keen, but not unpleasant, face. He had the air of one to whom success has
become habitual.

A few steps carried him out of sight. There was the distant sound of greeting at the front door, then steps on the stairs, and Mr. King and his guest passed with unnecessary briskness through the upper hall, and disappeared.

So swiftly had these events taken place that it was still only twenty minutes past ten when the two men entered Mr. King's room. From within their voices could be heard plainly, but no words could be distinguished. At five minutes to eleven they came out again and went downstairs. The chauffeur held open the door; they both stepped in; the car drove away.

Miss Webster sank back in her chair and fanned herself with the black satin fan which she always carried to church.

"Heavens to Betsy!" she said.

This, in Miss Webster's vocabulary was equivalent to swearing, and indicated the utmost perturbation of mind.

"Did you see that, Laura? *Mr. King went with him.*"

Miss Laura had seen that very thing and admitted it frankly. Following Miss Webster's example, she too leaned back and fanned herself with a copy of the *Universal Magazine* which lay beside her on the table. Miss Laura would not for anything have looked inside the covers of the *Universal Magazine* on the Lord's Day, but it did not seem wrong to use it for a fan.

"You know," said Miss Webster, "that *was* somebody."

"Oh, *yes,*" Miss Laura agreed.

"Somebody special, I mean," Miss Webster went on. "He made me think of some picture I've seen, but I can't think whose."

There was a brief silence. Then, presently, Miss Webster rose.

"I guess I'll go downstairs a minute," she said, "and speak to Mrs. Lyman. She said she found a handkerchief yesterday, and wanted me to see if it was mine."

Miss Laura Pennell started to speak several times and didn't. But when Miss Webster had started down the stairs, she fluttered across the room and stuck her head out into the hall.

"Oh, Abigail!" she called. "Abigail! If you should happen to think of it while you're there, you might ask Mrs. Lyman what that man's name was."

"Well—all right," said Miss Webster. "I will."

Miss Laura Pennell fluttered uncertainly back to her chair, then turned again with an apologetic resolution, and hurried out.

"Oh, Abigail!" she called. "Wait a minute. I guess I'll come too."

The man's name was Mr. Hetherton.

Miss Webster and Miss Laura Pennell hurried back upstairs as fast as their excitement would let them, and Miss Webster took down the well-worn copy of *Famous People* and whirled through the H's. She found Hetherton— Wakefield Irving Hetherton. There was a brief account of his life and a picture. Wakefield Irving Hetherton, editor-in-chief of the *Universal Magazine,* was a tall straight man with graying hair and a look about him of continued prosperity.

Miss Webster laid a lean finger on the picture.

"It is he," she said.

Miss Webster and Miss Laura Pennell had a very busy day. They had to collect all available data in regard to Mr. Wakefield Irving Hetherton, and report additional discoveries as they were made to an interested Mrs. Lyman. At two o'clock when Mr. Piper came in, they had to repeat the details of the day up to that point. At four o'clock, when Elizabeth Ames came in, they had to repeat them again. They had to look often at the covers of recent issues of the *Universal Magazine;* they decided that it would not be wrong even to open them to page one, where the name of Wakefield Irving Hetherton appeared. And in particular they had to fly to the window at the sound of every passing automobile, to see if Mr. King were returning.

Along toward night Miss Webster remarked openly that after all she had always thought that there was something rather likable about Mr. King in spite of his queer ways. Miss Laura upheld her cousin's statement, and added that she had often thought he might tell a good deal if he wanted to, and that she imagined that he knew awfully nice people.

"M-hm," said Mrs. Lyman. "Ye-us. I think that's so."

Mr. Piper said nothing.

Elizabeth Ames laughed.

Mr. King did not return until eight o'clock, and would have gone from the dark blue, or black, car directly to his room, if voices from the parlor had not called him back. They spoke to him after the manner of a chorus.

"Good evening," they said.

Then Miss Webster's voice detached itself from the others.

"Did you have a pleasant day with Mr. Hetherton of the *Universal Magazine?*" she asked.

She was herself not unaware that her question was a masterpiece.

"Yes," said Mr. King, pleasantly but not loquaciously.

"Business or pleasure?" Miss Webster asked again.

"Oh—both," said Mr. King. "We did our business while we golfed."

Then he went on up the stairs.

Miss Webster straightened herself a little in her chair, and said that she didn't see why he needed to be so close-mouthed about it. She added, however, that after all she supposed it was better to be too modest than to be always talking about yourself.

Elizabeth Ames laughed again.

The second event took place, so far as any definite time can be assigned to it, on Thursday, the tenth, at three-thirty, when the postman dropped the current issue of the *Universal Magazine* through the slide in Mrs. Lyman's front door. Mrs. Lyman picked it up and laid it on

the table in the living-room; to her undying regret she did
not look at it.

Miss Laura Pennell naturally made the discovery—Miss
Laura who read the magazines. She had heard the thump of
something coming through the letter slide, had known it
was the day for the *Universal,* and hurried down to get the
next chapter of Richard Dean Frothingham's serial, "The
Other Side of Main Street." Five minutes afterward she
gave a little shriek; Miss Laura Pennell had never before
made so loud and so sudden a noise. Miss Webster, from
upstairs, came running. Mrs. Lyman came running. Even
Annie, the maid, under the impression that Miss Laura
was having another of her spells, came running with the
bottle of aromatic.

Miss Laura was lying back in one corner of the divan
making little feeble gestures with the *Universal Magazine.*

No, she said, she was not ill.

No, she did not want the aromatic.

"Look," she gasped, and held out the magazine again.

They looked. Across the top of the first page, the title
of the issue's leading story stood out in large bold type:

THE TRAIL OF THE CHITIGAU

Below it in letters only a trifle smaller appeared the
name of the author:

JOHN BARTON KING

Even then, just for a moment, they did not understand;
indeed, it was the illustrations which first revealed to them
the full enormity of the truth. There were three pictures.
The first showed a girl and a man with a small mustache
sitting side by side on a divan, with three perfect ladies in
three straight-backed chairs facing them, and in the background a young man alone reading a magazine. The second
showed the girl and two men sitting on the same divan.

One of the men was bending forward toward the girl and making a kind of pattern with a piece of string. The third was a close-up of a man and a girl. It was not the man with the small mustache; he was taller and broader shouldered, with a round, serious, pleasant face. The girl was very lovely, with fly-away hair and dimples.

Miss Webster laid an accusing forefinger on the name of the author.

"King," she said. *"King."*

At that instant it was perhaps as well for Mr. King that he was at his office in town, where he did his writing.

During the day "The Trail of the Chitigau" was read an almost unbelievable number of times at Mrs. Lyman's. They were all there done to the life—humorously, and yet sympathetically, too—Miss Webster, her own ramroddy curious self, and yet obviously a born leader; Miss Laura Pennell, who read the magazines—rather sweet for all her fluttering and apology; Mrs. Lyman with her Southern accent from the West; Mr. Allyn Piper and his cat's cradles; and the hero; and the heroine.

At first every one was rather angry. They had been imposed upon; a scurvy trick had been played; they had been taken unawares—like having a picture snapped when they were not looking. Toward noon, however, a little change in the temper of the company began to take place. They began to feel less and less that they had been made ridiculous, and more and more that they had been made famous.

Miss Webster definitely sounded the new note at two o'clock when she said that after all there was no denying that Mr. King was *bright,* and that any one could see with half an eye that he was heels over head in love with Elizabeth Ames.

A half hour later the climax was reached.

"Do you think she's in love with him?" Miss Laura half whispered.

Miss Webster sat up very straight indeed. She spoke as one who has authority.

"I don't know," she said. "But *my* opinion has always been that she couldn't do better."

"M-hm," agreed Mrs. Lyman placidly. "Ye-us."

Miss Laura fluttered. Here was she, for sixty years a reader of fiction, now herself involved in a first-hand romance.

Before night it had been definitely decided that Mr. King was supremely clever.

Elizabeth came home at half-past five, and was met at the door by Miss Webster, Miss Laura Pennell, Mrs. Lyman, and the *Universal Magazine.* She was dragged almost by force into the parlor and made to read it on the spot, while the others sat in various points of vantage round the room and watched her expression as she read. At first she looked rather amused—once or twice she laughed; then she looked angry; finally an odd expression that no one could rightly interpret took the place of anger; only, as she neared the end, the bright color mounted and mounted in her face until it blazed there crimson when she finished and laid the magazine aside.

Elizabeth stood up.

"What did you think of it?" demanded Miss Webster.

"He's clever, isn't he?" Elizabeth replied ambiguously.

It was just then that Mr. Allyn Piper came in and was met in his turn by the delegation at the front door. Mr. Piper looked hot, as if he had been hurrying.

Miss Webster held out the *Universal Magazine*—waved it, indeed, before Mr. Piper's eyes.

"Have you seen it?" she asked.

"Uh," said Mr. Piper.

He continued down the hall toward his own room. Miss Webster followed.

"What did you say?" she asked again.

"Uh," repeated Mr. Piper.

"Because," Miss Webster went on, "if you *haven't* seen it, you can borrow this. I've got another copy."

Mr. Piper faced about with his hand on the doorknob of the back parlor; even the short walk from the front door of his own room had seemed to make him hotter-looking than he was before.

"The Devil you have!" said Mr. Piper loudly, and flung himself inside and slammed the door.

The little group in the hall stood rigid, frozen where it was with honest horror; a thing like that had never happened before at Mrs. Lyman's. Mrs. Lyman herself speculated vaguely as to whether she could get Mr. Piper out without really asking him to leave.

And then Elizabeth Ames laughed.

Strangely enough no one heard Mr. King come in at all. He came, by intention, inconspicuously, and crept up to his room on tiptoe. He did not come down to dinner. The fact is, he was busy packing.

It was Miss Laura Pennell who discovered the light under his door and knew that he had returned. She did not mention her discovery to any one, however, and presently, when the chance offered, she did an outrageous thing. Miss Laura walked up and knocked at a man's bedroom door.

Mr. King opened it.

"Good—good evening," stammered Miss Laura. She twisted her fingers together in an agony of embarrassment and apprehension, beginning already to edge away. "I—I just wanted to tell you how—how wonderful I thought your story was. I always wanted," she ended in a little rush, "to know an author."

From his superior height Mr. King smiled down at her—delightfully.

"That's mighty nice of you," he said. "You see—I rather thought—you might want to put me out."

"I don't," Miss Laura repeated. "I always wanted to know an author."

And then suddenly she came quite close to him and stood on tiptoe, and whispered.

"Miss Ames is going out by and by," she said, "but she hasn't started yet."

And then she whirled away from him and ran—literally ran—down the hall and into her own room and out of sight.

John King stood in his open doorway and stared after her thoughtfully. For a few moments he hesitated. Then he stepped quickly across the hall and knocked.

Elizabeth Ames opened the door. She was wearing a dark blue dress with a bright scarf, and there was a kind of gypsy quality in her beauty as she stood poised there on the threshold, her arms lifted a little against the casing.

"You've read my story," said John King.

"Yes," said Elizabeth.

Her expression to him, as it had been to the others, was utterly baffling. He was a little frightened by it, but he was not a man to give up without trying. He smiled at her—the wide irresistible smile that had always brought John King the things he wanted. But this time there was something in his smile, and in the look which he bent on Elizabeth Ames, that no one had ever seen there before.

"And in spite of that," he asked, "will you go to walk with me? It's"—he hesitated, then flung it out boyishly—"it's great down by the river."

Elizabeth Ames hesitated too for just an instant. Then she smiled back again at John King.

"Yes," she said. "I'll go."

COACHWHIP PUBLICATIONS
COACHWHIPBOOKS.COM

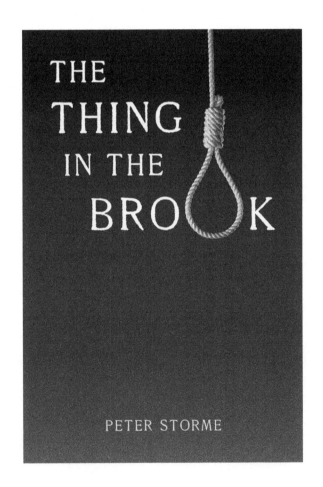

THE
THING
IN THE
BROOK

PETER STORME

COACHWHIP PUBLICATIONS
CoachwhipBooks.com

THE
RUMBLE
MURDERS

Henry Ware Eliot, Jr.

COACHWHIP PUBLICATIONS
CoachwhipBooks.com

DEAD
WEIGHT
ADDISON
SIMMONS

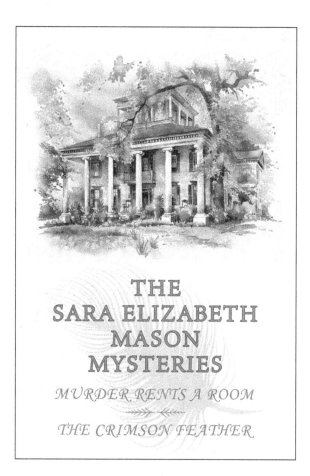

THE
SARA ELIZABETH
MASON
MYSTERIES

MURDER RENTS A ROOM

THE CRIMSON FEATHER

COACHWHIP PUBLICATIONS
COACHWHIPBOOKS.COM

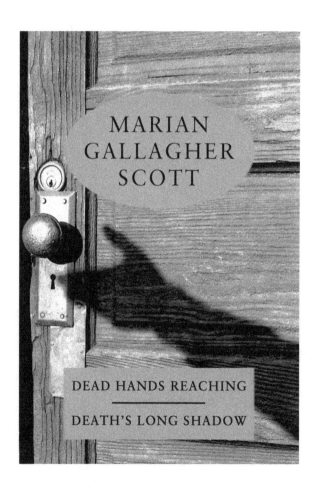

MARIAN
GALLAGHER
SCOTT

DEAD HANDS REACHING

DEATH'S LONG SHADOW

COACHWHIP PUBLICATIONS
CoachwhipBooks.com

COACHWHIP PUBLICATIONS
CoachwhipBooks.com

THE HOUSE THAT
JACK BUILT

with, MURDER IN AMBER

COLVER HARRIS

CPSIA information can be obtained
at www.ICGtesting.com
Printed in the USA
FSHW022247030620
70527FS

9 781616 464950